TO HOLD THE THRONE

A NOVEL OF THE LAST MACCABEE PRINCESS
AND KING HEROD THE GREAT

JONI OKUN

PALACE
PUBLISHING

To my beloved husband Neil, the wind beneath my wings.

CONTENTS

HERODIAN ERA ISRAEL

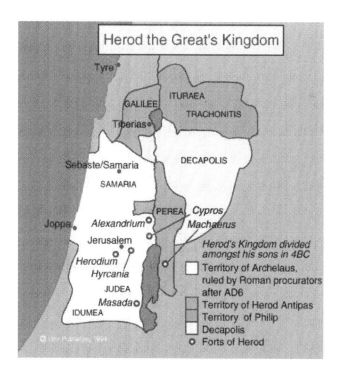

Herod the Great's Kingdom

Tyre

ITURAEA

GALILEE

TRACHONITIS

Tiberias

Sebaste/Samaria

DECAPOLIS

SAMARIA

PEREA Cypros

Joppa Alexandrium Machaerus

Jerusalem

Herodium

Hyrcania

JUDEA

Masada

IDUMEA

Herod's Kingdom divided
amongst his sons in 4BC

Territory of Archelaus,
ruled by Roman procurators
after AD6

Territory of Herod Antipas

Territory of Philip

Decapolis

Forts of Herod

HERODIAN CLAN

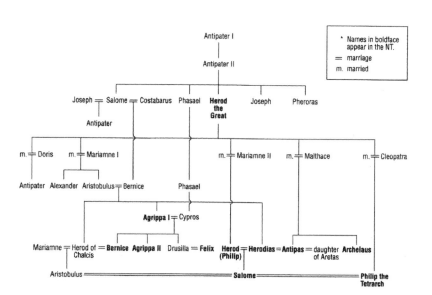

MACCABEE (HASMONEAN) CLAN

MACCABEE (HASMONEAN) CLAN

THE MACCABEES AND THE HASMONEANS (166 B.C.-A.D. 100)

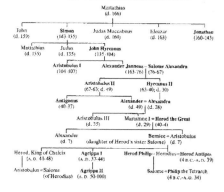

PROLOGUE

*K*ing Herod's guards force me up the narrow staircase to the top of the prison tower in Antonia Palace. In dazed disbelief, I look around the small chamber. A single, high window sheds a faint light on the furnishings, just a wooden stool, a small table, and a straw pallet on the floor. The walls are rain-streaked, and it smells of must.

Without a word, my husband's guards take their leave. Keys clink in the door lock. Boots clatter down the stone steps. Then, it is utterly silent. I am shivering. There is no hearth or brazier to warm me. I lie down on the pallet under a thin, ragged wool blanket. How did I, Mariamne, the last Maccabean Princess and the Queen of Judea, end up in this prison, my fate left to the whims of my husband, the mad king?

I am twenty-nine, not ready to die and leave my four children motherless in this brutal world. Their faces are crystal clear in my mind, as if they stood before me: Aristobulus, Alexander, Salampsio, and Cypros. My little ones need me. I long to be there to see them grow up, to give them the love they need, and to protect them, as best I can, from their father's brutality.

When I do leave this earth, whether soon or as an old woman, history may reduce me to a footnote, the wife of a despot king and the mother of his children. Yet like all women, there is so much more to my story than my husband and children. Roman leaders Antony and Augustus, and the Egyptian Pharaoh, Cleopatra, are the glimmering lights of the era, but I, too, will leave an indelible mark.

1

MARIAMNE, 41 BCE, JERUSALEM

*T*he night had finally arrived. My grandfather, the Governor and High Priest of Judea, was going to announce my engagement at this grand banquet in the Jerusalem Palace. This morning, Grandfather had signed the *ketubah* to arrange my marriage, and in moments, he would reveal the identity of my betrothed. My heart was hammering so loud I feared others could hear it.

From my red-velvet chair beside my grandfather's throne on the royal dais, a mosaic-tiled platform a few steps up from our guests, I could see the entire hall. My breath caught in my throat at the beauty and majesty of this vast ancestral palace, where Judea's Maccabee kings and queens, descendants of King David, had reigned for nearly one hundred years. Guards bearing torches stood along the high, white-stone walls. Hundreds of noble guests lounged on dining couches around tables cloaked in purple linens. Oil lamps suspended from the lofty ceiling, winking like a sky of stars, shed a golden radiance on their faces and silk robes.

Somewhere in the aristocratic gathering was the man I would soon wed. Who had Grandfather chosen? He would be a Maccabee, that much was certain. We have always married within the family to keep the royal bloodlines pure. I dearly hoped my betrothed was not my great uncle, an ancient widower who reeked of urine if one came too close. More hairs sprung from his nose and ears than his shiny head.

I hoped it would be my amiable and kindhearted cousin, Matthias, a lanky ginger beanpole. We often rode out on horseback in the hills around Jerusalem. I spotted him at the Maccabee cousins' table, close to the dais. Our eyes met, and he gave me his usual moon-eyed stare. His copper-colored hair, trimmed short Roman-style, shone fiery in the torchlight. I could do worse.

Three other cousins at the same table were also marriage possibilities. One was handsome but cold and arrogant. The other two were coarse and stupid, contemptuous of everyone, even our younger cousins. How a man treated those less powerful than he was said much about his character.

Beside me, Grandfather Hyrcanus slouched on the brocaded cushion of his citrus wood throne, its back and sides inlaid with amber and ivory designs. It is the same throne he sat upon when he was once king, before Rome, a decade ago, stripped him of his title and his crown.

The ermine collar of Grandfather's red velvet robe shimmered in the firelight as he rose with considerable difficulty. A hush fell over the aristocrats as he hobbled to the edge of the dais to address the gathering. Then, I saw it. Grandfather's gold silk turban had slipped down over an ear. It lay lopsided on his grizzled head. He did not adjust it, or even seem to notice the slippage. My cheeks grew hot. He was so often disheveled these days.

"It gives me great pleasure to welcome everyone to——"

Grandfather raised his white eyebrows. I swallowed hard. His decline had to be evident to his subjects. He had forgotten the occasion, again. His increasing confusion and bewilderment saddened me for its own sake, but even worse, it endangered the succession of our family line. Hyrcanus's unsuitability to rule was becoming apparent. However, my twelve-year-old brother, Aris, was not yet of age to take the reins of government. If Grandfather became too addled to serve as governor or died before Aris came of age, Rome would force Judea to accept an outsider to govern our country. We could not let that happen, no matter the cost.

I nudged my brother, who gave me a fleeting, resentful glance, and strode over to Grandfather. Aris whispered in his ear, and he nodded, absently.

"Oh yes ... Welcome to our feast in honor and celebration of Princess Mariamne's engagement."

I could not focus on my grandfather. I saw his lips move in welcome to his guests, but I heard only the roar of the sea as if I were listening to the inside of a seashell. Through sheer force of will, I stilled my trembling. My whole family appeared to be on edge. My brother's concern for me was evident in his dark-lashed eyes. Mother was bent forward, her back in an anxious arc. I felt our guests' eyes on me in my silver-cloth robe edged in rubies, made especially for this occasion. I could hardly bear the suspense. Please, God, let my future husband be a good man who would treat me with kindness.

"My dear granddaughter, Princess Mariamne, will marry Herod, son of Antipater the Idumean."

The floor swayed beneath me, and the hall spun. My belly hardened to stone. Herod was my grandfather's chief advisor and the Governor of Galilee. He ruled Judea in everything but his title. His lust for power was obvious to even our most simple subjects. Grandfather could not have selected a worse husband for me, especially now, when the future of our dynasty did not rest on firm footing. As my husband, Herod, that puppet of Rome, would be well positioned to challenge my grandfather, Governor of Judea, for his title.

As my father had lay dying from wounds inflicted by Roman invaders, he told me it was my duty to do my part to assure the dynasty's continuation, and the only acceptable spouse for me was another Maccabee. He had married his first cousin, my mother, Princess Alexandra. Both were progeny of royal lines. Even as his life ebbed away, he had managed to point out the importance of keeping the royal bloodlines pure.

Herod, however, was no Maccabee. He was the son of a Nabataean Princess and the grandson of an Idumean leader forced to convert to Judaism after Judea conquered his land. To many Judeans, forcible conversions were not considered genuine conversions. Herod was unqualified to partake in or even attend religious sacrifice and prayer.

"Come join the family on the royal dais, where you belong, Herod," Grandfather said, his voice quivering with joy.

At a table, Herod rose to his burly six feet. With spear-straight bearing, he ascended the dais's stone steps to join us. There was no denying Herod was a handsome man, well-muscled and strong of jaw, having the classical features of Greek sculpture. Beaming, he embraced my grandfather, kissed him on both cheeks, and turned to me, holding out his arms.

I loathed him. My body stiffened. I refused to stand or even meet his gaze, an insult, to be sure. He placed his big hands on my shoulders and kissed my cheeks. I shrank from his touch, and could not force a smile, though I knew a polite greeting was expected of me. Everyone fell silent as Herod took the carved wood, velvet-cushioned chair beside me without losing his proud bearing. I struggled to restrain an impulse to run as far from him as my feet would take me.

A cupbearer handed Hyrcanus a gold chalice. He raised it high. "Let us drink to the health of the Princess Mariamne and Governor Herod. Long live the newly betrothed!"

Those beneath the dais held up their silver goblets. "Long live the newly betrothed!"

We all sipped silvery-white Campanian wine, Rome's finest. Servants paraded in with steaming platters of lamb in date sauce, and my family repaired to the royal table, mid-dais. Herod seized the lounge beside mine, where Aris usually reclined. Already, my betrothed was scheming to take my brother's place.

The aromatic lamb was my favorite, but I could not eat, not tonight. I avoided Herod's glances and pretended to listen to my mother ramble on about how furious she was that rough seas had delayed an expected wine shipment from Rome.

"Mariamne—I hope you are not… unhappy about our

betrothal," Herod whispered to me in his preternaturally deep voice.

I could not bring myself to speak. Against protocol, I rose and made my way around the table to my grandfather's couch.

"I need to speak with you, privately," I said, leaning in close to his ear.

"Not now, dear girl," he said in his usual affable tone. "The new legate has just arrived from Syria. I must meet with him after I dine. Tomorrow morning, I will give you my full attention. That, I promise you."

He grinned and patted my head as if I was a child.

~

I rose early after a fitful sleep. Usually, I woke up ravenous, but that day I was too distraught to break my fast. I dressed in a fresh linen tunic and my favorite robe, blue silk with tiny pearls stitched down the sleeves. Perhaps it would bring me good luck in convincing Grandfather of the impossibility of the marriage he had arranged for me.

My stomach a tight knot, I raced across the courtyard to the king's quarters. Thracian guards, their spears and daggers hanging menacingly from their leather belts, blocked the arched doorway.

"Tell Governor Hyrcanus I must see him right away," I said with as much imperiousness as I could muster so early in the morning.

"He has been expecting you," a guard said with a faint smile, and he stepped aside.

I found Grandfather in his library, on a silk-cushioned, high-backed chair, hunched over a marble table. He studied an unfurled parchment bearing the seal of Rome. Sunlight streamed in from a high window illuminating the deep creases of his wizened face and his unruly tufts of cloud-white hair. Smiling affectionately, he motioned me to enter.

"Here comes my favorite granddaughter…"

I was too nervous to laugh as I usually did when Grandfather said those words. Still, I responded the usual way. "I am your only granddaughter."

"If I had ten thousand granddaughters, you would still be my favorite."

Our exchange had been the same ever since I was a small child. With each telling, the number of his imaginary granddaughters grew.

Grandfather's smile faded. "You are troubled, my dear. What is it?"

My heart pounded a rapid rhythm. "It is this marriage you have planned for me…"

"Marriage?" Grandfather's white brows furrowed.

Had he already forgotten? This did not portend well for me.

"Oh, yes," he said with a nod. He sorted through a heap of scrolls and held up the *ketubah* as if he was presenting a precious gift. "I have made an excellent match for you." His voice resonated with pleasure.

"No Grandfather, you have not. Herod is an old man. He already has a wife and a child."

Most patriarchs, even lowly ones, would balk at such a candid statement from a granddaughter, but Grandfather was an unusually kind and patient man.

"Marriages can be set aside, Mariamne. Herod will divorce Doress and marry you. He is in his third decade, the prime of his life, not old at all."

Herod had always treated me with the decorum due to a princess, but we had never uttered more than polite greetings when we crossed paths in palace halls. I hardly knew him. Then, I remembered something ominous. Herod had dined with my family last Sabbath. Over lentil stew, I had caught him staring at me in an assessing, calculating sort of way, his head cocked, his eyes intense. The memory of it made me shiver.

"Herod must think marrying me will bring him into the royal family and give him legitimacy to steal your throne. That is why—"

"Steal my throne?" Grandfather interrupted. "Never. Herod is my most loyal friend, just like his father Antipater was before him. He wants only to serve me."

I felt tears rising. Herod's scheming father, Antipater, had been a close ally of Pompey, then-leader of the Roman Republic. Antipater had flattered and cajoled Grandfather while acting as Judea's real leader. After Antipater had died, his sons Herod and Phasael succeeded him in governing our land in everything but title.

"Grandfather, Herod is no descendant of King David. He's not one of us."

Hyrcanus reached across the table and took my hand. "My darling, I do not think I will live much longer. Once I am gone, Herod is the only man in the land powerful enough to protect Aris's throne until he comes of age."

"But will he? People say he's Marc Antony's puppet on a string. He will always impose Rome's will on us."

"Herod and I agree on the wisdom of cooperating with Rome. We pay the price in blood when we defy the Roman Republic. Your father's rebellion cost him his life."

I burned inside, recalling what had happened to the Dynasty of Maccabean Kings.

Nearly one hundred years ago, Greek Seleucids conquered Judea, and forced us, at sword point, to worship their pagan god, Zeus, and to sacrifice pigs and other unclean animals on the altar of our Holy Temple. They executed circumcised men and boys, and they forbade all practice of Judaism. Our people fled Jerusalem and dwelled in caves, where they were free to live their lives in accordance with Jewish Law. Seleucid soldiers pursued them there. Judah Maccabee, my ancestor who was so fierce people called him "the hammer," led our people in a bloody, three-year battle against the Seleucids.

God heard our prayers, and Judah Maccabee's army drove our enemies from our shores. Maccabee monarchs ruled an independent Judea for nearly a century, and we could worship the One True God without foreign intrusion. Those days of freedom and plenty lasted almost one hundred years.

A decade ago, Rome imposed a bloody end to Judea's independence. My Grandfather Hyrcanus II was the King of Judea when his brother, Aristobulus I, besieged Jerusalem to steal my grandfather's throne. Rome's leader, General Pompey, took advantage of the civil war between the Maccabee brothers. He sent in the Roman Army, and they defeated us. I was only six when my father fell under the sharp blade of a Roman sword. The invaders sacked our Temple and plundered our city. They wrested Jewish independence from us and reduced Judea to a vassal state of Rome, a tribute-paying province under the thumb of a foreign overlord who chose our leaders. They allowed my grandfather to keep his throne as provincial ruler, but they took his crown and reduced his title to Governor of Judea.

Grandfather, however, never truly governed again. Rome gave Antipater the Idumean, their trusted ally, authority over our treasury. Antipater ruled in everything but name, and he placed his sons in positions of power. He appointed his first-born son, Phasael, Governor of Jerusalem, and Herod, Governor of Galilee. Together, these outsiders ruled my country and reduced my grandfather to a mere figurehead.

Judea's loss of freedom and independence cast a long, sad shadow over my childhood. It still weighs heavy in my heart. Plato says that one's essence is revealed in her name. My Hebrew name means "rebellious." I will never accept my family's downfall.

"Worry not, Mariamne," said Grandfather Hyrcanus, drawing me from my musings. "Herod has promised to honor and protect your brother's throne as he does my own." Hyrcanus gazed out his window opening with a dreamy smile as if he recalled a pleasant memory. "I have offered you to Herod as a gift."

"A gift," I said, incredulous.

"Yes, to thank him for putting down the rebellion against Rome in Galilee. Herod is loyal, and I reward loyalty." He took a small silk bag from his table drawer and handed it to me. "This is for you, my dearest granddaughter. Herod has asked me to give you this as a token of his great esteem."

I tried to still my shaking hands and reached for the silk bag. I opened it and pulled out a necklace. A single pearl gleamed on a golden chain. It was simple, yet elegant and costly. I slipped it back inside the bag and tossed it on the table. "I don't want it."

"I have ordered Herod to stay away from you until I say you are ready to marry. I have made you a fine match, my little princess. One day you will know this and thank me for it."

"Grandfather, please, please, do not force me to marry Herod."

His eyes lost their sparkle and his warm smile disappeared. "The *ketubah* has already been signed. I have work to do. Leave me now."

2

HEROD, 40 BCE, JERICHO

*I*n a desert valley in Jericho near the ancient palace, his opponent's blade came at him, slashing. With a battle cry that came from somewhere deep inside his chest, Herod swung his sword, again and again, but the younger man's grip on the knobbed hilt of his weapon stayed tight. As Governor of Galilee and the Judean leader's Chief Counsel, he could never let his challenger win. He fought with grace and skill until the other man collapsed on the ground, moaning. Herod, a master swordsman, raised his weapon in victory. His opponent, his chief guard, sat up on the rocky ground.

"I'm glad these practice swords are wooden," the guard said with a hint of a grin. "If they weren't, I'd be dead now."

After an interminable day of hearing border disputes between disgruntled date palm farmers, the physical release of swordplay relaxed Herod like no other activity except, perhaps, a visit to the whorehouse, but there were none here in the hinterlands of Jericho. He wished his guard a good night and scaled the steep, circular stairwell to his cramped bedchamber high in a palace tower, where he lodged whenever Hyrcanus's business brought him here. Though

Herod's titles were Chief Advisor to Hyrcanus and Governor of Galilee, like his father, Antipater, before him, Herod did the hard work of governing Judea.

After he married Princess Mariamne, he would tear down this near-ruin of crumbling stone and frayed tapestries, and build a far grander palace, Roman-style with white marble walls and intricate mosaic patterns on the floors. While his men were constructing it, he would sleep in the sumptuous Maccabee Palace in Jerusalem on a soft bed with a frame of inlaid gold and ivory. The most beautiful woman in the land would lie beside him, or better yet, beneath him.

When Governor Hyrcanus offered him his exquisite grand-daughter, Herod had been astonished. He had immediately seen the political expedience of the match and readily accepted. How could he refuse? As a member of the royal Maccabee family, there was no limit to the heights of power he might attain.

He peeled off his silk garment, heavy with sewn-in sapphires, and tossed it in a vibrant heap on the floor. After he married, he would have servants to remove the royal-purple lined togas he would wear. Stretched out on the uncomfortable straw mattress, Herod closed his eyes and thought about his betrothed. A year had passed since his engagement to Mariamne. He had kept his promise to Hyrcanus to leave her alone until the governor pronounced her ready to marry.

After they married, however, no one would be able to keep him from those lush breasts and her … an unwelcome thought about his wife broke his reverie. They were still married, though not for long. He could not help remembering Doress on their wedding night four years ago. The petite girl had been shy until he had taught her how to please him. He did not love her, but he had enjoyed her. Over time, his affection grew to something close to love. Now, he must let her go.

He pushed the image of Doress from his mind, and more diffi-cult, that of their first-born son, young Antipater. He would miss seeing the boy's round-eyed discovery of the world. But what man of sound mind would turn down the offer of a clear path to the throne, and in the bargain, attain the most beautiful girl in the land? He needed this marriage to reach his grand destiny, not only for his own sake but for the greater good of his country.

There was a tap at his door. "Are you awake?" called his sister, Salome.

Herod slipped on his tunic and opened the door to welcome her. The weak light of the oil lamp she held softened her sharp features, and she looked almost pretty.

"I hope I haven't disturbed you."

"No, come in and join me."

She alighted on a stool at the table and arranged her robes around her in her regal manner.

"I've pinched this wine from Governor Hyrcanus's famed wine chamber," Herod said, holding up an earthen vessel. He poured wine into silver goblets and handed one to Salome. "It's the finest Falernian, from a vineyard high on slopes of Mount Falernus."

"You honor me," Salome said with a smirk.

"I'm glad you've come. Night is lonely here."

His sister's face, sallow in the lamplight, had a strained look about it.

"I couldn't sleep," she said.

Herod sat down beside her. "Why?"

"When do you plan to divorce your wife?"

Herod did not want to think about Doress. He poured himself more wine. "Worry not. I'll divorce her well before my wedding to Mariamne."

"Spurned women can be vengeful," said Salome. "I've seen them do terrible things."

"Doress will want for nothing," said Herod. "I lavished her with jewels and gold when I told her I'm divorcing her. And I've already given her father a substantial settlement to soothe his wounded pride."

Salome raised her eyebrows and gave him a skeptical glance. "Perhaps it will be enough."

"I don't fear the little mouse Doress. She's pretty enough; she'll marry again in time. I might even arrange a favorable match for her."

Perhaps he ought to wait until she was no longer so spectacularly angry with him.

"Will you take your son into your household?"

Herod swirled the wine in his goblet and watched an amber-colored funnel form. Its rich berry aroma pleased him. "No, I won't irritate Mariamne with his presence or my former wife's. I'll exile them." He tried to push away the image of his son's dark eyes. How happy the boy was to see him at the end of the day. Thinking about young Antipater was making him uncomfortable, and Herod detested discomfort. He poured himself more wine and drank it in a single gulp.

"Do you plan to name your son as your heir? He's your father's namesake."

"The boy must take his place behind the sons I have on Mariamne. I hope there will be many." He imagined his betrothed with a belly big with his progeny. It made him smile. "Tell me, sister, why are you so concerned about Doress? You've always despised her."

She stared into the flame of her lamp, uncharacteristically quiet.

"Have I not answered your questions to your satisfaction?" asked Herod, with growing impatience.

Salome tended to sulk about his relations with women. It had always been that way.

"Mariamne is proud and haughty. I fear you'll be unhappy with her."

His booming laughter pierced the night's quiet. "Don't pity me. Mariamne is the beauty of her generation, the most prized bride of all. Royalty is always arrogant. It doesn't bother me."

Herod deserved whatever power and riches he might attain as a member of the Maccabee Family. He had earned it every day he had stood by the addled king's side, making the difficult decisions the old man ought to have made himself. He had earned it with hands stiff and raw from signing mountains of governor's proclamations, working well into the night while the leader snored. He had earned it as a battlefield commander and strategist who had led soldiers to victory, not once, but time after time.

"The princess is young and too beautiful for her own good. Every man will want her. Will it be hard for you to see them lusting after her?" she asked with a knowing grin.

"Men will keep their distance from Mariamne if they want to keep their heads." He poured more wine and swilled it.

"What will you do when other men turn her pretty, little head?"

"She better not turn it away from me," said Herod with a sly grin. "I plan to keep her satisfied. Anyway, her virtue is impeccable. My spies have confirmed it."

"But what about her mind? Stupid women never hold your interest for long."

"True, but you're wrong about Mariamne. She's quite intelligent and well educated. She took lessons in Rhetoric, Mathematics, History, and Philosophy for years alongside her brother. She speaks fluent Latin and Greek."

Salome gave him a grim smile and straightened her back. "Such an education is most unusual for a girl."

Herod remembered his sister's downcast eyes and trembling lips when he and his brothers had left her after breakfast every morning for lessons with their tutor. Their father would not let her join them.

"Do you think your engagement pleases Mariamne?" she asked, her head cocked.

Herod winced. During the past year, his betrothed had never once smiled when he had encountered her in palace halls. Her sour expression would have ruined the looks of a lesser beauty.

"It seems my betrothed isn't fond of me," he said, suddenly restless, drumming his fingers on the table. What misery a hateful wife might inflict on him.

His sister gazed at him with tenderness. "How could any woman fail to fall in love with you?"

Salome was a perceptive woman. From his youthful conquests to the more recent ones after his marriage, he had radiated confidence and power, the ultimate aphrodisiac. His sister came over to him and placed her small, soft hands on his shoulders.

"Judea will need a new leader. Hyrcanus is old. He can't live much longer, and he has no suitable heir," she said, kneading his tense back muscles with surprising strength.

Herod met her eyes. "What are you suggesting?"

"You ought to be the next Governor of Judea," she said with an impish smile.

"We think alike," he said, grinning. "Hyrcanus is near death. His only son, Alexander, is dead, and his grandson, Prince Aris, is but a child."

He took Salome's hand. She rested her head on his broad expanse of chest. "Did you know that on my twelfth birthday, an old Essenian Oracle stopped me in the marketplace. He told me I'd one day be crowned King of the Jews. I went home and told Father what he had said."

"What did Father say?"

"He said the old Essenian must have confused me with Phasael," he said, his smile bitter.

Salome gave him a knowing nod. "Father favored his first-born son."

The old hurt flared fiery in Herod's chest.

"Father thought Phasael was the son destined to bring glory to our family name. I don't know why. Of my four brothers, you were best at everything from studies to war games."

His sister was the only woman who had ever understood him. He lifted the vessel to pour more wine but found it empty. He slammed it down and stood up. "Father was deaf and blind when it came to his sons."

Salome nodded, grimly. "He lavished attention and affection only on Phasael, and not on you or our brothers Pherorus and Joseph. He hardly noticed I existed. You, Herod, should have been his most favored son. You are the one meant to lead nations." She nuzzled her head against him.

He smiled and embraced her. She was as delicate and lean as a little bird.

"You've always believed in me. I'll never forget how you used to stand up for me when Father blamed me for Phasael's mischief." He

tweaked her nose. "Have I ever thanked you for defending my
honor when our brothers would not?"

She chuckled and drained her goblet. "Our brothers were
craven. And Phasael was cruel when crossed. Father hated it when I
defended you against his lies. It cost me dearly. You know that."

Herod drew back and cocked his head. "What do you mean?"
"Why do you think Father forced me to marry Uncle Yusef? He
knew I despised the old goat. He did it to punish me for my
defiance."

"I'm glad you and Yusef are estranged. I need you with me.
Who else can I trust?"

Salome's eyes shone like amber in the dimming light. "You do
need me. The question is, do you need Mariamne? You can reach
the throne without her, Herod. I'll always be right beside you."

Herod considered his sister's words, and found Mariamne's
image forming in his mind. He wanted her. He wanted her body,
and her love, and all the prestige and gold that came with her family
name. He needed legitimacy only she could bring to his ascent. "I've
already signed the *ketubah* for our marriage," he said, with a helpless
shrug.

"I'm the one who will always love you with my whole heart and
soul, Herod."

"I know," he said.

The lamp, with only a shallow puddle of remaining oil, flickered
faintly. He stood with Salome in near darkness.

"The truth is, I want Mariamne, and I want Judea." How he
coveted the bewitching land whose name meant "tawny as lion
skin." Tawny it was, with its hills and valleys pale gold against the
flame-blue sky. He was going to make Judea the light of the known
world. Only he could transform it from the remote outpost it was
into a sophisticated land even Rome would envy and emulate. He
imagined himself, high on a portico of one of his many palaces,
gazing down at sprawling metropolis beneath him. He could see the
hippodrome for games and chariot races, the theater, the gymna-
sium. He could see the glorious temple he would build for God.

"Do you think Rome will ever allow you the crown?" Salome asked.

Herod chuckled. "This is the question that keeps me awake at night."

"You've shown your mettle, Herod, as Governor of Galilee. No one will ever forget how you crushed those brigands who rebelled against the king."

Herod smiled, remembering that day, on a bare hilltop on the shores of Galilee. He had sentenced an outlaw, Hezekiah, and his young followers to death for their revolt against Rome's rule. Herod had ordered Hezekiah beheaded and his men strangled. Despite their parents' frantic entreaties, he had refused to give the rebels trials although Jewish law required them before execution. He had watched the men die, one by one. He had made his own law. Never again would anyone doubt his power.

"I was terrified when the high court charged you with the rebels' murders," said Salome. "They could have executed you."

Herod had arrived at his trial clad in royal purple, flanked by an armed entourage of Roman soldiers. The chief judge's astonished expression when they marched into his hallowed courtroom was one Herod would never forget. "True, the judges could have ordered my execution, but they had the good sense to dismiss the charges against me. They despised me, yes, but they understood Rome's power."

"They did. Everyone knew Rome was behind you. They treated you with the respect you deserved. You were meant to lead us, Herod. But I worry. Our family has always been on the fringe of power. I think the Judeans will always consider us outsiders."

He slammed his empty goblet on the table. "That will change when I marry the Maccabee Princess. My subjects will embrace us. Once I am leading Judea, and my people have full bellies and purses heavy with gold, no one will dare to challenge my rule." Everyone was going to thrive when he was at the helm of Judea, as it could be, as it should be. He yawned, soothed by his own comforting thoughts.

Salome stood and stretched like a cat. It was not the first time Herod noticed how feline his sister was.

"Your eyelids are heavy, Herod, and my lamp burns low. I'll leave you now."

"Sleep well," he said, and he rose to open the door for her. "Tomorrow, I want to hear you play your harp."

"I will," she whispered, and slipped away.

~

*J*ust before dawn, Herod woke up in his Jericho Palace chamber to find his chief guard in a deep scowl, looming over his bed. "Wake up, Governor," he said, urgency resonating in his voice.

"What is it?" Herod mumbled. His mouth tasted sour and he needed the chamber pot.

The guard handed him the scroll: "News from your spymaster."

Herod sprang from his pallet. Bracing himself, he unfurled it and read.

The Parthians of Persia have invaded Judea and several other Provinces of the Roman Republic.

"No!" Herod cried. He punched the stone wall with a tight fist.In his fury, he felt no pain. "Rome is defeating them, of course?"

The guard shook his head. "No, they've already taken many of Rome's lands. They have the wealth and power of Persia behind them. Right now, thousands of Parthian soldiers are riding toward Jerusalem. Antigonus has bribed their king to let him rule Judea as a vassal state of Parthia."

"Antigonus? Mariamne's uncle?"

"Yes, the Parthian King has agreed to help Antigonus's army overthrow Hyrcanus and sweep out Rome."

"I leave Jerusalem for a few weeks and everything turns to camel dung. Where is King Hyrcanus now?"

"We've haven't been able to locate him."

Herod wrapped his sandal's straps around his thick calves. "I must drive the Parthians from Judea, and support Hyrcanus's continued rule. Send a messenger to Rome. We'll need soldiers and weapons."

Someone banged on the door. Herod instinctively drew his hand to his sword.

"Who goes there?" shouted a guard, his fists tight. "Say the code."

The knocker called out numbers, and the guard opened the door to a young envoy dressed in the blue and white livery of Judea's Army. Sweat streamed down his face. Herod's guard searched the man for weapons, and found none. Panting, the envoy held out a scroll to the guard. "This message is from the Parthian King."

Herod slid his sword into the girding leather around his waist. "It is raining scrolls this morning," he said, bitterly, and grabbed the writing.

We wish to broker an honest peace between the Hyrcanus and Antigonus to settle this matter and avoid civil war in Jerusalem. We care not which Maccabee governs Judea on our behalf.

I hereby summon Antigonus, Hyrcanus, Phasael, and Herod to appear before me on this day, just before sunset, at the trailhead of the king's hunting grounds north of Jerusalem.

Pecorus, King of Parthia

"Have Hyrcanus and my brother Phasael received this message yet?" asked Herod.

"We couldn't confirm it."

"This whole thing makes no sense. Spies tell me King Pecorus has accepted Antigonus's bribe to help him unseat Hyrcanus and to let him rule Jerusalem. But this message, from King Pecorus himself, makes it sound as if there is no such agreement."

His guard nodded, gravely.

"Someone is lying," said Herod, tersely. "We'll leave shortly for Jerusalem. Muster my entire guard."

It was already white-hot at dawn when Herod and his men mounted their stallions and set out for Jerusalem. It would be less than a day's ride if the weather held. At dawn, the newly risen sun looked as though it was floating in a pool of blood. But a red sunrise was a good omen for a soldier, was it not?

Herod had committed King Pecorus's troublesome summons to memory, and he mulled it over as he galloped toward Jerusalem. Why would King Pecorus, who has already profited from allying with Antigonus, suddenly turn neutral in the struggle between the old Judean King and his nephew, Antigonus? What did he have to gain? Had his spies lied or been misinformed about Antigonus's bribe?

On the road, halfway to Jerusalem, Herod figured it out. It was so clear to him he wondered how he had not grasped it earlier. The Parthian King was most likely gathering the leaders in one place to kill or imprison all except for the one who had given him a generous bribe: Antigonus. Herod was not going to let it happen. Abruptly, he ordered his men to halt. He dispatched messengers to find Phasael and King Hyrcanus and warn them not to appear at King Pecorus's meeting place and go unwittingly to their deaths.

Galloping under the searing sun, Herod thought about how quickly everything had changed. He had been so sure of his future last night, but now, only hours later, a massive boulder blocked his path. He must carefully consider his next move if he was going to survive.

Ah, safety, so elusive, so difficult to attain, and even harder to hold. If he was not safe, neither was his family nor Mariamne's. The thought of his betrothed in grave danger made his pulse race. Sweat soaked through his tunic. Antigonus needed every member of the royal Maccabee line out of his way; his first priority would be their slaughter. Herod had to rescue them from Jerusalem, and take them to a safe place before the Parthians or Antigonus reached them. Their rescue would be a risky endeavor, but what choice did he have? He must put Hyrcanus back on the Judean throne for at least a short time before he married Mariamne and took command, and so he must drive out the invaders and the usurper, Antigonus. Under Hyrcanus's rule, Herod was well on his way to ultimate power. But under Antigonus's regime, he was nothing but a dead man.

After he took his family and Mariamne's to safety, he would return and seize Jerusalem. The familiar thrill of the coming battle surged through him.

3

MARIAMNE, 40 BCE, JERUSALEM

*O*n the day the Parthians invaded Jerusalem, I awoke in the dark blue hour before dawn feeling strangely restless. Like every morning, my handmaiden Lila brought a spiced citron drink into my bedchamber and placed the silver goblet on the marble table beside my bed.

"Good morning, Princess Mariamne," Lila said.

I could depend on her warm smile no matter the time of day.

"Would you care to break your fast in your bedchamber this morning?"

I could not stay in bed one minute longer. "No, Lila," I said as she helped me slip into my tunic and silk robes. "I'll join my family on the terrace."

My mother said it is preposterous to consider a slave or servant your friend, but Lila was my closest friend, and she had been ever since we were children. Lila's mother had sold herself into royal slavery to pay off her dead husband's debts, and she served as one of the palace washerwomen. I first found Lila hiding behind her mother's robes. She had been too shy to talk to me until I took her hand and led her into the garden. I had her meet me there every day.

Lila's mother died when she was thirteen. By law, Lila would have to work as a slave until the governor deemed her father's debt fully paid. I had begged Grandfather to free her, and persuaded him to pay her to serve as my chief handmaiden. I cold never do without her.

~

O n the tiled and colonnaded southern terrace, the last vestiges of night-blooming jasmine perfumed the morning air. Potted miniature date palms on the terrace's edge waved in a gentle breeze. My mother, Princess Alexandra, and my brother, Prince Aris, were already lounging around the black granite table, its silver flecks gleaming in the morning sun. I reclined on my couch and ate honey bread and pomegranates. A handmaiden dusted breadcrumbs from my mother's face with a silk cloth.

"I was just telling Aris we must plan a feast," Mother said. "My wine shipment from Rome has finally arrived. Ship's crews are craven these days. They won't sail when there is even a hint of stormy weather. It wasn't like that when I was a girl."

My mother's callousness never ceased to amaze me. "Did you expect ship's crew to risk death to bring you your wine?"

She gave me a scathing look and turned away.

The sound of galloping hooves made my whole body stiffen. Early morning callers tended to bring bad news. Through the cypress trees on either side of the path, I saw a man in a blue uniform trimmed in white, one of Governor Hyrcanus's soldiers, riding at a fast clip up the stony path to the palace. The high bronze gate at the terrace's entrance moaned when the guard opened it for the messenger, who slid off his mount without a word. Once on the terrace, he fell to his knees, panting.

"Tell us," said my mother.

"The Parthians of Persia are attacking Jerusalem."

My breath caught in my chest. What army would dare to attack a province with the might of Rome behind it? The southern terrace was the best vantage point in the entire city; our palace loomed taller than any other building in Jerusalem, even the Temple. I looked out and saw no invading forces, only a few distant riders.

"Now? Where are they?" my mother asked.

"Our scouts say thousands of Parthian soldiers are traveling toward us as I speak," the messenger said. "Our spies expect the invaders to join Antigonus's Army later today. Together, they will vastly outnumber us."

Mother fanned herself. "How could this happen?"

The envoy kept his eyes fixed on the clay tile. "Governor Hyrcanus had intelligence from Rome that the Parthians were planning an invasion. They expected them to arrive later in the year, during the winter rains. They thought we had more time to prepare—"

"Yet here it is autumn, and there is not a cloud in the sky," my mother interrupted, her voice shrill. "Rome's spies have failed us."

The messenger bowed so deeply his hairless head nearly touched the tile before he looked up and met my mother's eyes. "There is more I must tell you. Your cousin Antigonus has seized our treasury and the high court. The Parthians have stolen Hyrcanus's throne, and they have appointed Antigonus Judean King and High Priest."

Trembling, I took my brother's hand. Aris's face was blank, unreadable. My mother, pale as an animal skull in the desert, sunk onto her couch and ordered a servant to fan her with a palm frond. I had never seen her as anything less than fierce and strong as a steel sword. "So my cousin has stolen my father's throne," she said, her eyes dull and distant.

"My grandfather was expected to ride home from Jericho Palace this morning." It was not my place to speak, yet I could not stop myself. "Is Governor Hyrcanus safe?"

The messenger hung his head.

"Answer her," said Princess Alexandra, staring hard at him. "Does my father live?"

"Governor Hyrcanus lives. But Antigonus found him on Jericho Road as he set out for Jerusalem and… he maimed him."

I cried out. Aris put his arms around me. "What happened?" my mother asked.

The man took a sharp breath and shut his eyes. It was as if he could not bear to see our faces when we heard his words. "The Parthians and Antigonus took Governor Hyrcanus captive less than an hour ago. Antigonus has bitten off Hyrcanus's right ear."

"Bitten off— the beast! How could our own blood do such a thing?"

Those were the last words I heard before I grew lightheaded and the world went black. My legs buckled and I fell to the terrace floor. I opened my eyes to see Lila's face, pinched in worry, hovering over my own. I sat up, and clung to her, crying. Horrific images of Antigonus's teeth gnashing at my grandfather's flesh raced through my mind. I could smell the spilling blood, hear his agonized cries, and feel the painful shock of it. Lila and Aris helped me over to a chaise. I could do no more than squeeze her hand in gratitude.

Ever since the first Maccabee ruled Judea, except during the reign of Queen Alexandra Jannaeus, the same person who was king also served as our high priest. A maimed man could not be a high priest. The brutal attack on my grandfather did not bode well for the future of our royal line.

"Where is my grandfather now?" I asked, my breath ragged.

"The Parthians have arrested him. They're taking him to prison in Parthia."

Tears I could no longer hold back coursed down my face. "Grandfather is an old man. How will he survive prison?"

Mother turned to me with eyes hard as the stone bluff beneath our palace. "Maccabees don't cry, Mariamne. We fight. Antigonus will die for this travesty." She turned to the messenger. "Rome will defend us."

The messenger shook his head. "Sadly, Rome has few soldiers stationed in Judea now. Antony has sent most of his army to defend Rome's borders from barbarians causing trouble again." The messenger met my mother's steely eyes with pity in his own. "The Parthians have already swept Rome from many lands."

It was inconceivable how any nation could take on the Roman Republic and emerge victorious. Since long before I had drawn my first breath, Rome had been unrivaled in strength and power.

"Our people will never accept that usurper on the throne," Mother said, her eyes wild. "We will crush him. I trust our generals are ready for battle, are they not?"

The messenger shrugged. "Antigonus is a Maccabee. We hear most subjects will be willing to give him their allegiance."

His words stung me to the bone. Would our own people refuse to support us?

"*My* line is the royal one," said my mother.

"Of course, Princess Alexandra, but Antigonus has well-bribed the Parthians. And he has probably bribed Jewish nobles and aristocrats to support him."

She snorted in disgust. "How much did that beast pay the Parthian King?"

"Antigonus paid him one hundred talents of gold and five hundred women, all daughters of high-born Jews."

"We must restore the throne to our family," my mother said, pacing up and down the terrace. The incessant scraping of her sandals on the terrace stone grated on my already frayed nerves. "To do this, we will need Herod."

For the first time that day, my betrothed crossed my mind. What if Antigonus and the invaders had already killed him? My throat went so dry I could not swallow. I detested the man, of course, but now, everything in our world had changed. We must fight not only the Parthians but also Antigonus and his followers, and many our own subjects. Some of our Maccabee kinsmen might shift their loyalty to my Uncle Antigonus when the Parthian king showed him favor. Perhaps the messenger was right, and people would care little about which line of the Maccabee family ruled so long as a Maccabee sat on the Judean Throne. Who besides Herod had the strength to save us from the swords of both Antigonus and the Parthian king? He was my family's sole chance for survival.

Then, a frightening thought struck me. If Herod lived, would he still want to marry me? With my grandfather no longer the leader of Judea, marriage to me would be a far different prospect from what he once had reason to expect. Now, perhaps, Herod might prefer to wed Antigonus's oldest daughter, ugly and thick though she was. And if he no longer wanted me, he had no reason to save my family. It might be better for him if we were out of the way. But no, I recalled with relief, our signed *ketubah* bound us. Only death could nullify it. I felt the color rush from my face. Herod might want to kill me to free himself.

"Where is Herod?" I asked, my voice quivering. I steeled myself for the messenger's response. For a few agonizing moments, I watched the man wipe his dripping brow with his sleeve.

"Antigonus and the Parthians have driven him from Jerusalem. We don't know where he is. The Parthians are coming for you. You have little time to escape. We have sent a message to Jericho Palace. Servants are preparing it for your arrival. We have called for coaches and wagons to take you and your retainers there. Please, ready yourselves to leave right away."

My mother, with eyes closed tight, nodded. "You may leave us." The messenger bowed, mounted his horse, and rode away. "Servants," Princess Alexandra called into the palace through the open door, "pack us for travel to Jericho Palace."

Three palace servants in brown homespun robes were peeking around the open mahogany palace door. Their eyes were bright with fear. No doubt, they had heard every word the messenger had uttered.

"Hurry up, and tell the others!" my mother cried. The servants scurried away.

"If only your father had not left me alone to see Aris to the throne."

The last thing I needed right then, when there was a good chance I would not live through the day, was to hear my mother complain about my poor, dead father. "The Roman Army executed Father. You speak as though he left us willingly."

"Your father failed to understand the benefit of cooperating with Rome. Revolt proved fatal to him."

"A Roman sword proved fatal to him," I said.

"And now your grandfather has gotten himself imprisoned. Always, always, the man is ineffectual."

I detested when my mother spoke ill of Grandfather. Even

though he had made a terrible match for me, I still loved him with all of my being.

She sighed. "I must go now and have the servants sew gold and jewels into the hems of our robes."

Squinting against the fierce glare of the sun, Aris and I looked down at the empty market. Shoppers usually crowded the fruit and vegetable stands at this time of day. The sight of the vacant stalls made me shiver. Not one mule or donkey plodded down the flag-stone roads. No water-carriers lugged their animal-skin bag down every byway, calling out prices. No shepherds drove bleating sheep up the road to the Temple for sacrifice. The familiar scents of cinnamon and frankincense were strangely absent. No sacrificial smoke curled from the Temple. There was only a sinister quiet.

People called Jerusalem impregnable, but was it? West of the walled city, sheer cliffs edged the Tyropoeon Valley. south and the east of the City, the deep Hinnon and Kidron Valleys protected the city from attack. However, north of the city walls, there was little to keep invaders at bay, only a moat and Bezetna Hill.

~

*a*ris and I stayed out on the terrace to watch for the carriages that would take us to Jericho Palace, fervently hoping they would arrive before the Parthians reached us. We squinted against the fierce glare of the sun, our eyes fixed on the horizon.

Hours later, Parthian soldiers, mounted on their great stallions, appeared on the horizon, riding hard toward us. Even from a considerable distance, I could see their metal helmets and chain mail glimmering in the sunlight. My tunic, soaked in perspiration, felt cold and wet against my skin.

"They're here!" I shouted into the palace.

My mother rushed out, her face wan with terror. "We must leave now, on our own. We cannot wait for the others to come."

"I'll order the servants to summon our carriages," said Aris.

"My good, clever son," my mother said, gazing at him adoringly.

I wondered how she could manage such a fawning smile at a time like this. Aris tore away to the carriage house.

Servants were packing carts and wagons, and burdening donkeys with large baskets of grain when they came. Through the canopy of cedar and palm, I saw what looked like hundreds of men riding up the hill toward our palace. I could barely breathe. They rounded a bend, and I had a clear view of a carriage with a mountain lion displaying sharp teeth painted in gold-leaf on the side. Roman soldiers in chain mail and domed helmets followed. Then, I saw Herod sitting sword-straight in the high seat beside the carriage driver. My betrothed was alive. Relief flooded me, body and soul. The carriage came to a halt beside the terrace. Mother's mouth fell in astonishment.

Herod peered down at us. His large hand, the same one that had taken mine when we had met in the courtyard the day after our engagement was announced, sheltered his eyes from the sun's glare. My mind raced back to that day. It was as clear as if it had happened an hour ago.

"I've promised your grandfather I'd wait for you to grow up, my beautiful Mariamne," he had said. His penetrating eyes, the pale green of new olives, frightened me. What transpired behind them was a mystery. I knew only what I had heard about him, and none of it was good. I pulled away; I did not want him to touch me. He had laughed as though we were playing a game.

A wave of repulsion for this aspiring thief of Judea washed over me. I could not let my confused emotions engulf me, not now, when our lives were in jeopardy.

"We must leave quickly," Herod said, his brow creased, his voice deep and resonant. "Antigonus and the Parthians will give chase when they arrive and find you gone. I'll take you to Masada. You'll be safe there."

Had I heard him correctly? I knew little about the high desert mountain plateau in the far south of our land near the Salt Sea, only that my Maccabee ancestors had long ago built a fortress at there. There was no wilder, more remote outpost in all of the land.

"Step into the carriage, quickly."

His voice held such authority not even my mother dared question him. He jumped down from the carriage with the ease of a young man. My mother smiled sweetly and held out her small, gloved hand, and Herod helped her into the carriage. When he took my cold hand, he gave me only the briefest of nods before his scowl returned. How he must be suffering. As the king's chief counsel, he was in grave danger. Antigonus and the Parthians would promptly execute him if they could catch him. Antigonus must consider him an enemy, at the top of his list of formerly powerful men to eliminate.

We settled on the carriage's silk-cushioned benches. There were window openings on both sides, and another in the front. I had a clear view of the bench where Herod perched beside the driver. How quickly life can change. Not long ago, I would have rejoiced at Herod's spectacular downfall. Now, with my world shattering into jagged shards, he had come to save us. I was deeply grateful to the man, that was all.

Herod turned around to glare at the servants in four-wheeled carts, and the baggage train queuing up behind his train. "Your servants and pack animals must be able to keep up with us, or we will leave them behind."

Lila was in one of those carts. "No!" I cried.

Herod looked at me with a bemused expression.

"We do need every bit of our baggage," said Mother. Her voice dripped honey.

Aris had only one foot inside the carriage when Herod ordered his driver to proceed. It lurched forward.

"Stop!" my mother cried.

I grabbed my brother's arm. With every bit of my strength, I pulled him into the carriage. The effort left me panting. Herod did not seem to notice.

"He meant to leave Aris behind," Mother hissed in my ear.

"I'm not hurt," said Aris. "Herod must have thought I was already inside."

"You are too kind, Aris," Mother said, without bothering to

lower her voice. "Herod wants you out of the way. You had better watch yourself."

I could only hope Herod had not heard her over the wail of the wind. Had he tried to leave Aris behind, or to maim him?

~

*W*e bounded down Palace Hill and flagstone roads, down the Cardo, past the Upper City's manicured villas, and through Tyropean Valley to the Lower City's maze of narrow alleys, toward the city gates. The ramshackle houses looked as if they clung together to stand upright. All through the eerie, empty city, nothing was as it had been yesterday.

When we reached Jerusalem's southernmost point, Herod nodded to the Roman soldiers posted at the gatehouse, and the carriage rushed through the open, arched Zion Gate onto the ancient road connecting Hinnom and Kidron Valleys.

When the gate clanked shut behind us, desolation overcame me. Even if I was lucky enough to survive, I might never see Jerusalem again. I wanted to remember the creamy stone of the city's turreted walls and towers against the blue shell of the sky. How had I never before appreciated its astounding beauty? I gulped back tears. I would not cry like a child and shame myself before my future husband.

"Why weren't the Parthians at the gate?" Aris called out to Herod.

"There were enemies at the gate," he said. "My advance men eliminated them."

I swallowed hard. Such killings were necessary to save our lives. Those men would certainly have executed us, given the opportunity. I knew that. Still, I was stunned by the nonchalance with which Herod told us of their murders.

We soon reached the countryside. Terrified our enemies were going to catch up with us, I barely registered the trees heavy with blue-green olives peppering the hillsides, or further on, the date and fig groves and the terraced vineyards, purple with ripe grapes. We

raced past fields of golden wheat and barley, and treeless, rocky hills
between villages that were no more than clusters of small stone and
mud-brick dwellings. Every hour, Herod's scouts rode up and
reported the progress of the Parthians' pursuit.

At one hamlet, women were drawing water from wells with
earthen jugs, washing clothing, grinding grain, and working an olive
press. A girl of around my own age sat at a table beside the village's
common oven, kneading bread. I wondered what it would it be like
to be that ordinary girl, to live in a one-room house above her family's donkeys and oxen stalls, to lay down each night on a straw-
stuffed sleeping mat. I envied her humble existence. It seemed less
dangerous and tumultuous than my own, but was it?

Once in the Judean Hills, we climbed through rugged rock
formations, crimson as old blood. Long past the Roman flagstone
roads, we traversed miles of ancient, rocky trails. Our exhausted
carriage horses began to slow. The driver whipped them, and their
cries of protest made me shudder.

Herod would not let us stop for dinner. Our enemies were too
close behind us, he said. Ravenous, I devoured the better part of a
loaf of bread as the carriage bounded forward. I had just finished
my last bite when I saw them in the distance. Hundreds of Roman
soldiers were riding toward us over the flat, barren terrain. Throngs
of young women followed, some on horseback, others on donkeys.
Many carried babies or young children.

"Who are all those women?" Mother shouted to Herod over the
hot wind.

"They're Jews from aristocratic families," Herod yelled back.
"Antigonus enslaved them and gave them to King Pecorus as a bribe
to let him rule Jerusalem. I sent soldiers to free them. Up ahead at
the fork in the road, they'll make the turn toward Samaria where
they will reunite with their families."

I detected a note of pride in Herod's voice. Having long heard
tales of his ruthlessness, this surprised me. Was this the same man
who had notoriously executed the rebel Hezekiah and his followers
without first giving them their trials as Jewish law required? Did he

deserve his ruthless reputation? To free five hundred women from slavery was, without a doubt, a compassionate act.

"My mother and sister are in the carriage at the end of their train bearing my crest," Herod asked. "They will lodge with your family at Masada."

"It's a fine son who takes care of his family," said my mother, drily.

Herod turned around and rewarded her with a radiant smile. Aris and I exchanged glances and grinned. If Herod had any idea how our mother had railed against him in the privacy of her own palace, he would gladly have thrown her to the Parthians.

I caught sight of Herod's family. His mother, Cypros, wore a Nabataean-style robe of bright blue silk trimmed in red and yellow. His sister, Salome, donned the white silk robes of a Roman aristocrat. Their kohl-lined eyes turned to me with curiosity. I wished I knew what they were thinking. I waved. Herod's mother gave me a nod and smiled warmly, but her daughter looked the other way.

"How rude of Herod's sister to ignore your greeting," whispered my mother. "She must show you respect. Does she not know who you are?"

"Please don't make trouble, Mother," I said. "She might be shy, or maybe she didn't see me."

"Oh, she saw you."

It struck me, then. Herod was confining us in a remote fortress in the desert for who knew how long to live with strangers who might detest us. Despite the heat of the day, a chill swept down my spine.

4

HEROD, 40 BCE, MASADA BOUND

On a desolate plain, the carriage containing his mother and sister took the fork in the road to merge with their train. The driver made too sharp a turn. The horses shrieked and bucked. The carriage toppled over and collapsed on its side with a sickening thud, throwing the driver and passengers to the ground.

The driver, Salome, and two handmaidens scrambled up without a scratch, but Herod's mother lay face down on the rocks, still as stone, her eyes shut. Herod leaped from his carriage. He knelt beside her and gently rolled her over on her back. Blood gushed from a cut on her forehead.

"Get me linen," Herod ordered. A soldier ducked into a supply wagon and rushed back with cloth Herod gently pressed against his mother's gaping wound. Blood quickly drenched it. He listened to her heart.

"Her heart beats, but she's barely breathing." He looked to his men with wild eyes. "Where's my physician? My mother is dying."

"He's at the end of our train. I'll get him," a soldier said and galloped off.

Images from his childhood flashed through his mind: his mother singing to him, kissing his scraped knee, her round face lighting up whenever he came through the door. She was leaving this ear. it was his fault. He had sent her down this perilous road into ha. open arms.

To make matters worse, this catastrophe was causing a delay that would give their pursuers time to catch up with them. Everyone one under his protection was in grave danger. Carriages and wagons emptied of riders, who gathered around to witness his despair.

"What a stupid, careless driver!" shrieked Salome as she pulled her mother's robes down over her ankles. "Herod, I want you to execute him."

The carriage driver cowered, fell to his knees, and bowed his head. "Please, please, let me live," he muttered. "I meant no harm."

From the corner of his eye, Herod saw Mariamne pushing through the crowd. She fell to her knees beside him and yanked off her silk headdress. He heard the viewers' collective gasp at her stunning act of immodesty. She made the silk into a pillow, and then gently slid it underneath his mother's head. Herod thought Mariamne's compassionate deed justified under the circumstances, even if it did expose her bare head. He admired how she seemed oblivious to the dark, shimmering curtain of hair falling loose around her heart-shaped face. She looked not at the astonished faces of the nobles and servants watching her, but only at Herod and his mother, motionless on the ground. Mariamne's dark eyes held great concern. That was the moment he knew her soul was as beautiful as the countenance she showed the world. Her kindness astounded him, and touched him, deeply.

"Ohhh," moaned his mother, opening her eyes slightly

"You live!" cried Herod.

With Salome's help, his mother sat up. She even managed a half-smile. Herod felt his tensed shoulder muscles loosen. Those watching laughed, giddy with relief. Herod lifted Mariamne's delicate headdress from the ground and tenderly placed it back on her head. Their eyes briefly met. He nodded in gratitude.

The ground trembled when a soldier galloped up to him. "The Parthians are close behind us."

There was no time to flee. Herod and his men must battle.

5

MARIAMNE, 40 BCE, MASADA

*H*erod mounted his stallion in one fluid movement. Without a word or even a glance at anyone, he and his men galloped toward the advancing Parthians. They charged down the road and around a bend, disappearing behind a craggy outcrop. All that remained was the cloud of ochre dust.

I found our wait in the eerie quiet of the bleak flatland harrowing. If Herod lost this battle, and he and his men did not return, we would all die. Only two guards had stayed back with us, too few to protect us from the perils of the desert. There were so many ways we could perish here. The wild boar, wolves, and leopards that roamed the land could tear our bodies to shreds with sharp teeth. We might succumb to heat, hunger, or thirst. If we managed to escape the natural dangers, brigands and bandits who plagued these lawless hinterlands could rob and murder us. I tried to stop myself from thinking such disturbing thoughts, and I prayed that Herod and our soldiers would survive our enemy's fiery arrows and sharp swords.

The guards allowed us to leave the carriages but warned us to stay close to them in case we were forced to leave quickly. Aris was pacing outside, between a guard and our carriage. My mother, stretched out on a carriage bench, had somehow managed to fall asleep. I tried to embroider a silk headdress, but my hands were shaking. I bungled stitches and pricked my finger. A rivulet of blood trickled down my hand and ruined my work. I tossed it aside and went to pace outside with Aris, back and forth, back and forth. Above the wind, I heard the distant screams of wounded and dying men.

〜

felt the ground rumble before I saw who was coming. Were enemy soldiers heading for us? Herod was the first to come into view. Sweet relief coursed through me. For the first time since he and his men had left for battle, I could breathe again.

The returning men, in the red livery and feathered helmets of Rome, formed two lines. Herod rode between them. They cheered for him and chanted his name. It was not the first Roman victory ritual I had seen, but it was the most thrilling.

Afterward, Herod rode up to our circled carriages. The dirt matting his face and beard could not mask his victorious glow. His armor looked pristine except for the swathe of dried blood across his chest plate. From the energy with which he bounded off his horse, I knew it was enemy blood, not his own.

"It was an utter triumph," Herod called, pride resonating in his voice, his eyes luminous. "We butchered every Parthian maggot that followed us here. We left no enemy alive."

The late afternoon sun cast long shadows on the brown mountain at which he pointed. "Someday I'll build a grand palace right here. I'll call it Herodium. The world will always remember my victory."

〜

n the blistering afternoon heat, we rumbled past giant boulders, deep gorges, and red mountains as old as time. Except for a few myrrh trees and isolated patches of scrub, the

barren land was nearly lifeless. A few antelopes and rabbits leaped
away as we approached. Never before had I been so far from home.

We reached Masada in the long shadows of the afternoon. Its
savage beauty left me breathless. Towering above its neighboring
mountains, Masada looked as if a giant sword had sliced off its
peak, leaving a diamond-shaped plateau. Now, I understood why
people called it impregnable. I could not fathom how any invader
could reach its lofty summit. Even more mystifying was how my
Maccabee ancestor, King Alexander Janneas, had built a palace
here almost one hundred years ago.

"We must leave our carriages at the foot of the mountain," said
Herod. "The Snake Path up is too steep."

My mother fanned herself languidly. "You don't expect me to
climb up, do you?" she asked.

Herod wiped the sweat from his brow with the back of his hand.
"Ladies can take a *lectica*," he said.

"A *lectica*? I've never heard of such a thing," my mother said.

"It's a leather sling with handles on both ends. In Rome, you see
many," Herod said. "You can lie on it, and guards will carry
you up."

I refused a *lectica* after Salome and Cypros refused theirs. Only
my mother took one. Her relative comfort, however, did not stop her
from complaining incessantly about the infernal heat.

Herod led our climb up the trail, a steep, narrow ledge twisting
ever upward. Guards and servants followed behind us, carrying
water and large baskets with food and our possessions. I concen-
trated on each step I took. If I slipped during my ascent, I would fall
a long, long way to an excruciating death on the rocks and boulders
far below.

The trail's end was a welcome sight after an hour-and-a-half-
long climb. A brown, sandstone castle rose up on the western end of
the diamond-shaped plateau. The entrance, between two crenellated
towers, was a worn wooden door, bleached and battered from years
in the punishing sun and wind. Smoke curled from the chimney of
the nearby cookhouse. The aroma of roasting meat drifted out. My
stomach rumbled with hunger; I could not recall my last meal.

To Hold the Throne   41

"Men, head for the barracks," said Herod, pointing to a row of stone dwellings up the path. He turned to face us. "I'm leaving thirty men here to see to your safety. Your Castellan is Salome's husband, Yusef. He will see to your needs."

"Don't call that man my husband," Salome said. "We're estranged. Did I not ask you to exile Yusef?"

Herod ignored his sister and pointed to the arched palace door. "Everyone, go inside the palace now, except Mariamne. You, stay here with me."

The sound of my name on his lips made me start. What did he want? I felt my face flush to the hot tips of my ears. With a disturbing combination of terror and excitement, I watched the others disappear inside the palace.

"Come," said Herod. With surprising gentleness, he took my hand. Our sandals crunched rocks on the barren ground. He led me uncomfortably close to the northern edge of Masada. Was he going to push me over? Ready to make my escape, I stepped away from the edge.

"Do you fear heights?" Herod asked, his eyes twinkling.

"No," I said.

I stood beside him in the hot wind and studied the sweeping view of dry, brown land and the silver glimmer of the Salt Sea beyond. I wondered how long we would have to stay in this barren place. It was a long day's journey from civilization. Herod's penetrating eyes softened when he looked at me. Had I not known better, I would have thought the man had tender feelings for me. Still, I could not force a smile. He stood so close to me. Was he going to kiss me? I turned my face away.

"Worry not, my beautiful princess. One day I will take you back to Jerusalem, I promise you."

Hope stirred. "When?"

"After I retake Jerusalem and Rome crowns me King. You will be my Queen and sit beside me on your throne."

"Did you say…" My breath caught in my throat. "Did you just say you want to be King of Judea?"

"No, I said I *will* be King of Judea."

My stomach was a bubbling pot. Herod planned to steal my brother's throne. I shook my head, vehemently. "Aris is next in line to rule. Grandfather Hyrcanus told me you had promised to safeguard my brother's throne until he comes of age."

He turned from me and stared at the sea. "Tell no one what I've said to you."

I bit my lip and fixed my gaze on the neighboring mountains. Waves of heat shimmered over them. By the time I found the courage to look at Herod again, he was taking long strides toward the Snake Trail.

How could I go inside the palace and face the others, knowing his terrible secret? I had no choice but to calm myself and go join them. I had to act as if nothing was wrong, as if Herod had not just totally altered every expectation I once had for my life. If I told someone, anyone, of his clandestine ambitions, he was sure to learn of it, with his army of spying soldiers and servants. He was famously brutal to anyone who dared to disobey his orders.

There was, however, another consequence of his ambitions. He planned to make me the Queen of Judea. I could see myself in cloth-of-gold robes and jeweled headdresses. My son would inherit the throne. I was going to be a mother of kings.

Remorse hit me like a javelin. How could I daydream about anyone other than Aris on the throne? It was my duty and my destiny to see my brother crowned, and to keep him on the throne where he belonged. I must keep Herod's scheme secret, even as I fought to thwart him.

～

Inside the palace, it smelled as though it had not been properly aired out in years. A fine layer of dust had settled on ornately carved chaises and their fraying cushions in the reception hall. Following the welcome sound of distant voices, I wandered through vast chambers on uneven stone floors.

In the first hall, two purple, velvet covered thrones on a dais presided over the room. I could imagine Queen Alexandra

Jannaeus, widow of Aristobulus I. there. Queen Alexandra Jannaeus had been an exceptional monarch, remembered for ushering Judea into an era of peace and prosperity. The next hall I passed through was grander still. Intricate marble designs in gold and white tile decorated the high ceiling, and dusty but colorful tapestries and faded frescoes adorned walls.

I found everyone at a long table in the banqueting hall. After I had washed in a bowl of water at the entrance and whispered my prayers, I slid onto an empty chaise beside my mother. Herod's mother and his sister lounged across the table. I had never before seen them among the guests and courtiers who often crowded the palace.

"I'm Cypros," said the older woman, a warm smile lighting up her deeply lined face. She came around the table and kissed my cheeks. "Welcome, dear daughter."

I nodded and returned her kisses.

"And this is my daughter, Salome," Cypros said.

Herod's sister gave me the cold stare of a dead fish in the market.

"Ah, the celebrated Maccabee Princess," Salome said. "I hear the angels sing of your great beauty. How delighted we are to lodge here with the former royals."

I recoiled from her. Why would Herod's sister say something so intentionally malicious? Was she opposed to the engagement? It puzzled me. My marriage to her brother could only elevate her standing in society. I forced myself to smile. "I hope you are both well after your carriage accident."

"What did Herod say to you outside?" asked Salome. My pulse quickened. I did not reply.

"Salome, I must remind you that you're addressing a Maccabee Princess," my mother said.

I gave her a searing glance. If only she did not feel the need to interject herself into everything and embarrass me.

"Herod will tell me, anyway," said Salome. "He tells me every-thing. We're very close."

Was she testing me? I turned away from her.

A stocky man with a bushy, graying beard swaggered in, a welcome intrusion.

Salome greeted him with a curt nod. "Yusef," she said. "Welcome, everyone. As my…wife Salome just told you, I'm Yusef."

"Estranged wife," said Salome with a dark look.

Yusef stared hard at her before he turned his gaze on the others. "I'm here to see to your care and provisions."

"How long must we stay here?" Salome asked.

"Until Herod comes for you," said Yusef.

"So we're his prisoners, then," my mother said.

Prisoners. The word made ice encircle my spine. We were at Herod's mercy, and we could only hope and pray he would be merciful to us.

"To the contrary, Princess Alexandra, you're all here under Herod's protection, which is something every one of you desperately needs. After you finish dining, go upstairs and choose your bedchambers."

Salome turned to Yusef. "I want the one farthest from you. I don't want you to think——"

Yusef paled.

"We'll take the royal apartments, the ones with the best sea view," said my mother. "Have our baskets sent up right away."

Salome rose, looming over my lounging mother. "As Herod's closest kin, the royal quarters are ours."

"You? The royal apartments?" my mother scoffed. "Our family is the one with royal blood, so we——"

"We are royal," snapped Salome. "My mother is a sister of King Aretas of Nabataea."

"Of course, I know," said my mother. "I also know you and your brother Herod are the progeny of an Idumean convert."

I cringed. How could she embarrass me so in front of my soon-to-be mother-in-law and sister-in-law? The woman was insufferable.

"My husband's family converted to Judaism generations ago," said Cypros with surprising calm.

"Because Judea vanquished his people and forced them to convert to Judaism or go into exile," my mother added. "My family ruled Judea for nearly one hundred years." She stood up with exaggerated regal bearing. "Yusef, kindly escort me to the king's apartments."

Yusef shook his head and chuckled. "I care not where you rest your head at night," he said, and left.

After dinner I was so exhausted I found the nearest bedchamber, neither large nor ornately decorated, and fell into bed fully clothed. The next morning at breakfast, I lounged with the others in awkward silence. I drank my beer and took a few bites of wheat cake and honey before I excused myself. I slipped away to the place on Masada's edge where Herod and I had stood together the night before. It seemed like a long time ago. Far below I saw the stark wasteland of brown and crimson boulders, and beyond, the silver glimmer of the Salt Sea.

Would I ever return home to the bustling streets of Jerusalem and its flagstone roads, thick with ox-carts and peddlers? How I missed the noisy morning markets, even the steady pounding of the blacksmith's hammer. I longed to see the blazing Jerusalem sunset turn the white walls of palaces and parapets gold, if only for a moment.

6

HEROD, 40 BCE, PETRA

*H*e could think of no man he would rather have beside him on his way to Petra than General Philippi. Herod was tall and broad-chested, with muscled limbs like tree trunks, but the general dwarfed him. Philippi, a mountain of a man, could easily intimidate or kill anyone who might threaten. And he prized Philippi's reticence. Herod detested men who prattled on endlessly about everything and nothing. Philippi rode and camped beside him in blessed silence. But now, there was something Herod must tell him.

"Antigonus has taken my brother Phasael hostage. I got word last night."

Philippi shook his head. His black eyes softened, and again, the men rode in silence.

If Herod only knew why Phasael had attended that meeting with Pecorus and Antigonus. Had he never received Herod's warning, or had he chosen to ignore it?

Ah, Phasael. Herod and his older brother had a troubled relationship. When they were children in the household of their father, Antipater, Phasael had often played mean and spiteful tricks on Herod and the other siblings. Phasael often accused Herod of the misdeeds, and he had suffered many beatings his brother had deserved.

As far back as Herod could remember, he and his older brother had competed for their father's attention and admiration. But their father had considered Phasael the golden son, and Herod was always second best. The old man should have accepted the truth, obvious to everyone else: Herod was better than Phasael at everything from studies to swordsmanship, from courage to character.

Antipater had long been Rome's close and trusted ally in Judea. During the civil war, when King Hyrcanus's brother, Aristobulus II, challenged him for the Throne of Judea, General Pompey had marched in, conquered the land, and made it a vassal state of Rome. Antipater had convinced Pompey to favor Hyrcanus over his brother as the local leader because Hyrcanus was weaker and more easily manipulated. Rome took Hyrcanus's crown and reduced him to territorial Governor of Judea, and appointed Antipater as his chief counsel. Antipater, however, essentially governed Judea.

When Antipater's sons came of age, he made Phasael Governor of Jerusalem and Herod Governor of Galilee. Of course, he had given Phasael the plum appointment over the most important part of Judea. The competition persisted into adulthood. Herod deeply resented his father's unfair and unjustified favoring of Phasael. Still, blood was blood. Herod owed it to his father, and to his family's honor, to save his older brother.

Remembering his father still hurt so much it knocked the wind from his lungs. Would he ever escape its agonizing grip? His grief was no longer as raw as it had been after his father's assassination four years ago when a political rival had poisoned Antipater at his own dinner gathering. With swift vengeance, Herod had hunted down the killer and slaughtered him with his father's sword. Though he had derived some degree of satisfaction from avenging the murder, Herod still felt his father's absence every day, an uncomfortable reminder of his fragile grasp on life despite his superior physical and mental strength. How easily someone, anyone, could end his life if he was not constantly vigilant.

"I'm going to ask King Aretas for gold to bribe the Parthians to

free Phasael. And I need more gold to raise an army to retake
Jerusalem for Hyrcanus and Rome. First, of course, I will rescue my
brother."

Phillip arched his thin brow. "Areas is not a king known for his
generosity."

"True. The king is parsimonious, but he's my mother's brother.
He won't tolerate the capture and imprisonment of his own blood."

Or would he? His kinsman was his best chance to raise the gold
he needed. If King Aretas refused him, he did not know what he
would do. His tense shoulders ached, and the long, bumpy ride
through the sweltering desert was not helping. They came across
tented villages of nomadic shepherds. Herod instinctively brought
his hand to his sword. Such tribes tended to be peaceable, but a
man has to be prepared.

By afternoon, the relentless sun and fierce winds made riding
almost unbearable. Sweat drenched Herod's robe and tunic all the
way to his skin. Stiff winds lashed him. Blowing dirt clung to his
face and robe, and the bitter taste of it lingered in his mouth and
stung his eyes. Still, the men journeyed on.

Close to sundown, they made camp in a deep valley that would
shelter them from the worst of the incessant bluster. Philippi built a
campfire and hunted a rabbit for their dinner. Herod watched him
adeptly skin his prey and roast the meat to fragrant perfection over
the campfire. Wordlessly, they dined and drank their sun-warmed
beer. The meat tasted delicious, but the bread they had brought
with them was already rock-hard. Still, Herod needed his strength,
so he ate it.

After dinner, he stretched out on a pile of animal skins and
watched the sun vanish over the lavender horizon. The desert
quickly cooled after darkness fell. Herod wrapped himself in his
wool cape. Sleep, however, eluded him. Philippi raucously snored
while Herod stared at the smoky clouds racing across the yellow
moon. His mind could not rest; images of his brother tore through
his mind. Were his captors torturing him? Starving him? He knew
he would have to reach Phasael quickly if he was to have any

chance of saving him. Setting him free was going to be a dangerous undertaking.

⁓

*T*he following afternoon, Herod and Philippi reached the rose-colored City of Petra. They rode through a narrow canyon between massive mountains and emerged to a sight that made Herod's soul soar. Magnificent buildings—treasury, court, temples, houses, and grand tombs—carved into the mountain's red sand- stone proved what was possible with tenacity and imagination. One day, his builders would use Rome's latest innovations to construct hippodromes, amphitheaters, and palaces. They would earn him the respect he deserved from his people and Rome's leaders. He could imagine even Marc Antony's jaded eyes brightening when he beheld the glory of Herod's creations.

But he was getting ahead of himself. First, he must persuade his royal kinsman to fund the ransom for his brother's release and his quest to take back Jerusalem from Antigonus and the Parthians.

Side by side on their stallions, they gazed up at Petra Palace.

"Let's hope King Aretas is in a generous mood," said Herod.

"He does have vast resources," said Philippi.

Petra controlled the commercial routes to Gaza in the West, Basra and Damascus in the North, and Aqaba and the Red Sea Ports. Every caravan of wood from Lebanon, glass from Sidon, fabric from India, and spices from Arabia must pay a toll to pass through Petra as it traveled to and from the Orient. Of course, King Aretas would help him. Any other outcome was inconceivable.

Herod dismissed Philippi, who left to lodge at the soldiers' barracks, and with a surge of excitement, he rode up the hill to the massive Nabataean Palace. The sight of it, towering over the city, dwarfing other buildings, made his pulse race.

The king's teenage son, his cousin Prince Ahmad, greeted him at the arched entrance. Herod embraced his cousin, lean and rangy, and kissed both cheeks.

"Do you remember when I lived with your family in this palace?" Herod asked. "You were very young then."

His kinsman smiled. "I don't remember, but my father told me he gave your family shelter here once."

"Yes, I was a teenager when King Hyrcanus's brother Aristobulus rebelled against him and defeated him. During the short time Aristobulus reigned as king, he banished my father, who had been Hyrcanus's chief advisor. Not long after, my father helped King Hyrcanus take back Judea, and my family could go home."

Though that battle for Jerusalem was not his victory, it was still a treasured memory, because it was his first taste of the sweetness of conquest.

All of a sudden, Ahmad's eyes clouded.

"Is something wrong?" asked Herod, with a vague sense of uneasiness.

"No," said Ahmed.

An old manservant came along and led Herod to his quarters. He felt the prince's eyes follow him all the way down the long hall. His lavish quarters, with shining marble floors and silk rugs, would have impressed the most sophisticated Roman. Had he not been eager to return to Jerusalem with sacks of gold, he would have been happy to linger in the Petra Palace. A vessel of spiced wine lay on the table. He poured himself a goblet and quaffed it.

The manservant bowed to him. "After you bathe, I'll bring your dinner to your quarters. The king will grant you an audience in the morning."

Herod nodded and poured himself more wine. He sat back on the plush, silk pillow on the marble chaise. If only the treacherous task ahead was not his alone. His two younger brothers, Joseph and Pherorus, were not blessed with his strength of character and battle prowess. Memories of Joseph made Herod smile. He had a special love for boy, only a year younger than he was, who had been fiercely determined to reach his older brothers' level of mastery in the classroom and on the imaginary battlefield of their youth. However, Joseph lacked the tenacity to stay with any particular pursuit for long; he soon lost interest and was off to the next. Last he had heard, Joseph held a position in Roman administration in faraway Venice.

Herod could not count on his youngest brother, Pherorus, either. He was firmly entrenched at his clerical worktable in Syria. In his sporadic correspondence, he seemed to be content in his dreary job, toiling as a clerk in Roman Antioch. Like Joseph, Pherorus was not equipped to rescue or to rule.

Herod was the only man who could save his brother and retake Jerusalem.

~

*I*n Petra Palace's Roman-style bathhouse, Herod soaked in the steaming water and considered how he ought to approach King Aretas. He could ask for gold in a straightforward way, or he might state his needs and hope his royal kinsman offered assistance. Either way, there were possible pitfalls. He decided to gauge the king's receptiveness in the morning when they met.

Back in his quarters, Herod found his dinner tray on the table. He drank another vessel of wine and wolfed down the fragrant roast fowl in fig sauce. Then he lay down, clean and sated, and fell into a troubled sleep.

Sometime in the early hours of the morning, he woke up to find a young woman standing over his bed. In the weak light of the oil lamp she held, he could see her long, straight hair, the color of ripe wheat. She opened her robe, exposing her full breasts. In his sleepy, drunken state, Herod recalled once spending an intensely pleasurable night with a prostitute who had looked much like her.

The woman smiled at him with berry-reddened lips. "I'm yours for the night, a gift from the king,"

Her thick accent sounded unfamiliar. From which faraway land had King Aretas captured this concubine?

"I wish to make you happy," she said in a heavy accent.

Herod's blood grew hot. He was married to Doress and betrothed to Mariamne, but nights of anonymous pleasure were a man's prerogative, and did not matter one sword hilt. He lifted his silk-covered blanket and invited her into his bed.

Whether or not a woman enjoyed sexual congress with him was not his concern, but did she have to lie as still as a corpse while he took his pleasure, and squeeze her eyes shut as if she was in terrible pain? It was a hasty coupling. He pulled away from her as soon as he obtained his satisfaction.

"Leave me now," he said, not bothering to hide his nakedness.

The woman's eyes grew coin-round with surprise. She snatched her tunic and scurried away.

Soon after daybreak, a servant summoned him to the king's hall, where Aretas received his guests and petitioners. Herod threw his shoulders back and kept his head up. It was essential for him to come across as a calm and confident leader of men. His future depended on it.

King Aretas and Prince Ahmad were already there, sitting with knees pulled to chests on a rug of shimmering reds and blues. The king had aged considerably since Herod had last seen him. His once coal-black hair was now silver as the twilight sea. Loose skin hung from his jowls. Herod could only hope the king's mind was still sharp and he was in a generous mood.

Herod greeted his royal kinsmen. The king motioned for him to sit down. A new and welcome serenity washed over him. He was among family. Of course, Aretas would help him.

"It's been years since we have last met. I hope you are finding your quarters to your liking?"

"Yes, I'm quite comfortable."

"What brings you such a long way from home?"

As if he did not know. He had spies, too.

"Antigonus and the Parthians have overtaken Jerusalem. They're holding my brother Phasael captive. I need gold to bribe them for his release. And I need more to raise an army to sweep the usurpers and invaders from Jerusalem, and to put Hyrcanus back at the helm."

"Antigonus is the son of King Hyrcanus's brother, Aristobulus, am I correct?"

"Yes," said Herod.

"Like his father before him, he has ousted Hyrcanus."

Herod's heart thumped a quickened beat. "Yes, Aristobulus overthrew Hyrcanus in a rebellion, but he ruled for only a short time before Hyrcanus retook Jerusalem with my father's help. Your gold will help assure Antigonus has only a brief reign as well. I must return the throne to the true Maccabee ruling line and help Hyrcanus restore stability to the region. To do so, I will need two hundred talents of gold."

"Your family has great wealth," said King Aretas with some annoyance. "Why do you come to me for funds?"

"My wealth is tied up in land. I cannot sell it quickly enough to raise the gold I need now."

The king sat in tight-lipped silence. He and his son exchanged unreadable glances. Herod's shoulders tightened.

"There is something I must tell you," said the king. "It's terrible news, Herod. You must brace yourself. Your brother Phasael is dead."

"Dead?" Herod repeated, his breath shallow, his throat suddenly parched.

"Your brother died an honorable death. When he knew his captors were going to kill him, he took his life into his own hands, and dashed his head against a boulder."

"And that killed him?" Herod could not believe his brother, a man of strength and power, was done in by a rock.

"No, but his injuries were grave," the king said. "Antigonus poured poison into his open wound. That is what killed him."

The chamber began to spin. Herod shut his eyes, tightly. He wanted to rage at the heavens. He wanted to carve out the heart of Phasael's killer with his sword. "My brother must have died in great agony, then," he said, quietly.

"There's no need for gold to free him now," said the King, too lightly.

Herod could no longer sit still. It felt like a knife had sliced open his chest. He needed, more than anything, to be alone with his grief. "Good King, I request your presence again tomorrow.

There are matters I must speak with you about...but now, I cannot."

"Of course," said King Aretas. "Your brother's loss saddens us, too."

Herod returned to his chamber. He drank a prodigious amount of wine while rain pelted his window shutters. The wine did little to dull his fury and his sorrow. His only comfort was the promise he made himself to avenge this unspeakable injustice, this rank insult to his family. His brother's murder strengthened his resolve. He could hardly wait to decimate his enemies.

～

*H*erod awoke at dawn. The clouds blanketing the sky were black as his mood. His stomach roiled. He pushed away his breakfast, and paced up and down, his sandals scraping on marble. The morning was nearly gone when King Aretas finally summoned him. They sat together, face-to-face.

"Thank you for postponing our visit until today," said Herod, his gaze resting on the monarch's heavy eyelids. "I still need two hundred talents of gold to raise an army and seize Judea from Antigonus and the Parthians. Please, good King, give or loan me what I need to do this."

The king's long silence made Herod's pulse race. "I'd like to help you, but sadly, I cannot."

Herod wanted to demand that he explain himself, but he held back.

"Antigonus sent me a message two days ago," said the king. "He warned me you would come to ask me for a war chest."

This could mean only one thing. A spy for Antigonus was among his men. Fury pulsed through every inch of Herod's body. He would root out the duplicitous ass and strangle him with his bare hands.

"Antigonus said he would attack Nabataea if I give you any assistance," said King Aretas. "The Parthians will join their battle against us."

Herod struggled to appear calm. "King Aretas, you are my kinsman. If you will not help me, who will?"

The king stared at him with eyes as dull as Salt Sea mud. "I won't bring war upon my country, Herod, not even for you."

He envisioned himself strangling his royal uncle and throwing him into a canyon where ravens would pluck the flesh from his body. However, he must leave such carnage to the realm of imagination. He could ill afford to make new enemies. He stood up and bowed low to the king and the prince before he took his leave.

Back in his quarters, Herod agonized about his next move. Was there another leader with ready gold who might support his worthy mission? One possibility, however remote, was the Triumvir Marc Antony, Judea's Roman overlord and one of the three generals who ruled the Roman Republic. Antony considered Herod a close friend and ally, he knew that, but to ask him for gold was taking a great risk, perhaps a fatal one, given the triumvir's volatile temper and impulsive decision-making.

7

MARIAMNE, 40 BCE, MASADA

*T*here was no shade on Masada, nothing green and growing to shelter me from the punishing sun and cool me. Incessant winds battered this bleak and barren place, night and day. How I missed Jerusalem, crowded with peddlers calling out their wares, and the clip-clop of beasts pulling wagons down stone streets. The quiet and emptiness of our remote dwelling place left me homesick and disoriented.

Even worse was the limited, stifling company of two old women, my brother, and Salome, the sourest of citrons. Herod's sister alternately sniped at or ignored me, while her mother sat grimly muttering worried words about Herod's welfare. My mother never refrained from the opportunity to interrupt me and everyone else with her esteemed royal opinion. Of course, Aris and I had each other to confide in, and we spent many evenings talking and reading by lamplight, and Lila listened to me and assisted me with her usual warmth and understanding despite her own displacement. At seventeen, however, I needed more, much more, in the way of society.

I mourned for my old life, the way it had been before the invaders and my duplicitous kinsman had upended everything. I should have been in Jerusalem, a princess of the palace, preparing for my wedding to some Maccabee cousin, selecting silks and brocades for my bridal wardrobe, and supervising the decoration of the palace apartments we would take after the ceremony. If only I could spend evenings with my cousins, as I once did, listening to harp and lute players, playing games, laughing. There had been a constant stream of fresh faces and interested men. My subjects had loved me, and even my detractors treated me with deference and respect. Why had I never appreciated my beautiful life, rushing between banquets and state visits and nightly musical entertainments?

Now, not a single handsome, eligible young man vied for my attention. The only men I saw, other than my brother, were the thirty or so guards and soldiers forbidden to speak to me. Most stood watch in palace towers around the edge of the plateau as if we were actually in danger of intruders. I doubted there were any other people around for miles, except for a few roving, peaceful Bedouins.

Samuel was the guard who spent the dark hours of the night in the hallway outside the bedchamber I shared with Lila. He was a handsome man of around twenty, with sand-colored curls and a smile that set his face aglow. I grew accustomed to his presence, and he began to blend into the hallway walls, but Lila was quite taken with him, and he with her. In the torchlight, I could see them exchange glances and flush. The spark of fire between them had nothing to do with the torch blazing in the hallway sconce.

"Samuel admires you," I said one night as I was laying down on my bed, and she was stretching out on her pallet in the corner.

Lila said nothing for a long moment. "It must be you he admires."

"Oh, no," I said, covering myself with a combed wool blanket. "It's you. His eyes follow you ..."

"Worry not, Mariamne. I won't leave you."

"You are a freedwoman, Lila. You can leave if you want. I would not hold you back from happiness."

The truth was I would be devastated if Lila left me to marry, if her face was not the first one I saw upon waking, and the last before falling asleep. How could I survive without her help and friendship?

"Do you miss Herod?" she asked. "Are you worried about him?"

"I don't miss him, but I do worry about him. I have this confusing mix of feelings, Lila. I'm grateful he rescued us from the Parthians' invasion." I loathed him, however, for his burdening me with his heinous secret ambition. The knowledge gnawed at the lining of my belly and kept me awake on many long nights. "We need him, I know that much."

We had heard nothing from Herod. Not knowing his fate or progress was maddening. If he still lived, he was seeking a war chest and raising an army to battle my treasonous cousin Antigonus and the foreign intruders. He might have already subjected my beloved Jerusalem to the ravages of war. It could be in ruins, and my home, the Jerusalem Palace, a pile of rubble and ashes. If Herod was dead, we had no protector, and my family would be the next to fall.

"I hope your dreams are sweet," Lila said.

"You, too," I murmured, and closed my eyes.

The quiet of desert nights unsettled me. Not even nightingales sang. With an ache deep in my marrow, I tried to remember Jerusalem's sunset, and how it washed the city's walls and gates in pink-tinged gold.

～

*E*very day, I did things I had never dreamed of doing. For one, I helped Rachel, our stout, congenial cook, in the garden. She taught me to plant and care for the vegetable patches. To my surprise, I loved working with my hands to water and weed and coax greenery from the barren earth. No longer was I a passive royal cared for by servants. I was contributing to our survival. It gave me a new pride. I quite liked the feeling.

One morning, before the searing afternoon heat drove everyone inside, Rachel and I were weeding lentil beans. I looked up to find Salome standing in the palace doorway. She gazed at us with large-eyed longing. That was when I realized Salome was lonely. I shaded my eyes with my hand and greeted her.

"Come join us," I said. "We would welcome another pair of hands."

Salome stiffened, wheeled around, and disappeared inside.

"Do you know why she's so cold?" I asked Rachel.

The cook shrugged thick shoulders. "I was a cook in Antipater's home when Salome and Herod were children. I don't recall her ever having a friend beside Herod. Those two often had their heads together, whispering. About what, I never knew. They always quieted when anyone walked in."

Salome's coldness baffled me. Her bloodlines were inferior to my own, yet I was willing to treat her as if she was a natal sister. Had I done something to offend or slight her? I could not think of anything. Perhaps her hostility was just awkwardness, and her brusque treatment was not personal. She did not know how to be a friend. I could teach her.

Determined to win her friendship, I gave a guard a coin to catch a yellow songbird and build a birdcage. I proudly presented the tiny, chirping gift to Salome. Without even looking at me, she brought the cage outside, unlatched the gate, and set the bird free. Her rudeness stung me. Nevertheless, I was glad to see the creature's joy as it soared into the sky.

~

I took refuge from my mother's constant grousing and Salome's snubs in the dovecote, a crude outbuilding that housed our doves. I fed the birds concoctions of grain, seed, and olive oil, and I swept up their dung to nourish our vegetable garden. It soothed me to reach into their cages and stroke their soft feathers and listen to their reassuring coos. When a mother with hatchlings died, I fed her babies bits of grain and drops of water and managed to keep them alive. In those moments, I could forget I was Herod's captive.

When the weather cooled, I decided to make one more effort to

befriend Salome. I invited her to come with me to care for the
doves. To my surprise, she agreed. However, when we arrived at the
dovecote, she sat outside and refused to come inside. Her face was as
stony as the steps on which she sat. I did not say a word to her while
I swept and fed the twittering birds. I fully expected her to leave, but
she stayed. I noticed how she kept scratching a red patch on her
elbow.

"My skin is dry here in the desert," I said. "Yours too?"

Salome nodded. "Every night I rub olive oil on my elbows.
They're red again by morning."

"I have something that will help you," I said. "I'll be right back."

I plucked a sprig of aloe from the garden and took it to the
kitchen and crushed it with a mortar and pestle, mixed it with olive
oil, and poured the concoction into an earthen vial. I brought it to
Salome. "Try rubbing some of this on your elbow every night before
you go to sleep," I said. "I do, and it's helped."

Salome regarded me with wide-eyed surprise. Gingerly, she took
the vessel and thanked me with solemn dignity. For the first time in
ages, I had hope we could be friends. We walked back to the palace
together in silence. I was about to enter my quarters when she called
my name. I turned to her.

"Why do you do servant's work? I don't understand you, Mariamne. You ought to conduct yourself like a princess. Royalty is
wasted on you."

~

One starless night, a servant summoned me to my mother's
chambers. She rarely sent for me. I entered with trepidation. Her quarters were lavish, by Masada standards. Silken rugs of
crimson and cobalt covered the stone floors. Faded tapestries
adorned the high walls.

My mother sat on a high-backed chair on velvet cushions,
mending a robe in the flickering lamplight. She looked up at me
with pursed lips and a furrowed brow. "How I hate mending," she
said. "Sit down, Mariamne. Help me."

I picked up a tunic from the stack and sat down across for from her. We could not replace worn and tattered robes and tunics, so we repaired our clothing as best we could. At home, the only time I ever lifted a needle was to embroider decorations on robes for my own amusement.

"I never dreamed I'd be reduced to having to do menial labor," my mother said with a thin sigh.

I shrugged and threaded my bone needle. "We need to speak, Mariamne."

My chest tightened. When my mother began conversations with this ominous introduction, trouble tended to follow.

"It's about your marriage."

I sat up straighter. "Have you heard from Herod? Is he coming to take us home?"

"No," she said, with a deep scowl. "There's been no word at all."

It seemed my mother was in a particularly foul mood. I doubted she had anything kind to say. A deep weariness settled over me, and I wanted only to sleep. "Can we talk in the morning? I feel a headache coming on."

She shook her head, rustling her silk headdress, and tut-tutted. "Our exile to this forsaken place is all your grandfather's fault. If he had been a strong king, Aris's succession to the throne would have been assured. But sadly, he's a weak and incompetent man."

A wave of fury swept over me like it always did when I thought about the downfall of my family. The Maccabees had independently ruled Judea for nearly one hundred years before the Romans conquered Judea and made my country a vassal state of Rome.

Sneering, Mother set aside her sewing, "Herod turned my father into a figurehead while he ruled Judea. Your grandfather failed to recognize his glaringly obvious ambition."

"I know this, Mother."

"Herod smiled and waved to our subjects during public events as though he already ruled the country," she said. "Your grandfather was blind and deaf to his threat. And he has grown weaker with each passing year."

"Did you summon me here to tell me that? Please, Mother. You know I hate it when you criticize Grandfather. If he still lives he's a prisoner in Parthia—an old and broken man." Despite the horrible marriage he had arranged for me, I loved him with all my heart.

"No one can break you unless you allow yourself to be broken. My father has permitted Rome and its puppets to destroy him."

"Grandfather is a kind and gentle man."

"He allowed Herod to act as our true leader," my mother said, with a flinty glower. "He allowed the Idumean to sign scrolls meant for his attention without even showing them to him. Before long, he will try to steal your grandfather's title as well. He promised my father he would protect Aris's ascent to the throne. He lied. Herod wants the throne for himself."

I felt myself flush, and fixed my eyes on my sewing. If I told her Herod had confessed as much to me she was likely to storm into the desert to find him and make everything worse. We would all lose our heads.

"Mariamne, always remember this. Your chief duty is to your family. After you marry Herod, you will be in a good position to manipulate him. You must do anything, and I mean anything, I ask of you to put your brother on the throne. If you cannot manipulate Herod and he proves to be a threat to your brother's sovereignty, you must eliminate him."

I looked at my mother with dazed disbelief. "Mother!" I cried, feeling my breath catch in my throat. "You expect me to kill Herod?"

"Of course, if other measures aren't fruitful."

"I couldn't do that. You know I follow God's Commandments."

"Then you will have to sway Herod to protect your brother's throne until he is of age to rule, and then turn it over to him."

"Do you think Herod is going to allow me, or anyone else for that matter, to manipulate him? This marriage has thrown me to the mountain lions."

My mother took my cold hand in hers. "Try to see the advantages of this marriage. Herod has many fine attributes. He's a handsome man and a fierce warrior. People say he's a brilliant general and a gifted scholar."

"He frightens me…"

"Frightens you? Why?"

"There's something about his eyes. They're penetrating, like he can see through—"

"Herod is intelligent. Intelligent men are often sharp-eyed."

I pulled my hand away. "I don't love him."

My mother gave me a bitter smile. "It matters not, Mariamne. Love is for peasants. Royals marry not for love, but to strengthen our positions. At your age, I was betrothed to your father, my cousin. Do you think I had any say in my engagement? I didn't even like him when we first married. In time, we fell in love. Perhaps you, too, will grow to love your husband."

The only thing I remembered about my parents' marriage was the frostiness between them, their long, stony silences, their raised voices. With Grandfather Hyrcanus and his wife, it had been different. I had seen the kind consideration they had shown each other, and the genuine happiness on their faces when they first saw each other after being apart. Theirs was the kind of marriage I wanted.

"Just don't expect Herod to love you."

I sat up straighter, bracing myself for the assault I knew was coming.

"He will admire your beauty, darling. Only a blind man wouldn't see it. But don't fool yourself. Herod would wed and bed you if you were the ugliest crone on earth."

I stopped sewing and closed my eyes. When I opened them, my mother was regarding me with the same disdain she had once shown the village idiot who had once fetched our water.

"You're a Maccabee Princess, Mariamne. You've had every possible privilege—the best education, the finest robes. You've lived in the most beautiful palaces in the land. Do I have high expectations of you? Yes, of course, I do."

She put a bony hand on my shoulder. It felt heavy. "Think of Aris—what a fine king he will make. He needs you, Mariamne, to

help him reach the throne. We all need you. This marriage is your
destiny."

8

HEROD, 40 BCE, ALEXANDRIA

*K*ing Aretas had refused to give Herod the gold he needed, but he had no time to sink into despair. He had a war to win. There was one other possibility. The Roman Triumvir Marc Antony might be willing to provide him with a war chest. Antony lived in Alexandria with his lover, the Pharaoh Cleopatra, so he must sail to Egypt and make a personal entreaty. This was no matter to entrust to a messenger.

Herod agonized about how Antony was going to respond. The mercurial statesman might smile and shower him with gold, or he might take a sword and separate his head from his neck, depending on his mood that particular day. Herod was certain, however, that Cleopatra, who ruled a vast and wealthy nation, would not welcome his presence in her country. Nor would she encourage Antony to grant his request. She despised him. Spies had reported overhearing her say as much to Antony. Herod had not yet met her, so her contempt must have been based on jealousy of his longstanding friendship with Antony. He was sure she wanted to undermine him so she could more easily persuade Antony to satisfy her lust to rule Judea, a land she and her Ptolemaic ancestors had long coveted and considered their due.

With a great foreboding, Herod set sail for Egypt.

~

*T*he ship approached Alexandria, and Herod caught sight
of Pharos Island. Once near the shore, he gazed with awe
at the lighthouse, a column of white marble towering into the sky.
Screeching seabirds dipped and dove around the statues of golden
angels ornamenting its upper reaches. Herod recognized it. It was
one of the Seven Wonders of the World. Years ago, his tutor had
shown him illustrations of the great structures of Alexandria. For a
moment, he forgot his perilous mission.

Farther down Alexandria Harbor, Antirhodus Island's massive
marble buildings glinted bone-white under the cerulean sky. The
brilliant sunlight made him squint as he identified Pharaoh's
immense Royal Palace and the Temple of Isis, boxy and pillared.
Cleopatra's liveried guards waved the ship into the Royal Harbor.
The crew unfurled a rope and dropped anchor.

~

*O*utside the arched entrance to Cleopatra's great marble
palace, Herod faced stern and suspicious armed sentinels.
Filthy and exhausted from his voyage, he wished he had first found
a bathhouse and had a long soak, drank a bottle of wine, and had
a good night's sleep before facing this ordeal, but it was too
late now.

"Yes?" a guard asked.

"I'm Herod, son of Antipater, Governor of Galilee and Chief
Counsel to Governor Hyrcanus of Judea. I'm here to see the
Triumvir Marc Antony."

"Pharaoh is not expecting you," another sentinel said.

"I hadn't the time to announce my coming. Again, it's Triumvir
Antony I've come to see, not Pharaoh."

The guards exchanged amused glances. The chief guard
dispatched a manservant to seek consent for Herod's entry to palace.

The manservant disappeared for a few uncomfortable minutes, and then returned and gave the chief a resolute nod.

"Leave your weapons here," a guard said.

Herod expected as much, but still, he felt naked without them.

Reluctantly, he handed over his sword and dagger. "All of your weapons."

With some hesitancy, Herod reached into an interior compartment in his robe and pulled out another dagger. The handle's inlaid rubies glinted in the bright sunlight. It had been his father's, and he prized it.

The guard nodded to a slave, wearing only a loincloth, who took Herod down a long hall to an airy bedchamber. Cloud-white marble floors met marbled walls of the same hue. Even the furs stretched across the inviting bed were blindingly white.

"Cleopatra will summon you to the garden when she's willing to see you," said the houseman.

Cleopatra? This confusion was most disturbing. How thick were these Egyptians? He must straighten this out right away. "As I have told the guards, I'm here to meet with the Triumvir Marc Antony, not Pharaoh."

"I'll return when *Pharaoh* tells me to fetch you," he replied with an insolent smile.

Herod's shoulder muscles tensed. The Egyptians were going to make this as difficult for him as they could. Then, it occurred to him that greeting Cleopatra before conducting other business was, perhaps, an Egyptian diplomatic custom. He nodded, politely.

$\backsim$

*L*ate that afternoon, two guards led Herod to the manicured garden behind the palace and asked him to take a chaise on the terra cotta tiled area beside the gold fountains. A heady perfume wafted from white lotus blossoms floating serenely in the fountain pool. On plump silk cushions, he surveyed the magnificent grounds, lush with vibrant flowerbeds and shaded by majestic date palms. It was beautiful, yes, but Herod could not enjoy it. His future, and the future of Judea, depended upon Antony's response. He drummed his fingers on the marble table beside him. Why was time passing so slowly?

His best hope was that Antony would accompany Cleopatra. He would greet her with respect and ask her to excuse herself so the men could speak privately. Might she take offense at such a request? Few women would, but Cleopatra was no ordinary woman; she was not expected to behave like one. She was known as a strong and decisive leader who well-ruled her wealthy and powerful nation. No other female in the known world held the vast power she did. Perhaps as important, she had the respect, and perhaps, the love of Antony, the most powerful man in Rome. Before Antony had been her lover, Julius Caesar shared her bed.

Despite her romantic alliances, Herod knew that Cleopatra's strength was based on more than taking Roman leaders as her lovers. Rome needed Egypt's wealth to finance its expensive military adventures, and Egypt needed Rome's protection. Pharaoh was known to be as shrewd and intelligent as any male monarch, and more so than most. She had Antony's trust, and his ear as well as his body. She was closer to Antony than he was, and their dalliance made Egypt even more powerful, and her, more dangerous. Therefore, he must tread carefully.

Could Herod charm her like he did most women? He hoped so. Suddenly restless, he jumped up and paced the terrace. He had long heard tales of Cleopatra's disarming allure, and he had never met a man she had not captivated. Of course, he was there for business with Antony, not for romance, so her magnetism was irrelevant.

A long hour later, Cleopatra swept in, flanked by slaves and servants. His chin dropped when he caught sight of her. Her beauty did not disappoint. She greeted him with a mysterious yet warm half-smile on her generous lips. Her kohl-lined eyes were astonishingly bright and clear, and her direct gaze, though unusual for a woman, was not intimidating. Glossy black hair cascaded down her back in long waves.

He did not want to stare, but how could he take his eyes from the white silk dress draped across her ample chest? A belt of glimmering gold pulled the dress to her narrow waist, and it flowed down like a silken waterfall over the curve of her hips to the floor. Her perfume, or perhaps her own scent, intoxicated him. With rare shyness, he bowed to her.

"I thank you, good Pharaoh, for your gracious hospitality."

She appeared to be delighted to meet him. Several emerald bracelets jingled on her shockingly bare arms when she offered him a soft, warm hand. Glimmering gold rings encircled her fingers.

"Welcome to Egypt, Herod, Son of Antipater. Antony will be sorry he missed your visit. He has business in Rome for the next months."

Pain deep in Herod's gut seized him. He stopped himself from drawing his hand to his aching belly. He could show no weakness. But Antony's absence was no less than a disaster. He had wasted valuable time journeying to Alexandria while Antigonus and the Parthians were growing more entrenched in their control of Jerusalem. He should have sailed straight to Rome to meet with Antony.

It was Cleopatra's fault he was in the unfortunate position of having to beg anyone for gold now. Antony would have seen the Parthian threat coming, and quashed it, had Cleopatra not bewitched him to tarry with her in Egypt for so long. Herod tried to mask his disappointment behind a deferential smile.

Cleopatra ordered her underlings away, and they scuttled to the periphery of the garden. She motioned Herod to the double chaise and stretched out beside him. With a snap of her fingers, servants swiftly filled two gold goblets with wine.

"To what do I owe this unannounced visit?" Pharaoh asked in a voice melodious as a musical instrument.

Should he tell her he had come to solicit Antony? No, he concluded, he would not. The truth would gain him nothing. Instead, he would massage the narcissism of a woman who had recently minted coins depicting herself as the goddess Isis. If he flattered her, she might be more likely to help him.

"I've come to tell you news I couldn't entrust to a messenger. The Parthians of Persia have overrun Judea."

Cleopatra smirked. "I am aware of this. The Parthians have ousted Hyrcanus."

"There's more. The Parthians have taken Hyrcanus to prison in Parthia, and they have appointed his nephew, Antigonus, the new King of Judea."

Cleopatra cocked her head, rustling the strands of jewel woven into her shiny hair. "How did Antigonus manage to steal Hyrcanus's throne?"

Herod brightened. She was listening. "When the Parthians invaded Judea, Antigonus bribed the Parthian King. He offered him five hundred daughters of Jewish aristocrats he had stolen and enslaved to allow him to rule as Judea's vassal king."

Her jaw dropped. Herod suspected he had just stunned a woman who was not easily stunned. His power to elicit such a response emboldened him. "I've freed those women, and returned them to their families."

"Ah, Herod, you are a hero."

The meeting was going unexpectedly well. Perhaps Cleopatra did not despise him after all. It seemed she admired him. Then, there was the possibility she was toying with him.

"Were you aware that Antigonus bit off Hyrcanus's right ear?"

"Bit off his... Oh, gods! Has Antigonus joined forces with the Parthians against Rome?"

"Yes," said Herod. Her mesmerizing eyes were taking him in with a look of wonder. Cleopatra would come to his aid; he could feel her empathy for him. He wanted to help her, too. There was no need to hunt down Antony. Confidence radiated from him. "Honorable Pharaoh, for Rome and Egypt, I'll rid the land of Persian intruders and take the crown back for Governor Hyrcanus, or in his absence, for his grandson."

Cleopatra smirked. "Oh, I see. You want to put *Aris* on the throne, do you?"

Herod swallowed hard. How dare she resort to sarcasm at his expense? He tried to conceal his distress. He did not respond until he could do so with calm. "Yes, I do."

She snapped her fingers, twice. Slaves instantly stepped forward and fanned them with palm fronds, a welcome relief in the sweltering heat of the afternoon.

Cleopatra's eyes suddenly clouded. "Does Princess Alexandra and her family still live?"

"Yes, I've taken them all to Masada. They're sheltering there with my mother and sister, under my guard." He sipped his wine. "You're acquainted with Princess Alexandra?" What hellish trouble was their friendship going to bring him?

"Oh, yes," she said, her smile mirthful. "Princess Alexandra is my dear friend. We have corresponded for years." She gave him a sardonic smile. "So, you rescued them, did you? How heroic."

Pharaoh's vacillating tone confused him. Perhaps she did loathe him. He must think only of his mission.

"There's still much work to be done."

"So, Herod, what do you want of me," she said, her gaze suddenly bored.

He cleared his throat. He would rather have been back on the rickety ship that brought him to Alexandria. "Good Pharaoh, I'll need gold to oust Antigonus and the Parthians and restore the throne to the royal line."

"You want gold? What a surprise."

"The Parthians are ambitious. They won't stop at Judea. They've already taken several other Roman territories. Eventually, they will attack your shores, too. If you grant my request, I'll defend our shared border."

"My answer is no."

His heart lurched; still, he forced an impassive expression.

She leaned in close to him. "I have a better idea, Herod. Stay here in Egypt with me. Antony tells me you are a brilliant military strategist. I will make you my highest general."

Her words nearly knocked him off his chaise. He thought of the life Cleopatra was offering: power, riches, and glory. He did not want it—not in Egypt. It was Judea he coveted.

"Cleopatra—"

"Listen to me, Herod," she said, and raised her hand as if to stop him. Her gold bracelets clattered. "I am giving you an opportunity to command the army of a nation larger and stronger than any other in our region."

Her offer confirmed what he had long suspected: his reputation for military excellence went well beyond his own country.

"If you stay here with me, I will reward you with riches beyond your imagination."

Her warm, radiant smile dazzled him. But he could not let her trap him in her treacherous web. Had she made the offer because she wanted his absence to weaken Judea, after which she could more easily persuade Antony to annex his land to Egypt?

Her dark gaze rested upon his face. "Gold, jewels, land, women, boys, I will grant you whatever it is you desire."

He allowed himself a moment to muse about the prestige and power that would come with his position as Pharaoh's top general. But it could never happen. At the helm of the Egyptian Army, Herod would shine, perhaps too brightly. And a close relationship with Cleopatra might make Antony jealous enough to put a blade through his beating heart.

"Forget the Maccabees," she said, tossing back a sleek lock of hair that had fallen in her eyes. "There is so much more we can do together here in Egypt."

Cleopatra reached out and stroked Herod's face with a long, slim finger. Herod could hardly believe what was happening. He hoped his expression did not reveal his shock. Still, he imagined himself peeling off her gown and laying her down. He wanted to feel her beneath him. He would like to hear her moan. No, he would not—could not—do it. But he could not rebuff her, either. From experience, he knew that a woman scorned could cause a man considerable grief. He forced himself to neither move toward her nor to recoil. It was a delicate operation.

"As much as I'd like to stay here with you, Pharaoh, I cannot. I've already signed a *ketubah* to marry Princess Mariamne."

Cleopatra quickly withdrew her hand and stood up, spear straight, with all the pride of her long line of highborn ancestors. "Ah, yes, Princess Alexandra's daughter. I hear she is a great beauty."

"She is," he said.

A harder look replaced her smile. "You dismiss my offer so hastily, Herod. Is it not enticing enough for you to even consider?"

"I'd like to assent, Pharaoh," he said with a helpless shrug, "but I have duties I must attend to at home."

Her eyes narrowed, ominously. "I know your sort, Herod. You want power. You will stop at nothing to attain the throne. I do not believe you have any intention of seeing Aris lead Judea."

Herod widened his eyes and tried to appear surprised. "You misunderstand me, Pharaoh. I mean, I have failed to make myself clear to you."

"You have made yourself abundantly clear to me, Herod. You are Antony's vassal king, not mine. Go ask him for gold. Oh yes, before you go, you should know that Anthony has permitted me to annex some Judean lands."

Herod swallowed hard. "Which lands?"

"Leave me now." With a self-satisfied grin, she waved him away as if he was her slave. "May the gods allow you safe passage."

The humiliation stung. Nevertheless, Herod forced himself into a prideful posture and bowed to her. He would not give her the satisfaction of seeing his abject misery.

"And may the gods watch over you, too, Pharaoh," he said. "Please—return my weapons to me."

She cocked her head. Long earrings jingled. "We will, eventually."

Two of Cleopatra's burly Thracian guards grabbed Herod's arms. They escorted him out of the palace and onto a ferry that took him across a narrow strip of water to mainland Alexandria, where a royal carriage waited for him. It all seemed calculated. She must have orchestrated his eviction before she had met with him. He squeezed between the two guards, and the carriage bumped down streets of the city. Oxcarts thronged the road, hauling everything from shirtless workers to clucking chickens. Peddlers calling out prices carried baskets piled high with citrons and vegetables. Shoppers crowded the markets. Smoke coiled above the cooking houses of the packed open-air cafes. The carriage came to a sharp halt at the port, and the driver motioned Herod to step down.

"My weapons?"

The older guard gave him a curt nod and reunited him with his sword and daggers. It was a relief to be armed again.

"I'll need a ship to sail me to Rome. Has the Queen of Egypt made arrangements?"

"No."

Sympathy softened the guard's small, sharp eyes. This miscreant pitied him. It was intolerable.

As soon as his sandals touched the pebbled ground, the carriage and its driver and guards left him there, alone, holding his own bag like a peasant. Herod looked around to get his bearings. Fishing vessels bobbed in the azure harbor's gently lapping waters. Anglers were returning to shore, their dragnets full of fish. Above the din of the screeching gulls swooping down to feast on discarded fish carcasses, he heard the shouted negotiations between fishermen and fishmongers. The harbor air smelled of a pungent combination of rotting fish and salt air. A toothless woman pushed a flopping, gold-headed fish she was struggling to hold at Herod.

"Bream here!" she called.

The woman's wig had slipped back, exposing her short-cropped hair. Egyptian women wore wigs on their near-bald heads to avoid lice. He waved her away and sank on a stone step to ponder his next move.

He must find his way to Rome before Antony returned to Alexandria. Antony's solo presence in Rome was going to give him a rare opportunity to make an appeal to the triumvir without unwelcome interference from Cleopatra. He had to leave right away if he was going to arrive in Rome before she could reach Anthony with a message asking her lover to deny him the gold he needed. As certain as the Nile flooding in summer, she would ruin him if she could.

Antony had every reason to grant Herod his request. He was, after all, offering to do Rome's dirty work—banishing the invading Parthians and the traitorous Antigonus from Judea in favor of Hyrcanus's line, a family that had long proven loyal to Rome. He knew he had Antony's respect; the triumvir had publicly recognized Herod as a brilliant military commander on several occasions.

That was when the thought occurred to him. It was time to make his ambitions known. Instead of asking Antony to allow him to protect Aris's throne, why not ask the triumvir to crown him King of Judea? His forthcoming marriage to Mariamne made him a credible contender for the Judean crown.

Exhilaration made his heart race. Of course, Antony would agree. The triumvir was an intelligent man; he had to know Herod was better suited than any other to rule Judea. After all, he had made sure Antony was well aware that Herod had long been the brains and brawn behind the feeble Hyrcanus. Was there any other man who had the experience and gravitas to command soldiers, and to govern men and territory? Was there any other man who better understood the political machinations of Rome and the importance of prompt and generous support and tribute? No, there was not.

Herod was clearly the best choice for King of Judea. Antony had to see that. Hyrcanus was languishing in prison, and even if Parthia released him, he would be too old and addled to rule, and as a maimed man, he could no longer serve as high priest. Aris, his twelve-year-old grandson and heir, was not going to come of age to take the crown for years. Rome had been rarely inclined to accept boy kings. Many did not live long enough to reach adulthood and the throne, and their uncooperative regents often proved difficult to dismiss when the boy kings came of age. He doubted Rome would agree to pour gold into establishing a Maccabee regency in Judea.

Two seabirds squabbled over a fish carcass. The larger bird made short work of the smaller one, leaving it mangled and bloodied on the shore. Herod was that stronger bird. He would leave the weaker ones bloodied in their wake, and they were all weaker than he was. Euphoria swept over him as he imagined his glorious destiny unfolding. He would marry the prize bride of her generation, and as king, he would transform Judea into the shining jewel of the Mediterranean, more magnificent than its most aristocratic elite could dare to dream. He would change his nation from the backwater it was to the brightest cog in the wheel of the Roman

Republic. He would prove he was the son his father should have favored.

Herod jingled the silk bag of gold that hung from his belt and soon engaged a ship to sail him to Rome. He knew what he had to do. Still, he dreaded it, because Antony was his last chance.

9

MARIAMNE, 40 BCE, MASADA

*M*onths after our arrival, we were still Herod's prisoners in the searing heat and howling winds of the high desert. The unforgiving sun burned and freckled my fair skin. Gardening made my hands rough and calloused. Frustration and boredom parched my soul. I was squandering the full bloom of my youth on a mountain plateau without the diversion of feasts or holidays. There was little to read or study, though we gathered in the palace on Sabbath mornings to recite the prayers we knew by heart. I was well on my way to becoming a sad spinster, trapped in the company of my family and Herod's, a world away from the civilities of Jerusalem.

Salome's unrelenting contempt added to the misery of my confinement. When I spoke to her, she either gave me a snapping retort, or she ignored me. Every rebuff drove me further away from her, and as time went by, I cared less and less about winning her friendship.

The most difficult part about life on Masada was the long silence from the outside world. We heard nothing from Herod or from anyone else. My betrothed could be waging a brutal battle for Jerusalem. If he died, my family and his own would soon follow. No

one else was strong enough to protect our families from Antigonus
and the Parthians.

Did anyone else know we were lodging at Masada? If Herod
had not told anyone where we were before he fell in battle or from
disease, there was a chilling possibility we would all be forgotten.
Would some poor souls come to Masada one hundred years from
now and find our skeletons?

I feared my betrothed's demise even more than I dreaded a
future in which he lived to challenge Aris's birthright. Still, my
Maccabee line was a determined lot. We would find a way to return
to rule.

I considered an escape. Was it possible? Could I venture out into
the Judean Hills with Lila and Aris? The desert—with its wild
animals and brigands and bands of vicious nomads—was not a
hospitable place.

Could I pay a soldier to take a message to my loyal Maccabee
cousins, begging them to come for me? Were there any loyal
Maccabee kin? Antigonus had, most likely, killed any who were
sympathetic to my line, or converted them to his banner under
threat. A messenger would face not only the brutal desert but also
the danger posed by invaders and people ravaged by war. Even if I
could find someone willing, I could not risk spending the gold my
mother had sewn into the hems of our robes on a plan unlikely to
bear fruit. Sadly, I had no choice, for now, but to stay on this
forsaken plateau.

～

*O*ne night, while the others slept, I slipped out to the edge of
the plateau, to the place where Herod had once tried to kiss
me. It seemed like a long time ago. Jackals howled, and clouds
shrouded the moon and stars, yet the night sky comforted me. There
was a world out there, and a chance, however slight, we might
someday be part of it again.

Knowing Herod's plan to steal the Judean throne weighed upon
me. I wished I had refused to speak with Herod privately, had not

given him the chance to tell me of his treasonous ambition to rule, on the day we had arrived at Masada. Then, I might not have suffered from a constant ache in my belly. But knowledge was power. Knowing of his scheme allowed me to devise a plan to stop Herod from executing it. I did not know what it was yet, but please, God, let me find a way short of the sin of murder. My family and my people were relying on me.

I heard footsteps. I looked up, and Lila stood beside me. Seeing her comforted me. My loneliness dissolved and blew away in the stiff winds.

"I worried when I woke up and saw your bed was empty," Lila said.

I turned to her. "I must survive, Lila. I must see justice done and restore the throne to my family."

With a sigh, Lila fixed her eyes on the distant Salt Sea gleaming silver in the moonlight. "Of course, you will survive and go home to fulfill your destiny. I know you will."

If I only had Lila's confidence. How did a wife undermine her husband's overreaching ambitions? "Herod can be quite brutal. I must be smart about it."

"You will think of something."

"I fear I will never have the chance to help Aris—and we will die here, Lila. What if no one ever comes for us, and we use all of our water and food? What if the winter deluge never comes, and drought dries our cisterns? I don't want to die and spend eternity here." I imagined my grave in the cracked, parched earth at the foot of Masada, and I shivered. "There is so much I must still do."

Lila nodded, solemnly. "One day we will return home."

"Do you want to return home, Lila? Would you rather marry Samuel and be a soldier's wife? I love you too much to keep you with me if you would rather be somewhere else."

Over the last weeks, I had often seen Lila and Samuel laughing together in the courtyard after dinner. They seemed to inhabit their own world, drinking each other in, oblivious to everything around them. When the soldiers did their daily drill in the open field, Lila looked out of the window and watched him.

"I hardly know him," she said, looking away.

To distract myself from these disturbing thoughts, I counted the stars. I tallied up to three hundred before the blazing tail of a shooting star caught my attention. I could not remember if a shooting star was a good omen or a bad one.

10

HEROD, 40 BCE, ROME

*A*t the Port of Alexandria, Herod hired a ship, weatherworn to a dull gray, sailing to the Port of Ostia near Rome. Once aboard, he gripped the rails while the vessel pitched in the harbor, creaking like an old man's knees. He usually savored the heady moment when a ship's captain barked orders to his oarsmen, and the ship skated away from the shore into the vast unknown, farther and farther out until the land disappeared, and there was nothing but endless sea and fresh salt air and squawking seabirds. But today was different. The gray sky was just a shade lighter than the water it met on the horizon. Leaden skies and cascading rain obscured his view.

A crew member with a spotty face and a deep frown approached him. "I have come to take you to your cabin, Sir, Captain's orders." He led Herod down an unsteady ladder of crude wood tied together with rope to a dark chamber large enough for only a sleeping pallet and a piss pot.

"This looks like servants' quarters," Herod said.

"Captain says you sleep here," the boy said, without meeting his gaze.

The crewman brought Herod his dinner and scrambled back up

the ladder without a word. A bowl of fowl and turnip stew sat on the tray, none too hot. It smelled terrible and tasted worse, but he was hungry, so he ate.

Soon after he took his last bite, he regretted it. To try to settle his churning stomach, Herod lay down on the straw-stuffed sleeping pallet, but his prone position gave him no relief. The roiling sea was more a swing than a cradle. He vomited into the bucket he had grabbed from a storage cabin. He had almost fallen asleep when a brazen rat darted out from the shadows and scampered across his bed. He smacked it with his staff, and it crumpled on the floor.

Between defending himself from rats and the ship's violent tossing, sleep never took Herod that night. That is why he was still awake in a dark hour of the early morning when the gale struck. Between claps of thunder, he heard the captain shouting frantic orders to the crew to adjust the sails, and he cursed at them for not working fast enough. They needed him on deck. It was rough climbing the ladder while ten-foot waves battered the ship.

Once on deck, Herod grabbed the rail to steady himself against the fierce winds. Lightning made day of night. He could see the captain, wild-eyed and drenched, motion him toward crewmen struggling to raise the sail. He let go of the rail and began to make his way toward them. A gust of wind knocked him flat on his stomach. He slid across the slick deck, but he kept his head and pulled himself upright when the rail wall on the opposite side stopped his slide.

"Tighten the mainsail," the captain called. "Now!"

Through sheer force of will, Herod made his way across the deck to the mast. He helped the crewmen work and carried out the captain's orders alongside the lowliest of crewmen.

The storm broke as suddenly as it had begun. Soon after a red dawn, Herod saw the blessed sight of blue sky and sunrise. On the main deck, He let his vast relief wash over him, feeling a rare fellowship with the captain and crew. Salt-scented air, the purest he had ever inhaled, made the world feel fresh and new again.

For the remainder of the voyage, there were clear skies, but strong headwinds made the trip take days longer than Herod had expected. The ship docked in Ostia, the port nearest Rome, a walled city at the mouth of the Tiber River. The captain whom he had graciously assisted had the audacity to ask Herod for more fare than he had earlier agreed to pay on arrival. Herod laughed and strode away, grateful to feel the firm ground beneath his sandals. He did not look back.

The voyage had not crushed him. Nothing would.

Herod engaged a *cisium*, a two-seated wagon for hire. He needed to bathe and sleep before he faced the Antony and the Roman Senate. "Take me to your finest inn," he told the driver.

Once through Ostia's western gate, his *cisium* joined the parade of wagons, carriages, and ox-carts rolling down the crowded roads. Vendors bearing heavy baskets hawked their wares. The odor of animal dung and emptied slop pots made him gag after weeks of breathing fresh sea air. From his wagon window, Herod studied the strange, multi-storied buildings of concrete brick that appeared to house multiple families. On the edge of town, they turned down a less-traveled, leafy street of large villas with tall pillars. The grandest of all was the Ostia Inn.

Inside the domed atrium, Herod strode across intricate mosaic floors and admired the bare-breasted goddess frescoes. A girl on the verge of womanhood greeted Herod. He wanted to run his fingers through her dark, shimmering curtain of hair and feel her newly budded breasts.

"Would you care to share quarters with other guests, or would you prefer a private chamber?" the girl asked.

"My own," Herod said.

Her uninterested stare disappointed him. Someday, everybody would know his name. They would be honored to meet him. Even Roman aristocrats would instantly recognize him from his distinguished face on the coins he would mint when he became king. He leaned over the table where the girl sat and jingled the silk purse hanging from his belt. "Care to warm my bed tonight?"

The girl's cheeks blazed. "Sir, this isn't that sort of inn," she said, and quickly summoned her brother to take Herod and his bag upstairs.

The chamber's furnishings were the height of Roman luxury. Marble floors, carved-wood chests, and tables of inlaid gold. The goose-down mattress was a world away from his straw pallet on the ship. In the evening, a servant brought him roast lamb and fine wine from the Alban Hills outside Rome. Then, for the first time in ages, Herod wrapped himself in soft linens and fell into a deep, dreamless sleep.

He felt much refreshed in the morning. His breakfast, bread still steaming from the ovens and a small heap of plump figs, awaited his attention on the table beside his bed. He filled his belly and engaged a *cisium* to take him into Rome.

On this shiny morning, Herod felt strong and his mind was clear. He was optimistic about the future, and the confidence he radiated would inspire Antony to see matters his way. The great wheels of his carriage rambled past patches of golden wheat and scarlet poppies, and the rising sun back-lit the wispy, purple-edged clouds. In the distance, he saw the famed arched aqueducts. They channeled water from upland springs all the way to Rome.

The carriage passed through the arched gate in the tall brick wall near Capitoline Hill, and Herod entered Rome. The glory of this moment would be etched in his mind, forever. Anything was possible in this magnificent city. The Via Sacra teemed with new, iron-wheeled *carruca* wagons carrying well-heeled men in togas and women draped in delicate silk robes of vibrant color. Oxen plodded along flagstone streets, hauling baskets of timber and stone, on their way to building sites on the burgeoning outskirts of the city. Masters barked orders to animals and slaves. Donkeys brayed. Down the road, smoke escaped from an open-air *propina* counter, where Romans queued up for bowls of bubbling stew.

If all roads led to Rome, then all Roman roads led to the Forum, the wide rectangle crowned by the pillared Temples of Saturn and Vesta, the Roman Baths, and the Orators' Platform. More merchants' shops than Herod had ever seen in one place opened off of columned walkways.

Herod left the *cisium* behind at the Curia Julia, where the Roman Senate met, and he climbed the stone steps to the entrance. Well-armed sentries in gold breastplates stood guard. From their prideful stances and elite airs, Herod knew they were patrician. He took a deep breath to calm his hammering heart. He would not betray his provincial origins.

"What is your business here?" demanded a sentry in a feathered helmet.

"I am Herod, Son of Antipater, Governor of Galilee. I've come to see the Triumvir Marc Antony."

"It is not possible." The guard pointed to the tablet he held in his meaty hand.

Herod hated the small man who got drunk on his power in his little corner of the universe. He wanted to squash the guard beneath his sandal like the insect he was.

"Please let Antony know I'm here," Herod said with forced deference.

Just as the guard opened his mouth, a barrel-chested Roman emerged from the building and swaggered over. Herod immediately recognized Antony, who had thickened some with age. His short-cropped hair was graying at the temples. The purple trim of royalty edged his linen tunic. Though Herod was elated to find himself in the triumvir's exalted company, he reined in his exhilaration.

"It's good to see you," said Herod with a nod and a dignified smile.

Antony held out his brawny arms and embraced him. "My friend, we haven't met since Bithynia."

Herod did not want to remember their meeting in Bithynia two years before. It was soon after Antony had defeated the Roman leader Cassius at Philippi and proceeded to Asia Minor. There, Antony had met with prominent Jewish aristocrats who complained that the growing power of Herod and Phasael was undermining Hyrcanus's authority. Antony had interrogated Herod about it, but he had defended himself well, and the triumvir had dropped the matter.

"Whatever has brought you this long way must be important," Antony said. "We will go to my villa where we can speak privately."

In the triumvir's gilded *carruca*, his painfully tense shoulders began to loosen. He hoped there was an afterworld where his father could see him now, perched beside one of the leaders of the world's greatest republic, approaching his villa as an honored guest. Herod was no longer the second son in the long shadow of his older brother. He was second to no one. He assured himself Antony would grant his appeal for gold. The triumvir needed to rid Rome of the Parthian invaders and their vassal king, Antigonus. He would make Antony see that he was the man to lead Judea.

He hoped Antony would remember that Herod's father had come to Rome's aid every time the leaders of the republic requested it, whether with gold or men. In fact, Antony still owed his family a substantial amount of gold for unpaid military service. But he knew that Antony's response would ultimately depend on his mood and the sharpness of his memory.

Antony's grand villa, at the summit of a hill near the Via Sacra, was only slightly smaller than Rome's public buildings, and nearly as grand. Life-sized silver and gold angel statues edged the entry chamber's marble walls. Just past it, in the atrium, vibrant frescoes depicting the gods stretched across the lofty dome. A small opening at the top, the *occula*, cast a shaft of light on the sparkling water in the marble pool beneath it. He glimpsed between interior pillars and saw the arched, airy entrance to the massive courtyard, where manicured flower beds opened white petals to the sky. Water cascaded down golden nymph-shaped fountains. So, this was how a great leader lived.

One day, he too would live in sumptuous comfort. He would recline upon soft pillows on marble and bronze chaises, like those on which the drunken, raucous Roman Senators were lounging. Wine vessels and bowls of grapes and figs cluttered the tables and floors. A slave boy offered him wine, but he waved him away. How he wished he could join in the drunken revelry, but he could not. It would be folly to dull his senses before he solicited Antony for title and gold.

Antony put his muscled arm around Herod's shoulder. "Senators, I introduce you to Herod, son of Antipater, Governor of Galilee and chief advisor to King Hyrcanus. Herod and his father before him have long been loyal to Rome. Let's welcome him to the capitol."

Swaying under Bacchus's influence, a balding senator raised his silver goblet in a toast. His eyes gleamed with admiration. "To Governor Herod, who has fought most bravely on our behalf, *salut!*" he slurred.

"*Salut!*" parroted the other senators.

Herod could have burst with pride, but he held back and gave the eminent Romans a mild half-smile. He did not want to appear to be unworldly.

A drunken senator ordered his slave boy to pour wine for Antony. Herod had to get the triumvir away from the inebriated aristocrats before he joined their drunken revelry. He could not afford to lose the opportunity for a sober conversation. Antony had been a surly and unreasonable drunk when last time they met.

"Might we first speak privately, Antony?" Herod asked under his breath.

"Of course," said Antony. "Follow me."

Antony nodded to his guard, who trailed them through the atrium to an inner sanctum, the library. Shelves full of scrolls lined the walls. Antony sat on a cushioned bench behind a mahogany table with inlaid silver flowers. He motioned Herod to sit on the marble bench across from him. Devoid of all expression, Antony's guard closed and locked the door. He stood spear straight beside his master, his brawny arms crossed against his chest.

"What brings you to Rome?" Antony asked.

"I've come to ask you to allow me to rid Judea and its environs of the Parthian intruders and their puppet king, Antigonus. I want to return Judea to Rome."

"Without question, the Parthians must go," said Antony. "But Antigonus is another matter. He's a Maccabee."

"Yes, but Antigonus doesn't descend from King Hyrcanus's royal line that has long ruled Judea. Antigonus is loyal to the Parthians, an enemy of Rome. He's bribed the Parthian King to allow him to rule Jerusalem."

Antony sat back in his chair and gave him a sidewise, assessing look.

"Soon I will marry King Hyrcanus's granddaughter, Mariamne."

Antony smiled. "She's lovely, I've heard."

"She is exquisite. If I ruled Judea, I could—"

"Hyrcanus has a grandson who stands next in line for the throne."

"He does, but Aris is a child, and I know Rome is reluctant to back boy kings."

"True," said Antony. "Too often their regents are slow to see the wisdom of cooperating with us. But here, I could make an exception. I'll appoint you regent to rule Judea until the boy is of age."

Herod felt his jaws clench. "A regent doesn't garner the respect of a king …"

Antony nodded. He put down the gold statue he was fiddling with and fixed his gaze on Herod. Now was the time. "Crown me King of the Jews, Antony. I will rid Judea of its invaders for Rome. I'll faithfully support Rome with soldiers and tribute, supplies, weapons, whatever the republic needs. I'll protect Rome's interests as long as I live, I promise you."

Antony's long, hard look unnerved Herod. If he walked away with nothing, he would soon be nothing but a hunted exile.

"I'm a known entity. The child Aris is not."

The triumvir leaned back and stroked his smooth chin. "I'll appoint you Governor of Judea, the same title old Hyrcanus held after we took his crown."

"If Rome crowns me King of Judea, I'll have stronger authority to enforce Jewish cooperation with Rome. The people will know I have the strength of the republic behind me." Herod knew his words were audacious, but his life and the welfare of Judea was at stake. The triumvir grew disturbingly quiet.

"It's long been my honor to support Rome," Herod added. "When I was Governor of Galilee, I swept out brigands who had rebelled against Roman leadership. Whenever asked, my father and

I came to your aid on the battlefield. Rome is still indebted to my family…"

Antony's dark eyes flashed anger. "I'm well aware of your family's loyalty."

Herod swallowed hard. He had gone too far. Had he stupidly ruined his chances with a few ill-chosen words? Instead of meeting Antony's narrow-eyed glower, he pretended to study the elaborate goddess frescos on the wall behind the triumvir. The son of Antipater would cringe before no one. His resolve returned. He straightened into a regal posture.

"Antony, please, let me help Rome. Make me King of Judea."

The triumvir dismissed his guard. Herod's breath caught in his dry throat.

Antony leaned in toward Herod "You've always been loyal to Rome. I have no reason to doubt you."

Herod closed his eyes for a moment. Euphoria flooded his entire being.

"It's customary to offer—"

Herod was prepared to play Rome's game. "How much do you want?" he asked with a level stare.

"Five hundred talents of gold, payable to me five years after you win back Judea for Rome. I'll send weapons and soldiers."

Herod nodded. "I'm aware you rule Rome in the West, Octavian in the East, and Lepidus in Africa. Will Octavian and Lepidus also… desire… a gift?"

"No, it won't be necessary," said Antony, averting his eyes. "We equally split gold we take in."

Herod had heard the three triumvirs tended to short-change each other, but that was not his concern.

"I'll present you to the Senate tomorrow," said Antony. "Senators no longer wield the power they once did, but they still appoint territorial kings."

Herod already knew this. He nodded, courteously.

"Octavian will be there, but Lepidus is off quelling a rebellion in the East. The Senate will vote on your confirmation. I'll see to it that they approve you."

Herod's soul soared. "Antony," he said, falling to his knees. "I'll serve you till the end of my days."

~

*T*hat night, Herod lay in bed, waiting for sleep to take him, when Cleopatra wandered into his mind, uninvited and unwelcome. Given the opportunity, she would stand in the way of his new position as King of Judea. However, there was not enough time for anyone, whether spy or messenger, to reach Cleopatra in Alexandria with news of Herod's ascent to the throne before Antony presented him to the Senate. Once the Senate accepted Antony's proposal, Cleopatra would be powerless to stop Herod from taking the throne. With immense relief, he drifted off to sleep.

~

*O*n the following morning, the Triumvirs Antony and Octavian, both clad in white togas trimmed in purple, greeted Herod on the Senate steps. Octavian was years younger and more taciturn than Antony. The triumvirs escorted him up a stairway to the windowless senate chamber, where the senators sat on three long, deep steps. The collegial chatter abruptly stopped when they strode in.

Antony motioned Herod to sit down on a wooden stool beside the leaders' podium. Octavian blathered on and on about matters that did not interest him. The scent of olive oil hung heavy in the air. Romans rubbed it on their skin and hair. It amused Herod to recall such a prosaic detail in the presence of these venerated politicians.

At last, Antony was asking the Senate to appoint Herod King of Judea. Through the speech, Herod kept his gaze fixed on the intricate tile design on the floor. He could not bear to look directly at the aristocrats who were determining his fate. If he did, his eyes might betray his utter desperation. It was essential that the senators see him as a strong, self-assured leader of men. Through sheer force of will, he stilled his trembling hands. He dared not lift his eyes until after the vote when Antony began to speak.

"*Rex Socias et amicus populi Romani.* We hereby declare you, Herod, son of Antipater, King of the Jews."

Herod gave the triumvirs and the senator a composed, kingly smile. Antony summoned him to the leaders' podium, and they signed the treaty appointing him Judean sovereign. He contained his ecstasy when the senators cheered. He had reached the pinnacle; he was exactly where he belonged.

"As you know, King Herod, Rome allows Jews and people of other religions in our territories to worship their own gods," said Octavian. "We ask only that your people worship our gods as well. Senators, join us in taking King Herod to the Temple of Jupiter. Together, we will make a sacrifice in the new king's honor, and we will ask Jupiter to give him strength and wisdom."

Herod's jaw tightened. News of his participation in a sacrifice to a pagan god was sure to enrage scores of Judeans when it reached Jerusalem. Already, his detractors did not consider him to be a Jew. Of course, he prayed to the One True God, and he considered himself Jewish, but he had to contend with political considerations most people could not begin to fathom. It would be an insult to refuse to accompany his venerable hosts.

The newly minted king strode out of the Senate behind Antony and Octavian. Flanked by senators and the army, they paraded up Capitoline Hill toward the Temple of Jupiter Capitolinus. Ordinary Romans in humble homespun packed the forum and strained to catch a glimpse of the procession, calling out cheers. To Herod, their accolades sounded as beautiful as his sister's harp music.

Through the open doors of the pillared temple, Herod could see the marble statue of Jupiter, the king of gods, portrayed as an old man with a bare chest and a full beard. Four spotless, white heifers with leaf garlands around their heads stood on the sacrificial altar.

"We now offer these beasts to Jupiter," intoned a wafer-thin priest. "May he bring the King of the Jews victory over Rome's enemies."

Herod watched the priest ritually kill the heifers with clean knife swipes to their necks. They fell, one by one, while the crowd murmured prayers to Jupiter. After temple workers skinned and butchered the beasts, the priests would offer their innards as a sacrifice on the altar.

That evening, Antony and Octavian hosted a feast in Herod's honor. The new King of Judea arrived early to the reception hall, a colonnaded government building emptied of all furniture except for long tables surrounded by sumptuously carved chaises. The building's white floors and walls of marble gleamed silver in the evening's last light streaming in from long windows. Herod greeted each arriving senator. The aroma of roasting meat drifted in from the kitchen. Slaves and servants were setting out vessels of wine and silver goblets when the triumvirs came in.

"Take the chaise between Octavian and me," Antony said to Herod, nodding to the middle one at the head of the long table. The Triumvirs Antony and Octavian stretched out on their respective chaises and propped themselves up on their elbows. Herod, watching them closely, did the same.

Antony raised his silver goblet of *conditum*, wine with honey, pepper, and saffron, in a toast: "To Herod, King of the Jews."

Senators raised their chalices and praised Herod in long, drunken toasts. After the last, Herod lifted his goblet. "Antony, Octavian, members of the Senate, your presence here this evening greatly honors me, and I thank you," he said, humbly.

Slaves glided in bearing steaming platters of rare meat from the heifers sacrificed earlier. They served other dishes Herod did not recognize. Unaccustomed to these particular delicacies, such as peacocks' tongues and sows' udders stuffed with kidney, he was grateful that the serving slaves announced the name of each dish they set on the table. Most tasted vile, but still, he complimented each new offering and forced himself to eat it.

"I had our chefs prepare our most elaborate dish for you," said Antony. "We stuff a chicken inside a duck, put the duck inside a goose, and the goose inside a pig. Then we stuff the pig inside a cow, and we roast them all together. We call it trojan horse."

Herod took a bite. "Delicious," he said, trying to hide his utter disgust.

"Ah, this one is the best of all," said Octavian as a slave rolled in a cart on which a roasted pig stood, propped up on its legs. Servants sliced open its belly. A bounty of sausage and fruit tumble out.

The unkosher pig flesh tasted strange but delicious. No one from home was present to witness his straying from Jewish dietary law, but he knew his people would soon hear of it and take offense. They did not understand political expedience.

The eminent Romans consumed copious amounts of food and wine. They purged themselves and returned to the table for more. By the time the juggling and sword-swallowing after-dinner acts ended, Herod craved his soft bed.

~

*A*fter days of senatorial bacchanal in his honor, Antony escorted Herod to the Port of Ostia in his *carruca*. The triumvir nodded to the sturdy-looking *libernia* gently bobbing in the harbor.

"The ship is yours, my friend," he said.

Its single white sail billowed out in a gust of wind. Herod had thought he was going to have to hire a ship to take him home. Antony's generosity moved him to throw his arms around the surprised triumvir.

"There's more," added Antony. He handed Herod a silk bag of fine jewels. "I'm also sending you soldiers. They will report to the hills north of Jerusalem and prepare for your siege of the city. You will need to recruit a thousand more men from your own lands. A true leader must be able to inspire men to join his banner."

Herod's heart was full. He kissed Antony's cheeks, and they wished each other well before he sailed away to begin his conquest of Jerusalem.

11

MARIAMNE, 39 BCE, MASADA

*S*amuel called on Lila every night during the twilight hour after dinner before he went on duty. I allowed her to invite him to the common area of my quarters and left them alone while Aris and I took walks across the length of the barren plateau. One blue-gray dusk, a flock of migrating doves caught my attention. We stopped to gaze at them.

"I envy how they can soar in the sky," I said. "Imagine the freedom."

"Speaking of envy, I've been wondering how you feel about your handmaiden's courtship with Samuel," Aris said.

"I do envy them. They have love in their lives. I doubt I will ever feel true love for a man."

Aris smiled. "Herod will fall in love with you. Any man would."

"But I don't return his love. I will never forgive him for…." I gasped, fearing too much had slipped out.

"What has Herod done?" asked Aris, his expression solemn.

"Nothing…yet. But you know he lusts for power."

Aris nodded. "He did act as territorial governor when our grandfather held the title."

If only I could tell Aris of Herod's grand intentions. I might feel lighter if I shared the secret, but I could not. For our safety, I must stay silent.

～

*O*n a late spring evening, Yusef was uncharacteristically quiet at dinner. Usually, he chatted amiably and steered the conversation to matters about which we could not argue, such as rain (was it coming soon or was it not) or the garden (should we weed more often and what other seeds should we plant)? He was the only lodger on Masada who could smooth out the awkward silences between Herod's family and my own. We all looked to him as the calm center of our precarious desert existence. He had never looked so troubled. His face was pale, and his brow deeply creased. I was curious why, but I was not alarmed, not yet.

After the cook had cleared away our wooden bowls, Yusef rose and cleared his throat.

"There is something I must tell you. Our food and water stores are beginning to run low. More than half of what we brought here is gone, and I don't know how much longer we can survive here."

My stomach twisted into a painful knot. An anxious rumble swept over the table.

"How did this happen?" my mother demanded.

Yusef took a deep breath and shook his grizzled head. "Herod told me we would lodge at Masada for only a few months. We have now been here over a year. As you well know, the winter rains never came. Our cisterns aren't as full as they should be at this time of year. Animals we once hunted have left the area for better watering grounds. The soldiers who hunt for us won't be able to bring back enough game to feed us."

"What would you have us to do, Yusef?" my mother asked. "Starve ourselves? Deny ourselves water?"

"No, but we must make changes if we are to survive. We'll have to eat smaller meals and drink less water. I'm going to send away most of our servants and some guards tomorrow. We will have fewer

mouths to feed. I'll keep only our most essential servants and
guards."

Lila, who was washing the dishes, went rigid.

"Which soldiers?" I asked.

"I'll make the decision later tonight."

"But who will take care of us?" asked Salome, aghast.

"We'll have to take care of ourselves," Yusef said.

Salome shook her head, vehemently. "You can't make us do
servants' work."

Yusef's eyes went as steely as the gleaming dagger dangling from
his belt. "You lodge here by the grace of Herod. My charge is to
keep you alive. You must do what I command."

Mother sniffed. "We are royals. Perhaps Cypros and
Salome…"

Yusef gave her a dark look. "Every person lodging on Masada
must do the work I assign. If you refuse, I'll cast you out into the
desert. You will have to fend for yourself."

~

Samuel was one of the ten soldiers Yusef was sending away.
When I found out, I begged Yusef to let Samuel stay, to
dismiss a different guard. He said he had already told each man
whether he was to leave or to stay, and he could not, in good
conscience, change these decisions now. It saddened him to tell me
this, he said.

I should have gone to Yusef the moment he had made his
announcement and implored him to let Samuel stay.

~

On the day the men were leaving, Samuel came by our
quarters. I quickly left so he and Lila could say their good-
byes in private. When I returned, I found Lila standing at the palace
window, watching Samuel and nine other men begin their descent
down the snake trail. When the sight of Samuel disappeared, she

sobbed. I embraced her, and I tried to comfort her, but she was, of course, inconsolable.

"Last night, Samuel told me he loved me and he wanted to marry me. He said he was going to return to his village, Shanan, north of Jerusalem, and I should go find him there once Herod frees us. He said he would wait for me no matter how long it took. I wanted him to take me with him. He refused."

I gave her a linen cloth to dab her tears. "Of course he did. It's far too dangerous for a woman to travel through a land at war."

"That's what he said," said Lila.

"One day, you and Samuel will be together," I said, sure of my words. I was sad for her heartbreak but grateful she was still beside me.

~

*L*ila and the other servants taught us how to do the myriad of tasks we had always taken for granted. Everyone was required, for the first time in our royal or aristocratic lives, to cook, clean, and wash clothes. Lila and I worked side by side, no longer master and servant, but fellow workers. Heartbroken, she was unusually quiet, but each day she grew stronger.

The sole remaining hunter showed Yusef and Aris how to use a slingshot to kill rabbits and other small animals on the plateau. We all learned how to garden and to draw water from the cisterns. If we wanted our allowance of food and water, we had to perform our duties.

We all responded differently to the tasks Yusef assigned us.

Princess Alexandra made a noisy show of offense whenever it was her turn to cook or wash clothing or garden, while Salome bore her work burden with scowling resignation. Cypros and Aris did their work pleasantly enough, but I was the only one who relished my new obligations. I found great satisfaction in turning a small heap of eggplant, turnips, and beans, into a thin but tasty soup. My newfound pleasure in cooking, however, did not compare to my joy in seeing the tender, green shoots spring from the earth.

No longer was I the passive recipient of all I received, but someone contributing to our survival. My hands, red and rough from long days of doing chores, were an unexpected source of pride. It was some relief to know I was doing something besides waiting for Herod to free us from Masada. The physical labor tired me and made it easier for me to fall asleep on hot desert nights.

Except for the barest of civilities, I ignored Salome whenever she made a rude or dismissive comment. It was rewarding to see her angry scowl after she tried, unsuccessfully, to quarrel with me. For a time, ignoring Salome led to a more peaceful existence. That is, until Yusef assigned Salome and me, with our handmaidens' assistance, to fetch water from the cisterns.

One sweltering summer morning when it was Salome's turn to fetch water, she claimed that she and her handmaid, Dreya, were too ill to work. Yusef ordered Lila and me to draw the water in their stead. Weeks later, Salome and Dreya were still "sick" whenever it was their turn for water duty. Until I could convince Yusef that Salome and her handmaiden were not genuinely ill, Lila and I drew all the water.

But that was not all. Salome began to leave her apartments in horrific disarray when it was my assigned day to clean the living quarters. She managed to spill every liquid flask in her possession, from perfume to the goats' milk she used to whiten her face. Then, she lay on her bed while Lila and I tidied her chamber.

Though I continued to ignore Salome's barbs and insults, she grew more and more brazen. One day I went to her bedchamber to clean and found she had emptied her chests and armoires and had thrown everything she owned into a massive heap on the floor. In a blatant attempt to humiliate me, Salome lay on her bed, smirking at us. Lila and I wheeled around and left.

*L*ate one evening at Masada, the ladies mended clothing by lamplight. Salome and I found ourselves alone after our mothers had retired for the night. I tried to speak civilly.

"I want to know why you are so unkind to me, Salome. Tell me, please."

She looked up from her embroidery with an arched brow. Her lower lip trembled. This show of vulnerability surprised me.

"You think you are superior to my family," she said.

"I am more highborn than you and your family, that is a fact," I said, patiently.

"I, too, have royal blood."

I could have pointed out that her father was an Idumean commoner, but I stayed silent.

"You don't love my brother," she said, her amber eyes narrowed. "You don't even miss him or care if he lives or dies."

"I'm very concerned about Herod's welfare and—"

"You don't deserve him," interrupted Salome. She pursed her lips and flounced out.

12

HEROD, 39 BCE, PTOLMAIS

*H*erod and Philippi made landfall in Ptolemais, a port north of Acre. They began their search for one thousand men to recruit to Herod's banner. Then, they must train them to be soldiers capable of facing Rome's enemies on a battlefield, no small task. Antony had already sent hundreds of Roman soldiers to set up camp just north of Jerusalem. However, Herod needed more men. He had not the luxury of time. He must seize Jerusalem swiftly, before the new rulers became too entrenched, and the people too accepting of their leadership.

With urgent resolve, they rode from village to village to enlist young men. No one recognized Herod in these far reaches, which was insulting, to be sure, but it did allow him to ride into towns and villages and attract little attention. Anonymity was essential: if his enemies got word about where he was and what he was doing, they would promptly hunt him down and kill him.

After nearly two weeks, only forty-one men had joined his army. At that rate, it would be a year before Herod could assemble a sufficient number of soldiers. He had to change his tactics. Lying on a hard pallet bed at a lonely village inn, Herod realized that recruitment would be easier if he could convince a powerful tribal leader to conscript his soldiers for him. He recalled hearing of a man named Levi Ashai, who owned vast lands, and ruled an alliance of several smaller landowners. He knew Ashai lived in a village just east of Samaria, but he did not know which one. He was determined to find him.

They traveled on horseback through leafy forests and lush meadows on their way to Samaria. The desert heat was a distant memory. They sought someone who could tell him where Ashai lived, and stopped to ask a peddler on the trail, and later, an oxen handler hauling stone, but neither knew.

Herod was beginning to wonder if there really was a man named Ashai when they came upon an unwalled cluster of mud-brick dwellings and a modest market, no more than a few fruit and vegetable stalls. An old man sat on a stool sharpening his spear. A young woman sat beside him at a rough-edged table, kneading bread. Herod rode up to them and threw the old man a coin. The old man left the coin on the ground and gazed up at him with a wary expression. The woman's almond-shaped eyes widened as she took him in, from his feathered helmet to his fine sandals, to his massive guard. How impressive he must look to these peasants in their ragged robes.

"Where can I find Levi Ashai?" Herod asked.

The spear-sharpener glowered at him. "What do you want with Ashai?"

Herod found the old man's audacity offensive, but he kept his face impassive. He needed his help.

"I've asked you a question," he said.

"Please, Papa, just tell him," the woman said, softly.

"Ashai lives in the stone house in the next walled town, Pomrain," said the old man. "It's not far down the road."

The young woman handed Herod and Philippi ladles of water from the nearby well, most appreciated after hours of riding. Herod tossed her a silver piece and admired her radiant smile. Had he more time, he would make the man an offer for the woman's company and tarry there with her for a while. He nodded his thanks and rode on.

Not long afterward, the high, thick walls of Pomrain came into view, and they rode through the open gate into a small square that had little in common with Jerusalem. Here, no arched or pillared structures sheltered vendors from the relentless sun. Townspeople looked at them with curiosity. No one said a word.

~

*A*shai's house was easy to find. It was the only stone structure in sight, far grander than the nearby wooden shacks. It was a good sign that the man had gold and influence.

Still, Herod loathed asking anybody for anything. Someday, he would be the one to whom people would come for help and favors. He would have the power to grant or deny requests as he saw fit. But he was not there yet. He must first ask the tribal leader to help him recruit men to his banner.

He knocked. An old man, thin as a rod, opened the door. He introduced himself as Ashai and ushered them into the courtyard. Herod expected Ashai to question him about the reason for his visit, but the ancient did not appear surprised to see him.

The tribal leader led the men into a courtyard, a dry and barren patch of land. Ashai sat down on a woven mat, his legs folded beneath him, in a sliver of shade. Across the courtyard, two women were spinning flax. The younger woman, who might have been a beauty but for her blackened teeth, worked a loom.

"Welcome," said Ashai. "I've been expecting you. I got word a great man was looking for me."

"Word of our arrival traveled swiftly," Herod said.

"It always does in these parts," said Ashai. "We look after each other."

Herod introduced himself and General Philippi, and they sat cross-legged on straw mats across from their host. Herod held out the treaty appointing him king. "Read this."

"I don't read," Ashai said, without a trace of shame.

"I'll read it to you, then. It says:

'The Roman Senate hereby appoints Herod, Son of Antipater, King of the Jews.'"

I've come to——"

"First, we eat," Ashai interrupted. "Then, we talk. You hungry?"

Herod was too hungry to be offended by the rude interruption. The food basket hanging from his saddle was nearly empty. He smiled, politely. "We would welcome a meal."

Ashai poured water from an earthen vessel over his hands into a clay bowl and murmured a prayer. He passed the bowl and vessel to Herod and Philippi, who did the same. A serving girl, whose hair was the color of ripe flax, offered him beer. She was too pale skinned to be native-born; a slave seller must have captured her in some far-flung land. She was lovely. Herod watched her small hands place a bowl of fish stew and bread in the middle of the mat. He wondered what else those hands could do.

He broke off a piece from the steaming-hot loaf of braided bread.

"Wait," said Ashai. "First, we pray." The tribal leader began to sway gently, back and forth. "Blessed art Thou, Adonai our God, King of the World, who causes bread to come forth from the earth," he murmured in Hebrew.

The men used their bread to scoop out stew from the common bowl. The fish tasted astoundingly fresh. A fisherman must have caught it that day in the nearby Sea of Galilee.

"To what do I owe the honor of your visit?" asked Ashai.

Good. Herod could come right to the point. "I must recruit one thousand men to my banner. For Rome, we will sweep the Parthians and their Maccabee stooge, Antigonus, from our lands."

The girl put a platter of cheese and figs between them.

"Care for more honeyed bread?" asked Ashai.

Annoyed, Herod shook his head. He wanted to get on with it.

"By God's word, our land belongs to the Jews, not to Rome or anyone else," said Ashai. "Tell me, why is a Roman overlord any better for my people than a Parthian?"

Herod knew he must proceed cautiously. Perhaps Ashai was not as smart as he seemed. Intelligent men tended to understand that Rome rewarded cooperative provincial kings with land and gold.

"With Rome behind my rule of Judea, we will all prosper."

"Some tend to prosper more than others," said Ashai with a shrug of his wizened shoulders. "Rome, Parthia, or another power, it's all the same to us. We tend to our sheep and goats. We plant. We plow. We reap. And we pay tax and tribute to foreign rulers. We're not a free people."

Herod tried to mask his irritation and keep his expression blank. He had thought this would be simpler.

Elder Ashai ate every fig in the wooden bowl, very slowly, one by one, with sun-browned fingers. "I hear the Parthians have crowned the Maccabee Antigonus Judea's king. Is that right?"

"It is, but King Hyrcanus's family is the true royal line. Antigonus is a pretender."

"My people don't care which Maccabee sits on the throne. It makes no difference to us. We're herders and farmers. We want peace. No matter which side we take, the other will burn our fields and steal our livestock."

Herod's growing exasperation was becoming more difficult to conceal. He felt a vein in his forehead throb. "We're going to cast out the Parthians and Antigonus. I'm sure you want to be allied with the victorious army."

Ashai cleared his throat and met Herod's gaze. "I'd prefer to stay neutral."

Herod shook his head, gravely. "That is not an option. If you don't join my banner, you team with my enemies. Landowners who support the losing kingdom will pay a high price."

"A high price? Do explain."

Herod looked deep into his watery eyes. "Your head and the heads of your family."

Ashai raised a brow and stroked his graying beard. He looked over at the small children at the other end of the courtyard, probably his grandchildren. They were drawing in the dirt with sticks and laughing.

"The men who lease my lands are farmers or herdsmen. Some are merchants and tradesmen. Not one of them is a soldier."

Herod smiled. "I'd expect as much. That's not your concern. I'll turn them into soldiers indistinguishable from Rome's."

Elder Ashai stiffened his back. "How much are you willing to pay my men for their loyalty to you?"

"I'll give them generous coin on signing. After our triumph, more gold will be theirs. To you I'll give a fourth talent of gold for every two hundred men you enlist. There will be more for you after we've taken Jerusalem."

"How much more?"

Herod smirked. Ashai drove a hard bargain. "After our victory, I'll give you half a talent for every two hundred men you recruit."

"Where will this gold come from?"

"Rome."

"But only if your army is victorious, of course," said Ashai.

"Fear not," said Herod. "We will triumph."

"King Herod, I will find you the men you need from my town and my tenants. People here are desperate. There was a drought last year. We had a poor harvest."

Herod beamed. Nothing motivated a hungry man more than the prospect of immediate coin.

"Your signing money will allow my people to buy grain from Egypt," Ashai added. "Their families won't starve. I'll do as you ask, but I do have one condition."

Who was this ancient bag of bones to give the King of Jews conditions? Herod refused to meet Ashai's eyes. It was far more pleasant to fix his gaze on the comely servant girl, who was standing on the flat roof now, hanging robes and tunics on a rope to dry. Her robes blew back in the wind, revealing her shapely legs.

"Your condition is?" he asked.

"Pay the gold you've offered me to the men I recruit for you. Divide it between them."

The old man said this as casually as he might discuss the price of wheat. He obviously had no fear of him, as he should. Herod would have relished breaking the ancient in half was he not in dire need of his services.

"It will be costly to make your raw recruits worthy of my army."

The old man lit his pipe, inhaled deeply, and passed it to Herod.

"You have already committed that gold to me. I can deliver you one thousand men, but those are my terms. The decision is yours."

Herod nodded. "I agree to your terms." He would punish Ashai for his insubordination when the time was right.

"Good," said Ashai. "I will begin recruiting tomorrow morning."

13

MARIAMNE, 38 BCE, MASADA

One late autumn afternoon, while walking back to the palace after caring for my doves, I saw Yusef on the northern rim, staring out at the Salt Sea, his brow drawn. He greeted me without smiling. Ever since our supplies began to run low, he had been a different man—serious and intense, but today he seemed to be particularly anxious. My skin prickled.

"What's the matter?" I asked. Yusef shook his head, grimly.

"Tell me, please. It will be our secret."

Yusef gave me a grateful glance, as if my interest lightened his burden, some. "As you know, last winter we had little rain. If the coming winter doesn't bring a great deluge, we won't have enough water to survive for much longer."

I looked up the white-hot sky. It did not host a single cloud. "The rainy season is almost here. Nights are getting colder—a sign the rains will soon come."

Yusef looked to the West, the direction from which winter storms blew in. "I think the deluge will be late this year if it comes at all. Even if it does, it might arrive too late to save us."

I tried to swallow, but my mouth had gone bone dry. "Is our situation dire?"

"It is. We must keep this quiet," Yusef added. "If panic sets in, people will hoard food and water. If that happens, we will all die."

I had an urge to break away and run. How did I, a Maccabee Princess, end up on this hellishly hot plateau, pondering whether starvation or thirst was going to take me?

"After dinner, I'm going to tell everyone we must ration our food and water. I fear rebellion. I don't trust Salome. I don't trust anyone here." He looked down at me with warm eyes. "Except you."

∽

The next morning, Yusef led us behind the palace to the small garden that had once bloomed green and plentiful. Without rain or sufficient watering, most of the vegetables had withered and died under the sun's brutal glare. Yusef said nothing at first. He looked from person to person. His taut, pale face showed the burden of his responsibility for our survival.

"I have gathered you here to tell you of my new decree," he said. "We have little water left. From tomorrow forward, every person will be allowed three small jugs of water each day, for drinking and washing."

"Three jugs are not nearly enough," said my mother, her expression appalled. Salome and Cypros joined her in a chorus of complaints.

Yusef took a linen cloth and wiped beads of sweat from his forehead. "We may not have to ration like this for long. Winter will soon come, and with God's mercy, so will the winter rains. For now, three jugs will have to be enough."

"Dismiss the guards," Salome said. "We will have more for ourselves."

"I've already dismissed as many guards as I can."

∽

*A*t dawn the following day, I stood at Masada's rim and watched the sunrise over the Salt Sea. For months now, a cloudless sapphire sky arched above us. We hoped and prayed and prayed for *mayim*, for water. Having sufficient water had never been a worry in Jerusalem; there were no rivers nearby, but abundant springs afforded plenty of water year around. Food and drink appeared, as if by magic, on palace tables.

As weeks passed, we grew even more desperate for rain. The cisterns were too low now to water our garden or to bathe. Every morning, I sponged myself clean as best I could with the little water I could spare, but only a true bath could wash away the sweat and grime of the desert. The small amount of water remaining in the *mikvah*, the sacred pool of water women bathed in after monthly courses, rose in mist and it went dry.

I would have given almost anything for a long, quenching drink of water. I tried to make my ration last by limiting myself to small sips from my daily allotment throughout the day, but it was not enough. My parched mouth and dry throat plagued me. I tried not to think about water but found I could think of little else. *Water, water, I must have water*, rang the constant refrain in my mind.

～

*T*he courtyard offered no shady reprieve from the sun's fierce glare. It was eight in the morning, and already, sweat trickled down my sunburnt face. Aris and I were weeding the few, limp vegetables still rooted in the parched earth. We were growing weaker each day from hunger and thirst.

I went to take a sip from my jug. It was empty. "It's only noon," I said, "and my water is already gone."

Aris's eyes held great compassion. He dropped his hoe and held out his jug. "Finish it," he said.

"No, it's yours. You need it."

"I want you to have it. Please, Mariamne, finish it."

With a grateful glance, I took the precious jug in my hands. In two swallows, I emptied it.

Aris's generosity touched me. I kissed his cheek. "You are kind."

"I'd do anything for you," he said.

"And I for you," I said, and took his thin hand in my own.

~

One day I awoke to see rainclouds blanketing the sky. Though weak from hunger and thirst, we had hope. We ran to open the cisterns and murmured prayers for *mayim*. A drizzling shower came, but moments later, the rainclouds cleared and the punishing sun returned.

A few days later, Yusef made another announcement. "I've just measured our remaining water. If we're judicious in our use, it might last us another two weeks."

"Two weeks!" cried Princess Alexandra.

"Yes, we must limit ourselves to two small jugs a day for all of our needs."

~

Winter was fast approaching. Night began to fall after a short twilight. I liked to slip outside, where everything was quiet, and I could think in peace, away from the long silences and constant bickering of people unsuited to live together. I looked to the blue-black immensity of the sky and reminded myself there was a world beyond Masada. Would I ever have a chance to see it? My long-carried fears weighed upon me. Had Herod taken Jerusalem? Did he still live? Did anyone else know Herod had taken us to Masada? Was he ever going to return for us and bring us home, or were we going to die here?

Back inside the palace, it was black as obsidian. There was not enough wood left to make torches. My family had been allotted one oil lamp only, and my mother kept it in her bedchamber. If I had my own lamp, the long nights might not seem so scary and endless.

In the morning, Lila and I went to the storage outbuildings to search for a lamp, but we did not find one.

"Oil lamps must be stored somewhere in this travesty of a palace," said my mother.

"Let's go search for them," I said, brightening at the prospect of an adventure. My life had devolved to the point where little changed from day to day.

Mother, Lila, and I set off. In palace storage chambers vast and small, we hunted for oil lamps. After nearly an hour, we had reached the only place still unsearched: the living quarters Cypros and Salome shared. In the long passageway leading to the entrance, a key glinted in a keyhole.

"I wonder what's inside," Lila said.

"Let's see," I said, and turned the mysterious key. What I saw made my mouth fall open. Rows and rows of jugs, filled to the brims with precious water, blanketed the floor.

"Salome did this," I said. "Who else could be so selfish?" Mother and Lila peeked inside. Both women gasped.

"I'm going to kill her," my mother shrieked. She snatched a jug from the floor.

"Put it back, Mother," I called out. "I'll bring Yusef here and show him—"

My mother thrust the jug into my arms and banged both fists on the main door to the living quarters.

Dreya cracked it open. "Salome is sleeping," she whispered. "No one is to disturb her."

My mother snorted and stormed past the girl. Lila and I followed her to Salome's bedchamber. Mother shook Salome awake and pulled her out of bed.

Salome blinked a few times, her brow knitted in confusion. "Am I dreaming?" she croaked.

"No, you water thief, this is our nightmare, not yours," my mother cried. She held the jug out to Salome. "We found the water you've been hoarding. How dare you!"

Salome tried to seize the jug. Mother resisted. They struggled. The vessel plummeted to the floor and shattered into dozens of pieces. More precious than gold, the water puddled on the floor, gone forever. My mother slapped Salome's face so hard the sound of it echoed off the walls. She hung her head and brought her trembling hand to her reddened cheek. Mother twisted Salome's arm behind her back.

From the sidelines, Cypros rushed in, her eyes ablaze.

"Take your hands off my daughter!" she shouted, hurtling herself into the fray. Salome and Cypros both pummeled my mother with their fists. I had to stop them before they killed her. I tried to grab hold of my mother. Salome slugged me. The shock of it hurt as much as the physical blow to my nose. Blood came pouring out. I grabbed a linen cloth from the tray on the table and pressed it to my nose. Lila and I rushed for help.

The hallway had never seemed so long. I raced down the halls and found Yusef.

"Come quickly!" I cried.

"Your nose is bleeding," said Yusef, his face pinched in alarm. "The women are fighting. Come with me."

The women still tussled, their silk robes a violent swirl of color. Yusef wrenched them apart. He held Salome back with one arm and Cypros with the other. Aris secured our mother, whose wig had slipped off, revealing wisps of white hair.

"All of you, out of my chambers!" Salome cried, her hair askew but her back spear-straight.

"You must see this, Yusef," said Princess Alexandra. Still panting, she beckoned him to follow her to the hidden jugs.

Yusef scrutinized the closet with a deepening scowl. "I'm sorry," Salome whispered.

She looked remorseful, but was she?

I handed Yusef the gleaming key to the chamber and saw him slip it into the purse hanging from his belt. "Salome, leave us," said Yusef.

She did, with her mother close behind her.

"How much more time will the water we found give us?" I asked.

Yusef shook his head, miserably. "Not much more than a week."

~

*H*aving little food left, we began to eat our doves. With every bite, I wondered whether the bird was one I had fed or stroked. The meat tasted bitter in my mouth, but I could not let myself starve to death. I had to live. There was much to do. I had to keep the deathbed promise I made to my father to protect the dynasty of his line. Each passing day without rain diminished my chances.

I looked to the heavens and prayed for *mayim*.

~

*O*ur cisterns were almost empty. The remaining food and water supply would last no more than a few days. Weak from hunger and thirst, we moved slowly if we moved at all. We lacked energy to do anything but the most essential chores. There was no longer any water to wash our bodies or our threadbare robes. We were all emaciated. My mother had lost her regal bearing, entirely. Wrinkles formed tiny canyons in her once-beautiful face. But it was the sight of the gaunt, hollow-cheeked Aris that hurt me the most. His ribs were visible under his tunic, and his once muscular legs were thin and bony.

The angel of death was drawing close. I could feel its feathery wings beating against me. Only one question remained. Would hunger or thirst take us? Either way, I prayed I would die before my mother and brother so I would not have to witness their agony. I could feel my mind slow and begin to shut down. Numbness set in, and I welcomed it. My approaching death no longer consumed my thoughts and dreams.

~

*T*wo days later, just before dawn, I awoke to a rumbling sound followed by a deafening crash. My first thought: the enemy was attacking. Trembling, I rushed to Aris's chamber.

"What was that?" he asked.

"The Parthians," I said. "We must go wake Mother."

I looked through the window in Aris's chamber, expecting to see flaming arrows. I saw nothing of the sort. What I did see astonished me. *Mayim!* Rain fell from swollen clouds tumbling across the sky. It was thunder we had heard, not enemy weapons. Relief pulsed through me with every heartbeat.

We all hurried outside. Everyone, from the highest royal to the lowest servant, was dancing in the rain, drunk with sheer happiness. I threw my palms to the sky and let the cooling deluge wash over my head and shoulders, filling me with joy. My sleeping robes clung to my body; I was soaked to the bone.

Aris spun me around with glee. "We're going to live!" he cried.

I opened my mouth and let the rain stream in. My thirst, however, was not quenched. I looked around for Lila to send her to the kitchen for some vessels to catch the rain. I found her among the others, twirling in the downfall, lost in her own jubilation. I did not have the heart to disturb her. I rushed to the kitchen and returned with a tray of earthen bowls I set on the palace steps. They quickly filled with newly fallen rain. I drank, and invited the revelers to take a bowl.

"Come with me, Aris," I said. I took his hand, and we climbed to the top of the highest tower. Our bare, wet feet slapped each stone step. Between the parapets, I scanned the land beneath Masada. Streams and eddies bubbled and whirled and flowed on what, only yesterday, was brown, parched earth. I had never seen anything like it.

～

*R*ain fell for eight straight days and nights. When it stopped, we rushed outside and planted lentils, onions, and eggplants on the northern terraces. Before the first green shoots emerged, wildlife had returned to the newly filled watering holes at the foot of Masada. Our hunter provided us with plenty for dinner.

14

HEROD, 38 BCE, ACRE

Once Herod had engaged the men he needed to liberate Jerusalem, he set up a training camp near Acre. He had little time to turn the farmers and tradesmen into soldiers capable of defeating the Parthian invaders and their pretender king, Antigonus. Marc Antony kept his promise and sent Roman commanders to his camp. They trained and drilled the recruits every day except Sabbath, when he allowed his men to pray and rest.

Herod was a constant presence on the drilling fields, barking commands, chastising the weak and the lazy, and rewarding those who excelled with his favor. Each soldier became proficient in the use of every weapon in the arsenal before the commanders decided which best suited the man's skills and temperament on the battlefield.

~

It was a lonely time. At night, when Herod lay in his camp bed, Mariamne's image often drifted into his mind. He closed his eyes and imagined the feel and taste of her lips, her body.

It would not be long before she was his. He intended to make her a queen, something even her royal family could not do. Through the blazing days of military exercises, Herod's thoughts and dreams of his princess strengthened his resolve to win.

One cold spring night when the sky was ablaze with a million stars, Herod warmed himself beside the campfire and drank a copious amount of wine. He was already half drunk when he heard trees rustling, and a man emerged from the woods. Herod instinctively pulled out his sword.

The young man laughed. Herod had heard that laugh many times before. "Is that you, Joseph, or is wine playing tricks on my mind?"

With a wide grin, his younger brother sat down on the ground beside him, his knees drawn to his chest. He leaned over and embraced his brother. When they were last together, Joseph had been a teenager.

Herod assessed the grown man, in the firelight. With his stocky build and patrician air, Joseph much resembled their father, Antipater. As a child, Joseph had been more inclined to read than to fence or to wrestle. Herod had thought he was soft. He did not understand why anyone would rather laze inside on a fine day than do swordplay in the open air. Still, Joseph was his blood, and therefore under his protection. If anyone had teased or taunted his younger brother, Herod beat him to a bloody pulp with his bare fists. Miscreants had soon learned to leave Joseph alone.

Herod had changed his mind about Joseph after seeing how hard he worked at his studies and at archery. To his surprise, his brother had looked to him, and not to Phasael, for praise or counsel. But Joseph was restive; as soon as he had been old enough to leave home, he moved from one Roman province to the next, taking low level administrative posts and leaving when they began to bore him. It seemed he had not the stamina to stay with any pursuit for long.

"I thought you settled in Venice, Joseph."

"I did, after I'd traveled the world," he said. "I got word Rome had crowned you King of the Jews, and you were going to war for Jerusalem. I want to join your army."

Herod studied his brother in the flickering firelight. He doubted Joseph had the resolve it took to be a great soldier. "If you join my army, you will have to train alongside my raw recruits."

Joseph nodded. "I know I have much to learn."

❧

*H*erod sent Joseph to drill under his toughest commander. It was not long, however, before his brother impressed the crusty Roman.

"Joseph is the finest archer in my contingent," the commander told him. "He has courage and great endurance. I have no doubt he will be a great soldier."

Herod gained a new respect for Joseph. He shared his fine wine with him on evenings when the commanders joined him to drink beside the campfire. One night, after the commanders had gone to their barracks for the night, Herod and Joseph stayed outside, warming themselves beside the still-glowing embers in the light of the golden quarter-moon.

"Do you remember the time Salome put a snake in my bed?" asked Joseph.

Herod chuckled. "She did? I don't recall."

"She tortured us," said Joseph with a mock shudder.

"Not me," said Herod.

Joseph smiled. "Salome loved you, and you alone. Remember how she was always trying to lounge next to you at dinner and get your attention? She loved you more than anyone, even her husband. No other man could ever please her."

"Uncle Yusef was too old for her. Father should never have arranged their marriage."

The thought of his sister, her loving eyes and her loyalty, warmed him. He wished he could hear her achingly beautiful harp music tonight.

❧

*A*fter months of drilling, the commanders assured Herod the newly trained recruits were ready for war. Once slovenly and lacking in discipline, his men now had the bearing and battle skills of Roman soldiers.

"Tomorrow, we will march on Ptolmais, Joppa, and Orhesa," said Herod, "and take these cities on our way to Jerusalem."

His men cheered heartily. Most of them were itching to fight. Over the next several weeks, Herod's army fought fiercely. Under his command, they swept the Parthians from every city, town, and village they attacked. They marched through Galilee and emerged victorious from a pitched battle.

"You've done well," Herod said, addressing his men after their final northern campaign. "We've lost men, yes, but far fewer than our enemies have. There is more we must do. Galilean rebels who survived our attacks have fled into caves high on the cliffs of Mount Arbel. Reaching them poses a challenge, but my army faces challenges head-on, yes?"

"Yes!" they shouted.

"We will not stop until our enemies are crushed!" His men hailed him. The sound of it was sweet.

~

*I*n his camp tent, Herod broke his fast with bread and cheese while he studied maps of Mount Arbel and its environs. Reaching the rebels who hid in caves carved into the mountain's steep rock face seemed impossible. The cave openings were small and too high for the infantry to storm. Spears, arrows, and projected weapons would not reach them from the ground.

Joseph came inside and sat down beside him. His brother's dusky eyes gleamed, and he gave Herod a bright smile.

Herod, trying to figure out a way to attack the un-attackable, did not want to be disturbed. "What is it, Joseph?"

"I've discovered a way we can reach the Arbel caves."

Herod shook his head. "Military strategy is well beyond your training and experience, Joseph. Don't concern yourself—"

"Hear me out, Brother. First, we build wooden boxes big enough inside for two soldiers. We attach long ropes to those boxes. At the summit of Mount Arbel, we use the ropes to lower the boxes, with the soldiers inside them, to the cave openings—"

"Even if our soldiers can reach the caves this way, the rebels will ambush them," interrupted Herod, shaking his head. "I must leave now. I have drills to run."

"Listen to me, Herod. There will be no opportunity for ambush. Inside each box, we will have an archer and a soldier wielding a long iron hook. First, they will throw lit torches into the caves to smoke out the rebels."

"Go on," he said, his eyebrows raised.

"The rebels will pour out of their caves to avoid the fire and smoke. Our archers will strike as many as they can. Those who remain inside the caves, our soldiers will hook like fish, pull out of the caves, and drop to their bloody deaths."

Astounded, Herod sat back and considered his brother's plan. It just might work. "Brilliant, Joseph," he said, ruffling his brother's dark, curly hair.

~

*H*erod would never forget the Arbel Caves attack. Soldiers lowered in boxes first tossed lit torches into the caves. Fire drove out frantic rebels, and their women and children, and archers picked them off, one by one. In their panic, many rebels tried to scale down the cliff. Archers' arrows sent them falling. Then, soldiers reached deep inside the caves with their great iron hooks, piercing the cowards' bodies. They pulled them out and dangled them, bloody and screaming, over the valley before they shook them free, and watched them plummet to their deaths on the jagged rocks below. Herod saw entire families leap to their deaths rather than face the sharp hooks of his soldiers.

The operation was successful beyond Herod's expectations. He

had to admit that despite Joseph's lack of military experience, he
had shown himself to be an exceptional strategist. As important, he
had proven that he had the strength and brutality necessary to win
battles. Herod made his beloved brother a general.

~

*A*fter the Arbel Caves victory, the Parthians sent in
reinforcements. A much larger force fought his army and
gave them strong resistance on the battlefield. He watched too many
of his men fall in battle. If he did not promptly acquire fresh
soldiers and weapons, he was going to lose them all. Herod knew
Antony well, and he was more likely to grant a personal request,
man to man.

He assembled his battle-worn men. "I must travel to Rome for
fresh soldiers and supplies. This army is too sizable to move
quickly, so half of you will come with me, and we will sweep the
Parthians out of the cities and villages on our way. The other half
of you will stay here in camp. General Joseph will be in
command."

His brother flushed with pride. What a relief it was to have an
adored brother he trusted.

"Those of you who remain here with the general must drill
daily," Herod added. "Defend any attack but initiate no battles until
I have returned from Rome with reinforcements." He turned to
Joseph. "That is a command."

~

*H*erod and half his army rode toward Rome. Passing
through Samosota, a town north of Syria, they came
upon Triumvir Marc Antony and his army battling the Parthians.
Antony's soldiers were fighting hard, but those still standing were
few. If Herod did not send in his army, the triumvir would soon go
down in defeat. Herod would save Antony. Indebted to him, the
triumvir would likely grant his request for more men.

"Go in," he ordered his soldiers. "Battle alongside the Romans. Defeat our enemies. Make me proud."

Swiftly, Herod's soldiers turned the tide of the battle. The enemy quickly fell to the combined forces, and Rome triumphed. An elated Antony embraced Herod like a brother.

"Herod, you have proven your worth to the Roman Republic," he said. "Men, let's have a victory march for our hero."

Antony paraded him between long queues of feather-capped Roman soldiers. Herod would never forget how they cheered him and called out his praises.

"Herod, to reward your courage and your assistance, I gift you land," said Antony. "Western Idumea and Samaria are now yours."

Ah, land, the most precious gift of all. Euphoria washed over him like a sea wave.

"Antony, I thank you," Herod added, "and I ask you for reinforcements of infantry and cavalry, and food and weapons, for our battle to retake Jerusalem."

"Whatever you want is yours," said Antony, with a friendly whack on Herod's back.

What could stand in his way now?

~

The next morning, in the Roman camp near Samosota, the fog was so thick Herod could not see his own feet as he made his way to the commanders' dining tent. He had taken only a few bites of hard bread when he saw his second in command heading toward him. From the man's deep scowl, Herod knew he brought bad news. His forehead vein pulsed as he took the scroll the commander held out to him. He read it. The earth dropped beneath his feet. The unthinkable had happened.

"Joseph is dead," Herod said. "He and his men attacked the Parthians in Jericho. He fell there— alongside most of the others."

He walked away from the commanders, whose offers of sympathy he could not bear. Outside, by the campfire, he watched the glowing embers from the night fire die. It had been a joy to reunite with Joseph and to watch him grow into a formidable soldier and military strategist. But his treasured brother had disobeyed his orders. Now, he was lost to him, forever. It set his soul on fire. He vowed to avenge his brother's death, no matter what it took. He could not wait to humiliate his enemies.

15

MARIAMNE, 37 BCE, MASADA

*T*he Parthians arrived on a cool dawn in late winter. On horseback and on chariots, hundreds of them poured over the horizon, riding hard toward Masada. Their pointed, gold helmets and dreaded long spears glinted in bright sunlight. My breath caught in my throat. "They're here," I cried out, though no one was around.

I heard the heavy footfall of our soldier's boots as they stormed up the tower stairs to take their positions on the ramparts. I ran to find Yusef. He was already at the highest lookout, glowering down on the soldiers riding in, though many were off their horses, pitching tents and making cooking fires no more than one hundred feet from the foot of Masada.

"What are we going to do?" I asked, barely recognizing the sound of my own quivering voice.

The intensity of Yusuf 's dark-eyed gaze further unnerved me. "I must speak with the families. Gather everyone in the tower chamber."

I ran to find my mother and brother, and then Cypros and Salome, and I led everyone up the tower stairs to a close, dark room where there were no windows, not even archers' slits. We waited there for Yusef to come. It seemed like a long while before he swept in, his face worn and haggard.

"The Parthians will attack. When, I don't know. Our chances of surviving are dismal. The enemy vastly outnumbers us."

I was suddenly lightheaded. The chamber began to spin. Salome and her mother clung to each other and wailed. My mother slumped into Aris's arms.

"The Parthians have already begun their siege," Yusef added. "They have blocked our trailheads. They will execute anyone who tries to leave Masada. Meat and supplies can no longer come up the Snake Trail."

"How are we going to live?" asked my mother, her eyes frantic. "We will have to eat whatever we can catch on the plateau."

Glaring at Yusef, my mother rose. "We can't live on small animals alone."

With a deep scowl, Yusef turned away from her. "Listen to me. When our watch sees the enemy approaching, I will blow the ram's horn three times. That will be your signal to come to this chamber. You will have some degree of protection here in this windowless tower. But know this. When the Parthians storm Masada, they will kill us all. So, make your peace with God now."

Descending the tower steps, no one said a word. In the morning's soft, buttery light, Masada looked incongruously beautiful. How could my adult life be over before it had ever really begun? I could no longer hold back my tears. I sat at the foot of the tower stairs and sobbed.

∾

The Parthians kept coming. Day after day, more soldiers rode in and joined their camp. Every morning, I stood at the edge of the plateau and watched them drill. Once they finished their military exercises, they milled around restlessly, looking disturbingly eager for orders to invade Masada.

Weeks later, the Parthians still had not attacked. When were they going to strike? I did not want to think about whether I would die by sword or flaming arrow, yet I did, obsessively. Chores went undone and we took care of only our most basic needs: food and water. Who wanted to weed a garden one might not live long enough to harvest? Who cared if our living quarters were clean when we would soon approach the Throne of God?

After dinner one evening, I found Yusef frowning as he paced the eastern ridge.

"Why haven't they attacked us?" I asked.

"I believe they're waiting for more soldiers to arrive," he said. "But they already have far more men than we do. How can twenty guards hold off hundreds of armed soldiers?"

Yusef smiled, ruefully. "They don't know we have few men. But we will give them a good fight."

~

Nearly a month after the first soldiers had set up camp, I woke up to the sound of shouting. I ran out to the promontory's southern rim. Yusef was already there, peering down at the enemy settlement. I could barely believe what I saw. With massive shovels, Parthian soldiers were pushing heaps of dirt up against the base of Masada. Pile by pile, the mound was growing high.

"What are they doing?" I asked with a shiver. "Making a ramp," said Yusef.

"Will they be able to build it high enough to reach us?"

Yusef shrugged. "We'll see. Even if they can't reach the plateau, any elevation will bring their weapons closer to us."

The Parthian presence hung over my head like a sword on a fraying rope.

16

HEROD, 37 BCE, JERUSALEM

The long, dry summer, the optimal season for war, had arrived. Herod and his army journeyed from Galilee to the Roman Camp to join the Roman soldiers Antony had sent. Their sprawling camp blanketed a ridge between two hills north of Jerusalem. Though his army was ready for battle, Herod hoped he might avoid war. Of course, he would use force, if necessary, but given a choice, he would rather not. The fewer subjects he killed, the more he would have to tax and rule after his victory.

First, he would try diplomacy. He arranged to meet with Mari-amne's Uncle Antigonus, who had bribed the Parthians to make him their local king. He had a tent hastily erected between his camp and the city walls for their meeting.

～

The morning Herod was to meet with Antigonus, he woke up from a leaden sleep to a rare, cool dawn and a chorus of crickets. He had a hearty appetite for the date cakes at breakfast. He dressed in his most kingly attire, a robe adorned with sewn-in sapphires and a belt of gold.

At the tent where Herod was to meet with Antigonus, the guards crossed their swords against him at the opening. He submitted to their inspection for hidden weapons. Herod and Antigonus had agreed, through their intermediaries, to leave their swords and daggers outside when they met. When Antigonus arrived minutes later, his guards similarly searched the Maccabee.

On a woven rug, bright with red flowers on a pale pink background, he and Antigonus sat across from one another. The tension in the hot, close space was palpable. Before Herod spoke, he studied Antigonus's classically beautiful face. His strong, square chin looked chiseled as a Greek statue. It was unfortunate. Herod had hoped to meet an ugly rival. But it heartened him to see that the man was weak, having spindly arms and legs, and a narrow chest. Antigonus was no soldier.

"All guards, leave us now," Herod said, flicking his hand as they filed out. "Wait outside." He turned to Antigonus. "Thank you for agreeing to meet with me, Uncle," he said.

Antigonus looked at him as if he had tasted something bitter. "Uncle? I'm no kinsman of yours, Herod, son of Antipater the Idumean."

"You will be soon. I'm soon to marry your niece, Mariamne."

The smug Maccabee's jaw fell. His astonishment made Herod grin. "I thought you knew." He handed Antigonus the treaty appointing him King of the Jews. "I've come to offer you an opportunity to surrender to my rule peacefully."

Antigonus studied the edict with large, dark-lashed eyes. "What do I gain for a peaceful surrender?"

"It's not about what you gain, kinsman. It's about what you will lose if you refuse my offer of peace. We will take Jerusalem by force."

Antigonus's face went crimson in his rage. "*Never* will I open the Gates of Jerusalem to you. Your edict no longer has the force of law. The Roman Republic has no authority to issue orders to Judea. Our overlord is the King of Parthia."

At the sound of Antigonus's raised voice, his guards clambered to the tent's entrance with hands on their swords.

"Stay out unless I call for you," Antigonus shouted.

Herod and Antigonus glared at each other with matching intensity.

"For the sake of your people, I urge you to rethink your position," Herod said. "Or you will bear the responsibility for turning Jerusalem's streets into rivers of blood. Your greed for power will kill many who need not die."

The Maccabee was panting now. "You dare speak of *my* greed for power? I'm the son of Aristobulus. I descend from Kings. Who are you? What priestly and kingly ancestors have you to name? You're a puppet on Rome's string."

Herod narrowed his eyes. "Spare your people your desire to avenge your father's disgrace."

Antigonus looked like Herod had struck him. "My father's disgrace?"

"Yes, his disgrace. Caesar appointed Hyrcanus King and High Priest of Judea. Your father coveted his brother's throne. He warred against his own blood."

"My father won that war. He took Jerusalem."

Herod snickered. "For a brief time, yes, but it wasn't long before Hyrcanus, with my father's help, took back what was rightfully his."

"Rome and your father needed a weak leader on the throne, someone they could easily manipulate. Hyrcanus was that weakling. My father was the strong, intelligent son."

"Aristobulus was not Rome's choice for King of Judea. Nor was he your mother's choice. The good Queen Alexandra Jannaeus appointed her oldest son, Hyrcanus, to succeed her."

Antigonus stood up and adjusted his robe with smooth, soft-looking hands. Clearly, they had never held a weapon on a battlefield. Herod quickly rose and stood akimbo. He was not going to let this man loom over him.

"Your father poisoned mine," said Antigonus, "and he had my brother Scipios beheaded. And you dare ask me to show you mercy?"

"I'm not asking for your mercy. I'm asking that you show the People of Jerusalem—my people—mercy."

"Herod, the people of Jerusalem despise you and Rome equally. We will defeat you."

"Antig-on-us! Antig-on-us! Antig-on-us!" chanted a crowd of people inside the city walls. The sound of it made Herod's intestines roil.

"My people will never submit to you," said Antigonus.

"You have given me no choice. I will take Jerusalem by force."

∽

*B*y the time Herod had returned to camp, all was quiet behind the stone walls of Jerusalem. Night fell, and a sea of stars winked down at him. He threw himself on top of his makeshift bed, a heap of animal skins. Jumbled images of the disconcerting day darted through his mind. If Antigonus wanted a battle, he would give him one he would never forget in the unlikely event he lived through it. Antigonus was, after all, no military man. He was a pampered Maccabee, a stranger to war. Antigonus was no match for his army and Rome's. However, the usurper did have the considerable strength of the Parthian Empire behind him. He had to consider the likelihood of Parthian reinforcements.

The Parthians had swept south from Central Asia one hundred years before and conquered the eastern half of Alexander the Great's empire. These pagans had long controlled many trade routes, and it made them wealthy and powerful. Now, they were seeking to expand their territory further into the Holy Land.

He tried to push away his political difficulties, and think only of Mariamne. Ah, what a woman she was. In his imagination, it was their wedding night. Mariamne dropped her robe, and…that was when the idea occurred to him. He should marry her before he besieged Jerusalem. Once they wed, he would be a full-fledged member of the Maccabee Royal Family. His subjects would have more reason to accept him as their king. As a bonus, the princess would sleep in his bed.

Herod had promised King Hyrcanus he would wait for the old man's permission to have the wedding ceremony. He did as the old king had ordered, and stayed away from Mariamne during their long engagement. At this point, however, Hyrcanus could hardly stop Herod from marrying her. If he still lived, he was languishing in some Parthian prison, unable to give or withhold his consent for the wedding. In any event, Mariamne was seventeen now, a grown woman, an age in which Hyrcanus most likely would have consented to the ceremony if he could.

Herod satisfied himself with his own hand and fell into a deep sleep.

~

*H*erod's spymaster arrived at dawn with a troubling message. A regiment of Parthian soldiers was riding hard toward Masada with orders to capture Mariamne and her family. Herod had to stop them.

With battle vigor coursing through his veins, he dressed quickly and strode over to General Sosius's tent. Sosius, the highest military commander in the Roman Republic, had arrived at camp a few days ago. At six feet tall, he towered over most men. His height, along with his burly frame and spear-straight carriage, might intimidate a lesser man. Herod insisted that the aide-de-camp who greeted at the tent opening wake the general at once. Before long, Sosius, haggard and grumbling under his breath, emerged.

"I must leave for Masada right away," said Herod. "I've just received intelligence that the Parthians plan to capture my betrothed, Princess Mariamne, and her family. They're in grave danger. I must take them to a secure place. Two hundred of my soldiers are accompanying me. While I'm away, have the men build siege engines and bulwarks. I want to be ready for the siege as soon as I return."

Sosius gave him the scathing look of a man unaccustomed to taking orders. "How long do you plan to be away? I haven't much time. There are rebellions on Rome's borders I must quell."

"I'll return as soon as I settle Mariamne's family and my own in Samaria."

Herod left without waiting for the general's response. He had to reach Masada before his enemies did.

17

MARIAMNE, 37 BCE, MASADA

I found a nest of newly hatched doves on my window ledge. The chirping creatures opened their tiny mouths to their mother. She fed them, beak to beak. I would never have the opportunity to bring new life into this world. Sadness swept over me.

Three short blasts of a ram's horn silenced the birdsong. My heart thrashed wildly. The Parthians were invading Masada. I hurried to the tower room. Yusef was already there. Both families and our servants rushed in.

"Our men are on the ramparts," said Yusef. "The battle has begun. Stay here for the duration."

"The ramp they built—will it allow them to reach the plateau?" I asked, barely recognizing the thin, shrill sound of my voice.

"It doesn't come all the way to the plateau, but it will raise the soldiers high enough to strike us."

"Yusef, please, I want to come with you," said Aris, standing up as tall as he could. "I can help. I'll run arrows to the archers."

Yusef gave him a curt nod. "Come."

"No!" I cried, but Aris was already gone.

I heard Yusef 's heavy footfall followed by my brother's lighter tread ascending the tower stairs to the parapets and harm's open arms. I should not have let him go. I should have barred the door and draped myself across it, if necessary, to keep Aris with me. Yusef was thoughtlessly risking the safety and welfare of our future sovereign. How could I sit still while my brother was facing the onslaught of spears and arrows?

I slipped out and climbed the stairway. From the open door at the top, I could see the ramparts. Yusef and his archers were raining flaming arrows down on the Parthians. Where was Aris? Panic shot through me. I peeked around a parapet to the desert floor far beneath Masada. It was a bloody abyss. Was my brother among those who lay mangled and slaughtered? It was too far down for me to see faces.

"Aris!" I screamed.

"Yes," said a blessedly familiar voice behind me.

I wheeled around. To my immense relief, my brother stood there, grinning.

"I thought you were dead."

"Yusef wouldn't let me out there with the soldiers," he said with a note of resentment.

"Good. You must protect yourself." I put my hands on his shoulders. "I cannot lose you, Aris. I love you more than anyone. Do you understand? You must stay safe. You're our future king. We need you."

I heard the sound of horses approaching. I looked out to see soldiers riding hard in our direction. Were they Parthian reinforcements? My breath came fast and shallow. We were all going to die. Everything grew blurry. I struggled to focus on the advancing chariots. Behind them, hundreds of soldiers on horseback thundered across the desert. When they drew closer, I saw they wore red tunics and feathered metal helmets. They were Roman soldiers, coming to save us!

Out of the oncoming horde, one golden chariot surged ahead. My heart hammered. "Herod," I whispered. He still lived. Relief coursed through me.

"What are you doing here?"

I wheeled around to see Yusef, his face thunderous. "This is no place for…" he said and turned to Aris. "I ordered you to stay inside the tower. Both of you—go down to the inner chamber and join the others."

"Herod is coming!" I cried. "I must see this."

"Downstairs. Now."

I held Yusef 's gaze. His black eyes softened. "Mariamne, I want to keep you—both of you—safe."

Aris and I exchanged glances and started down the tower stairway. We gave Yusef a few moments to leave, and then we hastened back up the stairs to witness Herod's glorious approach. He must have issued an order because all of a sudden, scores of Roman soldiers raced ahead and threw themselves into battle. Herod abandoned his chariot and jumped into the fray, viciously swinging sword and dagger, using even his shield as a weapon. Javelins and flaming arrows showered down on the enemy below.

In the haze of smoke and armor and clashing weapons, I lost sight of Herod. He had blended into the mass of men battling on the ground. Our lives depended on his survival. I mumbled a prayer for his safety and victory for his men. I kept trying to spot him until rising smoke from fiery arrows obscured my view and made me choke and cough. I had to get away.

I took Aris's hand and led him to the stairwell. I closed the door, and we sat on the floor up against the thick, cool wall. We held hands, and I closed my eyes and tried to shut out the horror I had witnessed. War had always been something I had heard about in the clean confines of family palaces. I had never been so close to its unimaginable brutality.

We went back out to the parapets when the sounds of battle no longer reached us. The sun had begun its descent over the western mountains. The ground was awash with blood and bodies. Only a few soldiers continued to fight. It was not long before the Parthians rode away in a hasty retreat.

"Victory is ours!" Yusef cried.

Herod clambered up the snake path in a confident stride. What would he expect when he saw me? A kiss? An embrace? Of course,

I was grateful to him for our survival, but the thought of touching him… How could I bear sharing his bed?

We descended the tower staircase to join the others just as Herod, battle-worn but triumphant, reached the open court in front of the palace. Ruggedly handsome, his face glowed golden as if lit from within. Or was it just the play of afternoon light on the dark curls around his helmet? Perhaps it was his elation over his victory. His beauty did not matter. I forced a nod and a smile in response to his surprisingly gentle gaze. His eyes lost their intensity and grew soft when they rested on me. To my astonishment, he approached me before anyone else.

"My love," he said.

Salome slipped between us. "Our hero," she said, and stroked her brother's cheek.

Cypros threw herself into Herod's arms and embraced him. "My son lives!"

Herod detangled himself from his mother and his sister. "You are greeting the new King of Judea," he said.

I brought a hand to my throat. This changed everything. I looked at my mother. Her jaw had fallen open, and her face was the color of a pomegranate.

"But that's not possible," my mother said. "Aris is next in line for the throne. Did Antony appoint you regent until Aris comes of age to rule?"

Herod gave my mother a triumphant smirk. "No. Antony said our land needs a man, not a boy, on the throne. Antony, Octavian, and the Roman Senate crowned me King of Judea. I wish you could have seen it. They paraded me down the Via Apian. Crowds packed both sides of the procession. Everyone cheered for me."

My mother fanned herself, vigorously. "As I've said, my son, Aris, will be our next—"

"The man who will be king after me will be a son I have on Queen Mariamne," interrupted Herod.

Queen Mariamne? I rather liked the sound of it. I could be the mother of kings. I could produce the man who wore the crown of

Judea. When I saw my brother's dazed expression, I felt immediate stab of remorse.

"Come, Herod," Salome said. "I've arranged for us to have wine in the courtyard."

Herod had not taken his eyes from me since he had arrived. "I must refuse you, Salome. I cannot bear to leave my exquisite princess."

Salome's face clouded. She stormed away, flanked by her mother.

Herod looped his arm through mine. "My love, let's have our wine on the terrace."

My mother left in a huff, and Aris followed. Herod and I stood together on a stony overhang jutting out from the western ridge. The heady scent of jasmine perfumed the air. Lounging on a chaise beside Herod, I watched the Judean Hills swallow the setting sun. Wisps of smoky clouds tumbled across the lavender sky.

"You miss Jerusalem," he said.

I turned to him in surprise. He sounded as though he cared.

"I know what it's like to miss home," he said.

"Do you?"

"When I was a boy, my family was forced to leave Judea quickly. Caesar murdered his rival, Pompey, and came to power in Rome. My father had been Pompey's good friend."

"Did your father think Caesar's men were going to come after your family?"

Herod nodded. "We escaped in the night and lived in Petra Palace for months as guests of King Aretas, my mother's kinsman. They were kind to us, but I hated leaving home."

Herod took my hand in his. He stared at my calluses and frowned.

My face and ears grew hot. "My hands are rough from all the work I did—"

Herod grinned. "You worked?"

"I did. There wasn't enough food and water for everyone during the drought. Yusef sent away most of our servants so our provisions would last longer. We all did chores alongside the few servants who had stayed."

Herod cocked his head and gazed at me with what looked like a new respect. "You learned what you had to do to survive, and you did it. You have become a strong woman, Mariamne. You make me proud."

This was the man who had stolen my brother's legacy. I pulled away from him. I longed for escape, and I longed for home. The pull was so strong it hurt. "I want to go home," I said.

Herod nodded, staring intently at the hills, a dark outline against a twilight sky the silver of Roman armor. "I'll take you back to Jerusalem after I have destroyed our enemies. I promise you."

~

The next morning, I said good-bye to Yusef, who was staying on with servants to close up Masada Palace. I would miss his warmth and wise counsel. I looked around for the last time at Masada's bleak, brown landscape. I would not pine for its scorching sun or its relentless winds and terrible isolation.

On the way to Samaria, our carriages and carts bumped along the gravel roads and wound through barren hills. The morning air was thick with the stench of horse and camel dung. Enormous jars of olive oil and dates burdened the plodding camels. As a particularly pungent caravan passed, I covered my nose with a piece of linen.

We traveled through a deep forest of myrtle and broom trees and emerged into rolling, green countryside. My stomach clenched when I saw the stopped carriage on the side of the road. Were they bandits? Two men jumped out and came toward us. One of the men handed Herod a scroll. They were messengers. I could breathe again. From inside the carriage, I heard Herod dismiss them. Afterward, he said nothing about what he had read.

The vineyards and olive groves looked much like those near Jerusalem. Around a bend, on the broad ridge where the Jordan and Tirza Valleys met, stood Samaria Castle. Its near-ruined towers leaned precipitously to the right, looking as though they might collapse at any moment. Heaps of gray stone lay beside the crumbling walls around the castle. It was hard to believe Samaria had once been the Kingdom of Israel's capital city.

At the castle gate, Herod turned to face us. "I must leave right away."

"What about the wedding ceremony?" my mother asked.

"Where are you going?" Cypros asked, her voice thin and strained.

"I got a message earlier today. Antigonus and the Parthians have invaded towns in the North. I am meeting my army there to drive them out." He turned to me. "Goodbye, my princess. I'll return to you as soon as I can, and we will marry."

I looked away and said nothing. Did Herod notice my disdain for him or mind it if he did? I did not think so. To him, I was merely property to advance his position. He left, and I breathed a sigh of relief for the delay of the wedding ceremony, which I feared and dreaded in equal measure. However, the possibility of Herod's death in battle frightened me even more than the wedding. Like Masada, Samaria Castle was far away from Jerusalem, and we were to lodge here without the protection of friends or trusted allies. We were still isolated and in danger.

Whether or not Herod won the war on Jerusalem, he might abandon us. After all, he was already King of the Jews. Did he need us at all, or was the former ruling family a hindrance to his future rule? Was he better off without us? He could let our enemies hunt us down and kill us. He could eliminate my family but save his own.

Stinging blades of cold rain began to fall. Everyone scrambled into the castle's vast reception hall. Its musty smell made it evident that years of dampness had settled into the high walls of stone. Small, high windows offered only weak light. The wind tore through cracks in the walls big enough to put fingers through. Even in my wool cloak, I shivered.

"It's so cold here," Cypros said.

"How can Herod expect us to lodge in this terrible place?"

"What choice do we have?" I said. "At least, we're safe, and we have a roof over us."

"We have not even that," my mother said, pointing up to the ceiling on the far side of the hall. Rain poured through a large hole and pooled on the floor.

～

*A*t Samaria Castle, our few servants did their best to make repairs and to keep the damp, drafty, near-ruin of a castle as clean and comfortable as they possibly could. Still, cold and darkness were our constant nemeses. Winter clouds shrouded the sky for weeks at a time, leaving the castle's interior a dim, nearly lightless place. Even at noon, I needed an oil lamp to see my embroidery. Even when every lamp burned, we walked in shadows. We wore our wool cloaks night and day.

Timeworn and broken furniture packed the palace's smaller chambers. Everyone slept in the cavernous reception chamber on rough homespun sheets stretched over straw pallets. Aris and the guards and male servants slept on one side of the hall, and women slept on the other. There was no distinction between master and servant, except that Herod's family and my own had the first choice of beds. No matter, they were all equally uncomfortable. A giant, makeshift curtain of stitched-together linens hung from the rafters, splitting the hall into two sections. It provided some semblance of separation, but nothing in the way of quiet or privacy.

It was a difficult time. My mother complained incessantly about our rudimentary lodging. I could feel Salome's hostile presence even when we ignored each other. Most evenings, we gathered around the hearth fire and listened to Salome play the harp she had found in one of the storage chambers. It was a mystery to me how a woman so heartless could create the music of angels.

～

*W*eeks later, without prior message or announcement, Herod returned to Samaria Castle. He had quickly dispatched Antigonus and the Parthians from towns and villages in the North. Now, it was only days until our wedding.

As the date drew closer, I could no longer contribute to conversations in the banqueting and reception halls. Terror of the marriage bed drew me inward. I had to spend the rest of my life beside my husband. The prospect daunted me.

Herod had given me bolts of fine silk he had bought from a caravan master just returned from the Orient. Lila sewed it into my exquisite wedding attire, replete with intricate, silver-thread embroidery and tiny diamonds. I spent the days leading up to the wedding going to fittings and selecting wedding jewelry.

My mother had retrieved some gold and jeweled necklaces and bracelets that had been sewn into the hems of her robes on the day we had escaped from Jerusalem, and offered to let me wear them at the wedding.

"You have been so quiet," Lila said as she attached the clasp on the sapphire necklace I was trying on. "What's wrong?"

"It's my wedding. There will be things….I will be expected to do."

Lila laughed. "I've heard wives learn quickly."

"But I don't want to learn with Herod."

She stopped combing. "It is your duty as his wife."

"Now you sound like my mother. I know there's no way around this marriage, Lila. There's a *ketubah*."

"Well, you don't have to like it," she said. "You won't be the first woman who didn't."

Lila made me laugh for the first time in weeks.

~

I did not speak to Herod again until our wedding day. On the morning of the ceremony, I purified myself in the *mikvah*, the ritual bath built on top of a palace hot spring. Afterward,

Lila perfumed me with rosewater and fragrant crocus oil. She wove ruby beads into my long braid and lined my eyes with kohl. Glittering rubies hung down my forehead from a gold-cloth band. Gold bracelets encircled my wrists and arms. A diamond pendant glittered from a gold chain around my neck.

For the first time since we had left Jerusalem Palace, I felt like a princess. Wedding guests packed into the palace courtyard. They gasped when I walked, with a regal bearing, down the petal-strewn aisle to the *chuppah*, a canopy covered with fragrant lotus blossoms. Herod stood beneath it with the grace and bearing of a king, his crown gleaming in the afternoon sun. He smelled faintly of frankincense and myrrh. The white, purple-lined robe he wore did little to hide the man of muscles and heat beneath it. I shivered and looked away.

"You're exquisite," he whispered.

My mother nodded to signal me to begin. With measured steps, I circled the groom seven times for the seven days in which God created earth and man. During the final circle, I grew dizzy and thought I was going to fall. Herod held out a hand to steady me. He slipped a gold ring on my index finger, the one that reflected the true path to the heart, custom said. But I could never give Herod my heart.

"Behold, you're betrothed to me with this ring, according to the Laws of Moses and Israel," Herod said in a strong, clear voice.

He kissed me with surprisingly soft lips. As the priest murmured prayers for our long and blessed lives, I promised myself I would never forget my mission. I must make this Idumean pretender fall, even though he was making me his queen, even though he was my husband. It was said that the gates of heaven are open to brides' and grooms' prayers on their wedding day. I prayed that Aris would prevail over Herod.

All of a sudden, the ceremony was over. The crowd pushed its way toward us and offered us wishes for a long and happy marriage. Herod and I politely greeted what seemed like the entire population of Samaria. I was as hot as a honey cake fresh from the ovens.

Damp tendrils of hair clung to my head beneath my veil. Still, I forced a smile and kissed guest after guest.

If only I could throw off my regalia and fling myself into the fountain pool. I imagined the feel of the cool water. The thought of it helped keep me smiling. I longed for peace and quiet, but at the same time, I hoped the guests would linger and delay our inevitable advance to the marriage bed.

Herod's mother and sister were the last to approach us. Cypros embraced us warmly. Herod reached out to his sister. She recoiled and gave him a cool nod, and followed her mother away.

"Salome, come back here," he called, but she was gone.

~

*H*erod opened the royal bedchamber door. Vases filled with roses perfumed the air. Carved-wood tables and chests had been polished to a high gloss. It was hard to believe no one had slept here for the last hundred years.

The day Herod returned to Samaria, I had overheard him order his guards to clear the ancient weapons stored in the castle's largest bedchamber so we could have privacy on our wedding night. His words chilled me, then. Recalling them did, too.

Herod closed the door behind us. It shut with a thump that sounded as final as the end of my childhood. I stood frozen in terror while he opened a window shutter. Darkness had fallen, and the full moon cast a soft, white light on the crumbling castle walls.

"The night is beautiful, like my bride," said Herod. He poured wine into silver goblets. "This is no occasion for date wine. We have the best, a Falernian from Rome."

We toasted and took a few sips, and then put down our goblets. Herod removed my veil. He stroked my hair and ran his hand down my back.

"Ah, the beauty," he whispered, his face aglow with undisguised lust. Herod lifted my chin and kissed me. Involuntarily, I pulled back, but he wrapped his arms around me and held me so close I could not move. Moments later, he expertly peeled my robe and tunic from my trembling body. How many times had he done this before?

"I'll be gentle," he murmured as he unwound my undergarments and tossed them on the floor beside my wedding robe.

I stood naked before him, feeling more vulnerable than I ever had before. I crossed my arms against my bare chest and shivered.

"Don't cover up your beauty." His whisper was hoarse with desire. "Turn around."

With hands as cold as well water, I did as he told me. I felt his eyes scanning my body.

"You're the most beautiful woman I've ever seen."

Herod dropped his mantle and his tunic. I had never seen a fully unclothed man before this night. The size of his excited male member surprised me. Herod slid his hands around my waist and pulled my body towards his massive wall of chest and muscle. We lay down, and he pushed his hardness into me. I felt the stab of pain married women had warned me about, but my discomfort did not last. He thrust himself into me, again and again, until he shuddered with his release and rolled over on his back.

"My young bride is a woman now. How does it feel?"

I was a woman now, a woman who belonged to this man with his smooth, confident airs. I turned my head away and did not respond. Herod searched the bed sheet for virginal blood and grinned when he found it. I would keep that bloodied sheet forever, folded neatly in a special chest, should the need arise to prove I was a virgin on our wedding night.

There was a knock at the door. "King Herod, Queen Mariamne, it's time for your wedding feast," called the manservant through the door.

~

*E*veryone rose to their feet and clapped when Herod and I entered the banqueting hall. We sat at the groom's table on a platform near the crackling hearth. The glow of one hundred mounted torches made patterns dance on the high walls of white stone. Guests in exquisite silks drank and laughed and chattered.

"Long live King Herod and Queen Mariamne!" courtiers called.

Herod's bright smile showed his delight. I wished I could slide through the tile floor and sink into the earth. After interminable toasts over wine, we dined. The familiar smell of cumin and coriander was of some comfort to me, but I could eat only a few bites of lamb stew from the bowl Herod and I shared.

"I thought you would have worked up an appetite in the bedroom," Herod said.

How was I going to bear a lifetime with this man?

Increasingly drunk as the night progressed, our guests slurred their good wishes. The grim set of Salome's face was in stark contrast to the other smiling, laughing guests. But I did not want to think about her, not tonight. I paid attention to those making toasts only when Aris stood up and raised his goblet.

"To Mariamne, the finest sister who's ever walked this earth, and to Herod. *L'chaim*, to life!"

Guests clinked chalices. I wondered what making that toast had cost Aris. He loathed Herod as I did.

During our dessert course of plump figs in wine sauce, Herod leaned toward me. "This is the greatest day of my life," he said.

Without waiting for my response, he left me and began to dance to the music of lyres and harps in the cleared part of the hall. The men circled Herod and clapped as he danced. My mother took me off to a curtained area for the women's celebration set apart from the place where men danced. There, I tried to lose myself in wine, dance, and song.

18

HEROD, 37 BCE, SAMARIA

*A*t dawn, Herod studied his sleeping bride in wonder. He could watch her all day. He loved everything about her, from her gentle kindness to the graceful way she glided across a room. Mariamne was his own jewel, a prize won, a lofty goal reached. She belonged to him now, body and soul. Not even death could part them.

Herod congratulated himself on reaching such dizzying heights. He had to concede that his father, Antipater, deserved much of the credit for his rise. The man had worked tirelessly to pave the way for his sons to rule Judea. He had also burned into his progeny the necessity of political alliance, and the wisdom of changing loyalties when expedient. His father had made himself indispensable to General Pompey. He had supplied the Roman with men, weapons, and gold, but he had smoothly shifted his alliance to Caesar after he defeated Pompey.

His father had also taught him a valuable lesson: loyalty invited reward. Antipater and a three-thousand-man army had rescued Caesar when he was trapped in a siege in Alexandria. To reward Herod's father, Caesar appointed him as the Roman Procurator of Judea, giving him the power over the treasury, allowing him to appoint his sons to high positions. Antipater made Herod Governor of Galilee, and his oldest son, Phasael, Governor of Jerusalem. Herod had flattered and ingratiated himself with Hyrcanus, making himself first an indispensable advisor, and eventually, the untitled Governor of Judea.

Now, with his father and two of his brothers at eternal rest in the family burial cave, it fell upon Herod to bring glory to the family name. What better way to do this than to join the royal Maccabee family? He was going to be the patriarch of a new, Herodian line of Judean Kings. Both Herodian and Maccabee blood would flow through his children's veins. His progeny would never be outsiders on the fringes of power like his own family was. Judeans would love and accept him now that he was a member of the Maccabee royal line.

As an added boon, his marriage brought with it the exclusive privilege of sleeping with Mariamne. All through the long months of battle with the Parthians and Antigonus, thoughts and dreams of her had sustained him. Even during the fiercest fighting in the North, her image hovered in the recesses of his mind. Through the bloody indignities of battle, she inspired his survival; the harder he drove his men to win, the sooner he could return to her. At night in his camp tent, he could have taken a camp whore, but he chose to satisfy himself by imagining himself loving her.

Now, the beauty of her generation, his own Maccabee princess, lay beside hm. He kissed her. She opened her eyes, large and luminous in the near darkness. He began to caress her. She went rigid at his touch. It did not seem his wife was fond of him. He attributed it to the virginal shyness of early marriage. His former wife was much the same way until he had aroused her passion, and she began to return his desire with her own. This morning, he had not the time to go slowly. With great need, Herod mounted her. Ecstasy. She averted her gaze from him. He shut his eyes so he did not have to witness her apparent misery.

Afterward, he tried to hold Mariamne, to no avail. She rolled over and turned her face away from him. Still, he hoped this morning's amusement was going to make him, months down the line, a father.

For a while, Herod lay there and listened to the soothing sound of his wife's steady breathing. Then, with the suddenness of an enemy attack, panic gripped him. What if Mariamne despised him, and planned to kill him and return her own family to rule? He sat up, stiff-backed. No, he assured himself, he was part of her family now. It would not be like that.

Tenderly, he kissed her forehead and rose to don his armor.

19

MARIAMNE, 37 BCE, SAMARIA

*T*he morning after the wedding, Herod's side of the bed was wonderfully cool in his absence. I rose and washed all vestiges of him from my body with a fresh linen and water from a silver basin Lila had, considerately, left beside the bed. I pulled on a white silk robe edged in purple. If Herod had already left for war, I would not have to see him for months. Of course, I wanted him to triumph. I wanted the Parthians and their stooge, Antigonus, gone.

Salome and her mother were in the banqueting hall. My mother-in-law grinned warmly.

"Good morning," I said, sinking into a chaise.

Salome smiled, but her eyes looked clouded and unhappy. "Are you not wondering where your new husband went?"

"I know he was—"

"He left without saying good-bye to you?"

It was a relief to be rid of him.

"My brother woke me this morning to bid me farewell," Salome said with a smug expression. "He told me he slipped out without telling you."

"Herod left for Jerusalem at first light," said Cypros, glumly.

War was coming. I imagined the leaping flames and charred

buildings of my beloved city. I heard people scream. I saw their frantic attempts to escape city walls trapping them inside. I clutched the sides of my chaise so hard my knuckles turned white. Thinking about an assault on Jerusalem left me desolate. If Herod was victorious, would I one day return to a ruined city I would not recognize? How many Judeans were going to die in the war?

"I'm sure Herod will take us home as soon as he can," Cypros said with a kind smile.

20

HEROD, 37 BCE, JERUSALEM

*R*oman General Sosius stood at the open flap of Herod's tent in the camp north of Jerusalem.

"Please, come in," Herod said.

Herod's aide-de-camp poured beer. They raised their mugs to victory in Jerusalem, and they drank.

"Several legions will arrive over the next few days," said Sosius.

Herod held his mug out, and the aide-de-camp filled it. "Good. I see my—our camp—is growing."

The general took a long swig of beer. "Have you turned your recruits into soldiers worthy of Rome?" he asked with a skeptical squint.

Herod nodded. "I've made warriors of peasant farmers and tradesmen."

During military training, Herod had worked his new conscripts as hard as any commander could work men. He had shouted drill commands long after his throat was raw and his soldiers were spent. When they fell to the ground in exhaustion, he made them rise and drilled them harder. He persisted until he was satisfied everyone was equipped to face the battlefield.

"But are they ready to fight alongside Romans?" Sosius asked. "I can assure you they will battle in lockstep with Rome's finest."

In fact, by the time his recruits had reached Jerusalem after winning several battles *en route*, they were feverishly loyalty to him, and itching for war.

Sosius's expression was unreadable. Was the eminent general doubting him?

"On our way to Jerusalem, we swept the Parthians from the North. We took every city, town, and village along our way."

New respect gleamed in the general's eyes. Herod prized it.

"We must attack Jerusalem right away," said Sosius. "A siege will be too costly in time. There are other revolts on the borders of the republic I must put down."

Herod drew in a deep breath and exhaled slowly. He must carefully consider his words; he could ill afford to offend this Roman general whom Antony held in high regard. However, he must get Sosius's cooperation. The general's strategy might serve his best interests—a quick departure from Judea to another unsettled border—but an armed struggle, with its inexorable bloodshed and loss of life, was not in his best interest, if he could avoid it. What Herod wanted was for the people to see they had no choice but to accept him as their rightful king.

"With respect, I disagree," said Herod. "We might have to fight, but we must first give Antigonus an opportunity to surrender."

"The people of Jerusalem ought to be punished for their resistance to you. You're Rome's chosen king, and diplomatic efforts have failed."

Herod looked at him, levelly. "I know Rome frowns on slaughtering too many of one's own people."

Sosius's lips formed a grim line. "I cannot tarry too long in any one land."

Herod tried to control his mounting frustration. "I can't be king of a people I've made extinct. We will begin with a siege."

The general's glower did not intimidate him. "Then this siege is yours to command," said Sosius.

Herod smiled. That was precisely what he wanted.

~

*O*n the first day of the siege, Herod felt a heady mixture of exhilaration and dread. It was time to make the Judeans recognize him as their sovereign. He would force them to see his superiority over Antigonus in weapons and soldiers. If Antigonus had a shred of sense, he would know the hopelessness of his predicament and surrender.

Herod and General Sosius climbed the city-taker, a fifty-foot, fortified siege tower in the new circumvolution wall his army had built. This new barricade surrounded Jerusalem's stone walls and let his army draw close enough to city walls and watchtowers to intimidate the soldiers defending them. Roman artillery could easily reach Jerusalem, but most of Herod's fighting positions were beyond the reach of Antigonus's inferior weapons. Herod confirmed that ram tortoises, wheeled catapults of timber and rawhide, and battering rams were ready. Then he blew four sharp blasts on his ram's horn to capture Antigonus's attention. From his vantage point, Herod could see the people stop milling about inside the city walls. A hush fell over them, and they turned their terrified faces toward the siege tower.

"Antigonus," Herod bellowed. "Can you hear me?"

There was no response.

"Answer me, Antigonus," demanded Herod.

Again, the only sound was the wind shrieking around the siege tower.

"This is Herod, King of the Jews," he called in a loud, clear voice. "Antigonus, surrender now, or we will starve you into submission. No one will be permitted to enter or to leave Jerusalem. We will allow no food or water to come through your gates or over your walls."

After a reshuffling of men perched on top of Jerusalem's nearest section of wall, Antigonus, his handsome face pale and solemn, came into view. "We will never surrender to you, Herod, son of Antipater the Idumean," he shouted.

"Soldiers, take your positions," Herod thundered. "The Siege of Jerusalem has begun."

~

*D*ay and night, Herod's soldiers watched Jerusalem's towers and walls, and studied the activity inside the city. Lengthy days grew to weeks. Herod's soldiers grew edgy and eager for battle. At the end of the fourth week of the siege, General Sosius summoned Herod to his barracks. The eminent Roman was sharpening his sword. The hard set of his jaw gave his weathered face an even more formidable look. He sharpened his blade, again and again, and did not bother to look up. Standing before the great man, Herod felt like a schoolchild called out for misbehavior. He was unaccustomed to this feeling, and he did not like it. Finally, the general spoke. "Tell me, why hasn't Antigonus surrendered as you said he would?"

"His surrender will soon come," said Herod, shifting on his feet. "Jerusalem's grain stores are low from last winter's drought. It is a Sabbatical Year, the seventh year the people have planted and harvested. By Judean law, they must let those fields lie fallow. They should be close to starvation by now."

"I can't stay here much longer. Judea is not Rome's only troubled vassal state. We will attack the city tomorrow at dawn."

Herod kept his lips pressed together until he was confident he could speak civilly. "General, I know you have Triumvir Antony's respect. You have mine, too. But I'm the Sovereign of Judea. Antony sent you here to support my position. I will decide when we invade Jerusalem."

Sosius's eyes burned fire. He gave Herod a tight smile. "You're a vassal king of a Roman Province."

Herod wasn't going to let the general's conceit and his selfish itch to leave Judea ruin his chance for victory.

"For now, we will wait," Herod added, decisively. "If Antigonus doesn't surrender during the next two weeks, we will attack."

Sosius gave him a curt nod.

~

Two weeks later, the war began. Herod rose in the darkness before dawn with a surge of battle vigor, a sensation he always felt before he must fight and kill or face his own death. He channeled his fury toward Antigonus for refusing to surrender into anticipation for the opportunity to destroy him. When sunrise cut its bloody gash on the horizon, Herod was in full armor.

Before the battle began, Herod gathered his officers and soldiers around him. The sight of the men he had trained into hardened warriors filled his heart with pride. In their red tunics and feathered helmets, they were indistinguishable from the Roman soldiers who would fight alongside them.

"Our war to free Jerusalem commences!" Herod shouted.

His soldiers hailed him. "I'll tolerate no looting or rape," he called. "Kill no ancients, women, or children. Now, begin. Archers!" Soldiers rained down flaming arrows, striking the enemy, whether on walls or on the ground. From Herod's vantage point, high above the fray, he could hear people scream as dwellings and stores and public buildings erupted into flames. The individual blazes found each other and joined to create a giant conflagration that rose high above the city. Herod stared at it in awe. It was unfortunate their leaders had not the sense to accept him as King of the Jews. It was going to be expensive to repair and rebuild the city once he took the throne. All of the ruin and carnage was unnecessary.

From Jerusalem's walls and turrets, Herod's soldiers returned fire from siege towers. Many of his warriors and his enemies fell screaming to their deaths. It looked as though the entire city was burning.

Parthian warriors, in peculiar armor that looked like connecting fish scales, began to pour out of Jerusalem's towers and replaced Antigonus's fallen. Perched on the wall, the foreign invaders yelled battle cries in their harsh tongue as they poured boiling oil on his soldiers on the ground below. Those struck screamed in agony. Many stayed prone on the ground. Parthian fighters leaped from Jerusalem's walls, landing on top of his men.

Herod had to make a bold move or he would soon lose the battle. He descended from the tower, taking the steps two at a time, and galloped, stiff-backed on his stallion, to the edge of the battlefield.

"Stand up and fight!" he shouted at his men.

The men who still stood battled, sword to sword, dagger to dagger. The air grew thick with smoke, and it was difficult to see through the haze. More and more Parthian soldiers rushed in, replacing their fallen. Herod steeled himself and maintained his calm even as fires raged, arrows flew, and daggers and swords pierced flesh.

"Siege engines!" Herod commanded. Sweat streamed down his face. "Crush those walls!"

Battering rams launched massive stones into the city and struck the North wall. The impact was deafening, but the ancient walls stayed intact. Again and again, shooting stones rammed into the ancient walls.

"We need to bring in the catapults," Sosius said.

Herod nodded. "Catapults!" he shouted. "Northern wall!" It was the weakest section.

The catapults struck. The old stones trembled, but the wall did not fall. The strength of the Maccabee fortifications impressed him. But after several more strikes, the northern wall gave way. Archers and infantrymen did not need scaling ladders to storm the city. They pushed aside the crumbled stone and invaded. It was not long before the road was red with blood.

As Herod watching the carnage, memories of his wedding night incongruously flooded his mind. He wanted Mariamne right then with a passion that both astonished and exasperated him. Before Mariamne, no woman had ever occupied his thoughts while on a battlefield. It was unacceptable, intolerable. She was, after all, just a woman.

Herod squeezed his eyes shut, and willed away his thoughts, but his wife's image kept sweeping back into his mind. She must have bewitched him. Why else would a king be unable to free his mind of a woman during battle?

~

*A*s time passed, the enemy soldiers still capable of fighting did so with a tenacity that astounded Herod. But the numbers of battle dead and gravely injured grew. Ultimately, Antigonus and the Parthians could not hold back Herod's Army.

Two long, bloody months after the first battle of the War on Jerusalem, a commander galloped into camp and came to a dusty halt. Soot caked his face, and blood streaked his armor. Clutching a scroll, he slid off his stallion and bowed low to Herod. "We've taken and secured every Parthian and Maccabee stronghold. Antigonus has sent you this a message."

God, please let it be a surrender. Herod unfurled the papyrus.

On Behalf of the Parthians and the People of Jerusalem, We Offer King Herod Our Unconditional Surrender.

"We're victorious!" Herod shouted. Ecstasy coursed through his entire body. Jerusalem was his.

The commander galloped back to the near-ruined city. Minutes later, soldiers on foot led horses into camp with fallen and wounded soldiers draped over their backs. The dead piled high. Herod ordered the injured wrapped in linen bandages. He wished he could do more. He knew most were going to die.

"I'll send Antigonus to Rome," said Sosius, grinning for the first time in weeks. "Antony will exile him."

Herod nodded. However, he could not afford to let Antigonus live. Even in exile, the Maccabee would pose a threat. He might try to garner support in Rome for a return to his rule. Hastily, Herod sent a messenger to Antony, along with a bag of gold and a request that he order Antigonus's execution He soon received intelligence that Antony had the Maccabee usurper strangled when he was passing through Syria on his way to Rome. It was the first time Rome had executed a conquered king to protect his successor. Antigonus's execution proved Rome's high regard for Herod. He would not disappoint them.

After Antigonus's defeat, the Parthians quickly retreated from Judea. Herod's conquest of his kingdom was complete. The usurper, Antigonus, was dead, and Herod was the king. Now, his glorious reign could begin.

21

MARIAMNE, 37 BCE, SAMARIA

*L*iving at Samaria Castle was like standing on a cliff in a strong wind. If I did not brace myself, I could easily lose my balance and plunge to the ragged rocks below. As difficult as it was to live in near-ruined quarters with hostile people, anxiety over what new hardship would befall us next was even harder to bear. Herod had taken us from Masada to Samaria, both remote places far from home.

From time to time, Herod sent Yusef cryptic messages. "*At war*," the last one said, and that was all. So, we knew a battle raged in Jerusalem. I could only imagine the chaos and carnage it must have brought to my beloved city.

My family was going to face trouble if Herod lived through his seizure of Jerusalem or if he died in battle. I was most apprehensive about my brother. Herod had to see Aris as the chief obstacle to his reign. No doubt, my husband was capable of making a thorn in his world disappear, and what was Aris if not a thorn? Everyone knew what happened to those who stood in Herod's way. Some tended to have life-ending "accidents," or they disappeared or he ordered them crucified. Others, like the rebels against Rome in Galilee, he had publicly strangled without trial. To protect Aris I had to outsmart my brilliant husband and his army of spies, advisors, and henchmen.

〜

*T*he ladies spent most afternoons mending robes and tunics in the reception hall. Night or day, we needed the light of an oil lamp to see our stitching. One chilly afternoon, Cypros and Princess Alexandra put down their sewing and left to supervise the cooks' dinner preparation. Salome and I found ourselves without other company. I strained for something civil say as I placed a finished robe on top of the pile on the table between us.

"Your stitching is lovely," I said. It was no lie. Every stitch was the same size, not messy or pulled too tight like my own.

Salome smiled. Perhaps this could be the beginning of a friendship. If only I knew what was to come. Placing a finished robe on the table, Salome knocked over the oil lamp. The pile of robes and tunics it fell on burst into flames.

"Fire!" I cried.

My mother and Cypros rushed in from the kitchen.

"Mariamne knocked over the lamp," Salome shouted, pointing to me.

My face grew hot with fury. "You're a liar, Salome. You were the one who knocked it over."

"Servants, hurry, put out the fire," called Salome.

Lila ran for salt. She poured it on the blaze and quickly extinguished it. All that remained of our long hours of sewing were smoking ashes.

Frustrated tears welled in my eyes. "How dare you accuse me of something that you did, Salome. You're horrible—"

"The fire is out," Cypros interrupted. "All is well. There is no need to argue."

With a smug expression, Salome linked arms with her mother, and she and Cypros left. Lila stayed close and gave me a comforting smile, but the other servants stared at me accusingly as they cleaned up the mess. They believed Salome's word over mine.

Salome's false accusation shook me to my marrow. She had lied to implicate me and extricate herself. How far was she willing to go to hurt me? Was her loathing entirely personal, or would she have despised any bride Herod had taken? I suspected the latter. Sly, possessive Salome would not warm to any bride of Herod's. It was as if she wanted him for herself. Yes, I realized, that was the trouble. Salome wanted who she could never have, and she hated me for being his wife.

~

*a*t night, I lay in the darkness on my uncomfortable straw pallet and listened to the sound of the women sleeping around me. Some snored, others mumbled, and a disturbing few ground their teeth. The clamor prevented me from falling asleep until late into the night. I longed for the privacy of my own bedchamber. How little we appreciate what we have until it vanishes.

One night, I struggled to fall asleep for an unusually long time. Thoughts and worries tumbled through my mind. Long months in close quarters had exhausted us all. My mother, a tightly pulled thread nearing its breaking point, lashed out at whomever was closest to her, and usually, it was me. Sharing the same air was enough to make Salome bristle at me. But Aris concerned me the most. He had been unusually quiet and distant. I had to speak with him, privately.

I pushed aside the makeshift curtain that separated the women from the men and crept over to the place where Aris slept. I kissed his warm cheek and woke him.

"What?" he whispered with half-closed eyes. "Follow me," I said, softly.

We slipped out of the castle. I led Aris to a high point on the Samarian Ridge near the old brown tower. On the edge of a boulder jutting out from the hilltop, we sat huddled together, in comfortable silence, against the cold and the darkness. The moon shed luminous, white light on Jezreel Valley. His face glowed opalescent.

"It seems something troubles you, lately, Aris. What is it?"

He hung his head. "You don't want to know."

"I do. You can tell me anything."

Aris sighed so deeply it sounded as though it came from his belly. "I don't want the Crown of Judea."

His words shocked me, but I knew he did not mean it. He was just young and feeling overwhelmed. "To be king is a great responsibility," I said, my voice quiet and firm. "Rule seems frightening to you now, but when you come of age, you will be ready for it."

Aris shook his head, slowly. "The truth is, I'd be satisfied—no, ecstatic—to serve only as Judea's High Priest. I don't want the throne."

"But who is better suited than you, our crown prince, to lead us?"

Aris shrugged thin shoulders. "What I want to do is study *Torah* and lead prayer and sacrifices. I want to be a priest."

I shivered. "You're too young to know what you will want when you're a grown man."

He shook his head, gravely. "I am sure about this. I won't change my mind."

"Aris, it's your destiny to take the throne. We cannot deny our destinies." A sense of peace came over me. I knew my reason for living was to see my brother king.

Aris's sad eyes looked incandescent in the moonlight. "I don't want to be King of Judea. Your ambition to make me king will destroy both of us. It will enrage your husband and ruin your marriage. It could even kill you… I want you to stop it."

I fixed my eyes on two deer loping across the valley. I envied their freedom.

"You are our queen," Aris added. "Should I ever take the throne, what will happen to you? This troubles me. Let Herod be king, but please, encourage him to appoint me high priest. It will be enough."

"Are you saying this because you fear Herod's wrath?"

"No, I am saying this because it's the truth."

Unwelcome royal ambitions stirred inside me. I pushed the rogue feelings down and shook my head. "Aris, you're the one meant to lead us. It's your birthright." The massive stone on which I sat was digging into my skin. I shifted my weight. "I'll never rest until you are king and the crown rests firmly on your head."

"As I said, I don't want—"

"I have a plan, Aris. First, I will have Herod appoint you high priest. Our nobles will never let Herod serve as high priest. He hasn't the priestly bloodlines."

"True."

"Our people have come to expect the high priest to also serve as king. Once they see you in this post, they'll demand Rome put you on the throne."

"You're not listening, Mariamne. I want to be the high priest, not king."

"Judeans will support you, Aris. Rome will crown you king to avoid civil war in Jerusalem."

Aris sadly shook his head. He would feel differently about his destiny when he was older, I was certain. Meanwhile, I would try to persuade Herod to appoint my brother high priest. If I had trouble, my mother might persuade Cleopatra to use her influence with Antony. If the triumvir ordered Herod to make the appointment, he would have no choice but to comply. As high priest, Aris would be well on his way to the throne.

I was going to return my family to our birthright, no matter what it took.

22

HEROD, 37 BCE, JERUSALEM

*A*fter Herod took Jerusalem, his first priority was the restoration of the war-ravaged Maccabee Palace. He could not bring his wife home until the palace was worthy of her. He worked two shifts of men around the clock to rebuild the charred and ruined reception hall and king's apartments. He brought in the most eminent Roman artisans to create mosaic floors in black and white geometric designs. Rome's most celebrated fresco artists painted lush landscapes on the palace walls. For months, Herod lived with the constant noise of construction and a parade of workers.

In the end, it was worth the trouble. Scores of builders, stone masons, and carpenters used the latest Roman innovations to make the palace more luxurious than the one Mariamne had left. There was still much rebuilding he must attend to in the city, but the Maccabee Palace was ready for royalty. Herod ordered a heavy guard to escort his family home.

∾

*A*utumn winds swept down from the mountains on the bright morning his family was returning to Jerusalem. They finally blew away the war's lingering odor of smoke and ruin.

From the palace entry, Herod watched the carriages from Samaria roll up to the Maccabee palace, now his own. He hurried out, ecstatic to see Mariamne again. He lifted her from the carriage, twirled her around, and set her down. She was shockingly reedy and pale, but still lovely.

"Have you been ill?" he asked.

She shut her eyes and shook her head.

Once inside, Mariamne barely looked at the restoration he had so painstakingly undertaken on her behalf. She hardly glanced at the vibrant frescoes on the walls, or the intricate patterns on the mosaic floors, a new Roman style used for the first time in Jerusalem.

It was not until much later, after everyone else had retired for the evening, when he and Mariamne were lounging on chaises, sharing herbed wine and grapes, that her troubled eyes met his own. "On our way here, everywhere I looked I saw charred buildings and crumbled stone. It distresses me so to see Jerusalem in ruins."

Her words stung. "For months I've done nothing but oversee the restoration of this palace. There's more we must do, yes, I know that, but I've made your home the jewel in Jerusalem's crown. I've given gold to those who needed it to rebuild their homes and shops, but it will take time."

Mariamne's wan smile, noticeably strained, was hardly a show of appreciation.

"Now that I have rebuilt the palace I will make Jerusalem the grandest city you've ever seen," Herod added. "Rome has given me Samaria to reward me for ridding the land of Parthians. You are the queen of a land much larger now than it was during your grandfather's reign."

*G*iven her earlier ambivalence, Herod was not confident his wife would welcome his advances that night. Despite his great need for her, he forced himself to proceed slowly, to gently undress her, and to linger with kisses before he allowed himself to go further. She did not respond with enthusiasm, to be sure, but he attributed it to their long separation. Still, their reunion brought him intense pleasure, and he had her several times before exhaustion took him.

Never had a woman incited such consuming lust in him. In the weeks that followed, he had her in the morning and again at night, and in the afternoon when his schedule permitted.

~

*E*very day except for the Sabbath, Mariamne went with Lila into the lower city, where the peasants dwelt, to help them rebuild. They cared for the children of the city's poorest, freeing the women to help men lay new mud-brick or stone to fix their war-ravaged hovels. They also spent hours delivering bread baked in communal ovens to families in need.

Mariamne insisted on wearing plain homespun when she worked. After a long day, she returned to the palace as fatigued and filthy as any lower city dweller doing laborers' work, chatting and laughing with that handmaid of hers. Mariamne was too comfortable with that Lila. They were entirely too close for master and servant, not a good idea if a master was to retain control. But Mariamne did not seem to want to control her handmaiden. Herod did not approve. Yet he admired his wife immensely. She did not boast about her good works or seek attention or recognition for it. Her grit and her compassion fascinated him. It showed him the purity of her soul.

The resilience she had learned, in her determination to survive drought and starvation on Masada, had strengthened her character. Herod also prized her delicate beauty, her intoxicating balsam scent, and the mystery of her smile. But now, he knew Mariamne was

much more than an exquisite face and a luscious body. Inside, his
wife was a kind and loving soul, a rare princess, indeed.

Herod had not expected to fall in love with her, but he did.

~

*O*ne night, as they lay in bed together, Mariamne sat up. It
was highly unusual that she would meet his gaze.

"I must talk to you, Herod."

He yawned loudly. They had already made love, and he wanted
only to sleep.

"It is important to me that you listen."

"Yes?"

"I would like for you to appoint Aris high priest. He is of age
now, and fully qualified."

"I have already appointed Hananel as our high priest."

Hananel was a descendant of the family that provided Judea's
high priests before the Maccabee Dynasty.

"Place the man in another prominent position. Please, Herod.
This is important to me."

Why must she meddle in matters outside the womanly realm?
"Hananel has a lifetime appointment."

"So did Hyrcanus. Sometimes, things change. You will consider
it, Herod?"

"Of course," he said, to quiet her.

~

*D*id Mariamne love him? He suspected she did not. She
had never shown him affection or even a hint of fond-
ness. She performed her duties as a wife, yes, but with a certain reticence. He had thought it was due to her modesty and shyness, but
after years of marriage, he doubted this explained her lack of
enthusiasm. For the first time in Herod's life, his own physical satisfaction was not enough. He wanted, no, he needed Mariamne to

love him as he loved her, deeply and wholly. He was a resourceful man who got what he wanted. He must find a way to her heart.

23

MARIAMNE, 36 BCE, JERUSALEM

*I*n the oppressive, mid-summer heat, I was painting a courtyard fresco of a garden in which nothing terrible ever happened, where one's own kin would never steal a throne, where family brought joy and comfort rather than treachery and deceit. Tranquility set over me as my paintbrush flew across plaster walls on which I painted verdant cypress and palm trees. Lila brought in an earthen vial of powder. She mixed it with water to create peacock-blue paint.

"You found me lapis lazuli—a rare pigment."

"I didn't buy it in our market. I found it in Shanan, a village north of Jerusalem."

"Doesn't Samuel live in a village north of Jerusalem?"

Lila looked unspeakably sad. "Yes, before he left Masada, he told me his home was in Shanan. I stopped there to search for him. He wasn't there. He has moved to a farm in the far north with his family. No one could tell me where. He didn't wait for me, Mariamne, as he had promised."

"Oh Lila, I'm sure you're disappointed. I'm sorry..."

I was annoyed to find my mother approaching. I wanted to finish my conversation with Lila, and then paint a cloudless sky before the plaster dried and the paint would no longer stick. I kept my paintbrush moving. "What is it?"

"Leave us, Lila," my mother said. "Mariamne, stop your foolish painting. You must see this letter I'm sending to Cleopatra. The idea for it came to me last night in a dream."

With a frisson of dread, I put down my paintbrush. "What are you scheming now, Mother?"

"Scheme? I don't scheme. I look after my family. Cleopatra cares about our welfare. She understands that the throne belongs to us. She will help us."

With a deep sigh, I took the scroll.

Dearest Cleopatra, Queen and Pharaoh of Egypt,

My son, Aris, is now seventeen years of age, and he is fully qualified to assume his rightful place as Judea's High Priest. Though I have made King Herod aware that our high priests have long descended from the Maccabee royal line, he has refused to appoint my son. I would be most grateful if you would kindly persuade Triumvir Antony to force Herod's hand in this matter. Should Antony order Herod to appoint my son high priest, the king will have no choice but to do as the triumvir commands.

Please know, dear Cleopatra, how much I treasure our friendship.

Princess Alexandra Maccabee

I looked around to see if anyone had heard us, and was relieved to find no one else around. "Don't send this, Mother. It will never reach Cleopatra. Herod's spies will intercept it and give it to him."

"Worry not. I'll send it with a trusted servant. He will take it by ship, and put it directly into Pharaoh's hands. We must all take risks in this life if we are to gain anything. Don't you want to see your brother become the high priest?"

"Of course, I do, but a subtler approach might be more effective with Herod, I think."

My mother bristled. "This is too important a matter to leave to Herod's whims," she said before she swept out.

Trouble was nigh. I felt it in my core.

~

That night, I went to purify myself in the *mikvah*. I was in the hall, on my way back to my chambers, when I overheard Herod and Salome speaking to each other in the library.

"...So I killed them," Herod said.

I drew in a sharp breath. I had to hear this. I dared not peek inside the library for fear they would see me. Heart thrashing, I pressed myself flat against the wall beside the open door, and I listened.

"You had no choice, Herod," said Salome. "You couldn't let those forty-five *Sanhedrin* judges live. They signed their own death warrants when they refused to swear oaths of loyalty to you. They chose to die."

A sharp pain made me draw my hand to my aching stomach. How could he have done such an evil thing? Did I know this man at all?

"No king would have done otherwise," Salome added.

She would have agreed with Herod had he told her the sky was green and sheep were pink. I could easily picture her adoring gaze.

"As usual, your political instincts are correct, Salome. But my wife won't see it that way. She'll be—"

"Don't worry about what your wife will think. She's a witless, pampered pet."

I was not shocked to hear Salome insult me. Still, it made me burn.

"You're wrong," said Herod. "My queen is a good woman, and quite intelligent."

"The little princess may have done well in her lessons, but that means nothing. She has no idea what it takes for a king to hold a throne. Don't trust her, Herod. She's bitter about her family's decline. She wants to put her brother on the throne."

Herod did not respond. He must agree, then.

"I'm the only one you can trust, Herod. I'm the only one who will always look after your best interests. There's nothing I wouldn't do to keep you on the throne, nothing."

"I know that," said Herod. "I prize your devotion."

My husband and his sister disgusted me.

"I've sacrificed everything for you, Herod. You are my whole world."

The long silence after Salome spoke made me intensely uncomfortable. Were they embracing, or worse?

"News of the judges will spread quickly," Herod said. "It always does, even when every witness is sworn to secrecy. People will squawk."

"They will."

"The executed judges were aristocrats. They owned substantial estates. My subjects will say I executed them for treason because I wanted to confiscate their property."

"It doesn't matter what they say. You're the man who rules the land. The judges' estates are yours now."

"Their gold will go a long way toward funding my building plans."

I could easily imagine my sister-in-law's triumphant smile.

Herod was silent. What if he suspected I was eavesdropping? I should leave, I knew that, but I wanted to hear more.

"You have turned the judges' treason into a boon for our nation," Salome said.

Again, they subjected me to a long, disturbing quiet. "Shall I play my harp for you now, Herod?"

"Yes, it soothes me so," he said.

Still leaning against the wall, I listened to Salome play the music of angels. Again, I wondered how this malevolent woman could create music so sublime. I had to escape before they discovered me. I dared not pass the open door, so I crept in the opposite direction to the back stair.

24

HEROD, 36 BCE, JERUSALEM

When Herod slipped into bed later that night, Mariamne was already sleeping. Her long hair cascaded across the pillow and the linens. He adored her. He grew rigid at the sight and scent of her, and reached out for her breast but stopped short when she opened her eyes, and he saw how they glittered with fury. What fresh hell was she going to bring him? She wrenched herself away from him. He did not need this trouble.

"What's the matter?" he asked.

"I know what you did, Herod."

Candlelight flickered on either side of their bed, illuminating the soft curve of Mariamne's cheeks, her lush lips. He did not want to discuss politics with her. Other activities would be far more pleasurable.

She sat up. "You executed *Sanhedrin* judges. How could you?"

"Judges must be loyal to me," he said, bristling. "The men I executed were all Antigonus loyalists. They refused to take an oath of loyalty to me. Twenty-six of the seventy-one judges still live."

"What a generous man you are to allow all twenty-six their lives."

His wife dared sarcasm at his expense? "You must understand,

Mariamne. I had to remove those perfidious fools. They had lifetime appointments. A king must fill the court with judges whose loyalty he can depend on."

She shook her head, sadly. "I've known most of those old, learned judges since I was a child. Tell me, how did you kill them?"

Her obvious disgust distressed him. He reached out for her again. She tensed and pushed his hand away. They could be experiencing rapture at this very moment instead of having this most uncomfortable conversation. Women were impossible to understand. Still, he did not like displeasing Mariamne. But as King, he had done what was necessary.

"They were strangled," he said. "Now let's not argue anymore."

She twisted away. "I know why you killed them. You wanted to confiscate their estates to fill your treasury."

"I executed the judges because I couldn't trust them, but of course, I need their gold. How do you think kings become wealthy?"

She flung herself out of bed and slammed the door behind her. Herod jumped up to pursue her. He would make her understand. He called out her name in the hallway, but she had disappeared somewhere in the vast labyrinth of the palace. Too tired to search every chamber for her at this late hour, Herod returned to bed and instantly fell asleep.

The next morning, Herod found his wife sleeping in nearby guest quarters, her wool blanket pulled to her chin. He dared not disturb her for fear she might continue the tongue-lashing of the night before. Gazing at her tranquil face, recalling her words, he questioned himself. Should he have just exiled the traitorous judges? Had he gone too far? No, he concluded, he had not. He had done what was expedient. He respected Mariamne's intelligence, but how could she understand the threats a king faced and the decisions he must make?

∾

*O*n his way to the banqueting hall to break his fast, Herod stopped off at the library. Like every morning, he shut and locked the door, so he could read the scrolls his spies had intercepted. Herod had long offered gold to servants and messengers who brought him writings—whether on animal skin, tablet, or papyrus—entering or leaving the palace. After he read them, he would send most on their way. If it served his purposes, he burned them.

On the top shelf of the bureau at the far end of the library, Herod pushed aside the works of Aristotle and Plato and felt around for the key. He unlocked the top drawer of the marble chest. Ah, good, a papyrus scroll laid there. He unfurled it. The writing closed with Cleopatra's ornate signature.

> *My dearest friend, Princess Alexandra,*
> *I offer you my full support should you wish to launch an armed rebellion against Herod. The man is a power-mad upstart who badly needs reigning in.*

Herod's head throbbed. The Nile viper wanted to overthrow him in favor of the Maccabees. Equally infuriating, she had called him a 'power-mad upstart.' It was ironic, indeed. Pharaoh was as power-mad as any leader who had ever walked this earth. However, unlike members of his own family, Cleopatra had not had to muscle her way to supremacy, descending as she did from a long line of Ptolemy Kings who had handed her power on a platter of pure gold.

He continued reading.

> *Do not concern yourself with Antony. Should you accept my offer of assistance, I promise to bring the triumvir around. He, too, will support your rebellion.*
> *Cleopatra, Pharaoh and Queen of Egypt*

Herod seethed. How satisfying it would be to put his hands

around the Cleopatra's long, graceful neck, and strangle her. His first instinct was to throw the scroll into the licking flames of the hearth. However, he had never before found a message from a foreign sovereign offering to support an armed uprising against him. Should Antony's relationship with Cleopatra ever go sour, and he hoped it someday would, he would offer the triumvir this letter. Then, Antony would know how confident she was in her ability to influence the most powerful man in the world.

It struck him that Princess Alexandra had not asked for Pharaoh to support an armed insurgency against him. Cleopatra herself initiated this disturbing offer to help oust him. It was not a homegrown Maccabee plot. He locked the scroll away.

A month ago, a spy had intercepted a message Princess Alexandra had sent to Cleopatra. In that scroll, his mother-in-law asked her to persuade Antony to order Herod to appoint Aris High Priest of Judea. It never reached Cleopatra; Herod had burned it.

~

*I*n the banqueting hall, Herod found Princess Alexandra lounging on her couch, alone at the long table. She smiled and greeted him pleasantly. Her smile was, indeed, a rare occurrence, though she ought to do so more often. It changed her appearance, entirely. Despite the lines and crevices charting her face, he caught a glimpse of the beauty she had once been. Had she not already seen him, he might have slipped into the kitchen. The cook's company would have been preferable to facing the insults and demands of his mother-in-law. His discovery of Cleopatra's recent correspondence made it even more difficult for him to conduct himself with civility toward this ancient javelin of a woman.

"Herod, how nice to see you," said Princess Alexandra in a voice sweet as the honey cake she was eating.

The woman's usual lack of deference made it plain she loathed him. There must be a reason for this newfound warmth. She wanted something.

"Come join me at my lonely table," she said.

Her table? Who had paid for the carved-marble chaise with silken pillows on which she lounged? Who had spent his gold on the long granite table, and the exorbitantly expensive Greek silver angel statues? His mother-in-law was a parasite who consumed his delicacies, wore expensive silks he had bought, and slept on fine linens in his palace, all the while despising him and scheming to oust him. What a curse the woman was.

Herod sank into the plump pillows of his chaise at the head of the table. Servants hurried over to serve him beer and honey cake. He dined in silence, averting his eyes from Princess Alexandra's unctuous gaze. If he ignored her, perhaps she would let him break his fast in peace, or better yet, leave.

"I'd like to discuss something important with you," she said. Herod's shoulders tensed.

"As you know, Herod, Maccabee Kings have long served as our high priests, but you cannot."

How well he knew. On his first morning on the throne of the restored palace, the most revered Jerusalem priests had paid him a visit. They told him, in no uncertain terms, that he lacked the necessary bloodlines to serve as high priest. His first inclination had been to order their execution, but he had restrained himself, and leaned back on his throne to consider his response.

Despite the religious leaders' assumptions about the strength of Herod's faith, he did believe in God, at least in a vague sort of way. Still, he knew that neither his level of religious dedication nor his lineage was strong enough to qualify him for the post. Should he take this lofty position, he would garner the antipathy of the powerful priests and aristocrats who thought him unqualified, and risk their rebellion.

His was a new dynasty. He did not have to bind himself to time-worn Maccabee customs; he had separated the offices of king and high priest, and granted the highest religious post to Hananel, a descendant of the line of high priests who had occupied the posts before the Maccabees had come to power. A kings' decision could not satisfy everyone.

"Do you know why my father, King Hyrcanus, can no longer

serve as our high priest if the Parthian king releases him from prison?"

Did the woman think he was ignorant of Jewish tradition? "Of course," replied Herod with considerable irritation.

"Because my cousin Antigonus bit off his ear. Do you know why he attacked my father like a beast of the desert?"

"Because a streak of madness runs through your family," Herod said with a sidewise grin.

"No. Antigonus did it so my father could never again be our high priest. A man in this position must have no physical flaws."

Herod knew he was going to soon face indigestion because of this most unpleasant woman.

"I know of a physically perfect man," added Princess Alexandra, as if this epiphany had just occurred to her. "Aris is seventeen now. He would make a splendid high priest. The people adore him. They call out their praises to him wherever he goes."

So, the old cur was licking his sandals because she wanted to thrust her precious son into power. Never would he willingly place Aris, the golden prince and last male scion of the ruling Maccabee line, in the lofty position. There was no denying Aris was learned and devoted to God. Nor was there any question that the Judeans loved him. They clung to him with the same persistent adoration with which Romans attached themselves to their favorite gladiators. The people respected his intelligence and learning, and believed his unearthly beauty showed God's favor.

"The Judeans will love you for appointing him."

Princess Alexandra was utterly transparent. She was conniving to oust him and retake Judea for her own line. If he appointed Aris high priest, a bid for kingship was sure to follow. Judeans had long been accustomed to seeing the same man serve as both high priest and king. Did she think he was stupid enough to make an appointment that would inexorably lead to his demise? From the hopeful gleam in her eyes, he saw that she did. He was not going to let it happen.

"As much as I'd like to appoint Aris high priest, I cannot. I've already put Hananel in the position. We can revisit the matter after he dies."

Princess Alexandra's face fell. Her eyes ceased to shine. "Dies? The Babylonian is nothing if not young and healthy. He won't be going anywhere soon unless…."

"Unless what?" interrupted Herod. "Are you suggesting I execute him to further your ambitions for your son?"

She suddenly brightened. "That is unnecessary. You can change the law, Herod. You're King. Who will stop you? Set Hananel aside and make my son the high priest."

The woman's boldness astounded him. What choice did he have but to put her in her place?

"As I've told you and your daughter many times, my answer is no."

Princess Alexandra dropped the piece of honey cake she was eating and thundered out. He vowed to rid himself of her when the time was right.

~

*M*uch to Herod's chagrin, his wife's chilly treatment persisted. She slept with her back to him and nudged him away when he made advances. He could easily overpower her and take what belonged to him, but he would not do that to her. Mariamne declined his invitation to join him on the terrace for evening wine. At dinner, she made lively conversation with everyone at the table but him. When he directed a question to her, she gave him a terse reply. She refused to meet his gaze. It was as if he was invisible to her.

After a few weeks of such treatment, Herod was so in need of a woman's body he considered threatening Mariamne that he would invite concubines and prostitutes into the palace if she continued to deny him. He longed for her, and wanted her love, but what could he do about the executed judges? He could not bring them back to life or return their estates to their families. He had already spent their gold on weapons to strengthen his arsenal.

One evening, Herod found Mariamne at the vanity table in their bedchamber. Lila was brushing her hair, glossy as oiled furniture, in the soft lamplight. He longed to reach out and stroke it, but stopped himself; he did not want to face her likely rebuff. He sent the hand-maiden away.

"Join me on the terrace, Mariamne," he said.

With a tight jaw, his wife followed him out, her silk robe billowing behind her. Previously, she had refused his requests, but she could not ignore a command from her husband the king.

Servants had set out a vessel of her favorite Falernian wine and a tray of the sweet figs he knew she loved. Herod grew hopeful when he saw her eyes brighten at the sight of them. He waved away the servants and filled her chalice with wine.

"Please, sit down," he said.

The sinking sun set the horizon aflame, and the scattered clouds were a delicate mauve. He could not recall a more magnificent sunset. He looked out to the Tyropoeon Valley and the cliffs beyond, bathed in golden light. Mariamne sat stiffly beside him with a blank expression, with lips pressed together and hands folded in her lap. Why had God made women so difficult?

"I know you're angry about the judges," he said.

"Am I furious you summarily executed forty-seven learned men? Yes, of course, I am."

"I'm sorry you're angry." He wanted to take her in his arms and make love to her.

She blinked hard. "But are you sorry you executed the judges?"

Herod thought about how much his mother and sister would miss him if he had died but quickly dismissed his misgivings. For the sake of marital harmony, he would tell his wife a harmless lie.

"I'm sorry," he said.

She gave him a hint of a smile. "Do you have genuine remorse for killing those judges, Herod?"

"I do," he said, tersely. Not true, but if those words might restore harmony in the bedchamber and banqueting hall, so be it.

"Are you truly sorry?"

She was beginning to irritate him. "I've said I am."

She slid away from him. "I don't believe you."

"What can I do to make you believe me?" asked Herod.

"Do something kind for the judges' widows and sons."

Herod had immediately seized their gold and used it to refresh his armory. Next week, he planned to take their land and livestock. Pleasing his wife was going to cost him, dearly.

She looked away from him, through the evening mist to the bare, tawny hills in the distance. "At the very least, let their families keep their land and possessions."

Herod grimaced at Mariamne's overly generous and unprecedented request. Her widened eyes, luminous with hope, gazed into his own for the first time in a long while. How could he say no?

"If I agree, will I have your forgiveness?"

She nodded.

"Then I will do as you ask," he said. He swept her into his arms. She felt small and soft against the broad expanse of him. His soul soared.

"Herod, I think your love for me is making you a better man."

He forced a smile. Had his wife not considered him to be a good man before?

"I'm forgiven, then?"

"One day you must answer to God," she said, "but yes, I forgive you."

He took her hand and led her to their bedchamber.

25

MARIAMNE, 35 BCE, JERUSALEM

The searing summer heat was now only an unpleasant memory. The gentle autumn winds were most welcome in my condition. I was with child. It was as if the burgeoning creature inside me had leased my body, and I no longer controlled it. Someone else forced me to eat an inordinate number of nuts and dates. The same small irritant in my abdomen demanded I sleep every afternoon and made me dash to the privy too often.

Herod showed me a facet to his character he let few others see. At night, he rubbed my swollen feet with rose oil. He strolled with me through the gardens, thought such ramblings bored him. I could never forgive him for stealing my family's throne. I did, however, appreciate his acts of kindness.

"You're carrying a son," an Essenian seer told me one day when I was in the market with Lila.

Deep in my soul, I already knew this.

*T*hat night, I had a dream.

I was a dove. From my perch on the ramparts of the palace's highest tower, I soared into the air and felt my heady freedom. Joy coursed through me as I flew, bright white against the cerulean sky.

Suddenly, I lunged toward the rugged rocks in the canyon far below. I wanted to fly high and glide across the heavens, but I could not rise. Just once, please, God. A sense of profound loss swept over me.

Stabbing pains broke through the echoing chambers of my dream. I woke up. Was it the baby's time to come?

"Lila!" I called. "Go get the midwife."

Before long, Elzea stood over my bed with a reassuring smile. No one had brought more babies into the world than she had. I knew I was in skilled hands, but still, I quaked with dread. Women often died in childbed. Another sharp pain made me cry out.

"Leave us, King Herod," said Elzea, pointing to the door. "Only Lila can stay."

The king nodded like a well-behaved child. Elzea was the only person in the world who could issue Herod orders with impunity. He kissed my cheek and left just before I suffered the next excruciating spasm.

Would my baby—my precious baby—and I live through his perilous journey into the world? I reached out for Lila. "I'm afraid," I whispered.

"Of course, you are," Lila said, squeezing my hand. "Every woman in childbirth is afraid."

The midwife put a cool cloth on my forehead. "We all enter this world the same way," she said. "God willing, you will have a great blessing to show for your pain."

I prayed it would be so.

~

"*Y*ou have a son!" cried Elzea.

After hours of excruciating labor, Prince Alexander was born. His robust cries filled my heart with delight.

The midwife cleaned and swaddled my baby in linen, and gently placed him in my arms. A fierce love for this child bloomed like a rose. My heart nearly ruptured with joy.

Tears pooled in Lila's dark eyes. "I will love this child as I love you."

Though exhausted, I mustered enough strength to squeeze her hand.

Herod came in and sent everyone else away. He kissed my forehead and knelt beside the baby basket. He stroked the baby's face. His hand looked immense against our child's tiny, ruddy cheek. Gingerly, he took his new son in his arms and held him.

My husband's love for me was softening the edges of his roughness. The tenderness he had shown me during my pregnancy, and his gentle, wondrous gaze on our new son, confirmed my conviction that loving me was making him a better man.

Alexander began to cry and root for a breast. Herod returned him to me with a relieved glance. Hungrily, the baby took my nipple and fed, while my husband gazed at us in wonder.

"Our mothers and Salome would like to meet our son," said Herod.

I shook my head. "The child and I are tired," I said. The moment was too precious to ruin with his sister's hostile presence.

I looked into my son's eyes, wide-open and fixed on mine. I vowed to him I would be a good mother, unlike my own, who had not concerned herself with her young children. When she deigned to speak to us, she took a sharp, dismissive tone. I asked God to help me be a steady, loving mother of kings. Was it not every royal mother's dream to see her son wearing the crown of his nation? The baby opened his tiny mouth and yawned. It was difficult to envisage him with a crown on his hairless infant head. The thought made me laugh.

Then, guilt seized me. How could I even imagine such a thing? My very purpose in life was to see my brother to the throne.

Did I want to see Aris crowned king with the same fierce longing I did before my son was born? I was not certain that I did, and it troubled me.

26

HEROD, 35 BCE, JERUSALEM

*H*erod wanted Mariamne beside him. Even when he heard his subjects' petitions in his presence chamber, the vast hall where he met with foreign dignitaries and humble petitioners alike, he had his wife sit next to him on her throne. Having her near brought him a sense of calm. As important, he could keep an eye on her. Late one afternoon, the last petitioner of the day was droning on about how he wanted compensation from a sheep stealing neighbor when a guard burst in, dragging Princess Alexandra by the arm.

Mariamne's mouth fell open. "Mother?"

"Let me go, you lowly fool!" Princess Alexandra cried, struggling to escape the guard's grasp.

Herod nodded to the guard, who loosened his grip.

"Most esteemed King, I've caught servants carrying a coffin out of the palace. I ordered it opened, and Princess Alexandra lay inside, quite alive. She had this scroll in her hand."

Herod read the parchment, and his face reddened. "So, Cleopatra has arranged for a ship to meet you at the Port of Jaffa to sail you to Alexandria." He turned to his wife.

"Were you aware of this? Did you conspire with your mother to plan this act of treason?"

Mariamne paled and shook her head. "I knew nothing of this, Herod." Tears flowed down her face. "Why did you do this, Mother?" she asked.

Herod wondered if Mariamne's incredulity masked her involvement in this treason. Was she genuinely distressed, or was it a show for his benefit? He stroked his dark beard.

His mother-in-law held her head high and smoothed her robes. "I simply wanted to visit Cleopatra. I knew you would never let me go."

"I would have consented had you asked," said Herod. The truth was he would never allow his mother-in-law to journey outside of Judea. The mere thought of Cleopatra and Princess Alexandra with their heads together, conspiring against him, gave him indigestion.

A courtier came forward from the shadows. He handed Herod a painting of Aris on a small slab of wood. The portrait well-captured the prince's loose, shining curls, his straight nose, and his strong chin. In the background, winged angels hovered above him. Herod was astounded; Jewish law prohibited the display of human likenesses, because images could be worshipped, or could represent idols.

"We found this painting inside the coffin," the guard said.

"Why did were you taking this painting of your son with you?" Herod asked.

His mother-in-law averted her eyes. "Pharaoh asked me to bring a painting of Aris. Cleopatra has always been—interested—in my family."

"Tell me the true reason," thundered Herod. He relished toying with her as a mountain lion with his prey.

Princess Alexandra looked down and said nothing.

"If you won't tell me, then I will tell you," Herod said. "You wanted Antony and Cleopatra to see your son's rare beauty. You thought that once they saw his face, they would summon him to Alexandria and crown him King of Judea." Antony appreciated both beautiful women and men, and Princess Alexandra knew that.

His mother-in-law regarded him with an innocent expression. "I don't understand what you mean. I would never undermine my own daughter's husband."

Of course, she understood. Her wounded countenance did not fool Herod, but still, he was puzzled. How had she made these deceitful arrangements when his spies purportedly brought him every message coming into and leaving the palace? She must have bribed some trusted servant to put her writings into Cleopatra's own bejeweled hands. Perhaps she had planted other confiscated correspondence to mislead him.

"You climbed into a coffin and bribed your servants to sneak you out so you could sail to Alexandria. Did you think you could successfully execute such a plan?"

His mother-in-law covered her face with her hands and wept. Did she think her show of false distress would move him? Her deviousness was exceeded only by her lack of common sense.

"Please don't hurt her," Mariamne whispered.

He gave his wife a scathing glance and turned his attention to her mother. "From now on, guards will watch every move you make, day and night. You will never set foot outside this palace again without my permission."

Princess Alexandra began to wail. Now, her tears were real. She fell to her knees. "Keep me here under lock and key, I don't care. But please, let Aris go to Antony and Cleopatra."

He would never let the young Adonis charm Antony and Cleopatra as he had everyone else. "It's not possible. I need Aris here."

"Need him? You don't even allow him to attend council meetings."

He could not bear to look at this woman a moment longer. "Guards, get her out of my sight. Take her to her quarters."

His men pulled Princess Alexandra away, screaming.

"Leave me now," he told the guards and couriers.

In silence, everyone except Mariamne filed out of his presence chamber. He looked into his wife's eyes. That was when he knew. She had not only known about her mother's treason, but she had also helped orchestrate it. They all wanted to oust him; even his beloved wanted him dead. He shook his head and strode out.

The gardens behind the palace were in full, scented bloom, but he barely noticed the shimmering water cascading down from the golden fountains, or the purple bellflowers, vivid against the brown hills beyond the gardens. It was clear to him now. So long as even one Maccabee lived, he could never rest easily on his throne. Princess Alexandra would be first on his list, but killing her was not an option, for now at least. Her friendship with Cleopatra protected her. Without a doubt, the Egyptian crocodile would make him pay with his life if he executed her friend. Enemies did not help a king hold a throne. Still, he could imagine how sweet it would be to see his mother-in-law's face turn purple as a head of cabbage when his hands tightened around her neck.

27

MARIAMNE, 35 BCE, JERUSALEM

*A*fter Herod questioned my loyalty, anxiety gripped me with the sharp talons of an eagle. My husband had made his mistrust known not only to me, but also to every courtier and guard who had witnessed him question whether I had schemed with my mother to plan her escape from the palace. Herod's men had convicted me of treason without a trial. I felt their steely eyes on me, watching, accusing.

To add to my unease, Herod was becoming quicker to point the finger of suspicion at anyone and everyone. With each passing day, he grew increasingly paranoid. He forced his guards to proclaim oaths of loyalty, even though they had already done so the day before, and the one before that. Nearly every month, he accused his spymaster of disloyalty, and sent him into exile, replacing him with yet another short-lived spymaster. He stationed guards in the cookhouse to prevent anyone from slipping poison into his food or drink. Even so, he refused to eat or drink until no fewer than three royal tasters survived bites or sips.

Herod's suspicion extended to me. I often caught him staring at me, his face pinched, his eyes questioning. When I asked him what was wrong, he fell silent and sullen.

Months after my mother's escape attempt, I was drifting off to sleep one night when Herod shook me awake.

"Tell me the truth, Mariamne. Did you know your mother was trying to escape Antonia Fortress? Did you plan it with her?"

"I knew nothing of her plans. I have told you this, Herod."

"But how can I believe you, Mariamne, how can I?"

Soon, Herod was snoring, but I lay wide-awake. His questioning of my loyalty was, I had to concede, justified. I was scheming to put my brother on the throne. Aris, however, was a reluctant future king. I hoped I could, one day, persuade him to accept his birthright and to fight for it. For now, I would be satisfied to see him as high priest, and I would keep trying to convince Herod to make the appointment as the first stage in my plan to make him king.

An uninvited image of my son, Prince Alexander, in an ermine lined coat, the gold Crown of Judea atop his shining curls, eclipsed my thoughts. I pushed the image away. Still, a strange coldness penetrated me to the bone.

~

*A*ris was my anchor to the world, my dear pet, and my weighty dynastic responsibility. He was the only person to whom I could speak in total candor. No one listened to me the way he did, with his head cocked and his eyes fixed intently on mine, full of merriment or empathy, depending on the direction of our conversation. We met most frequently in the afternoon, meandering in the courtyard gardens before we took our honey cake and beer.

On a late spring stroll with Aris, the perfume of the waning bell-flowers was a poignant reminder that the summer sun would soon shrivel any living thing in its blazing path. Usually, we conversed about any number of things, but today, Aris was unusually quiet.

"What troubles you?" I asked.

Abruptly, he stopped walking. "You said when I came of age I'd want to be king. I'm of age now. I still have no desire to rule. The priesthood is where I should be, Mariamne. You and Mother must believe me, and stop scheming to make me king. After Herod dies, your son will wear the crown. A half-Maccabee king is good enough for me. I want it to be good enough for you, too."

I gave him a long look. "Our mother will never accept this."

"Since when has Mother been happy about anything?"

He was right. Torn between my mother's expectations, my own traditional bent, and my brother's heart, I wanted to weep. Seeing Aris to the throne was my chief purpose in life. If I stopped striving for that, who was I?

"You have a son, Mariamne. One day, when he is king, I will be a proud uncle."

"I want to see you content, Aris, truly I do. But we cannot forget the long line of kings our family has provided Judea. The crown is your birthright. You cannot turn away from it."

~

When the sun began to cast long shadows on palace walls, we lounged in courtyard at a table between the flowerbeds, their red blossoms in full bloom. Our mother joined us.

"Another honey cake?" I asked.

Aris shook his head, but Mother sniffed and turned away from me. She had been cool to me ever since she had tried to sneak out of the palace to sail to Alexandria, and Herod had placed her under guard.

"Your daughter has asked you a question," Aris said.

"I have no daughter," said Princess Alexandra. "A true daughter would never let her husband put her mother under constant watch."

A mist had crept in, shrouding the courtyard in near darkness. I had just taken a bite of my second honey cake when I noticed the old man, hunched and emaciated, in the arched doorway. A linen bandage was wrapped around his head, covering his right ear. He began limping toward us. His sweet smile and crinkly eyes looked familiar…

"Grandfather Hyrcanus!" I cried, and I ran into his arms the same way I did many times when I was a child. I rested my head on his narrow ridge of shoulder. Happiness flooded my soul. My entire family was back together again.

"Welcome home, Grandfather," said Aris, his eyes burning bright.

Even my mother was smiling. "You're too thin, Father. Didn't they feed you in prison?"

My grandfather gave her a wan smile and nodded. He looked a decade older than he did when last I saw him. His eyes had lost their light. It hurt to see the sad shadow of the man he had once been.

"It seems he's forgotten how to speak as well," Mother said.

"It doesn't matter," I said. "Grandfather is home now." I piled his plate high with honey cakes. I longed to hear him tell us everything that had happened to him since we had last been together, but he did not say a word.

"Mother," Aris blurted after a long quiet. "I've asked Mariamne to stop scheming to make me king. I'm asking you to do the same. I don't want the throne."

My mother cried out. She shut her eyes and shook her head. "You cannot forget your destiny, Aris."

"My dream is to serve as Judean High Priest for all of my years."

"I agree you should begin your ascent to the throne as our high priest, but you must eventually rise to the throne. It belongs to you. Blood determines destiny."

"Herod will appoint me, someday," said Aris, shifting on his chaise. "I'm studying hard. I will show him I'm worthy of the post."

"My darling boy, you're too naive for your own good." My mother's eyes were flinty arrowheads. "Herod has stolen what is ours, and he fears us because of it. You're the last scion of the royal line. Herod will always despise you. He will always want to do away with you." She leaned in close to me. Her breath fell hot on my face. "But he loves you, Mariamne. Only you can persuade him to make the appointment. You must do more than ask him, Dear. You must convince him, the way only wives and concubines can."

I felt myself blush. I looked to my grandfather to come to my defense, to tell my mother to leave me alone, but he just stared at us with benign pleasantness. He would never defend me again.

"Use your womanly wiles. Remember Michal, your father's favorite concubine? She still lives in a house my husband had bought for her. I will send a servant to bring her to your chambers to advise you."

A dark look crossed Aris's face. "It's not right for you to interfere in Mariamne's marriage even for—"

"I'm only trying to help you take what is rightfully yours," she interrupted, and nodded to her servant, who brushed the cake crumbs from her lips with a silk cloth.

28

HEROD, 35 BCE, JERUSALEM

*H*erod found some aspects of ruling Jerusalem riveting, but hearing petty petitions about border disputes between farmers, and deciding the compensation due to herdsmen for stolen goats, was mind-numbing, and quite frankly, beneath him. If such matters did not interest the high court, why must he, the supreme leader of the land, burden himself with them? Still, it was royal tradition to hear subjects' petitions, so hear them, he did.

Back in palace apartments after a long day of petitioners, he looked forward to wine on the terrace with Mariamne. Where was she? She knew he liked her there to greet him at the end of the day. A servant handed Herod a scroll. With irritation, he grabbed the writing and waved the servant away.

My Husband,
I've gone to the baths. Care to join me there?

Would he care to join her there? Oh, yes, he would. He could think of nothing he would rather do. A vision flashed through his mind of Mariamne luxuriating in the hot bath water, steam rising around bare shoulders, her body shimmering in the torchlight.

Herod crunched down the pebbled path to the newly built bath-house, free-standing in the Roman tradition. In the anteroom, he dropped his clothing on the tiled floor. Usually, he would have servants undress him, but tonight, he was in a hurry.

Inside the columned pool chamber, he treaded as softly as he could to the water's edge. Blazing torches cast a shimmering white light on the pool of water. Mariamne was facing the opposite direc-tion, humming in her sweet voice. She bobbed in and out of the water while he enjoyed the view from behind. He was the luckiest man alive.

That was when it struck him. If he found Mariamne intoxicat-ing, other men must. They all wanted her. How could they not? Some men gave her wistful, longing glances, while others coveted her with undisguised lust in their eyes. The thought of it made a fire blaze in his belly. Mariamne belonged to him and only him. No other man would ever have her, on earth or in heaven. He possessed her, body and soul.

Herod decided to surprise her. Stealthily, he slipped into the bath. The warm swirl of water felt good on his tense shoulders. He moved his lean, muscled body through the water toward Mariamne, trying not to make a sound. But the small wave he made must have alerted her. She shrieked and turned to him.

"Herod, you frightened me," she said, laughing.

Grinning, he swept her into his arms. She embraced him and gazed up at him with large, luminous eyes. Joy coursed through his entire being. He took her face in his hands and moved his face toward hers.

She pulled away. "Herod, I want to speak with you —"

"Not now," he interrupted, and he kissed her, long and deep. Her lips tasted like almonds and honey.

She yanked away. "Herod, please listen to me. I need you to appoint Aris high priest."

Stung, he untangled himself from her. So, this was why she had lured him to the baths. "Mariamne, I cannot appoint your brother. We already have a high priest with a lifetime appointment. I've told you this before—"

Her eyes glittered in the torchlight. "Banish Hananel in favor of my brother. Our people will love you for it." She pressed herself against his broad, flat expanse of chest.

He pulled away. "Your mother put you up to this, yes?"

Mariamne chuckled. "Well, you know my mother."

Unfortunately, Herod knew her only too well. He knew she despised him even as she relentlessly tried to wheedle him into making her son the highest religious leader in the land, the first part in her all too transparent ploy to return the land to Maccabee rule.

"Appoint him, and you will make me happy."

Herod embraced Mariamne from the back, rubbing his hands over her smooth, flat belly. He could not wait to fill her womb with more children.

Mariamne turned to him. "Say yes. We will celebrate right here."

"I never said I'd —"

"Shhhh," said the woman. She wrapped her shapely legs around his waist and did not give him an opportunity to finish his sentence.

~

One rainy afternoon soon after Mariamne's seduction, Herod was signing government edicts in his library when an Egyptian envoy presented him with a wooden writing tablet. "This message is from the Triumvir Marc Antony, Your Highness."

Herod tensed. Good news rarely came by Egyptian envoy. He motioned for his guards and courtiers to leave. With trepidation, he read the words carved in wax.

> **Herod,**
> **Cleopatra has received some disturbing**
> **correspondence from Princess Alexandra of Judea**
> **informing her that you have appointed Hananel the**
> **Babylonian to serve as Judean High Priest though there is**
> **a Maccabee of royal lineage, fully qualified and of age,**
> **desirous of the appointment. I command you to**

promptly dismiss Hananel and to appoint Aris high
priest of your province.
   Marc Antony

Shuddering with rage, Herod kicked his scepter across the
length of the chamber. Antony's order was most unorthodox. Rome
rarely imposed its will on the religious affairs of its territories.
Leaders of the Roman Triumvirate—Antony, Octavian, and
Lepidus—allowed client states to worship as they wished so long as
they paid Rome tax and tribute. And paid, he had. Cleopatra must
have convinced Antony to issue the command.

Every fiber of his being resisted Aris's rise. He did not want him
too close to the throne. Herod's subjects still had no love for him,
and little appreciation for the law and order and the peace and prosperity he had brought to the land. Spies informed him an increasing
number of his subjects wanted him gone. Once the Judeans saw
Aris in high office, he had little doubt they would agitate to place the
Golden Maccabee on his throne.

Herod could crush any rebellion, of course. Time and time
again, he had done so on behalf of Rome. However, he did not
want to put himself in a position where he would be forced to put
down an insurgency against him. There would be a hefty political
price to pay to Rome if he used the brutality necessary to crush a
revolt against his own people. As important, his subjects would
dislike him more than they already did.

Still, what choice did he have but to obey Antony's command?
But first, he had tension to burn. He summoned a petty administra-
tor, one of his wrestling partners. On grounds near the palace,
Herod wrestled his opponent, and pinned him, again and again,
until the man, utterly exhausted, could not rise from the straw mat.
He left the administrator panting on the ground.

After Herod bathed, he dressed in his royal regalia, a robe lined
with mink fur from the Orient, and he summoned Aris to his presence chamber. His brother-in-law soon stood before him, his face
white as bones in the desert. How satisfying it was to see the Golden
Maccabee trembling before him. Aris's display of discomfort almost

made his unsavory task enjoyable. Herod stared at him for long seconds, watching him squirm. If Aris feared him, he was smarter than he looked.

Herod cocked his head. "Do you know why I've brought you here today?"

"No, King Herod."

Let him wait. He snapped his finger and asked a servant to bring him grapes. He slowly ate them, one by one, until the silver platter was empty. He never took his eyes away from Aris, sweating rivulets and plainly miserable, waiting in silence.

"I have decided to appoint you High Priest of Judea. You will begin to serve right away. I have just dismissed Hananel."

His brother-in-law's jaw dropped. Then, he straightened his posture and gave him a brilliant smile. In the band of sunlight spilling in through a high window, Aris had an angelic glow. Why did the damnable Maccabee have to grow more radiant with each passing day?

"Thank you," Aris said, humbly, his voice shaking. "Your trust honors me. I will not disappoint you."

Herod nodded, graciously, a frozen smile on his lips.

"Please know, King Herod, I want to remain high priest for life. Throne and crown, I do not want."

If Aris thought Herod believed him, he was mistaken.

~

*H*erod let Mariamne believe she was the one who had persuaded him to appoint her brother High Priest of Judea. In truth, it was not his wife who had persuaded him. If he could help it, she would never know that Antony had commanded him to make the appointment.

29

MARIAMNE, 35 BCE, JERUSALEM

*G*od answered my prayers. Herod made Aris our high priest. Seasons spun the web of time. Every Sabbath and on Holy Days, it thrilled me to see my brother, the holiest man in the land, stand before the people at the synagogue's brass altar, and hear the gathered chant his name.

Handsome and charismatic, Aris riveted the people. Herod's love for me moved him to make Aris our high priest, a decision that proved he was a changed man from the one I had married. Of course, some subjects were outraged to see Hananel dismissed, but no king could please everyone. The discontent of the few was but a small swell in the sea.

Now, my brother led the most elite priestly order that had the exclusive right to pass through the great bronze pillars and enter the Temple's innermost chamber, The Holy of Holies, the dwelling place of God. It was this venerable place, fashioned from pure gold, that held the Ark of the Covenant. Aris said the Temple's lofty ceiling seemed to reach the heavens, and exquisite carvings of palm trees and angels ornamented the cedar-paneled walls.

Herod, sullen and irritable lately, began to bristle at my delight whenever my brother led prayers or sacrificial blessings. He was even on the first day of the Feast of Tabernacles, five days after the Day of Atonement when our family ascended the steps to the Temple, and the crowd in the courtyard parted like the Red Sea to let us through. His sour expression stayed fixed on his face as we passed the panels of carved-ivory lions, oxen, and cherubs in the temple's outer court, and the priests' great washing basin mounted on the backs of twelve bronze oxen. Herod was grim even as we skirted the hewn-stone Temple itself. He did not smile and wave to the crowd gathered for a sacrificial offering, as I did, as I had urged him to do.

We led our subjects to the Temple's sacrificial altar. Aris came forward, splendid in his long, priestly robe of white silk and gold-thread embroidery. In his deep, resonant voice, he led prayers over the heifers and lambs, the day's sacrificial offerings. Beneath his high headdress with inlaid gold decoration, his radiant face made me swell with pride.

"We gather here today to celebrate the abundance of God's blessings, and to remember the Israelite's Exodus from Egypt, intoned Aris. "Our people dwelled in temporary shelters, or taber-nacles, on their way to the Promised Land, as our pilgrims do today."

My brother's words and his presence filled me with grace.

~

*A*fter prayers, thousands of residents and pilgrims crowded into the Temple Courtyard area for the most sumptuous feast of the year. Babylonians wore black robes and Phoenicians dressed in striped attire. Persians donned flowing silk brocaded in gold and silver. All were Jews who had come to Jerusalem to pray and feast. The scent of roasted meat and fresh bread filled the air.

Guards stationed at wall gates turned away lepers, and required foreign guests to bathe in the ritual baths before they entered. We dined in the open air on the sacrificial beef and lamb, and a host of the abundant harvest's dates and pomegranates, all of which Herod had bought with his own purse. My mother and grandfather sat beside me, their eyes fixed on Aris's every move, their faces aglow with pride. Cypros and Salome sat mirthless and silent across the table. After the prayers, scores of people crowded around Aris expressing their delight in his appointment.

My mother fanned herself languidly. "See how they love our Aris?"

Herod grunted and turned away, glowering. Aris's appointment had been a resounding success, so why did Herod look so grim? If he truly loved me, as he said he did, would he not be pleased to see how happy it made me?

"What's wrong, Herod?" I asked. "Please, tell me."

He pointed a thick finger at Aris, at a nearby table with the other elite priests. "We dine here alone while my people hang on your brother like flies on rotten fruit."

I squeezed his hand. "You were the one who appointed him. It's your wisdom they celebrate. They are grateful to you."

Herod's eyes turned cold as spring water. "My subjects, grateful to me? Not a single one has thanked me for anything, not even this feast. They don't even see me when your brother is around."

"They wrong you, Herod," said Salome, with righteous indignation.

"No matter how much I do for them, they show me no appreciation."

"Herod, please…" I said. If he would be quiet, I could hear Aris lead the chorus of priests singing psalms.

~

*M*uch to my relief, as the weeks passed, Herod showed no further signs of jealousy. Though he continued to bar Aris from council meetings and other matters of government, he warmed toward him at family gatherings and even began to show him the affection of a brother. He invited him to take the most honored chaise at the head of the table, beside his own, at feasts.

On other occasions, he permitted my brother to join us on the terrace for wine. Herod smiled and laughed more in Aris's company than he did with anyone. He had just needed time to grow comfortable with my brother at the religious helm.

30

HEROD, 35 BCE, JERUSALEM

*W*ith the birth of his son and heir, the Herodian Dynasty rested on solid ground. Herod knew this ought to please him, but it did not. At one time, he had wanted sons, but now he could not bear the thought of ever handing his crown and scepter over to anyone, even his own blood. When Herod watched baby Alexander's valiant, if initially unsuccessful, efforts to walk, he had to admire his son's show of determination. Yet he knew in his heart that this tiny amalgamation of himself and his beloved could never measure up to him. No one could.

Everyone died; Herod knew this objectively, but in the deepest recesses of his soul, he did not believe his heart would ever cease beating. He was a man who met life with extraordinary strength and stamina, and he seldom fell ill. On the few occasions when did, he pushed himself to rise from his sickbed and take care of his responsibilities. Men who gave in to weakness or infirmity disgusted him. He could not imagine himself weakening. He was godlike, different from other men.

On a steamy morning after a great deluge of rain, Mariamne persuaded Herod to join her in the nursery. He stood beside her over their sleeping baby's crib, and they watched him for what seemed to him, an eternity. He took his wife's hand and began to lead her away. The baby started to wail.

Mariamne turned from him with the speed of hummingbirds' wings and went to the child. She lifted him up and made a shameless fuss over him, although the nursery servants who hovered around his crib could easily have attended to his needs.

Herod lounged on a chaise and watched Mariamne rock the baby and sing him soothing songs. The excessive amount of attention she paid this small, demanding creature exasperated him. He knew why. She loved Alexander more than she loved him. The baby began to squall.

"Nurse!" Herod called.

A squat woman of middle age scurried over and took the baby from Mariamne, who gave the child a longing glance. Herod grinned. Now, his wife was his. He took her hand and led her to the royal apartments. Gently, he undressed her, noticing the changes in her body. There was a newly acquired softness to her belly. Her breasts had fallen, if only slightly. Such changes meant little to him; his desire for her was undiminished.

Afterward, Herod watched her sleep. The woman, a beauty inside and out, belonged to him, forever. Ever since Marc Antony had forced him to appoint Mariamne's over-glorified brother high priest, there had been a genuine thaw in their relations. He could not call her loving, but she seemed resigned to her role as his wife. It had to be enough, for now. If not for her obsession with the child, and her brother's needling presence, life would have been almost perfect.

31

MARIAMNE, 35 BCE, JERICHO

fter a year of construction, the new Jericho Palace was complete, and we moved there in early autumn. We planned to lodge in the warm climate of the Jordan Valley oasis, east of Jerusalem near the Jordan River, during the winter. I had not wanted to abandon the old castle of my ancestors, but once we began living in Herod's newly built palace, his enthusiasm was contagious. I quickly warmed its airy beauty.

A year ago, Herod visited Jericho to settle disputes between local shepherds and farmers. He had returned home determined to build a larger, more luxurious palace in the verdant land of date palms and balsam groves.

"I like the old one," I had told him. I did not understand Herod's obsession with constructing more magnificent palaces than those already standing.

"It's small and old-fashioned, and quite unworthy of my status."

"Where will you build the new one?"

"On the clifftop. We'll have a magnificent view of the mountains."

"But the synagogue stands there."

"I'll raze it and build a better one. Wait until you see it, Mariamne. When it's finished, it will rise up on both sides of the stream. Can you imagine? I will build you a colonnaded courtyard to rival those in the finest Roman palaces, and fortify it with towers and crenellations. Why are you frowning, my love?"

"I will miss the old one. My family often lodged there when I was a child. I have good memories…"

"Surely the place bored you. What was there besides balsam and date groves?"

I smiled, remembering. "Aris and I liked to play games in the palm groves. We chased each other and screamed like loons. We hid behind trees, and jumped out and tried to frighten each other."

Herod gave me a long, icy stare, as he often did when I spoke of my brother.

Soon after, he began to spend evenings with the architects and engineers he had brought in from Rome to design the new Jericho Palace. These meetings left Herod exhilarated, even after a long day of kingly duties. Once construction began, he often journeyed to Jericho to oversee its progress, rail at the slow pace, and see that nothing was less than meticulous.

Now, Jericho Palace was complete. Once we had settled in, we invited Jerusalem's six priestly families, also spending the winter in Jericho, to join us for our first feast to celebrate the season's abundant harvest. I found myself caught up in the excitement of hosting. Servants were still rushing about, sweeping, and polishing wood furniture to a high gloss with balsam-scented olive oil, when our guests' parade of carriages rolled up to the palace entrance.

"Welcome, welcome," Herod cried as people stepped down from their carriages into the unusually warm evening. He took them through a grand entrance between stone towers into an atrium with a domed ceiling and a small *occula* at the top. Early evening sunlight streamed in from long windows. The atrium pool glowed golden. Admiration and jealousy registered on our guests' faces as they murmured their compliments.

"Good King, this is undoubtedly the most spectacular palace in the Roman Republic," said a family patriarch, Mayer Ben Ami.

Other men strove to outshine ben Ami's compliments with their own. Herod took them as his due with gracious nods. In the back garden, framed by blooming beds of hyacinth, narcissus, and roses, Herod directed the visitors' attention to gold fountains of winged angels, spilling water into a large pool shimmering blue.

"It's a true oasis, is it not?" Herod asked.

Everyone agreed that the garden and cerulean pool created a lush desert haven.

Herod guided everyone through an arched doorway to the massive banqueting hall. Roasted lamb scented the air. He pointed out the wall frescoes, painted to imitate marble and cut stone, then drew their attention to the red, black, and white, mosaic floors. "I commissioned Rome's finest artists to fashion these floors. They used thousands of *tesserae* tiles to make geometric patterns. It took forty men nearly a year to complete."

Duly impressed, our guests took every opportunity to flatter the king. Herod's expression of smug satisfaction amused me. He relished their fawning, obsequious compliments. He either did not recognize how many dripped with jealous insincerity, or he did not care.

"Ah, what a lovely evening," said Herod. "Aris, take the young men to the pool before dinner for a swim."

Through the open window, the large fountain pool glimmered red in the waning sunlight. Something about the strange color made me shiver.

"I'd welcome the opportunity," said Aris, flush-faced and grinning. He grabbed a wine jug from the table and led the raucous group, most of whom were already well on their way to inebriation, out the back door.

"I wish you had not invited the boys to swim right now," I whispered, nodding toward the steamy galley, where cooks were making a racket moving lamb stew from pots to serving platters. "We're about to serve dinner."

"Let them have their fun," said Herod, smiling indulgently. "They can dine afterward."

From my place at the table by the window, I could see revelers slip off their robes. Wearing only tunics, they leaped into the water, one by one. They whooped with delight and called out to each other. Aris was still young, but now that he was serving as high priest, I no longer thought of him that way. It pleased me to watch him enjoying boyish amusements.

I was sipping wine when the joy-filled cacophony in the garden pool suddenly went silent. Then came a horrific scream. Something was terribly wrong. I jumped up. The others followed me out.

With dread, I watched two guards drag a man from the water and lay him on his back on the ledge beside the pool. Who was it? I edged in closer, and gasped. Aris lay on the wet stone. His wide-open eyes were glassy. His face was purple.

"No! No! No" I shrieked in unbearable anguish.

"Revive him!" my mother cried.

I crouched down and tried to shake my brother back to life. His wet skin felt cold to the touch. His body was stiff. It could not have hurt more had a sword sliced out my heart.

Herod pushed his way through the crowd. "What happened?" he demanded.

No one responded. Herod put his hand on my brother's chest and shook his head. "Aris's heart no longer beats," he said, his voice quivering. "He's with God now." He nodded to his guards, who gathered around my brother's body.

How could this have happened? It made no sense. Aris had been a good swimmer. Someone must have held him under water. Who would do this? Everyone loved Aris. There was only one man who would benefit from Aris's demise: the one who shared my bed. A fresh wave of horror washed over me.

My mother fell to the stony ledge and clung to her son. "Wake up!" she cried, frantic and weeping. Two burly men tried to pull her off. She fought them like a feral cat.

"Take Princess Alexandra to her bed," Herod told his guards. "Bring her wine. Make sure she drinks it. Someone must stay with her."

Herod put his arm around my quaking shoulders. I did not want him to touch me, but I forced myself not to recoil. I could not reveal what I suspected, not yet. For now, I would say nothing that would endanger me and what remained of my family.

My husband's guards placed Aris on a litter and carried him into the palace through a side entrance. It was too much. I saw black and crumpled to the ground. The next thing I knew, Herod was pulling me up. He tried to hold me while I sobbed. I let him.

Mercifully, the guests left quickly. The family gathered in the reception hall. We had little to say to each other. I could hear my mother ranting and wailing in her chamber. I stayed until I could no longer bear to watch my grandfather's white-knuckled, stoic show of grief. I needed to grieve in private. Herod tried to follow me.

I shook my head. "I need to be alone," I whispered.

He nodded, and I left for our apartments.

I sobbed until sleep took me. I woke up several times that night. Each time, I found Herod's blazing eyes, full of concern, fixed on me. Should I have feared for my own life? Perhaps, but I was too grief-stricken to care. It was inconceivable that I would never again, in this life, see Aris. Our entire country would share my grief at his untimely death.

The next morning, my mother stayed in her chambers and did not join us in the banqueting hall. Grandfather Hyrcanus arrived late, wearing his sleeping robe. Never before had I seen him undressed in a common chamber. Then, I noticed. Grandfather had lost his hair. Last night, he had had a full head of silvery-white hair. Now, he had not one strand.

"What happened to Grandfather's hair?" I whispered to Lila with alarm.

"Grief can make people lose their hair overnight," she said.

The former King of Judea touched his bare, pink scalp. His eyes clouded, and he blinked, absently. "I must ask your grandmother what has happened to my hair."

These were the first words Grandfather had uttered since his return from prison. His wife's bones had been at rest in an ossuary in our burial cave for the last ten years.

My stomach in knots, I could not eat. I returned to bed. At noon the next day, I still lay there. How could I rouse myself to live in a world without Aris? Only sleep brought me oblivion, welcome in my state. I was still asleep when I felt a presence. I opened my eyes. Herod stood over me, smiling too brightly.

"The funeral is tomorrow. I've bought Aris a sarcophagus. It's beautiful, Marianne. It has inlaid roses of rubies with emeralds stems — it's fit for the prince he was."

The words, "Prince he was…" echoed in my mind. Aris was.

$\sim$

The open, gilded carriage carrying Aris's body rambled down the old Roman Road toward the family burial cave outside the Damascus Gate. I walked beside Herod behind the carriage, feeling numb. My dazed state was nature's kindness. Had I been able to feel the magnitude of my grief, I would not have been able to stand.

My family, flanked by scores of Judeans, followed us on foot. Everyone was wailing, Herod the loudest. Never before had I seen a grown man grieve with such fervor, not even Grandfather Hyrcanus, when his adored wife passed away. Herod's watchful gaze never left me. Our procession paused from time to time to recite psalms while lyres played.

The Maccabee burial cave's classic, pillared façade had been hewn into the bedrock, Herod's strongmen carried Aris's body into the cool, shadowy interior. I breathed in the scent of aloe and myrrh rubbed on Aris's linen shroud. With reverential quiet, the crowd—weeping family, aristocrats, and peasants—packed in with the family.

In the weak light of the cave opening, pallbearers placed Aris's body on a rock shelf, the same one on which my Maccabee ancestors had lain for a full year after their deaths. I shuddered at the sight of it. One day, my bones would rest on that same shelf. A year from now, I would return with my family to fill Aris's ossuary with his bones, where they would spend eternity alongside those of our other long dead.

Priests began to utter a Hebrew Prayer for Aris's eternal soul.

"Wait!" Herod cried. He laid his crown and scepter on the ground near Aris's feet.

The crowd gasped at the king's dramatic show of respect. But I knew my husband. He was a theatre performer in a show of respect and humility, and the depth of his love for Aris, so they would not suspect him of having a role in the drowning.

A priest nodded to us, and my mother, Grandfather, and I tore our robes in a display of grief, a funerary custom of my people. Herod, too, turned his robes to tatters, but he did not fool me.

In a sudden panic, I could not breathe. I had to escape the cave. But how could I leave my little brother there, all alone with our ancestors' bones? It felt terribly wrong. Still, I acted on my compelling need, and pushed my way through the mass of mourners, and stood outside, trying to catch my breath.

Moments later, the funeral was over. The living poured out of the burial cave. Herod's men rolled a massive stone up against the entrance.

Goodbye, sweet Aris.

~

*W*hen we returned to the palace after the funeral, I climbed back into bed and drew my silk blankets over my head. Herod strode in, holding a wine vessel.

"Come with me to the terrace" he said. "We will have a special wine tonight."

Herod led me to the chaises. He sent the servants away and offered me wine. I shook my head. He filled his goblet and swilled it, again and again, until the vessel was empty. Herod rarely over-indulged, but this, of course, was no ordinary night. Had his unbearable guilt compelled him to reach this drunken stupor? My husband rarely regretted anything. More likely, he needed to escape his terror of accusation and conviction for my brother's murder.

He staggered to the edge of the terrace. In a strange, rough voice, he bellowed words I could not understand. It seemed as if he was in some far away, hellish place. He stared intently at the dark outline of the Judean Mountains and then turned to me with a cold, hard-set face. I sensed danger. I called in Lila and other servants. Quickly, I said good-night to Herod and locked myself inside a guest bedchamber.

~

The next morning, I awoke to swallows chirping in a nest on my window ledge. Out my window, lamb-white clouds tumbled across an azure sky. The beauty of the day, washed fresh by night, seemed to mock my misery. I could not lay still; I jumped up and dressed, and took a stroll in the garden. I heard male voices. They were too far away for me to listen to what they were saying. I followed the sounds to the nearby wrestling grounds.

Herod and his burly wrestling partner stood on the mat, facing each other, with their heads together, laughing. They must have been between matches. Herod looked altogether too happy for a man who had, only the day before, sent his brother-in-law to his eternal rest in a burial cave.

I hid in the shadows of the viewing benches and watched Herod and his opponent begin a new match. Each man grabbed his other's limbs. Herod soon struck down his adversary, and held him down while he struggled to rise. After long seconds, my husband raised his fist in victory.

Disgusted with Herod, I returned to the palace. Everyone had finished breakfast. Lila had left me a plate of bread and dates. I had not eaten much before the funeral, so I forced myself to take a few bites. Mother had not emerged from her bedchamber since the funeral. Worried, I went to see how she was faring. Her chamber door was closed. Her handmaiden, Adina, paced the hall outside her door.

"Is my mother sleeping?"

Adina's doughy face puckered. "She does nothing but lay in her bed and stare at the wall. She hasn't eaten a morsel, or shed a single tear."

We all grieved in our unique way. As a young girl, I had sobbed for weeks after the Romans executed my father.

Aris, who had also adored our father, had retreated into himself, sullen and silent, unreachable for weeks.

"You must be exhausted, Adina. Find another handmaiden to relieve you. Go get some sleep. I'll take care of my mother until fresh servants come."

Adina nodded gratefully and shuffled off. With trepidation, I opened my mother's door. She lay in her bed, as still as sculpture, facing the wall. The quiet of the bedchamber felt like a living, sinister presence.

"Mother, turn around," I said in a soft voice. "Please, I want to talk to you."

She did not respond. I climbed over my mother to see her face. It was as white as dove feathers. Dark half-circles hung in the loose flesh under her red-lined eyes. Tears choked me. I lay down beside her.

"Mother, can you speak?" She blinked and said nothing.

Was I going to lose her, too? I had to do something. I jumped off the bed, and rushed to the kitchen and ordered the cook to prepare my mother's favorite dish, lamb stew in lentil sauce. I reminded the cook to add an extra pinch of turmeric, the way she liked it. When it was ready, I insisted on bringing it to her myself.

"Look, Mother."

Princess Alexandra turned around.

"I can feed you."

She shook her head.

"Drink some water, at least."

I opened my mother's parched lips and poured a small stream of water into her mouth. She spat it out on her silk blanket. A dark stain bloomed.

I felt tears rising. "Don't you want to live? I've lost my brother and my father. I can't lose you, too. You must drink some water."

She sat up, grabbed the water vessel, and took a long, steady swig. "Come closer," she said in her raspy, unused voice, "in case anyone is listening."

I looked around to see if there were spy holes in the walls. There were none.

I was relieved to see my mother's familiar scowl return.

"Listen to me, Mariamne. Herod murdered Aris. I'm sure of it. He must have ordered his strongmen to drown him." She took a sobbing gasp. "Aris would never get drunk enough to drown in that puddle of a pool."

My jaw clenched so hard pain shot through my face. A sudden swell of sympathy for her arose. The poor woman had lost her only son. "I think so, too. Eat your lamb, Mother." She took a few bites. "Is there anything you know about this...execution...that I don't?"

"Not specifically, but a snake will always be a snake. Herod has shown his brutality, again and again. He betrayed your grandfather's friendship and stole our throne. He executed forty-seven innocent judges and who knows how many more people have died at his command. Your husband will kill again. Who will be next? Me? You? Grandfather? Herod needs Maccabees out of his way, Mariamne, every one of us. Our lives are in danger."

I nodded, sadly.

"Don't speak a word of this to anyone, not yet. If you do, Herod will execute you for treason. We cannot accuse him of Aris's murder until we can show Rome he arranged it. First, we must see to our own safety."

"You must leave this dangerous man, Mariamne, and take the children and me with you." A semblance of a smile appeared. "We will go to Alexandria. Cleopatra will help us."

"First, you must get well."

"If my father wasn't a weakling and a fool, our family could have held the throne."

"Don't disparage Grandfather for being unable to conquer the Romans. Who could?"

"Rome took Judea because my father was weak. None of this would have happened if your grandfather had been a strong man."

It was the same hate she had spewed a thousand times before. "You're so bitter about the past—"

"How can I not be bitter, Mariamne? I was born to the ruling

family on both sides. Pure Maccabee blood runs through my body.
Now, we live and die by King Herod's mercy, and that evil man is
anything but merciful."

"Shhhh. He has spies everywhere."

Her eyes were flinty arrowheads. "Listen to me, Mariamne. I
want you to slip wolfs' bane into Herod's wine. We must rid the
world of him."

"No. I won't violate God's Commandment. I hope you won't
either. There has to be another way."

"His servants would never let me near his food and drink. But
you…"

"We must proceed carefully. I don't want the rest of our family
to join Aris in the burial cave.

My mother sat on the edge of her bed, her posture as straight as
a Roman soldier's. She appeared strangely refreshed. "You still have
a family duty to strive for—"

"Strive for what?" I interrupted. "Aris is dead. We can no longer
put him on the throne. He never wanted it, anyway. Alexander is
next in line to be crowned king. We must protect his throne and—"

"You're willing to allow an Idumean mongrel to rule our land?"

My jaw dropped. "Mongrel? You are speaking of my son and
your only grandson."

"It is a fact that Alexander doesn't have pure Maccabee blood as
we do," she said. "Judea's king's veins should run pure— it's been
that way for nearly one hundred years."

I turned to leave. I could not look at my mother another minute.
"You're as terrible a grandmother as you are a mother."

Her eyes filled with tears. "Your brother didn't think so. Aris
loved me."

"You wish I'd died instead of Aris." Her stony silence confirmed
it. "You've never loved me. You barely noticed my existence until
you could use me for your benefit."

"It's not true, Marianne. Didn't I give you the best education
any princess ever had? You learned everything your brother did,
right alongside him. Your father didn't think girls should have an
education, but I fought for you."

"I'm grateful for that."

"Heed my words, Daughter. We'll never be safe here so long as Herod lives. Kill him. You and I can rule together." With an imperious grin, she dismissed me. "Keep in mind what I've said. You will know when the time is right."

"We must make plans, sensible plans, to take the throne. We must persuade Rome to make me regent for Alexander until he comes of age to rule."

"I am the oldest living Maccabee of the royal line. We must persuade Rome to appoint me queen."

"You would take the crown from your own grandson?"

"Do you want the tradition of a pure-blooded Maccabee dynasty to end with Hyrcanus? Would you shame your ancestors this way?"

"King Herod has already ended the Maccabee dynasty. I will stay with him until we are ready to move against him. It will be difficult, but until then, I must remain his wife in every sense of the word."

32

MARIAMNE, 34 BCE, JERUSALEM

*N*early a year had passed since Aris's death, and my life was still an endless sea of grief. I had spent so many years striving to put him on the Judean throne. His glaring absence made me question my own life and purpose. I found the answer in my son. I must see to it that he reaches the throne, even if he was only half Maccabee. His veins flowed with my blood. It was enough for me, and I would see to it that the Judeans accepted him.

Little by little, I stepped back into the world. I did my duty in the bedchamber and submitted to Herod's needs, a strain though it was. Mother and I had to see Herod brought to justice, and at the same time, keep our lives. It was a delicate operation.

We had to show Rome that Aris had no enemies and that no one, except for Herod, had reason to want him dead. Hananel, the former high priest who had lost his position to Aris, had taken his family to Babylonia, where they had lived since Babylonia had defeated my country five hundred years ago. The Babylonians had sent most Judeans to their native lands. Priests who corresponded with Hananel said he had been appointed a senior priest in his community. By all accounts, he was happy. The few supporters he had in Jerusalem were men of religion, not murder.

Herod, however, was a different story entirely. The stability of his reign was at stake, and he was ruthless enough to order Aris's elimination. But could I prove this without speaking to Herod's guards and strongmen? They would not confide in me, and would certainly tell him I had been asking questions. I could not confront Herod with an accusation until I was prepared to defend myself and my children, which I could not do without Rome's protection.

My mother sent a scroll to Cleopatra accusing Herod of arranging Aris's execution. We hoped Antony's lover would persuade him to summon my husband to Alexandria to face murder charges. I hired an envoy to sneak the correspondence out of the palace and put it directly into Pharaoh's hands, and prayed that Herod would not intercept the writing. Tensely, we waited for a response.

~

I was with child again. The child should have made its squalling entry into the world already, but the little one stubbornly clung to my womb. I was restless in my discomfort, and did not sleep well during this unusually warm winter, Herod was off quelling a rebellion against Rome in the South. What a relief it was to have him away. An enemy sword or arrow could take his life, which would swiftly solve the problem of his kingship. If my husband died, I would present a request to be appointed Prince Alexander's regent to the Roman leader Marc Antony, and if he allowed me, I would rule the country until my son came of age.

Just thinking of my regency made my heartbeat quicken. I would be a good queen, like my esteemed ancestor, Alexandra Jannaeus, who had reigned for nearly a decade over a peaceful and prosperous Judea. Could I persuade Antony to back me, and not my mother, if Herod fell in the rebellion? Mother would whisper her intention to be Queen of Judea in Cleopatra's ear, and beg her to persuade Antony to appoint her queen.

Such concerns, however, were premature. Deep inside, I felt

with cold certainty, that Herod was going to survive and return home.

~

*O*ne morning, I lumbered down the steps to break my fast. In the banqueting hall, I found Salome alone at the long table, dipping her bread in peppered olive oil. I took the chaise at the opposite end of the table, as far from her as possible. A servant poured my beer and set out plates of dates and honeyed bread.

"Will you require anything else?" the servant asked. I shook my head.

"May I join the garden harvest?" the servant asked. "You may," I said.

"Could Lila help? All hands are needed today."

"Lila has gone to Chenna to care for her sick aunt," I said. She had departed a week ago. I missed her.

"Leave us now," said Salome. She waved away the servant and gave me a long, assessing look. "I heard your grandfather released Lila from slavery before her mother had worked off her father's debt. Is it true?"

"It is. Lila has been a paid servant since she was ten."

"Ah, so she's free. And you actually think she will return to you?"

"She said she would. I trust her. But she doesn't have to come back."

Salome shook her head in disgust. "You've never known how to conduct yourself like a princess."

I ignored her disrespect. Neither of us uttered another word or even looked at each other as we finished breakfast. When I stood up to leave, I caught Salome glowering at my mountain of a belly. Fear pulsed through me. Was she giving me the evil eye? A sudden stab of pain made me double over. Water gushed and puddled around me. I heard myself panting. "Go get the midwife. The baby is coming."

My sister-in-law looked at me sidewise, like she was considering her response.

"Hurry, please!" I cried.

Salome stood up and stretched, and strolled toward the door. Why was she moving so slowly? It seemed like a long time before I heard the sound of the great door creaking open and shut.

"Please, someone, please help me!" I cried out.

No one came. Then, I remembered. The servants were in the kitchen garden, and Princess Alexandra and Cypros were at the market with their servants. I should have asked Salome to call them in before she left. Even if no one knew how to deliver a baby, I would not have been alone in my peril. I could do nothing but wait for the midwife.

I had a strong urge to lie down. I curled up on the cold marble tiles of the floor. Another excruciating wave of pain swallowed me like a riptide. Where were Salome and the Midwife Elzea? They should have been here by now. Tears streamed down my face. Would I have to deliver my own baby? I had no idea what to do. The best midwives in the land delivered Maccabee babies. The next pain could not have hurt more had an ox cart rolled over my face.

Then, I heard the blessed sound of footsteps. One of the cooks stood over me, her plump hands drawn to her mouth, her eyes round as coins. "Oh, no," she said.

"Get Elzea," I whispered, barely able to speak.

She rushed out. The next pain came just seconds after the last. It gripped me with the strength of a lion and did not subside. I felt a strong urge to push. The baby was coming. I was going to give birth unaided on the floor in the banqueting hall. The baby was going to die, and so was I, because of Salome's unthinkable cruelty.

The cook and Elzea charged in. My agony prevented me from feeling even a shred of relief at the sight of them. The horror on Elzea's face made my heart hammer harder.

The midwife examined me. "The baby is crowning," she said, and wheeled around to the incredulous cook. "She needs clean linens and fresh water. Go quickly."

With the cook's help, the midwife slipped a linen cloth underneath me. "Push harder than you've ever pushed before," she said.

I did. My second child entered the world, pink and squalling.

"A son!" Elzea cried. "Good Queen, you have given your husband another beautiful child."

I gazed at my baby with wonder and whispered a grateful prayer. "He's as handsome as his uncle Aris. I will call him Aristobulus IV."

Though spent and aching, I was ecstatic. My baby lived, and he appeared to be healthy.

"We need to get you into bed," said Elzea. "Then the grandmothers will want to meet the young prince."

"I'll go find them," said the cook. "And Salome, too."

The sound of my sister-in-law's name made me recoil. "Tell me, did Salome come for you earlier?"

Elzea shook her head.

Why had Salome not fetched Elzea? What might have detained her along the way? Had a lion mauled her? Had a brigand raped her? I was sure it had been nothing of the sort. Herod's sister had intentionally failed to bring me the midwife I so desperately needed. I had long suspected that Salome despised me, but now, I knew the extent of her hatred, and the cruel and dangerous measures she was willing to take to hurt me.

~

J awoke from sound slumber to hear my sister-in-law's footsteps clattering down the hall.

"Salome!" I called out.

She stopped, and coolly regarded me from the doorway. Not a trace of remorse was evident on her unsmiling face.

With considerable difficulty, given my post-birth state, I pushed myself up to a seated position. "Why didn't you bring the midwife as I'd asked you to do?"

"Do you think I'm so far beneath you that you can issue me orders?" asked Salome. "I'm not your servant."

"My baby and I could have died," I said. I was too exhausted to fully express my fury. "You're heartless, Salome. I'm going to tell Herod of your cruelty."

Salome's narrowed eyes glittered with menace. "If you mention a word of this to Herod, I'll tell him about all of the lovers who visit you in the night when he is away."

Lovers? I had done nothing to give her such an outlandish idea. "You're a liar, Salome. Say whatever you want to Herod. I don't care. He'll know it's not true."

Salome raised her thin, ginger eyebrows. "Will he? My brother will believe me. He always believes me."

If she accused me of adultery, might Herod believe her? He certainly trusted his sister. And any man's attention to me, no matter how innocent, incensed him. I shuddered to think of his rage. Still, he must learn of his sister's malicious neglect. She was not worthy of his trust; he must know it. Salome's mistreatment went well beyond mere envy.

"You're in love with your brother," I said. "How very sad for you."

Salome stepped back and blinked hard. She opened her mouth as if she was going to speak, but instead, she pursed her lips and hurried away.

~

*I*t was clear that Salome posed a danger to me, and by extension, to my children. My sons' lives could be in jeopardy. If the woman could abandon me during childbirth, was she not entirely capable of killing my children?

That night, Salome invaded my dreams.

A voice whispers in my ear, "Go see them…" I wake up and rush to the nursery. I am too late. My two little boys are dead, stiff and cold in their beds.

I woke up from the vivid nightmare with my heart thumping and my tunic wet with sweat. I slipped on a robe, grabbed a torch and a bag of gold from a locked marble chest, and rushed to the nursery.

In the torchlight, I first saw two-year-old Alexander. I put a hand on his cheek and felt its reassuring warmth. His moon-round face looked calm and cherubic as he slept. His chest rose and fell with each steady breath. Baby Aris lay on his back, very still, his eyes wide open. I gasped. Had my worst fears come to fruition? Then, his gaze locked on mine, and he gave me a sweet, toothless smile.

My babies lived. Joy flooded my soul. In my immense relief, I could breathe again. I needed to feel the new infant close to me. I lifted young Aris to my chest. He began to wail. Leah, the night nurse, rushed over from her pallet in the corner.

"Queen Mariamne, I wasn't expecting you," she said.

I ignored her and held my baby close, breathing in his milky scent. His heart was beating a comforting rhythm against my breasts.

"I've come to speak with you about the nursery," I said. "You must deny entry to anyone but me. I'll arrange for guards, night and day." I untied the bag of gold hanging from a ribbon inside my robe and put it in Leah's hands. "This is for you. Say nothing to anyone about my orders."

Leah's eyes lit up. "Good Queen, I'm grateful, but it isn't necessary… I'll gladly do as you ask without—"

"I want you to have it," I interrupted. I had to lavish Leah with so much gold Salome could not possibly offer her more to let her into the nursery to harm my children. "There will be more when the boys reach their next birthdays."

"Thank you, Good Queen," Leah murmured.

"My guards will put a new lock on the nursery door within the hour. No one besides you and me will have the key. Do you understand me?"

Leah's brow creased. "But why— "

"That's none of your concern. Just follow my orders. If any harm comes to my children, I will know who is responsible."

33

HEROD, 34 BCE, JERUSALEM

*H*erod returned to the Jerusalem Palace after months of battle in the South. The rebelling tribes had given strong resistance, and it took longer to defeat them than he had anticipated. Weary and dirty from long months of fighting and the arduous journey home during the winter deluge, he wanted to soak in the bathhouse before he faced his wife. He hoped their time apart had thawed her ice. He wanted her love.

He rounded a corner near the door to the bathhouse, and there she was, in full flesh. He wanted to touch her, smell her. She had no smile for him. He reached out for an embrace. After an uncomfortable pause, she wrapped her arms around him. She felt good in his arms, but she pulled away too soon.

"Hello, Alexander," he said to the toddler who sat cross-legged on the rug and played with a small carved wooden cart. The child looked at him as if he was someone he did not know.

"Say hello to your father, Alexander."

"Hello," the child said, without looking up from his toys.

Herod knelt beside the child and tousled his curls.

"Come meet your new son," Mariamne said. She took him to

the nursery, where the baby slept in a raised basket. "See, he's as handsome as his uncle was. I've named him Aris."

Herod looked at the infant, and his heart froze. It was eerie how much he resembled his namesake. He even had the same earthy scent. Was young Aris, now swinging his tiny fists and making cooing noises, the dead Maccabee returned from the grave to haunt him, to taunt him, to punish him for murder? He felt the child's forehead to see if he was, in fact, a ghost, but his hand met soft baby skin, not air. He shrieked and glowered at his father, accusingly.

He ought to be ecstatic about his new son. His dynasty now rested on a stronger footing. Young Aris was second in line for the crown. If Alexander did not survive childhood, another prince stood in the Herodian line. But he wanted only to turn away from his second-born son.

"Don't you want to hold the baby?" Marianne asked.

"After I bathe," he said.

Her face crumpled. Herod knew he had disappointed her, and he did not want to make her sad, truly he did not, but his visceral revulsion for the newborn namesake of his dead brother-in-law was too strong for him to pretend to love the child. He kissed Mariamne and left for the baths.

～

*T*he next morning, Herod woke up with a throbbing headache. The image of his infant, who looked startlingly like his dead uncle, immediately sprang to mind, and it troubled him. Why should he have to bear the child's unwelcome presence? He could foster him out. But Mariamne would balk at the suggestion, and he did not want to make her miserable. No, he would not send his second son away, but he must keep the boy away from him.

After breakfast, he went to the library to read the accumulation of scrolls piled high on his writing table. He had just started when Mariamne approached, her face unusually pale and serious, her skin pulled tight over her cheekbones.

"I need to speak to you in private," she said, her tone firm.

Herod was in no mood for a conversation. Voices only worsened the pounding ache inside his head. "I have work to do."

"This won't take much time," she said with a level stare.

He would oblige her in hopes she would soon go away. He dismissed his guards and courtiers and led his wife into the reception hall. They sat on side-by-side chairs near the crackling hearth.

"Herod, I want you—I need you—to encourage Yusef to divorce Salome."

His shoulders grew taut. "Why?"

"It's time your sister remarries and has children and a home of her own. She must be lonely."

"Salome, lonely? She's never complained about her lot or asked me to arrange another marriage for her," he said, his palms massaging his temples. He had not the time for such nonsense. Mountains of scrolls awaited his signature. The bickering of women did not interest him.

Mariamne stared at her hands, folded in her lap. "I don't feel safe with your sister in our home."

He frowned.

She shut her eyes, tightly, as if she could not bear to look at him. "Your sister did something terrible, Herod, when you were off battling in the South. I was with Salome at breakfast the morning my birthing pains came. Our mothers were out, and all the servants were in the garden, harvesting. I asked Salome to go get the midwife. She didn't do it, Herod. She abandoned me in childbirth. Had the cook not come along when she did, your son and I would have died on the banqueting hall floor."

"Are you asking me to believe that my sister intentionally endangered you and my son? She must not have heard your request, or she didn't understand what you had asked her to do."

Mariamne shook her head. "Salome heard and understood me, I can assure you. She deliberately neglected to help me. That's not all, Herod."

He stared at his work table. He did not want to hear any more. "Salome threatened to tell you lies if I told you of her cruelty."

His back went rigid. "Salome would never lie to me."

"She said she would tell you men visited my bedchamber while you were away. Of course, it's a lie, Herod."

His eyes narrowed. "You took lovers?"

"No, I did not. I've never been unfaithful to you. Salome threatened to tell you this lie if I told you about how she had abandoned me in childbirth. She wanted to stop me from telling you the truth."

"Who visited you? I want names. I'll crucify them all."

"Herod, listen to me, please. You are and have always been my only lover. Your sister is a dangerous woman. I can no longer bear her presence in my home. Please, send her away. It's best for all concerned."

He gave her a scathing look. "Never." He ordered his manservant to bring in Salome.

His sister soon strolled in. "Yes?" she asked, with a sunny smile. "Tell me, Salome, did men visit my wife's bedchamber while I was away at war?"

Salome gave Mariamne a long, hard look. "What did the Maccabee woman tell you?" she asked.

"Tell him, Salome," said Mariamne, "how you threatened to tell my husband lies."

"Lies?" asked Salome, aghast.

"Is this true, Salome?" Herod asked.

His sister's face was smooth in its innocence. "The queen never asked me for help. And I have never said anything to her about lovers. I have no idea why she would tell you such deceitful lies." She started to sob. Herod opened his arms to her, and she rested her head on his chest. His sister was a little bird in need of his protection.

Mariamne blushed and shook her head, vehemently. "Your sister is lying."

"Listen to me," he said. "I'll never banish Salome from our home. She's a woman estranged from her husband. I'm responsible for her."

His wife gave him a searing look. "Salome has another brother. She could live with Pherorus in Syria." She turned to Salome. "You are no longer welcome in this palace. It would be better for our family if you left right away."

Herod felt his fury mount. "Better for our family, you say? Salome is a member of our family. Would her exile be better for our mother or for me? I think not. Enough. Salome stays."

"You love your sister too much, Herod."

"A man cannot love his sister too much."

"Yes, you can. And it's blinded you to her true character."

Never before had he seen her eyes glitter with such rage. She pointed a finger at Salome. "Your sister is a menace, Herod. If you let her stay, she will be the undoing of our family."

Now, she had gone too far. No one, not even his beloved queen, was going to tell him what to do. He stood up and loomed over her, glowering. Mariamne's face fell, and she ran away, weeping. He did not relish making her unhappy, but he must overrule her audacious request. His sister was the only one, besides his mother, whom Herod could trust. He needed her.

~

*A*lone on the southern terrace, Herod reclined on a silk-cushioned chaise and quaffed his wine while rain slapped the wooden awning above him. Mariamne was already asleep. She had been retiring for the night earlier and earlier. It seemed she wanted to avoid his company. Perhaps her infidelities had left her wracked with guilt. Had his sister been there with him, he would not have this terrible ache of loneliness.

He reflected on his sister's devotion. Had he been keeping Salome by his side at the expense of her own happiness? He recalled asking her several times if she wanted to marry again. She had always insisted that she wanted only to be there beside him, to help him and protect him from the many who coveted his throne.

Here, with his vast lands stretched out before him, Herod felt safe. He had been cautious about every word he uttered about Aris in his wife's presence so as not to let anything slip. It was a strain, to be sure. But here, on his own, with the peaks and valleys of his land framed in the terrace's arches, he could congratulate himself on the smooth execution of his plan for his brother-in-law's execution.

He knew he had to do it. His subjects had loved Aris too much. Handsome, brilliant, and absurdly amiable, the golden Maccabee had posed an unacceptable threat to his kingdom's stability. The two executioners he had dispatched to the pools dressed as aristocratic young men had murdered Aris with cool efficiency. They had waited until the others were engaging in such drunken horseplay that no one noticed them holding the prince under water until he was dead. If Mariamne ever learned of his part in her brother's death, her love would dry up like a creek bed in summer. Losing her would feel like someone had scooped out his heart and lungs. She must never, ever learn the truth. The two men who had drowned Aris could not talk; Herod had ordered his guards to strangle them on spurious treason charges less than an hour after they had pulled Aris's dead body from the pool. No one would ever learn of Herod's orders, if not from his own lips.

What a relief it was to have Aris gone. Herod could breathe freely, now. Every Sabbath through the High Holy Days, beginning with the Jewish New Year to the Day of Atonement ten days later, he had despaired at the Judeans' near-reverence for the Maccabee. Even worse, it was plain to see that his wife, like everyone else, loved Aris more than she loved him.

With this single act of political expedience, he had shown his father in heaven that he, not Phasael, was the fiercest and most intelligent son, the one bound for greatness. His father should have recognized his superiority. The old man had been wrong to favor Phasael, to groom him for greatness, and to give him the best of everything, from the biggest slab of meat at dinner to their dead grandfather's sword.

Now, Herod was the only son who could bring glory to the family name. Phasael was dead, and Joseph had fallen in battle. Pherorus, his sole living brother, was a good-natured sort who could keep accounts well enough, but he had neither the heart nor the stomach to battle and lead men.

To hold a throne, a king must eliminate threats to his rule. How could he meet his grand destiny while his brother-in-law still lived? Aris would have met Marc Antony at some point, and who knew how far his brother-in-law's charisma might have taken him with the most powerful man in the known world. Herod was not willing to find out. The short period that Aris had served as high priest had been enough to show him it was only a matter of time before the Judeans would rise in revolt and demand that Rome crown him King of the Jews. Rome would oust him and put his wife's brother on his throne. Herod would have lost everything—everything—had he not stopped Aris's beating heart.

Uneasily, Herod paced. He knew many thought he was too mistrustful of his subjects, but was he? In the most recent the many efforts to overthrow him, a group of subjects had taken it upon themselves to travel to Rome to complain to Antony about him. They said Herod was moving Jerusalem away from its religious roots and turning it into a city too much like Rome. They resented the theater and hippodrome he had built. They found Roman culture and entertainment foreign and offensive. Spies told him Antony was soliciting opinions about him from high-ranking Judeans.

It saddened him how his subjects failed to appreciate his efforts to take Jerusalem from the backwater it once was to the thriving, modern city it had become. He had hired thousands for his building projects, and their purses were heavy with gold. But still, they worked against him.

He hoped, in time, the image of Aris's waxy, plum-colored face, eyes wide open and eternally frozen in horror, would no longer haunt him. He kept forcing the gruesome vision down until it dissolved into the recesses of his mind, only to later reappear. When he had a fresher kill, this torturous vision would cease. It had always happened that way.

Restless, Herod sauntered over to the quarter rail of the terrace. He drew comfort from the stark beauty of his land. He wished Mariamne did not grieve so for her brother. Her sad, forced smiles were like daggers in his chest. She ate so little Herod wondered how she could survive. He could feel ribs where there was once softness.

She submitted to his needs, as a wife must. But it was as if she bore him with grim determination, an insult to be sure, when he wanted her passion to equal his own. He ought to be the most important man in her life, but she loved her dead brother and her two sons more. Perhaps she did not love him at all.

In a fit of rage, Herod flung his wine vessel over the terrace wall. He heard the faint sound of it shattering to pieces in the canyon below. In the distance, the spilled wine looked like a ribbon of blood.

34

MARIAMNE, 34 BCE, JERUSALEM

*N*ow, I knew. No matter how outrageous Salome's lies and accusations, Herod was always going to believe his sister's word over mine. No matter how horrible his sister's actions, he would refuse to see them as such. His acceptance of Salome's spurious allegations of my infidelity astounded me and left me reeling. He had not listened to me. He had not believed me. He had not protected me. I had long thought that Herod's love for me had changed his character, but now, I questioned the belief. Who was this man I had married? Did I know him at all? Can one person ever truly know the heart and mind of another?

Despite my outrage and disappointment, I kept my emotions buried deep inside. I had sons to raise. I wanted, more than anything else, to do it well, and to live to see my son take Judea's Crown. So I pretended nothing was wrong while I waited for Cleopatra's response to my mother's letter. If Cleopatra persuaded Marc Antony to charge Herod with Aris's murder, Herod's life would soon be in the triumvir's hands. But if Antony refused to charge Herod, and told Herod of the letter my mother had sent, my husband would probably execute my entire family.

Worry was aging me before my time. My looking glass reflected new wrinkles and gray hairs.

35

MARIAMNE, 33 BCE, JERUSALEM

From the terrace of newly built Antonia Fortress, I took in the sweeping view of Jerusalem. Northwest of the Temple, perched on steep, impregnable bedrock, our new home of white stone rose higher than any other building in Jerusalem. Though fortified towers graced the four corners with lofty ceilings, airy chambers, and a vast courtyard, it was the most luxurious place I had ever lived.

Herod built Antonia Fortress on the land where the ancient stronghold, David's Citadel, had once stood. Pompey had destroyed it when Rome invaded Jerusalem. Antonia Fortress rose over Maccabee ruins.

"It's the way of kings to build over former kings' ruins," Herod said.

~

The unseasonably warm spring turned into a blazing summer. Months after my second son's birth, I was once again with child. Sick for the first few months, I could not sleep and my mind was in a constant fog. Later in my confinement, my belly ballooned to twice the size it had been during my previous pregnancies. I wore robes especially sewn to accommodate my gargantuan proportions. I took to dining in my apartments with my mother and my grandfather to avoid meeting Salome in the common halls and chambers. I knew too well she was capable of harming my baby and me.

One blessing was that Herod was rarely home. He spent weeks in Jericho during the balsam harvest and returned home for just days before he left again for Masada, where hundreds of workers labored on his massive building project. Once again, my husband was destroying palaces my ancestors had built, and he was replacing them with larger, more sumptuous ones. A month before I was due to give birth, Herod returned home. I was embroidering a tunic for the poor when he strutted in, his face flushed, his eyes shining.

"Mariamne, I wish you could see the compound I'm building on Masada. It's massive. There will be a synagogue, two palaces, barracks, and cliff-side terraces. I will build a wall around the perimeter stronger than the world has ever seen. I return tomorrow, and I'll stay there for the next months to oversee the new master builder I've brought in from Rome."

I hid my joy.

~

*W*hen my time came, I sent Lila for the midwife. While I waited for her, I dutifully began to push, as Elzea had instructed me to do the last time I had given birth. The midwife's assistant, a girl who looked too young to know much about childbirth or anything else, arrived first. She examined me and gasped. "Stop pushing, or your baby is going to fly across this chamber before the midwife arrives."

Elzea swept in just as the pains grew unbearable. At sunrise, my daughter was born, red and bawling. I wanted a girl child so badly I dared not admit it to myself. I had already provided my husband

and country with a royal heir and a spare. This beautiful baby, with tufts of coppery hair and blazing, dark-blue eyes, belonged to me.

The midwife pressed on my belly with two fingers. Her eyes widened.

Her expression alarmed me. "What's the matter?" I asked.

She squeezed my hand. "Another baby is coming."

Twins, double joy! What a gift God had bestowed on me. The cries of my two rosy girls rang through the night. Along with my welling of love for them came relief. The tiny, demanding lodgers no longer occupied my body. I named the firstborn Cypros because her eyes sparkled like those of my mother-in-law. I called the second girl Salampsio simply because I liked the sound of it.

~

*A*fter I visited my children in the nursery, I had Lila set up my pigments and mix them with water. She wetted the wall plaster in the courtyard. I had an image of a ship on the great sea fixed in my mind. I had to paint it. Through fast brush strokes, I sketched out a boat on the water and a green spot of land in the distance.

"Is that Alexandria you are paining?" my mother asked.

I shrugged. "I keep dreaming of a ship on water, sailing to a faraway city."

"Perhaps it portends our future, and our family will sail to Alexandria. Cleopatra will help us take back our throne. I don't know why she hasn't answered my letter. She usually responds right away. I wonder if she ever received it. I sent it with a messenger I trusted. He told me he had placed it in her hands. Perhaps he lied, and Herod bribed him to turn the scroll over to him."

"If that were true, Herod would have confronted us about it by now."

"So why hasn't Cleopatra written? I hope she isn't ill."

The more time that passed, the less likely it was that Rome was going to act against Herod. Still, my mother had, through Cleopatra, made Rome aware of Herod's complicity in Aris's murder. So if Antony had learned of my mother's letter to Cleopatra, and told Herod about it but did not charge him for Aris's murder, our necks were on the line. Herod would promptly dispatch Grandfather, my mother, and me.

HEROD, 33 BCE, JERUSALEM

*B*y the light of his library's hearth fire, Herod studied General Ptolemy's eyewitness account of Alexander the Great. He marveled at the Persian's leader's extraordinary military campaign through Asia and northeast Africa hundreds of years earlier. By the age of thirty, Alexander had created an empire that stretched from Greece to Egypt to India. Herod read voraciously; he wanted to learn everything he could from the world's great kings and emperors.

His guards interrupted his reverie when they ushered in an Egyptian envoy. Herod took the scroll the man offered. He unfurled Antony's message with hands grown suddenly cold.

> *Greetings, Herod,*
> *I have divorced Octavia and married Cleopatra. The wedding gift I have given her includes Jericho's balsam and date groves. I will, however, permit my wife to lease the groves to you at a price she determines. I have also gifted her the lands of Gadara, Hippos, Samaria, Gaza, Antriedon, Jappa, and the Tower of Stratom.*
> *I know you share our joy in our glorious union.*

Marc Antony

Herod shut his eyes and swallowed hard. It was happening. Cleopatra was stealing his land. What would Antony give away next, Jerusalem? He smiled at the envoy. "Send Antony and his new wife my best wishes for a happy and prosperous marriage." He lifted the nearest small statue from his writing table, an exquisitely crafted bucking horse of pure of gold, and put it in the envoy's hands. "Give them this gift as a token of my highest esteem."

The Egyptian nodded officiously, bowed, and backed out.

~

That night, Herod could not sleep. Under a panoply of bright stars, he paced the stone walkway on top of the massive wall surrounding Antonio Fortress. At sunrise, he found a dove's nest tucked under a parapet. In it were three eggs the pale blue of the morning sky. Its presence irritated him. He had not given the bird permission to nest in his castle. The ramparts belonged to him, like everything else in his palace and in his nation.

He picked up the eggs and hurled them, one by one, into the valley below. Every creature in his kingdom, large or small, lived or died by his hand. In his new calm, he considered the implications of Antony's wedding gift to Cleopatra. The loss of his land holdings enraged him, but what recourse did he have? Antony was within his rights to make such a gift. Any objection would only court his wrath. He heard light footsteps on the tower staircase. His wife stepped out on the walkway, shivering in her white linen sleeping robe. In the moonlight, she shone like a pearl, ethereally beautiful. They sat down together on the low ledge of a parapet.

Sleep evades me," he said

"Me too," she said. "Is something on your mind?"

"Antony has married Cleopatra. He's given her some of my lands as a wedding gift. I've lost Jericho and my income from its balsam and date groves."

She raised her eyebrows and nodded.

"The date groves lie in some of my most fertile lands, and balsam bark and oil are a great source of our wealth. Antony will allow me to lease these lands back from Cleopatra for whatever usurious price she offers me. I fear our treasury will shrink considerably while my groves enrich her coffers."

"You have other sources of wealth."

"Cleopatra has always had more land and gold than I do. Now, she has even more, and I, less. My spies tell me she has designs on all my lands. Her charms blind Antony to reason. Her greed threatens me."

"Friends pose less danger than enemies," said Mariamne. "Nurture your friendship with Antony. Tomorrow, I will send the newlyweds our Egyptian-gold wine goblets."

Herod smiled. His wife had sharp political instincts when it came to royal etiquette, a subject he was not highborn enough to know. "I've already sent the Egyptian envoy with a wedding gift. Let's send the goblets, too, on the next caravan to Egypt. I must remind Antony and Cleopatra of my loyalty."

~

*H*erod and Mariamne sat on their thrones in the presence chamber. Herod had just finished hearing villagers' petitions on sheep and horse theft allegations and petty border disputes. After the last petitioner of the day, a messenger donning Egyptian robes held out a scroll. Herod was tired, and in no mood for trouble, especially from Egypt. Had Antony purloined more of his land and gifted it to his avaricious new wife? With trepidation, he read.

> **Marc Antony of the Roman Triumvirate hereby summons Herod, son of Antipater, to report immediately to Alexandria to answer to charges for the murder of Prince Aristobulus III, Grandson of King Hyrcanus of Judea.**

A vein throbbed in Herod's forehead. If Antony found him guilty, he would execute him on the spot. He stole a glance at Mariamne, right beside him. It did not matter that his insides were turning to jelly. He must appear calm and dignified. "Everyone, except Queen Mariamne, leave this chamber now."

Courtiers and petitioners scurried out, and he and his wife were alone.

"What is it, Herod?" asked Mariamne. "Your face has lost all color."

Herod's mouth was so dry he wondered if he would be able to speak. He took a gulp of citron juice, and immediately felt nauseated.

He considered his approach. Must Mariamne know? Could he hide the summons from her? She would, at some point, learn of his murder charge. Such news tended to spread swiftly. Nothing is truly secret in this world. Cleopatra would inform Princess Alexandra, who would promptly advise Mariamne. If he did not tell her, she was going to learn from someone else, and he would not be able to control the way someone else presented it to her. Best she should hear it from him.

"Antony has summoned me to Alexandria."

Her eyes grew big and round as silver coins. "Why?" she asked.

"He has accused me of responsibility for Aris's death," he said, avoiding eye contact. "It's preposterous, insulting."

Mariamne bounded off her throne and wrested the scroll from Herod's hands. "Let me see this." She read it and looked up at Herod in horror. "Murder," she whispered.

"Cleopatra must be behind this spurious charge. She wants me dead. You know that."

She shook her head, looking down at the letter.

He mustered outrage. "I didn't lay a hand on your brother." He took her cold hands in his and kissed them. "Antony's accusation is false. You were there. You saw everything. Your brother drowned. It's tragic. I grieve for him, still. Surely you won't let Cleopatra cause trouble between us?"

His tight-lipped wife stiffened and backed away from him as if he was someone to fear.

"How dare you doubt me," thundered Herod, but she was already gone.

~

*H*erod trudged over to the bathhouse. Alone there, he undressed and slipped into the warm, enveloping water. Behind thick stone walls, he might be able to rage at the top of his lungs about the indignity of Antony's accusation.

Mariamne's reaction to the murder charge infuriated him. He knew who was behind it. To do him such harm was well beyond the capabilities of doddering old Hyrcanus, but the former king's brazen daughter, Princess Alexandra, was another story, entirely. He could well imagine his mother-in-law's tear-stained scroll, another one that had somehow slipped by his spies, begging Cleopatra to persuade Antony to accuse him of murder.

Everyone was aware of Pharaoh's strong influence over Antony, and how she loathed the triumvir's friendship with him. Cleopatra did whatever she could to undermine him whenever the opportunity arose. After he had turned down Cleopatra's offer to stay in Alexandria to serve as her chief general, his spies had overheard her tell her underlings she despised him.

Cleopatra and Princess Alexandra—what had he done to deserve these two dragons?

In the weak light of a single torch, Herod bobbed up and down in the balmy water, the rich steam rising around him. Still, he could not relax. How could he? His very existence was in jeopardy. Had he handed Cleopatra the rope with which to hang him? He thought about it, and concluded that no, he had not. He had been careful. No one could have even a shred of evidence implicating him. None existed. No one knew he had arranged his brother-in-law's murder except for the killers themselves, buried in unmarked graves.

"I'll never let them destroy me!" he screamed. His words reverberated off the bathhouse's marble walls. Had anybody heard? He looked around and was relieved no one was present.

After his bath, Herod dressed in royal apparel, white silk robes lined in royal purple, and his golden crown. It was time for him to confront Princess Alexandra. He summoned his guards and the old cur to his presence chamber.

His mother-in-law approached his throne. He turned the full power of his penetrating stare on her pale, pinched face. "I'm sure it comes as no surprise to you that Antony has charged me with murder for Aris's death."

She did not bother to feign surprise.

"You're responsible for this travesty. I can think of no one else in the land who would have the audacity to make false accusations and involve Antony and Cleopatra in your son's tragic demise."

Princess Alexandra's visage went red with rage. "Did you think, Herod, son of Antipater the Idumean, that you could kill my son, the Crown Prince of Judea, with impunity?"

Herod rose and descended from the throne platform. With fists tightly balled, he loomed over his mother-in-law and pointed his scepter at her, stopping inches from her chest. She took a step backward and lost her balance. She would have fallen without a guard's assistance.

"You pushed Antony and Cleopatra to accuse me of murder— it's treason!"

Princess Alexandra's defiant glare raised his ire. His guards stepped forward, ready to seize her.

"God saw what you did," she said, pointing a gnarled finger at him.

"Your son's death had nothing to do with me."

"Aris would never have drowned in that puddle of a pool if your henchmen hadn't held him under water." All of a sudden, she bolted toward him. His guards blocked her with crossed swords. Tears streamed down her wizened face as she struggled in vain with his brawny men.

"You couldn't stand how the people loved Aris, could you,

Herod?" she said between sobs. "You knew they would oust you in his favor. So, you killed him."

Herod swallowed his mounting anger. He must appear to be in command. "I'm afraid grief has addled your mind."

Princess Alexandra smiled bitterly. "My mind is fine, I can assure you. No doubt your spies have made you aware that Cleopatra and I correspond. Of course, I told my dear friend you drowned my son. But it was she who involved Antony."

"Which was certainly no surprise. Congratulations on your success. You stirred the brew of trouble for me even as I suffer my own grief for Aris."

She threw her head back and laughed. "You, suffer grief? The only skin you care about is your own."

How he would delight in wrapping his hands around her wrinkled little neck. How he would relish squeezing it and seeing her crumple like a rag doll at the foot of his throne. How he would savor seeing her body twitch as life left her. But now was not the time. He pointed to her. "Guards, take this woman away."

Herod signaled his courtiers and servants to leave with a wave of his hand. Alone again, he paced back and forth across the marble floor, his mind racing. How had the correspondence reached Cleopatra? Long ago, he had ordered his spies and servants to intercept every letter or document entering or leaving Antonia Fortress. What wily ways had Princess Alexandra used to send her message to Cleopatra, without his detection? He would question every servant until he found the one responsible for this breach. Someone would pay.

He must prepare to leave Jerusalem to face Antony's charges. Who could he trust to govern while he was away? His uncle and Salome's estranged husband, Yusef, was the first man who came to mind. After Salome had left him, the kind and sensible man had continued to work as a clerk in Herod's administration. Yusef had never given him any reason to doubt his loyalty. He summoned him to his presence chamber. The white-bearded old man soon appeared before him.

"I must leave soon to stand trial in Alexandria. Antony and

Cleopatra have made false accusations against me. I'm blameless, of course, but the charges against me are serious. If Antony finds me guilty, he will execute me."

"But surely that won't happen," said Yusef, his brow knitted with concern. "As you have said, you're innocent."

Herod nodded, grimly. "I'm appointing you viceroy in my absence, Yusef. You are to hear and rule on my subjects' petitions. I am giving you the authority to conduct all matters of state."

Yusef 's eyes grew shiny with delight. "I'm honored, King Herod."

"By law, the king or the queen must co-sign edicts…"

"Yes, I have thought of that. You will meet with Queen Mariamne every day for signatures."

"Thank you," said Yusef with a bow, his voice deep and quivering with emotion. "It's a tremendous honor to serve you. As always, I will do what you ask of me."

～

*T*he day before Herod left for Alexandria, he heard subjects' pleas in his presence chamber. He was apprehensive about the upcoming trial, and it was difficult to focus on the parade of people, all wanting something, who came before him. Something about the last man of the day, a bony ancient with bare feet, a thin, wispy beard, and soulful eyes, touched Herod.

"What brings you here?" he asked.

The old one stood quaking before him. "Honorable King, drought has killed my village's wheat crop. There will be no harvest in the South this year. I fear our village will starve this winter. We need gold to buy grain from farmers in the North. Galilee had rain this year, and a good harvest. We can buy grain from them if you will kindly help us."

"Are your neighboring villages suffering as well?" Herod asked. "They are, Your Highness."

Herod was not going to let his people starve. "Where's my treasurer?" he asked, searching the crowd of couriers lingering on the fringes of the chamber.

A short man with a ponderous belly shuffled forward.

"I want the treasury to buy two hundred barrels of grain from Galilee. Distribute it to every western village in drought," Herod said.

"You have already earmarked the remaining treasury funds for war," said the treasurer.

Herod stroked his dark beard and nodded. "Ah, yes. War funds are sacrosanct."

"There's the Temple Treasury, Your Majesty. Or you might raise taxes."

To raid the Temple Treasury was out of the question, and the people would likely revolt if he raised taxes. He could easily crush any protest, but Rome did not smile on a king who used force against too many of his own subjects. He was already widely disliked; he did not need to generate more enemies. With much of Judea in drought, there was little in the way of crops to tax.

He looked levelly at the old man. "I'll give you gold from my own chest. Buy grain and deliver it to those in need."

"You're giving him a gift from your personal funds?" the treasurer asked, incredulous.

"I am."

The old man's eyes filled with tears. He folded himself into a deep bow. "Thank you, good King Herod, thank you. We will be eternally grateful for your kindness."

Herod nodded, beneficently.

Would his act of compassion and generosity finally make his people love him? He doubted it. No matter how many kindnesses he bestowed upon them, he would feel the contempt behind their obsequiousness. They did not accept him as one of their own. Many did not even consider him a Jew, because his family had been forcibly converted to Judaism when Judea vanquished his grandfather's native Idumea more than a generation ago. Nothing he did pleased his people.

Ah, the people, his biggest headache. They said they wanted law and order, yet they called him ruthless when he separated heads from necks to enforce Roman Law. The previous year, he had cut taxes by a third, more than any other king before him. He also began building the world's most modern seaport, Caesarea Marittima, near the ancient Port of Acre. Had more than a few subjects thanked him or even noticed? Their ingratitude maddened him.

He wished his subjects could understand how political considerations required him to build temples dedicated to Roman gods in cities outside Jerusalem, and how the vast and expensive improvements he was going to make on the Temple more than adequately compensated for his nod to Rome's gods. The magnificent new temple would outshine everything built before it, a worthy tribute to the One True God.

He could only wonder how it might feel to hear his people call out, "Long Live King Herod!" when he rode down the street in his golden carriage, or when he stood on his southern terrace, waving benevolently.

It was folly, he reminded himself, to indulge in self-aggrandizement and daydreams when he might soon face execution.

~

*A*t the height of summer, when the sun seared everything in its unforgiving path, Herod left for Alexandria to stand trial for the murder accusation. He kept his eyes fixed on the Judean shore as the ship slipped away from the land, its sails billowing in a steady breeze. Would he ever see his homeland again? There was a good chance he would never return.

About one thing he was certain: Cleopatra wanted him gone. He figured her plan to encourage Antony to eliminate him went well beyond revenge for his rejection of her offer, and her conviction that he was not fit to wear royal robes. If Antony executed him, Pharaoh could annex his lands without obstacle. Love-addled Antony might well gift his beloved Herod's entire nation to her as a token of his enchantment.

Herod shook off these discomfiting thoughts and reminded

himself of his grand destiny. As the greatest Judean King who had ever worn the crown, Herod would lead his people in peace and prosperity, and build structures and entire cities so magnificent that immortality would be his. Before he could do this, however, he must convince Antony he was innocent while concealing his rage for the audacious charge based on nothing but the finger-pointing of the old crone, Princess Alexandra.

Antony and Cleopatra could not possibly have a shred of evidence against him. He had a firm alibi, and he had seen to it that no one who knew the truth still lived. As always, the image of Mariamne hovered in the upper reaches of his mind. After he had put her mother under constant guard, Miriamne had treated him with coldness, brushing away his advances and refusing to speak to him. He would try to make her love him if Antony deigned to allow him to return to Jerusalem.

After hours of swift sailing, windless skies slowed the vessel's progress. For days, it bobbed in the sea like a wooden bath toy, with little forward movement, giving Herod too much time to think and worry. Was this difficult voyage an omen of what was to come?

Once near the Egyptian coast, the winds finally strengthened. The craft glided on a tranquil sea past massive marble buildings, bone-white against a stark cerulean sky, into Alexandria Harbor. Herod tried to shake off his sense of impending doom.

He disembarked at the port, fully expecting Antony and Cleopatra to be there to greet him. They were not. He keenly felt the insult of their absence. Abject, he sat on the stone steps and watched squawking gulls dip and dive into the sea while he waited for a royal vessel to take him to Pharaoh's Palace.

It was not until the afternoon sun was at mid-descent when a gilded boat slipped into the harbor. A painted likeness of Cleopatra stretched across its side. The sight of it made Herod's stomach cramp. A servant in white and gold Egyptian livery ushered him inside. Sailing down Alexandria's Royal Canal, the vessel glided past the pillared House of Isis gleaming in the sunlight. From childhood lessons, he knew Isis was the goddess of funerals as well as the

protector of Kings. Would she protect him, or usher him to his
funeral?

Pharaoh's massive marble palace, surrounded by high palms,
stood alone on a verdant island. An unsmiling servant took him
through the back door, the same one tradesmen and servants were
using, another shocking slight. He escorted Herod to his quarters, a
plush prison with white marble floors and a wool-stuffed bed.
Cleopatra's servants brought in steaming bowls of fattened fowl and
beef in fig sauce. Hunger brought him directly to the table, where
he tasted the flavors of exotic spices. Could it be cumin and garlic,
and perhaps some cinnamon? There were chickpeas and lentils, and
a salad of lettuce, cucumbers, and onions, far more than he was
able to consume in his uneasy state. It was, perhaps, his last meal.

Herod drank an entire vessel of wine and quickly fell asleep. He
had a nightmare of his own beheading, in which he felt the
agonizing pain of the sword's sharp blade, and saw his blood spilling
over the platform. He awoke after a fitful slumber to dawn's
lavender light. Breakfast was already on the table near his bed. He
bit down on a hard, gritty chunk of buttered bread, and felt a sharp
pain. He felt a loose tooth in the back of his mouth with his tongue.
How could the Egyptians eat such stone-hard rubbish? He pushed
the food away.

From an open window, he watched a black asp slither across the
lawn. Another bad omen? The sound of his door creaking open
made him start. Two imperial guards stood in his doorway.

"Time for trial," a guard said.

Herod's legs felt unsteady as Cleopatra's guards took him past
the granite statues of Pharaoh's eminent ancestors, Egypt's former
Pharaohs. Two great stone lions crouched on both sides of the
entrance to her presence hall. Their yellow-jewel eyes seemed to
follow him accusingly.

Antony and Cleopatra peered down at him from the throne dais
in the massive hall of marble floors and walls. Herod's forehead vein
pulsed as he forced himself into a prideful posture. He bowed and
gave them a polite nod. Pharaoh's cool gaze made clear her disdain,
but Antony's expression was blank, unreadable.

"You look terrible," said Cleopatra, taunting him with a snide smile. The folds of her white dress with a gold-cloth bodice flowed elegantly to the dais floor. Her elaborate headdress, tall and bright with emeralds and rubies, struck Herod as funny, but he held back his inappropriate urge to laugh. Just nerves. He bowed.

"You, Pharaoh, look more beautiful than ever, my ageless friend." She did have a satisfied glow about her.

She rewarded him with a hint of a smile, but her kohl-lined eyes remained stony.

Antony's fingers drummed absently against the arms of his throne. Herod knew the Roman well, and he did this when he felt uncomfortable. The triumvir's obvious distress in seeing his long-time ally standing before him on a murder charge heartened Herod and gave him a glimmer of hope.

"How do you answer, Herod?" Antony asked. "Did you, or did you not, kill your brother-in-law, Aristobulus III, Grandson of Hyrcanus II ben Maccabee?"

Herod forced himself to look into Antony's sharp brown eyes. "I did not."

"Have you evidence of your innocence?" Antony asked.

He handed the triumvir an animal-skin bag of scrolls he had brought with him. "Men who had attended my Jericho feast have all attested that they were dining with me at the time of the Maccabee's accidental drowning."

Antony read them silently and, with a knowing look, handed them to Cleopatra. She perused them and, one by one, dropped them at her feet. A servant scrambled over to collect them.

"We are aware, Herod, that you did not drown Princess Alexandra's son by your own hand," said Cleopatra, sounding exasperated. "But did you order your servants or guards or anyone else to drown Prince Aris?"

Beginning to believe his innocence, Herod resented the audacity of this accusation. He met Cleopatra's piercing gaze. "I did not." Humbly, he hung his head. "Aris's drowning was a tragic accident."

Cleopatra sat arrow-straight on her throne. "You thought your people's love for Aris threatened your hold on the Judean Crown, did you not?"

"No, Pharaoh. I loved Aris like a brother. Had I believed he posed a threat, I would not have appointed him high priest."

Antony's expression went hard, menacing. "You appointed Aris high priest because I had commanded you to do it."

Herod knew he had blundered, perhaps fatally. By sheer force of will, he stilled his trembling limbs. He must appear innocent; his life depended on it. He fixed an innocent gaze on Antony.

"Poor Princess Alexandra, to see her beloved son murdered on her own son-in-law's orders."

Cleopatra was a fine one to talk. How he longed to recite the list of Pharaoh's kin she had murdered to seize her position of power. In her ruthless quest to rule Egypt, she had a hand in the execution of three of her four siblings. The Egyptian throne had long gone to the survivor of the Ptolemaic siblings' bloodbath.

"The matter is most unfortunate," said Herod. "However, I did not kill Princess Alexandra's son, nor did I order anyone else to kill him."

Cleopatra gave him an icy smile with lips stained red by berries. She was enjoying his ordeal. "It is said that you have done many brutal things to your people. Would you agree?"

He was going to die, but he would defend himself so long as he had a heartbeat. "I do what's necessary to enforce Rome's law and to keep order, as every provincial king of the Roman Republic must do." With his back spear straight, Herod fixed his gaze on Antony. "May I remind you of the loyalty I've shown you, both in tribute and on the battlefield, whenever you required my assistance?"

Antony cocked his head and gave him a long look. "It's true, Herod. You have been a good friend. The Parthians would have defeated us in Samosota had you not sent in your army and turned the tide in our favor."

Herod bowed low to the triumvir. "I was honored to support you. Like my father before me, I will always be loyal to you, Antony. Gold, men, whatever you need is yours for the asking."

Antony rose to his feet and grinned, his relief plain on his smooth face. "Enough. We have nothing at all connecting you to Aris's death. You have swept the Parthians from your lands as you promised you would." Unapologetic, he turned to Cleopatra. "We need vassal kings we can depend on."

She drew back in surprise.

"I believe your words," Antony added. "From this day forward, you are a free man, exonerated of all charges."

Herod knew he should contain his joy, but he could not stop himself from beaming at Cleopatra's outraged expression. Her fury tasted as sweet as honeyed bread.

Antony laid his thick, hairy hand over Pharaoh's. "It's over, my love. I have made my decision."

Cleopatra stormed out of her presence chamber, flanked by her entourage of slaves and servants.

The Roman triumvir turned to Herod with all of the warmth of a gracious host to a welcome guest. "I hope you will join us for dinner and entertainment this evening?"

Herod nodded and thanked him. He returned to his quarters and, with sweet relief, collapsed on his bed.

∾

The next morning, Herod broke his fast in Cleopatra's marble-domed banqueting hall. Life-sized, winged angel statutes lined the edges of the vast chamber, impressive indeed. He still had a headache from last night's overindulgence in fine Roman wine. Dinner had been lavish, with a myriad of Egyptian delicacies and a performance by a troupe of Chinese acrobats. How remarkable that a body might twist itself in so many directions. It was an awkward evening, however. Maintaining her chilly demeanor, Cleopatra did not speak to him, while Antony treated him with the warmth of a long-time friend and ally, and proudly introduced him to royal and aristocratic Egyptians.

Then, a dignified and strikingly handsome stranger stood beside his chaise. The man had cloud-white hair and the strong jaw and

symmetrical features of a Greek god. He introduced himself to
Herod as Nicholas of Damascus.

"I'm a court historian," Nicholas said, bowing. "I've tutored
Pharaoh's son for years. He's just gone off to study in Rome. I'm
leaving today to seek another position."

Herod motioned to the couch next to his own, and Nicholas
lounged there.

"Antony has often spoken to me of your keen intelligence, King
Herod."

It occurred to him that if this erudite Roman joined his household, he would have an intellectual equal with whom he could
discuss the political vagaries of the republic and elite Roman opinion. He might even engage him in debates on some of the subtler
points of Greek Philosophy. Most important, the eminent scholar
could author the history of his reign.

"I'd like for you to serve as my court historian in Jerusalem,"
Herod said.

Nicholas looked up from his breakfast and met his eyes. "I am
not inexpensive," he said.

"Name your price," Herod said. Immediately, anxiety struck
him. What if Mariamne found this eminent Roman appealing and
wanted him? The handsome historian might tempt his wife. They
could become lovers. Intolerable! The thought of it made him
seethe. Still, Herod wanted, no, he needed, this highly intelligent
man to write an insightful and flattering record of his reign.

Herod found a brilliant solution to his quandary. He brought
Nicholas into his household, but he hid him from his wife in a
remote corner of the South wing, an area of the palace she had no
reason to go. Only when his wife was lodging at another palace did
Nicholas have the freedom to roam Antonia Fortress's common halls
and chambers. When Mariamne was home, he confined Nicholas to
the South wing. His queen need never know of the handsome
Roman's existence.

37

MARIAMNE, 33 BCE, JERUSALEM

*B*y the glow of lamplight, Lila and I were embroidering my new silk robes. No one else was around. The hearth fire crackled, and the light of the oil lamp cast a warm glow. "You have been so quiet lately, Mariamne."

"Hmmm, yes. I have much on my mind." Herod was away in Alexandria answering to murder charges for my brother's death. I was on edge about the future. Whatever Antony decided, my family had a difficult road ahead.

"Tell me what's wrong."

Perhaps the cozy intimacy of the evening loosened my tongue. I knew my secrets were safe with my handmaiden. "If Antony absolves Herod of guilt and sets him free, the man who most likely killed my brother will come home. Who would he kill next? What if my mother is right, and Herod wants to murder all of us with Maccabee blood in our veins?"

"Oh, Mariamne," said Lila, her voice soothing and full of compassion.

"So, if Antony releases Herod, it means he still has confidence in him, and we won't be able to recover the crown while Herod still lives. And Antony or Herod will swiftly execute us for asking for it."

"Do you think your family is in danger of execution?"

"I do. Mother wrote to Cleopatra to ask her to persuade Antony to charge Herod with Aris's murder. We can only hope she and Antony have stayed mum about the letter. Herod will kill us all if he suspects our involvement."

"He will," said Lila, nodding.

"But if the triumvir finds Herod guilty at trial, he will execute him. Then my family would be without protection from outsiders as well as from other Maccabees who would gladly kill us to keep us away from the throne. Any successor to Judean rule would, first and foremost, need my family out of the way. Then, I would ask Antony to make me Alexander's regent until he comes of age to rule. But Rome doesn't like to set up vassal regencies. Alexander is still very young, so my regency would be a long one. I doubt Rome will agree to it."

"If Rome refuses to appoint you regent, as Herod's widow, Rome could make you the ruling queen."

I nodded. "I'd rather rule myself than have my mother crowned queen. She desperately wants it. Cleopatra is her friend. She will ask Pharaoh to persuade Antony to make her queen. I cannot let that happen. She would be a despot. Her rule would be disastrous for all Judea."

"We will have to wait and see what happens with Herod," Lila said.

"Yes," I said. "And it is so hard to wait."

38

HEROD, 31 BCE, JERUSALEM & NABATAEA

*A*fter Antony dismissed him, Herod returned to Jerusalem. Mariamne was polite enough, but there was no warmth in her smile. She slipped away whenever he tried to embrace or kiss her, and she refused to let him love her as a husband should love a wife. To avoid him, she often left to lodge in other palaces. Her enduring chill puzzled him. Antony had absolved him of the murder charge, yet his wife continued to treat him as if she believed he was the man responsible for her brother's death. More than anything, he wanted her to love him.

To distract himself, he spent many evenings with Nicholas, who was becoming a trusted friend. If he was not listening to Salome play her harp or attending palace entertainments, he spent his evenings with Nicholas. They had spirited debates on Greek Philosophy and Rome's political intrigues while downing wine. Their invigorating discourse took him back to the rigorous but rewarding scholarship of his youth. Nicholas was good for him; he knew that. A king must have, above all, a sharp mind.

One night in his library, Herod and Nicholas were lounging side-by-side on silk-pillowed chaises. They shared a bowl of sweet figs and had a vigorous debate on Plato's *a priori* concept and the nature of recollection. Herod scored his final, winning point, and threw back an entire goblet in victory. His wife found gulping uncouth, so he took particular joy in doing it when she was not around.

Then, the smile left Herod's face. "There is a matter I must discuss with you, Nicholas."

"Yes?"

"Cleopatra's pull on Antony is strong. He can't—or won't—resist her. My spies tell me he's lingering too long in Egypt and neglecting his duties at home. Octavian is incensed, and the Senate is losing patience with him."

Nicholas nodded. "Antony divorced his Roman wife Octavia, Octavian's sister, to marry Cleopatra. Relations between the triumvirs have never been worse."

"Pharaoh's influence on Marc Antony sickens me," said Herod. "Antony has allowed his lust to overpower his rational mind and his sense of self-preservation. He will do anything for Cleopatra. Whatever she wants, he gives her." Herod stroked his dark beard. "They tell me she's trying to sway Antony to grant her more of my lands."

"Antony probably has more pressing matters to concern him," said Nicholas. "Both Antony and Octavian want to be Rome's sole emperor. War is coming."

"I will pledge my support to Antony, of course," said Herod.

"Let's hope you will be backing the winner," said Nicholas.

A hard knock on the door startled him. "Yes?" Herod called.

His guard stood in the doorway. "Pharaoh's envoy has an urgent message for you."

"Enter," he called. The lamplight threw a pale yellow wash on the papyrus the envoy handed to Herod. He read it to Nicholas.

Nabataeans are, once again, attacking your southern villages, looting, stealing, and burning homes and public buildings. They are angry that Rome's new trade routes have bypassed their territory. The Nabataeans are no longer collecting gold from Caravans' use of their roads and purchase of food and lodging, and they are lashing out. Antony wants you to send your army south to keep them in line. Most of Rome's soldiers are not available. They are away fighting other skirmishes and border incursions.

To show my gratitude for your loyal support, I will send you my finest general and additional soldiers to your camp in Nabataea.

Cleopatra, Pharaoh and Queen of Egypt

Herod looked up from the scroll and met Nicholas's worried gaze. "Whatever ails the Nabataeans, they cannot invade Roman territory with impunity. We will ready our army for war."

~

When the torrential winter downfall dissipated, and the sodden ground gave way to the first crocuses of spring, Herod and his commanders were ready to head south for war in Nabataea. However, the day before they were to leave, Cleopatra arrived on Herod's doorstep without invitation or advance announcement. Accompanying the Pharaoh were her contingent of guards and courtiers, all hungry, thirsty, and in need of lodging. Herod was in no mood to entertain Pharaoh and her entourage.

As graceful as a swan, draped in gold silk and jeweled in gold and lapis, Cleopatra glided into the Antonia Fortress reception hall. Herod greeted her with kisses on her soft, smooth cheeks. Behind his diplomatic smile, he seethed at the unwelcome surprise. She smelled of *balsoma*, the prized Ein Gedi perfume worth more than its weight in gold. To Herod, it smelled like trouble.

Cleopatra looked around the massive hall, and her black eyes gleamed with avarice at all she surveyed. She lifted statues from tables to take a closer look at them, and circled Herod's favorite life-sized statue, an angel of pure gold. Had she been a dog, she would have squatted and marked it to claim it as her own.

"How lovely, Herod," Cleopatra said as she nodded toward the angel statue. "I'm glad you have the good taste to adorn your palace with Egyptian gold."

"It was a gift from Marc Antony," he said. "He knows I favor Egypt's gold—the best in the world. Please, Pharaoh, come join me for wine in my lotus garden."

She followed him into the courtyard garden, where beds of delicate white blossoms perfumed the spring air. The soothing sounds of the fountain's cascading water and the hum of cicadas seemed to mock the uneasiness he felt in Pharaoh's mercurial presence.

He took a silk-cushioned, marble chaise. Cleopatra waved away her hangers-on to the periphery of the garden, and she lounged beside him. His servant poured her his finest Falernian wine into a silver goblet. Herod caught her almost imperceptible nod to her cupbearer, who took a discreet sip. Then, Pharaoh smiled at Herod as if she had not just insulted him.

"Surely you don't think I would poison your wine," said Herod.

"Never," said Cleopatra, meeting his eyes, grinning too brightly. "Just as you, King Herod, have no reason to mistrust me."

Herod cleared his throat. "Tell me, what brings your Royal Majesty here to the fringe of Roman settlement?"

A shadow crossed Cleopatra's face. "That greedy bastard Octavian wants to oust Antony and Lepidus and rule Rome as her sole emperor. He has declared war on Egypt."

Herod felt his pulse quicken.

"Octavian is furious because Antony has set aside his sister, Octavia, to marry me," Cleopatra added. "But greed is the real reason Octavian is no longer willing to rule as a member of the triumvirate and share power and riches. He wants it all for himself."

Herod's shoulders tensed. This could be the end of the world as he knew it. He cleared his throat. "As always, you and Antony have my full support. Soldiers, supplies, weapons, anything you need is yours for the asking. And I'll gladly take my place among your generals."

Cleopatra lifted her perfect eyebrows. "Once we triumph over Octavian, I will see to it that Antony amply rewards you."

He grinned broadly. Now was his chance, and he was going to take it. "My offer is a standing one, but I do have conditions."

She cocked her head. "I am listening."

"Return my coastal lands, and my date and balsam groves Antony has given to you, and then I will take my army to Nabataea."

Cleopatra blinked hard. "For your loyalty, I will return your lands and groves. I will have the documents drawn up as soon as I return to Alexandria."

He would confirm it before he took his men to do battle for her. "Now, how can I be of assistance to you and Antony? I would gladly postpone the Nabataean campaign to join you and Antony against greedy Octavian."

She stared at him with large, dark, spellbinding eyes. What was she scheming now? How he despised every shiny black hair on her arrogant head.

"Antony wants you to do something for me when you are in Nabataea," said Cleopatra, her face set hard. "King Aretas owes me tribute. He has not responded to the measures I have taken to collect it. After your victory there, and I am certain it will be a victory, I want you to pay a visit to Nabataean King. Wrest what is mine from his coffers. Have your most trusted men bring me the gold."

Herod tried to keep his face impassive while he considered Cleopatra's audacious request he could not refuse. Was she conniving to destroy him? He could not confirm that the command came from Antony without insulting her, and Antony made those who insulted Pharaoh pay dearly. One thing was clear. She was sending him on an underling's errand when a civil war loomed. If it would not guarantee his execution, he would gladly ready her for mummification.

Burning inside, he bowed to her. "I'm at your service."

"Thank you, Herod. Tomorrow I will send my best general and one thousand soldiers to your camp. I must return to Alexandria in the morning."

"So soon? What a shame. I've arranged for a banquet in your

honor this evening." He had not, but now, he would. He would serve her his finest delicacies on golden dishes.

She smiled. "Lovely. I will go to my quarters now."

After Cleopatra left, Herod went up to the ramparts, where he could pace and think in blessed silence. It rankled him that she was sending him to lead a relatively minor campaign while barring him from the more significant struggle between Antony and Octavian. She knew Herod's army would outshine hers if she allowed him to join them. She was not going to let him attain the status of Antony's war hero as he once did in Samosota.

That night, Herod's servants and slaves hurried to arrange Cleopatra's feast, complete with lute players and theatre actors for her amusement. It cost him a fortune, and a great deal of dignity.

∼

*A*ll summer long, his army battled the Nabataeans. The Egyptian general and the soldiers Cleopatra had promised to send him never arrived. Herod, invigorated in his fury, won several early battles without Egyptian support. During a particularly pitched fight, he watched in astonishment as Cleopatra's highest-ranking military commander, General Tutakhan, and hundreds of Egyptian soldiers, distinctive in their chain-mail armor, rode out alongside the Nabataeans to fight against Herod's army.

That night, Herod lay in his camp bed and seethed about Cleopatra's betrayal. She had deceived him, and now, Herod was losing. He questioned whether Antony had asked Pharaoh to send him to battle in Nabataea, or if she had lied to undermine him. Perhaps Cleopatra wanted to force Judea and Nabataea to thin each other's ranks in battle so she could later convince Antony to divide the spoils and let her rule both war-weakened nations.

He vowed he would never again let Cleopatra deceive him. Her promises were camel dung to him now. He could not kill her, so he must outfox her.

∼

*W*eeks later, in the starless darkness before dawn, cold rain fell like small blades on Herod's back. He was leading his men to the Nabataean Army's camp. A thick blanket of fog shrouded the enemy's tents and concealed their approach.

At first light, his army attacked and defeated the Nabataeans in less than an hour. Not one enemy soldier was left alive. The battle proved decisive in the victory over his southern neighbors. As a condition of peace, Herod collected the tribute their chastened king owed Cleopatra, and he sent trusted commanders to Alexandria with the gold. In the rosy glow of victory, Herod headed home, certain Nabataea would not trouble Rome again. Despite Cleopatra's treachery, Herod had won.

39

MARIAMNE, 31 BCE, JERUSALEM

With Herod away at war in Nabataea, I could breathe freely again. Every morning, I took my children and their nurses to the gardens. We played games, hiding behind trees and bushes, searching for each other. I cared not that the nurses, who pushed my daughters in strolling carts, pursed their lips in disapproval at my childish behavior. When I tired of the children, I sent them back to the schoolroom and the nursery, and I painted.

On a warm spring morning in the courtyard, Lila was preparing a rare ruby pigment, mixing ground rubies with water, and I was wetting down the wall plaster when my mother made an unwelcome appearance. She often approached me with a serious topic when all I wanted to do was to disappear inside the rhythm of my brush-strokes and the beauty of the world I painted.

"Mariamne, we must make plans. Herod will die in battle and—"

"How do you know Herod will die in battle? Herod has survived many wars."

"Well, it is possible. Whether he dies or not, now that Antony has absolved him of Aris's murder, we must find a way to unseat him and persuade Rome to appoint me queen."

"You know I disagree with that plan. It is Alexander who will be Judea's next king, and it is I who should be his regent."

"What do you know of governance, Mariamne?"

"I know as much as Aris did. I studied alongside him. Of course, he was more of a religious scholar than I was. Neither of us ever had the opportunity to attend council meetings. But I have a fine mind, Mother. You have said so yourself."

"Actually, your grandfather is the oldest surviving Maccabee of the ruling line, and so he should be declared king," my mother said. "But he is old and addled, so I will be the one to rule Judea."

"The Judean Crown will rest on the head Rome selects," I said, keeping my paintbrush moving.

My mother brightened. "I know! I will write to leaders of neighboring nations, and ask them to support my father's claim to the throne."

"Your father is not capable of claiming the throne, so you will be lying."

"You know nothing about politics."

"Please don't send anything to anyone, for now. Let's first see if Herod survives, and then we will better know how to proceed."

~

When Herod returned home from the Nabataean War, I avoided him. I left any chamber he entered. I spoke to him only when he directly addressed me. Each day, I learned of his schedule and circumvented his path. In bed, I firmly pushed him away so many times he stopped making advances. Every time I was forced to look at him, I saw the corpse of my beloved brother.

Herod often traveled to oversee the progress of his many building projects. These were my happiest times. I felt free of the oppressive yoke of his presence. When he returned home, I often left with the children and lodged elsewhere. I could hardly bear to share the same air with Herod.

Meanwhile, my husband was sinking deeper and deeper into unreasonable suspicion and fear for his life. He thought everyone was out for his blood. His excessive fear extended to me. I was returning from a ritual bath one night when Herod summoned me to his library.

I took a few steps inside. "Yes?' I asked with trepidation.

Herod met my gaze. "Tell me, Mariamne, why you treat me with such disdain?"

I said nothing. It was not the time to confront Herod. Before I did that, I needed to have a plan to protect my family.

"What I don't understand is why you still think me guilty of your brother's demise. The Triumvir Antony himself has absolved me of the murder charge. I've told you I'm innocent. It pains me, my love, that you don't believe me. My word should be good enough for you. If you loved me as a wife should love a husband, my word would be enough."

He was staring at me with alarming intensity. I shuddered to imagine what he was thinking.

"Well, have you anything to say?"

I struggled for the right words. I could not express my true convictions and expect to live.

Herod's face fell. "So you will not discuss your brother's accidental drowning death?"

What was there to be gained by discussion? Aris was dead at my husband's command, and I would be next on his execution list if I pressed him too hard on the matter.

"No," I said, softly.

A look of sorrow crossed his face. "Leave me now," he said.

40

HEROD, 31 BCE, JERUSALEM

To Herod's chagrin, his beloved continued to spurn him. When he joined her in their bedchamber, no matter how early he retired, she was already sleeping or pretending to be asleep. Her rejection left him frustrated, and in serious need of a woman's comfort. What choice did he have but to satisfy himself with prostitutes, and with other women who were happy to make themselves available? Backed-up seed was ruinous to a man's health; everyone knew it.

He had caught every one of Mariamne's mistrustful glances when she thought he was not looking. One stormy dawn, Herod awoke to see his beloved's burning gaze upon him, her head cocked, and her eyes questioning. Panic gripped him with the sharp talons of a hawk. What was she thinking? Was she planning his murder? Was she scheming to take the reins of power for herself or her mother? Fear competed with more tender, loving thoughts, and all he could see was the beautiful woman who lay beside him.

～

*S*leep evaded Herod. One night, after trying to fall asleep for hours, Herod arose and paced in the library. How could a man rest when so many enemies plotted to stop his beating heart? They coveted his throne, and they would stop at nothing to attain it. He must unmask the treasonous bastards, every one of them, and kill them.

He dispatched scores of informers to comb the streets for rebels. The mere whisper of a scheme against him earned the traitor torture and an agonizing death. Every time he eliminated a would-be usurper, another sprang up like a weed in a garden. As many times as he beat them down, more surfaced. He was, perhaps, safer on the battlefield than he was in his own land.

41

HEROD, 30 BCE, JERUSALEM

*H*erod was on his way to the reception hall when Nicholas approached him. What was his court historian doing outside of the South wing? He had warned the man to stay away from the common areas of Antonia Fortress when Mariamne was home.

Nicholas's ashen face alarmed Herod. "What's wrong?" he asked.

"Brace yourself, Herod. I've just received disturbing news from Rome. Antony and Cleopatra have lost their naval battle near Actium. Octavian has utterly defeated them."

Herod felt the blood drain from his face. Lightheaded, he sat down.

"Both of them are dead. Cleopatra has taken her own life with the venom of an asp. Antony has died by his own sword. Lepidus, too, has been defeated. Octavian is now the sole Roman Emperor."

Herod jumped up and paced the floor, his sandals scraping marble. He massaged his throbbing forehead. "Defeated. Dead. Antony had tarried too long in Egypt. Drifting away from Rome was folly."

Nicholas shook his head, gravely. "Yes, and Octavian's naval power was superior to that of Antony's and Cleopatra's Armies combined."

"Had Rome and Egypt let my army fight alongside them, the outcome would have been different."

"Perhaps," said Nicholas.

Perhaps? Had he heard his court historian correctly? He turned the full intensity of his glower on Nicholas.

"Of course, it would have been different, King Herod."

"I simply cannot fathom a world without Antony," said Herod. "I'm finished. I've never fought against Octavian, but he must be well aware of my years of loyalty to Antony. He's going to execute me."

"Hide out for a few months," said Nicholas. "Octavian will be too preoccupied establishing his new regime to chase after you. Later on, perhaps a year from now, go to him. Make your apologies. Beg him for mercy. He might let you live."

Herod lumbered out to the terrace, heavy with the weight of his future. Nicholas followed. Both men stood silently at the rail. Herod studied the landscape, from the deep valleys, brown in the summer's drought, to the distant mountains peppered green with olive trees. Everything he beheld belonged to him, but only so long as Rome was on his side. He had to keep it that way. But could he?

"If I go into hiding, Octavian will know I'm trying to evade him. He won't rest until he finds me. I have no choice, Nicholas. I must go to Rhodes right away and pledge my loyalty to the new emperor. I'll ask him to forgive me for my alliance and friendship with Antony."

"King Herod, please, reconsider," said Nicholas, a shadow crossing his face. "I think it's unwise to put yourself at sword's length from Octavian so soon after he has defeated your friend. He could execute you on the spot."

"He might. But Antony is no longer my friend, nor is he Octavian's enemy. He's a dead man."

"How are you going to persuade Octavian to forgive you for all of the gold and soldiers you have showered on Antony these past years?"

"Ah yes, the gold. I must bring along sacks of gold."

~

*T*hat night, Herod left his slumbering wife in their bed and climbed up the dark, winding staircase to the highest tower. Once at the summit, he looked out. The full moon beamed a river of white light on the temple and dwellings and the city walls around them. He mulled over whether he should listen to Nicholas and elude Octavian for a while. His court historian was intelligent and well informed, but Herod's instincts told him he ought to meet with Octavian soon, and throw himself at the new emperor's mercy. To do so, however, meant risking his life.

If his subjects were solidly behind him, Octavian would probably consider that when deciding whether he was going to allow him to keep the throne. But sadly, his people still had little affection for him. He had once believed Judea would accept him after he married into the royal family. It had not happened. He thought they would accept him after he cut taxes, kept the peace, and fattened their purses with wages from working on his building projects. He had built an astounding new skyline in Jerusalem that impressed even the most sophisticated Romans, and he had given generously to the needy. But still, the people had not accepted him. Herod knew this was due to their limitations, and not because of any failings of his own.

His subjects were blind to the Roman advances he brought them. They called him a ruthless brute. They said the new theatre, hippodrome, and coliseum, and the temples to Roman gods he had built in other cities were an affront to God and their way of life, that he showed little respect for Jewish tradition. Their relentless discontent posed a significant threat to his future as king, particularly during this perilous transition period at the dawn of Octavian's rule. Herod wished his subjects could understand that imposing order and the rule of law on a nation was never a bloodless pursuit. Enemies lurked everywhere. Paid ears brought him news of complaints heard from the most elegant villas of the Upper City to the most dilapidated shacks of the Lower City, from the marketplace to the synagogue steps.

They all coveted his throne. Only days ago, his spies had told him of a rebellion developing in the outskirts of Jerusalem. Herod had summarily crushed its leaders. He did not, however, kill the people who merely slandered him with their wagging tongues, but did not scheme to kill their king. He did, however, confiscate their land and gold and sell their children to the slave market.

His spies reported that complaints heard on the street were rare now, but Herod did not believe them. Perhaps they, too, were out for his blood. He would not let them steal his crown. He would outsmart them all. He would continue to show no mercy to those who dared to whisper of rebellion.

But then... There was the even thornier problem; the one that made his heart gallop in the dead of night. It was the woman who lay beside him in bed who posed his most significant threat. She and her mother both coveted his crown. Their positions as queen and queen mother were not enough to satisfy the Maccabees. His mother-in-law was not even the least bit subtle about her lofty ambitions. As for Mariamne, as much as he loved her, if she made a move against him, he would have no choice but to eliminate her. The very thought of this possibility caused him intense pain. No, it would not come to that.

A gust of wind thrust him forward. He steadied himself and sat on a turret. What if the wind swept him off the ramparts to the stones and boulders far below? What if Mariamne found him there, a mangled mess of bones and blood? Would she weep for him? Or would she rejoice in the streets? Perhaps she had never loved him. The thought filled him with rage. He smashed his fist into the closest turret and watched blood stream down his hand.

～

The next day, he found Salome in the reception hall, strumming on her harp. Listening to her play soothed his soul like nothing else. Her music was pure and true, like she was.

"Don't worry about meeting Octavian, Herod." She gave him a sly grin. "You have inherited our father's talent for gaining the trust of important Romans."

Herod laughed. "Our father knew how to shift alliances when necessary. Remember how he had supported Cassius, then switched to Julius Caesar when he became the leader?"

Salome nodded. "The best thing Father did was to persuade Rome to crown Hyrcanus the Judean King rather than his brother, Aristobulus."

Herod nodded and smiled. "Yes, because Father could more easily influence Hyrcanus. Aristobulus was the stronger and more intelligent prince."

"Father ruled Judea in all but title for years. But he was never a king. You have already surpassed him. I know Octavian will have confidence in you."

He nodded to his sister, who always knew the right words to comfort him. But he knew the truth. If he could not win over Octavian, he was a dead man.

~

Herod had to arrange for someone to rule in his stead while he was in Rhodes meeting Octavian. Yusef had done an excellent job as his viceroy two years ago when he had journeyed to Alexandria for the murder trial. Herod summoned him to his library. After Yusef arrived, Herod dismissed his guards and locked the door.

"Tomorrow, I leave for Rhodes to ask Octavian to let me keep the crown. I'm appointing you viceroy in my absence."

Yusef flushed. "Thank you, King Herod," he said, smiling.

"There is one additional duty I'm assigning you this time. My mission in Rhodes is a dangerous one. There is a good chance Octavian will execute me. If you learn from a reliable source that Octavian has executed me, there is something you must do."

"Anything you ask."

"You must kill Mariamne."

Yusef 's jaw fell. "You want me to—"

Herod looked at him, levelly. "I do. If Antony executes me, take Mariamne's life. Strangle her."

"I-I don't understand…"

"You see, Uncle Yusef, my love for Mariamne is so great I cannot bear the thought of her with other men. Nor can I face the world to come without my love. She belongs to me, in death as in life."

"I see," mumbled Yusef, his eyes fixed on the mosaic floor.

"This is an order."

~

*A*fter his conversation with Yusef, Herod felt the taut muscles in his shoulders begin to loosen. If he met his end in Rhodes, it was of some comfort to know that no other man would ever possess his wife. Someday, he and Mariamne would dwell together for all eternity in the Kingdom of Heaven. He closed his eyes and envisioned her soft, warm hand holding his as they approached the Throne of God. If he could not make her love him again in this life, she would love him in the next. Of that, he was certain., it was of some comfort to know that no other man would ever possess his wife. Someday, he and Mariamne would dwell together for all eternity in the Kingdom of Heaven. He closed his eyes and envisioned her soft, warm hand holding his as they approached the Throne of God. If he could not make her love him again in this life, she would love him in the next. Of that, he was certain.

42

MARIAMNE, 30 BCE, JERUSALEM

The morning after Herod left for Rhodes to meet with Octavian, Lila brought me citron juice and threw open my shutters. Outside the window, black-edged clouds amassed over the city. Was it storming at sea? Perhaps Herod's life was in danger before he even met Octavian.

Lila pulled my red silk robe over my linen tunic. "Would you like for me to braid pearls into your hair this morning?" she asked.

I nodded, my mind hundreds of miles away. "Herod is on his way to Rhodes to meet Octavian, Rome's new Emperor. He's going to ask Octavian to allow him to keep his crown. He is in danger Lila. Octavian might not forgive Herod for his friendship with his vanquished enemy, Antony. He could execute him."

Lila twisted my jeweled braid around my head and pinned it up like a crown. "Do you think he will?"

"I don't know. My husband knows how to flatter and charm those who might further his interests. Words they want to hear pour from him like honey. The great lap it up like a thirsty dog. But Octavian might be another story."

I felt a heady lightness. Herod might never come home.

43

HEROD, 30 BCE, RHODES

*H*erod was so nervous when he approached Octavian he nearly soiled his undergarments. The new emperor was not particularly tall or muscular, and he walked with a distinct limp, but his sharp, unnaturally bright eyes showed a keen intelligence. The great man frowned and gave Herod an assessing stare. He did not appear to like what he saw. His face was tight and his mouth, a grim line. Was he going to kill him on the spot?

In hopes of impressing Octavian with his humility, Herod removed his crown and laid it alongside his scepter at Octavian's feet. He said nothing but bowed low to the most powerful man in the world. Then, he stood up and met Octavian's intense gaze. "Emperor Octavian—Augustus—I ask you to look not at whose friend I was, but at the loyalty I've shown my friend."

The emperor's face registered surprise. With a slight smile, he nodded.

That was when Herod began to hope that Octavian would spare his life. "Allow me to keep the throne of Judea, most venerated one, and I swear to serve you with the same loyalty and honor I had once served Antony." Herod pointed to a chest of gold his men had brought just inside the chamber. "Please take this gift as a small token of my esteem."

The emperor began to move toward him, but Herod did not flinch; his fear of the great man had soared away like a dove newly freed from a cage.

Octavian lifted the crown and scepter from the floor. With his own hands, he set the crown on Herod's head and handed him the scepter. "Herod, my friend," he said, "you will remain King of the Jews. I know you will be the same faithful ally to me that you once were to Antony."

Elation swept through him. He was going to live and continue to be king because Octavian respected his past loyalty to Antony. In his relief, he felt as though the emperor had lifted a massive stone from his shoulders.

"I return to you all of the lands Cleopatra seized from you— Gadara, Hippos, Samaria, Gaza, Antriedon, Jappa, the Tower of Stratton," Octavian added. "I also give you the Golan Heights to rule. You will have the weapons and soldiers you need to defend Judea for Rome."

"As vassal King of Judea and your humble servant, I will always defend you. Hail, Augustus!"

Octavian was far more generous than Antony had ever been. With the additional lands the emperor gifted, Herod's kingdom was now close to the size it had been in the days of King David.

Herod fell to his knees. "I thank you, Augustus. I will serve you all of my days."

44

MARIANNE, 30 BCE, JERUSALEM

While Herod was in Rhodes, I spent most days painting frescoes on shaded courtyard walls. Lila mixed water with ground pigments of jewel or ochre to make the paint. The only time I knew true peace was when my brush met wet plaster, and I captured the beauty of nature with torrents of color. I had to work quickly; I could paint only while the plaster was still wet.

When painting no longer soothed my soul, I visited my children in the nursery. Every day, I watched them change and grow. Each new word they learned and step they took delighted me. Through their bright, innocent eyes, the world looked fresh and shiny, and infinitely lovelier.

I often found five-year-old Alexander, a serious child, in his father's library, reading, or trying to read, one of the thousands of scrolls. In a few years, I would have to part with him. Herod was going to send him to school in Rome. For now, he belonged to me.

Despite my terror and dread during little Aris's birth, he had grown into a calm and gentle child, quick to smile and laugh. When he saw me coming, he flashed a smile as bright as a full moon in a cloudless sky, and he held out his arms to me. My copper-haired twin daughters felt soft and warm against my chest when I embraced them. When they grew fidgety, I sat down on the nursery floor and stacked wooden blocks with them. Just looking at my children brought me the most profound joy I had ever known.

Every time I returned to my living quarters after visiting them, I felt a sense of loss in their absence.

~

*W*e spent most evenings sewing tunics and wool robes for the poor. My mother chatted amiably to Cypros while my mother-in-law and her daughter sewed silently. From Salome's pale, sad face and her new quietness, I could see how devastated she was by Herod's dangerous undertaking.

"Will you play the harp, tonight?" Cypros asked. "It is such a comfort to hear your lovely music."

Salome shook her head. "I will play again when Herod returns." She turned to me with narrowed eyes. "You share my worry about Herod's welfare, don't you, Mariamne?" she asked, mockingly.

I ignored her.

That night, I lay sleepless in my bed, agonizing about what would happen if Octavian executed Herod. An empty throne invited takers; there would be no lack of them. My duty was to keep the crown in the family. I would do what I could to convince Rome to appoint me Alexander's regent until he came of age to rule. But if Octavian refused to set up a regency, my family was in the gravest danger. Any newly appointed king would swiftly eliminate my entire family. That much was certain.

~

*E*very day, Yusef and I met in the banqueting hall. Over earthen mugs of beer, we discussed each scroll he put before me for signature. He treated me with kindness, and to my surprise, he was interested in my opinion. It was rare to find a man who respected a woman's mind. Still, ever since Herod left for

Rhodes, Yusef had an uncharacteristic seriousness about him I attributed to the weight of his responsibility as viceroy.

Late one afternoon, the rain lashing Antonio Fortress sounded like stones were pelting the closed shutters. Yusef handed me the final scroll.

"Perhaps you can advise me on how to settle a matter some petitioners have brought to me."

"Go on," I said.

"It's a thorny problem. Avram and Jared both fish the River Jordan. Jared claims Avram's sons drive him away from the more abundant fishing areas as soon as they see him. They must all make a living. How would you resolve this, Queen Mariamne?"

I carefully considered my response. "Advise the men to fish the more abundant waters on alternate days."

He nodded, in serious concentration. "It's a fair solution, I think."

"What are the other petitioner's complaints?"

"The usual. Tenants must pay their landowners a third of their harvest, and the king takes a third. They keep only a third of their crop. Most want their taxes forgiven or reduced, so they have enough food to last the winter."

"I hope you have given them your assent."

Yusef smiled. "You're too kind. We'd have an empty treasury we gave everyone everything they wanted."

I watched Yusef tie together the edicts we had signed with ribbon. The melancholy set of his face worried me.

"What's wrong, Yusef? You can tell me."

He took a long swig of beer and wiped his mouth with his sleeve. "I was thinking about how much Herod adores you. Salome has never loved me the way Herod loves you."

"Do you still love her?"

Sorrow fell over Yusef"'s face. "She's tired of me. She wants a divorce. I've held her off for years. I was hoping she'd change her mind, but now, she's threatening to lie to Herod if I don't divorce her."

"What would she say?"

"That I've been unfaithful to her, and she will see to it that Herod executes me."

"So, Salome would see you die to get her way," I said, bile rising.

"Oh, yes, my wife excels at lying. Why I still love her, I cannot explain. But you and Herod, you two have the greatest love of any two people I've ever known."

With a quiet smile, I nodded. I was not about to divulge my marital difficulties.

"King Herod speaks of you with such adoration. He even said —" Yusef 's mouth snapped shut, and his face turned crimson.

I sat up straighter. "What did Herod say to you, Yusef?"

He shifted on his chaise and scratched his long beard.

"Tell me."

"He said he loves you so much he needs you with him in heaven," Yusef blurted.

A chill snaked down my back. "What do you think he meant by that?"

"He loves you, that's all," Yusef said, his face strained and tight. He picked up the signed scrolls. "I must go now."

I stood up. "Please, wait! Answer my question."

"I can't," he said with a sad shrug, and he began walking out.

I could not let this go. "I have not dismissed you, Yusef. Tell me what Herod said."

Yusef stared down at his worn sandals. It seemed he could not bear to look at me.

"Herod told me…he told me I must kill you if he doesn't return from Rhodes."

I could barely catch my breath. "My husband wants me dead?"

Yusef returned to the table and sat down beside me. "No, no, you have misunderstood. I mean, I haven't made myself clear to you. Herod wants you with him always *because* of his eternal love for you. You see, he can't bear to part with you, even in death."

My breath caught in my throat. "How does he propose you kill me? Strangulation? Hanging? Crucifixion? Did he tell you to take a sword to my belly, or my neck? Does he want you to roll my head at my children's feet?"

"Queen Mariamne—"

"Do you intend to carry out what he's asked of you?" I interrupted. "Will you murder me if Herod doesn't return?"

His silence told me his answer. "Leave me, Yusef."

After he left, tightness seized my chest. I needed to breathe cool twilight air if only to assure myself that I still breathed. I climbed the narrow, coiling stairway to the northern tower's highest reaches. On the walkway beside the battlements, I looked out to Mount Bezetha and the Kidron Valley, hazy in the low clouds, and considered Yusef's words. How outrageous it was for Herod to claim he had ordered Yusef to end my life because he loved me. A man who truly loved a woman would not, could not, order her death. I was just the next Maccabee on his list to eliminate.

I dared not tell my mother. She would most likely say or do something foolish and make everything worse. The burden of this horror was mine, alone.

~

"My Queen, I have news."

The sound of Lila's voice in the still of the night startled me. I had no idea anyone had seen me slip away to the parapets. Moonlight made my handmaiden's face shimmer pearlescent.

She moved in close enough for me to see her sad, dark eyes. "The cook went the marketplace today. People were talking about King Herod."

"What are they saying?"

"They say Herod is dead, executed by Octavian's sword. The cook said the whole market was talking about it."

My knees went weak with relief. Herod's death would free me, and indeed, the entire country from his paranoia and his bloodlust. But could I believe it? His demise had been reported many times over the years, but he always returned unscathed. The peril did not seem real given Herod's sharp mind and his preternatural strength and vitality. "It's only marketplace gossip … I won't believe it until I hear it from a reliable source."

"Come inside, Queen Mariamne," Lila said. "It's late, and so cold up here."

"I'm going to stay. Leave me now, Lila." Her footsteps echoed down the stairway.

If Herod were dead, I would be next. Yusef would soon come for me. Might I convince him to disobey Herod's orders? I felt certain Yusef did not want to kill me. Such violence was not in his nature, but as the Queen of Judea and the mother of four children, I could not afford to find out. If I was going to live, I had to lock up Yusef. I returned to my bedchamber and called for my guards. Two burly Thracians rushed in.

"Find Yusef immediately. Take him to the prison tower. Chain him to the wall. Keep him there until further orders. Do it!"

The taller guard looked puzzled. "King Herod said we're to take orders from Yusef only."

"I'm your Queen. I issue my own orders."

"I'm sorry, Your Majesty," said the older, more grizzled guard. They turned to leave.

"Wait!" I cried. I pulled off my necklace, an intricately carved golden turtle with emerald eyes on a gold chain. I held it out to them. "If you refuse to do as I ordered, I will send you to prison. Or you can take my necklace and do as I command, and keep your freedom. The choice is yours."

The men shuffled their feet. "It is quite nice," the tall young guard said with a sheepish grin.

"Take it to the goldsmith in the morning. He will pay you well for it."

The taller guard reached out for the necklace, but I yanked it away. "Not so fast," I said. "First, take Yusef to the dungeon. He must have no means of escape."

The guards exchanged glances with each other and nodded. "No torture," I called out as they were leaving. "I want him well fed. He must have blankets and water. Go quickly, and close the door behind you."

I did not want to hear Yusef screaming as the guards dragged him away.

~

*T*hat night, I had a strange dream:
          I was a dove, soaring above Jerusalem. Joy surged through me as I glided in the air over Herod's funeral procession. My husband's mangled body lay on a gilded litter. I swooped down low and saw his face, still in death.

~

*Y*ou didn't come to breakfast," Lila said, her brow creased, handing me a plate of lentil beans and a silk handkerchief for my tears. She sat down on the stool next to my bed and took my hand.

"I didn't know my husband at all," I said.

"What do you mean?"

"Before Herod left for Rhodes, he ordered Yusef to strangle me if Octavian executed him."

Lila gasped, her hand cupped over her mouth. "No!"

"Tell no one," I added. "I thought Herod's love for me had changed him, Lila, but I was wrong. He died the same ruthless man I married."

A shadow of terror darkened her face. "Does Yusef know Herod is dead?"

"Don't worry. He can't hurt me. I locked him up in prison."

My handmaiden drew back. She looked at me as if I was a stranger.

"Prison?"

"I had to do it, Lila. I'm not going to let him kill me."

~

*L*ater that day, my mother burst into my bedchamber, smiling radiantly. "Have you heard the wonderful news, Mariamne? Herod is dead. Octavian executed him. A sailor who had recently returned from Rhodes confirmed it. Oh, what a joyful day! The Maccabees will rise again."

"A sailor in the market? It could be just gossip."

"The tyrant is dead. People will rejoice in the streets. We must go quickly and arrange to have the Roman Senate appoint King Hyrcanus as Herod's successor. I will, of course, rule in his stead. This is the chance we've been waiting for, Mariamne. We must seize it."

"We must wait to hear it from a reliable source before we take any steps—"

"Our time has come, at last," she interrupted. "Come with me to the Legions' Camp. I'll order the Roman general stationed in Jerusalem to take us to Rome. We must arrange for your grandfather's smooth succession to the throne. I have already asked the Nabataean leader to encourage Rome to appoint my father king, and to support our return to rule."

"You have entangled King Aretas in this? You may have just signed our death warrants. If Herod is not dead, this is going to infuriate him."

"You never appreciate anything I do."

"We must do nothing until we get official word of Herod's execution. Emperor Octavian will choose Herod's successor."

I intended to see to it that the emperor crowned Prince Alexander king and appointed me as my son's regent until he comes of age.

"Fine. I'll go see the general myself." She wheeled around and left with all the dignity of a monarch.

The general, however, must have refused to take my mother to Rome, because within the hour, she returned to Antonia Fortress and slammed her chamber door. For nearly a week, she did not emerge and had meals sent to her quarters. When she reappeared, she did not say a word about going to Rome.

~

*T*he following day, just before sunrise, I felt a presence in my bedchamber. I opened my eyes and saw a tall and muscular man, slightly darker than the darkness surrounding him, looming over my bed. It was Herod, staring down at me with a broad grin. My heartbeat quickened. Was I still dreaming? Was his ghost haunting me? No, I concluded, unless an apparition could smell of clean sweat and saddle leather, just like my husband. So, Herod lived. A ghost would have been less frightening. I sat up and pulled my sleeping robe tightly around me.

"We heard Octavian executed you."

Herod chuckled and shook his head. "Reports of my demise are premature. You shouldn't listen to the idle market talk."

With dull dread, I watched Herod remove his robe and tunic. He lay down beside me, collected me in his arms, and gave me a long, deep kiss. His hot, sour breath disgusted me. I wanted nothing more than to break away from him and run away as fast as I could. When I could no longer bear it, I pulled away. He sat on the side of the bed and lit a lamp, then poured himself wine from a vessel on the night table. He drank until the goblet was empty. I considered confronting him about his arrangement for my murder, but it was not the time. I was too tired to be cogent.

Herod's face was aglow. "I could not have schemed more brilliantly. I wish you could have seen it, Mariamne."

"Octavian has accepted you as our king?"

Herod nodded with the glee of a young boy.

"Please, Herod, I need to go back to sleep. We can talk later."

Herod lay down. To my surprise and immense relief, he almost immediately began to snore. However, I lay beside him for hours, restless, pondering how much I had to lose if I angered him. Yesterday, I had taken my sons to the gardens. I saw their joy as they ran around the manicured hedges, laughing and calling out to each other. I must tread carefully. My children and I needed each other.

~

he morning after my husband's midnight return, I went to break my fast and found Herod in the banqueting hall reclining beside Salome. With their heads close together, they were whispering. The sight of them sickened me. No doubt, Salome was stirring up trouble. Herod frowned at me, and they fell quiet. My spine tingled. I had a premonition I was in imminent danger.

"Join us," he said, his voice cold and dull. I took the silk cushioned chaise across from them.

"My sister just told me you and Joseph were lovers while I was in Rhodes, pleading for my life."

My stomach lurched. "I've never been unfaithful to you," I said, in a clear, poised voice. I turned to Salome and gave her a withering look. "Again, your sister has lied to you."

"See how calm, she is?" asked Salome, pointing at me. She's guilty. An innocent woman would have cried out at the injustice of a false accusation."

As incensed as I was, I would not prostrate myself and beg my husband to believe my innocence.

"See? Your wife barely denies her guilt," Salome added. "She reeks of it."

"I have no reason for guilt," I said, still composed but fighting back my tears at the injustice of the accusation. My sister-in-law's smug presence was intolerable. I turned to her. "Leave us now, Salome. I wish to speak with my husband privately."

She glanced at Herod, who nodded. She curled her lip and went away.

Furious, Herod jumped up and strode over to me, his fists balled. My pulse roared in my ears. He was going to strike me, and not one guard or servant was in sight. The worst thing I could do was to show him how frightened I was. He stopped only inches away. Still, I held myself with pride.

"Salome told me she saw you steal into Yusef 's bedchamber, night after night," he said, bitterly. "She heard you two moaning in..." He choked on his words.

I took a few steps back in. "It's not true, Herod. Why do you believe your sister's lies? She hates me. She will say anything to hurt me. You should know that. The only time I saw Yusef was when we were signing edicts. Salome wants to cause problems between us, and she also wants to dispose of Yusef."

He snorted. "Salome is my blood. She never lies to me."

She never lies to him? Her deceit would have been apparent to a woodpecker. "Your sister wants you all to herself, Herod. She's in love with you. Don't you see it?" It felt so good to say it to him.

"That's ludicrous," he said. "You're are just trying to deflect from your adultery."

"As God is my witness, I have never committed adultery. And Yusef has never made an advance toward me. We are both completely innocent."

"Yusef will die for betraying me."

"No, Herod. Please don't kill—"

"No man betrays me and lives. My life was on the line in Rhodes, and here you were, in my palace, whoring yourself."

His words took my breath away. "How dare you speak to me like that." I could not hold back. "You, who left Yusef orders to strangle me if you did not return from Rhodes."

Herod went white. His chest rose and fell with each panting breath.

"Yusef told me."

"Did he tell you this falsehood when you lay with him in our bed?" he bellowed.

"I have never lain with him or any man but you, Herod. He told me of your orders when we were signing edicts in the banqueting hall."

"What did he say?"

"He said you couldn't abide separation from me, even in death, because of your great love for me. He considered your murderous orders an expression of your eternal love."

Herod looked like a wounded young boy. "It is." He leaned forward and reached for my hand. I stepped back. Chastened, he hung his head. "My love for you is so strong, Mariamne, that I cannot fathom being without you, in life or in death. I will never let another man possess you."

"Love, you call this? It is no loving act to order your viceroy to end my life. 'Thou shalt not kill.' You are aware of this Commandment?"

"Of course, I am. Do you think I'm not one of your people?"

"You had no trouble participating in sacrifice to a Roman god after Antony crowned you king. You have eaten the flesh of pigs in Rome. You have built temples in our own country to pagan gods."

"Enough!"

My fury felt like a thorny briar in my chest. "And you murdered Aris."

He froze. "I had nothing to do with Aris's accident."

Serenity settled over me. I was no longer afraid. "You ordered my brother murdered just as you ordered my execution."

Herod looked at me as though he was seeing me for the first time. There was a glint of admiration in his eyes. "Who told you these lies?"

"It's the truth, Herod, and you know it." He was a brutal, ruthless man, willing to spill anyone's blood, even my own, for any threat —real or perceived—against his rule. "You acted like a player on a stage at my brother's funeral with your false show of grief."

"You have the audacity to condemn me as a murderer after Antony himself did not find me guilty? Treason!" thundered Herod.

His words had little effect on me. "Antony's verdict doesn't make you innocent in God's eyes or my own. You hated my brother. You knew people would never love you as they loved him. You feared his rise to power. So, you killed him."

"You must be careful, woman, what you say—"

I would not restrain myself. "Aris was kind and wise and pious, everything you're not, Herod. You were jealous. You couldn't stand the attention people lavished on him. You hated how much they loved him. You knew it was only a matter of time before they rose up in revolt against you and demanded Rome put him on the throne. You had to eliminate him, just like you have eliminated hundreds of threats, real or imagined."

"A King must protect his throne," he said, gruffly.

"You're not a true king like the Maccabee Kings were. They ruled an independent Jewish nation for generations. But you, you dance to the music Rome plays."

"Have you forgotten the buildings and the entire cities I've constructed to advance this backward land, and the fortresses I've built to protect you and your thankless family? And you dare to tell me I'm not one of you?"

Suddenly, I was shivering cold. Tears streamed down my face. Trembling, I crossed my arms over my chest. I expected Herod's fists to come flying at me. Still, I could not bring myself to try to appease him.

He turned from me and headed toward the door. "I must speak with Yusef."

"You'll find him in chains in prison. I sent him there so he couldn't kill me when it was rumored you were dead."

"I'll see him there."

"Wait!" I called. "Promise me you won't kill Yusef. He's as blameless as I am. He meant you no harm."

I thought I detected a brief nod.

~

That night, I slept in guest quarters behind a door I barricaded with furniture. The next morning, in the banqueting hall, I saw Salome resting her head on her mother's shoulder and heaving great, moaning sobs.

"What happened?" I asked.

"Yusef is dead," Salome cried. "Herod's beastly guards strangled him last night."

"Oh, no," I said. Unsteady, I reached out for the table to keep my balance.

Salome blew her nose into a linen cloth her handmaiden held. "I can't believe my husband is dead. I didn't want to be his wife, but I never wanted him to die."

"You are as responsible as your brother for Yusef"'s execution," I said. "You sentenced him to death when you told Herod lies about his fidelity."

The rims of Salome's eyes were red, and her face, flushed and splotchy. She gave me a wounded look. It was all for show. If she felt any emotion, it was gratitude toward Herod for ridding her of her unwanted husband. She had her freedom now.

"How dare you speak with such impudence to the King's sister."

"I am the Queen. It is you who must show respect."

Like his disgraceful sister, Herod had no respect for human life. Where was he? I had to find him and express my rage. I knew I was provoking a bear, but I was too incensed to hold back. His manservant told me he had left an hour ago for Jericho Palace.

Herod still had not returned by late evening. By then, I had accepted the futility of confronting him about Yusef 's murder and thought it best to stay as far away from him as I could. I locked myself in a guest chamber. When I finally fell asleep, I had terrifying dreams of a raging fire consuming Antonia Fortress. I tried to escape, but Herod's guards kept pushing me back into the flames.

The next morning, I woke up to the cacophony of Herod kicking in my door with such brute strength it gave way and crashed to the floor. I fled to a far corner of the chamber, and crouched down, my arms wrapped around my knees. Was he going to rape me? Kill me?

To my astonishment, Herod knelt beside me. He looked at me tenderly, took my hands, and pulled me up. "Don't be afraid of me, Beloved," he whispered.

I forced myself to meet his eyes. "You promised me you wouldn't kill Yusef."

"I promised you nothing," he said.

～

I moved into a guest bedchamber and had my servants pile furniture up against my door every night to prevent Herod from forcing his way in. For days, I did not rise from the bed, and I ate only bites of the meals Lila brought me. Emptiness filled me, heart and soul, but my mind raced. How naive I had been to think Herod's love for me could tame him. Brutality was the very essence of this man, rooted in his very soul. He was a liar and a murderer. Like a scorpion with a venomous sting, he was a killer who would act in accordance with his true, bloody nature so long as he had a heartbeat.

After a few days, I began to leave my new quarters from time to time. I was careful always to have someone with me in case Herod crossed my path. On nights the family dined together, I refused to meet his gaze. I left any hall or chamber he entered, and slept alone, on the other side of a barricade of piled furniture.

～

A week later, I was on my way to visit the nursery when one of Herod's manservants handed me a scroll summoning me to the library without accompanying servants. My stomach tightened. Why did he want me to come alone?

Herod opened the library door and ushered me in. He, too, was alone. Where were his guards? I expected him to start railing at me about something, real or imagined, but to my surprise, he took my cold hand.

"I miss you," he said with a ragged sigh.

I forced myself to look at him, though every instinct told me to run.

"To deny me your love is the cruelest thing you can do. There is no other woman I want."

I could not bear to look at him a moment longer. I pulled my hand away and turned to leave, but he grabbed my arm and clenched it. My throat was so dry I could not swallow.

"I can't stop thinking about you, Mariamne. Day and night, I see you in visions. They often come, now. They torture me. I want you to love me—"

"Herod, your crimes against my family have ravaged me to the depths of my soul. I will never forgive you for stealing the Maccabee throne and for murdering my brother and Yusef."

There was something vulgar and wild in his glare. I wrested myself from his grip and started toward the door.

"Wait! Listen to me, Mariamne. As long as I live and breathe, I must protect my throne. Anyone who threatens my rule must die."

That was when I knew Herod was going to kill me. I had to find a way to escape.

HEROD, 30 BCE, JERUSALEM

*H*erod's rift with Marianne caused him the deepest anguish he had ever known. To escape his misery at home, he threw himself into large-scale building projects. He journeyed to Sebaste, an ancient city in Samaria that Octavian had given him to restore. He rebuilt the entire city in Roman style, with a grand Cardo lined by six hundred columns, and a forum, basilica, stadium, temple, hippodrome, and theatre, all surrounded by walls and gates. When Herod was not in Sebaste, he lodged on the coast near Caesarea Marittima, a new city and seaport he was planning. An innovation in cement made undersea construction possible. He was going to build the largest and most modern port in the Roman Empire.

Herod had hoped that if he gave his wife time, she would return to him, body and soul, but it had not happened. It was quite the opposite. The rift grew into a chasm. Only on the High Holidays and at the Feast of Tabernacles did Mariamne join him at the banquet table in Antonio Fortress, where she sat beside him in stony silence, her smile icy.

She had turned him away from her bedchamber so many times he finally stopped trying. His bed was cold and lonesome. To solve this quandary, he acquired three nubile young concubines, Amina, a raven-haired beauty, Hialeah, a Slavic captive with fair skin and golden hair, and Dhalia, a ginger. He set them up in Antonia Fortress's remote southern wing, some distance from his wife's apartments.

His visits to these women of firm, delectable flesh brought him pleasure and physical release, to be sure. They charmed him, flattered him, and fought each other for his attention, but they could not satisfy his yearning for Mariamne. When he was with his concubines, her image hovered in the corner of his consciousness. When he drilled his soldiers, there she was, a faint smile on her beautiful face. When he heard petitioners or sat in interminable council meetings, her dark eyes flashed at him. Her heady fragrance scented the air. The woman haunted his every waking moment.

During the concubines' first weeks in the fortress, he hid them well. Mariamne seemed unaware of their presence. Then it occurred to him that they might make her jealous or guilty about her failure to perform her marital duties. He encouraged the women to lounge around the common halls when his wife was at home. To his mortification, Mariamne did not seem to care that strange women in her home were sleeping with her husband. She even amiably conversed with the concubines, apparently untroubled by their presence.

~

*I*t was Herod's spies who found the former King Hyrcanus's treasonous correspondence. On papyrus, Hyrcanus written to the Nabataean King, imploring the old man to help him retake the Throne of Judea should Herod die in Rhodes. Herod questioned Hyrcanus and Princess Alexandra. Both denied writing or knowing anything about the letter. Had Mariamne forged it? He had no choice but to confront her. With an odd combination of excitement and rage, he strode into her apartments and found her at her vanity table. Lila was braiding emerald beads into her hair. She quickly rose when she saw him, her exquisite face frozen in fear.

"Leave us," he said to Lila, the annoying handmaiden who always seemed to be around.

Alone now, he moved toward Mariamne for an embrace, his arms open. She stiffened and stepped back. Angry self-righteousness obliterated his sadness. He wanted to hurt her. "My men have intercepted a letter your grandfather Hyrcanus wrote to the King of Nabataea," he said, and held out the scroll. "Read it."

With a wary glance, she took it.

> *Dear King Aretas,*
>
> *We have long been allies and have come to each other's aid when necessary. I will soon need your support. As you may know, Roman Triumvir Antony is dead. Octavian is the sole Roman Emperor. King Herod has gone to Rhodes to ask Octavian to allow him to keep the Judean crown. However, given King Herod's previous loyalty to Antony, it is unlikely that Octavian will consent, and will, most likely, order his execution.*
>
> *Should Octavian execute King Herod, I plan to retake Judea. As Rome holds you, King Aretas, in the highest esteem, it would help my cause considerably if you would encourage Octavian to support my return to the Throne of Judea.*
>
> *Hyrcanus II*

Herod threw the letter on the table. "This is an act of treason, Mariamne."

"My grandfather did not write that letter," she said, her voice quivering. "He couldn't have. He's incapable of such duplicity. He's simple now."

Herod's eyes narrowed. Mariamne had the innocent look of someone hiding something. Perhaps he could intimidate her into confessing. "If your grandfather didn't write it, then someone forged it. Was it you?"

"Of course not, Herod."

"I see. Your mother also denies forging the writing, and so do you, so I must take Hyrcanus's signature at face value. Tomorrow, the *Sanhedrin* will try him for treason against the king."

She paled. "But Grandfather is innocent."

He must crush the Maccabean threat. "Guards, take Mariamne, and her mother and grandfather, to the East wing," commanded Herod. "I want the Maccabees under constant guard."

46

MARIAMNE, 30 BCE, JERUSALEM

*I*n a state of dazed disbelief, I watched servants carry all of our worldly possessions to the far reaches of Antonia Fortress's east wing. Frayed rugs, long-faded tapestries, and worn furnishings crowded the dusty quarters I was to share with my mother and grandfather. My new bed was an old sleeping pallet with a lump the size of a camel's hump in the middle.

"Send for my children," I told a guard.

"They are to remain in the West wing—king's orders."

"No!" I cried. "I must have my children with me."

The guard averted his eyes and shook his head.

"I need to speak to my husband. Please, ask King Herod to come to see me."

~

*H*erod did not return.

Except for a few servants, our handmaidens, and the dour-faced parade of guards, my mother and I lived in total isolation. We needed Herod's permission to leave the east wing, even to walk in the gardens or on the fortress grounds. We were not allowed to shop in the market or to attend sacrificial offerings. Guards shadowed every step we took.

I was sick with worry that Herod was going to charge my grandfather with treason. I had protected my mother at my grandfather's expense. I could not bring myself to tell him my mother had forged the letter, though I never said she did not.

My only consolation was seeing my children playing in the garden beneath my window opening. I shouted greetings to them. Alexander and young Aris smiled and called out my name. I blew them kisses and told them I loved them. My girls, Cypros and Salampsio, held up their arms when they saw me. I would have given anything to hold them. When their nurses caught them looking up at my window, they promptly took them away.

My children's young memories, however, faded as the months passed. Or perhaps, Herod had corrupted them. I wondered what lies Herod had told them about why I was no longer in their lives. My boys began to respond to my exuberant greetings with wary glances and before long, they completely ignored me. My girls no longer recognized my face. Their indifference was the worst heartbreak I had ever known.

Every day, I sent another message to Herod begging him to let me see our children. He never responded. After several months, I stopped asking. It was plain that if I wanted to see them, I would have to take matters into my own hands.

One quiet morning, after a servant told me Herod had left for Masada, I watched the guard change through my open window. No one was paying attention when I slipped out of the East wing and down the hallway to the nursery. Exhilaration coursed through my entire body. I was going to see my children again. I felt fully alive for the first time in months.

In the nursery doorway, I saw a beautiful sight. My little girls sat cross-legged on a woven rug, dressing their baby dolls. Little Cypros looked up at me as though I was a stranger, but Salampsio gave me a gummy smile that made my heart lurch. Did she remember me?

Furtively, I stepped inside the nursery. That was when the guards appeared and crossed their swords against me.

Through an open door, I could hear the melodic timbre of my sons' voices reciting Latin verbs tenses. I had to see them. I tried to push past the guards.

"You cannot enter on orders of the king," a sentry barked. "Step aside and let me through."

At the sound of my raised voice, my daughters began to wail. I had not meant to make them cry. My sons stood in the schoolroom doorway staring at me with wide-eyed terror.

"You must return to your quarters," said a guard who looked strong enough to toss a tree.

"No!" I cried. "I must see my children."

They bound my hands behind my back with a leather band and pulled it painfully tight. My wrists stung. They escorted me to the East wing, untied me, and left without uttering a single word. The clank of the lock closing was the saddest sound I had ever heard.

47

HEROD, 30 BCE, JERUSALEM

$\mathcal{H}$erod's litter carried him back to Antonia Fortress after the former King Hyrcanus's trial and execution. The letter he had written to King Aretas was nothing less than treason. Any man who plotted to seize the throne was doomed to death; everyone knew it. The fact that the letter's author was his wife's grandfather mattered not. What choice did he have but to recommend that the Sanhedrin judges sentence Hyrcanus to death?

And yet….Herod could not drive back memories of how, in his gentle way, Hyrcanus had taught him everything he knew about ruling a nation. The old king was at least as instrumental as his father had been in helping him to reach this pinnacle of power. However, the student had surpassed the teacher. Would anyone disagree that he was a far better king than Hyrcanus had ever been? At least, the old king had been intelligent enough to recognize his shortcomings, and to rely on Herod's advice on everything from military strategy to matters at home. Hyrcanus had given him the freedom to rule on his behalf. But his letter to King Aretas revealed his mentor had schemed to take his place. He had dealt with him, accordingly.

When Herod had come to the East wing to take the former king to trial, he told Mariamne and her mother that he was taking the old man on a hunting trip. Everyone involved in Hyrcanus's imprisonment and trial was prohibited, on pain of death, from speaking openly about it. He would keep the guilty verdict and execution secret until he broke the news to Mariamne and Princess Alexandra. He was proud of his decency in this regard when he approached his wife and mother-in-law in the garden. Under the sheltering fronds of a date palm, the women were embroidering. Herod did not recall permitting them to leave the East wing. He must remember to punish their guards for being too lax.

Mariamne stopped sewing and looked up at him. "You're back early. Have the guards taken Grandfather to our quarters?"

"We didn't go on a hunting trip. We were at the *Sanhedrin*. The judges have tried your grandfather for the letter he wrote to King Aretas."

Mariamne's mouth fell open. "The *Sanhedrin*?"

"Yes, the Court has found him guilty of treason."

Mariamne dropped her needlework to the ground. Herod picked it up and tried to hand it to her. She swatted it out of his hands and sunk to her knees with a plaintive cry. "Please, Herod, spare my grandfather's life."

Herod looked down at the kneeling woman. The jewels woven into her hair glimmered in the sunlight filtering through palm fronds. She belonged to him, but he could not have her. He placed a hand on top of her head. "Hyrcanus is already dead," he said.

Mariamne's face crumpled. She shoved his hand away, dropped to the ground, and wailed. Princess Alexandra lay sobbing beside her.

Herod hated the animal sound of their grief. He turned to leave.

"Stop!" called Mariamne.

Herod twisted around.

His wife's eyes were red from crying, and her face splotched with red patches. "You won't rest until you've killed every last Maccabee, will you, Herod?" she called out.

"The High Court sentenced your grandfather to death, not I."

Her glower held venom. "You have packed the Court with men

who have sworn their allegiance to you. They did what you ordered them to do."

His forehead throbbed. "The court has applied our nation's laws and put a traitor to death."

"So, you bear no responsibility for killing a kind old man, your wife's grandfather, your children's great-grandfather, a king who did so much for you. Is this what you are saying?"

He had heard enough. It was time to go. His architects were waiting to talk with him.

~

*H*erod strolled through the gardens on his way back to Antonia Fortress. Roses in full bloom scented the air. How peaceful it was to walk here. Still, amidst nature's magnificence, he felt profound sorrow. If his wife truly loved him, she would understand why Hyrcanus had to die.

48

MARIAMNE, 30 BCE, JERUSALEM

*A*fter Herod executed my grandfather, I trudged through a deep valley of grief. My heart ached for the loss of my grandfather, and my outrage about the injustice of his execution lingered for a long time. I kept thinking about the horror of his final moments. Hyrcanus had been a good man who cared deeply about his people and his country. He deserved to grow old in peace, with his family around him.

Furthermore, I longed for my children with pain that was physical. Would Herod ever release my mother and me, or were we going to die here in this remote, lonely corner of Antonio Fortress? I filled my hours sewing or reading the scrolls servants brought me from the library, but these activities of hand and mind did little to keep me from longing for my children and my freedom.

My mother was mired in her own sorrow, which was, of course, far more vocal than my own. I grew so weary of her incessant complaints and lamentations, I rarely listened anymore. One evening at dinner, tension weighed heavy in the summer air. After we finished our plums stewed in honey, she subjected me to a virulent tirade I could not ignore.

"Your husband has stolen my family's crown, but it was not

enough for him. Oh, no. He had to murder my son and my father. Who will he kill next? Me? You?"

For once, she was right. My husband had placed a target on the royal Maccabee line. We were all in peril.

"I'm trying to figure out a way we can slip away from the palace with the children."

My husband's mind was fast deteriorating; he was sinking into paranoia, fearing everyone wanted to do him in. He considered my mother and me his chief enemies, and with the regularity of rising tides, Herod eliminated his enemies.

~

*W*hen night fell, I extinguished my oil lamp and lay down. Lila was already snoring softly on her pallet in the dusty corner of my cramped bedchamber. I tossed around my lumpy bed, considering ways to escape. How could we elude Herod's guards who followed us everywhere? Even while in the privy or our bedchambers at night, they stationed themselves outside closed doors. And if we did manage to escape without getting captured or killed, where could we go?

If we were peasants, we could live a normal life. I would have a life of hard work, but I could raise my children... Yes, that was it. We would disguise ourselves as peasants. I shook my handmaiden awake. "Lila, listen, I'll speak quietly, so the guards don't hear me. I need your help. Promise me secrecy."

"I'd die before I'd reveal your secrets," Lila whispered, her eyelids heavy with sleep.

I squeezed her hand. "I know you would. Here's my escape plan. I'll tell the guards I've sent you back to your village to care for your grandmother. Go there, and ask your uncle to arrange to for lodging for us. I'll repay him with gold. Make sure he tells no one my family will live there after our escape."

Lila's eyes flashed in the darkness. "Escape? Please, no. It will be the death of us."

I shook my head, vehemently. "I won't let that happen. And I will amply reward you, Lila, you and everyone else who helps me. Someday, you will be a heroine of all Judea for saving us."

Lila sighed and hung her head. "I'll leave tomorrow at first light."

I gave Lila a kidskin bag of silver coins. "Bring back peasants' homespun for my mother and me, and small tunics for the children. We will disguise ourselves."

"Princess Marianne, please, listen to me. No one escapes from Antonia Fortress. Soldiers and guards are posted everywhere—towers, grounds, and gates. How can we possibly do this?"

"Don't concern yourself with how," I said. "The less you know, the safer you are."

I had much to do before the escape. Most importantly, I would purchase loyalty and favors. Herod's frequent absences, overseeing his building projects, gave me the opportunity. I was grateful for my mother's foresight in sewing gold and silver coins into the hems of our robes before we left the Maccabee Palace for Masada.

~

*W*atching Lila leave for her village, I felt hopeful for the first time in months. My family was going to break away before Herod killed us. We were going to live a new life. The following day, however, doubts began to plague me. My plans could quickly go awry, and the penalty was death. Still, I must be brave. No one else was going to save us.

A week later, Lila had still had not returned from her village. I began to wonder if something terrible had happened to her. Only a short time ago, as a queen I could have ordered an army of men to find her, but no longer. Herod had reduced me to a prisoner. I could do nothing but wait for Lila to return with our disguises and pray the guards I bribed to look the other way had not informed Herod.

49

HEROD, 29 BCE, JERUSALEM

*H*erod lay alone in bed, pining for Mariamne. Her aloofness was driving him mad. He had not seen her since he had sent her to the East wing, but she was always on his mind. More often now, he chose to think of her and pleasure himself rather than dally with his concubines. He only had to close his eyes to see her face and her body, to smell her intoxicating scent. He imagined the rapture of their bodies joining together, and he rode waves of ecstasy until he spilled his seed.

Mariamne might despise him, but her feeling did not change the fact that she belonged to him. She was his wife. She should be with him. He woke his servant and had him carry the torch while they strode down a hallway of dancing shadows to the east wing and Mariamne's bedchamber. He tapped on her door. She did not respond. Was she sleeping? He would surprise her. He took the torch and sent the servant away.

Once inside, he took a moment to admire her. There she was, in full flesh, her breasts exposed, her breath soft and rhythmic. Long, dark tresses fanned across her pillow. Herod placed the torch in the wall mount and sat on a stool beside her bed. He watched her chest rise and fall. No matter what heinous acts she did, he could not stop loving her.

At last, her eyes fluttered open. She gasped and pulled the blankets to her neck. "Get out!" she cried, pointing to the door.

Humbled but still dignified, Herod returned to his apartments. Back in his cold bed, he wondered how he could win back his wife's favors. There were sound reasons why Aris had to die, why he had to issue Yusef orders to kill her, and why he had to relieve the world of Yusef and Hyrcanus, the traitorous scourges. He had to find a way to make her understand he had done everything *because* of his deep and abiding love for her. The two of them could never, ever part, in life or in death. Heaven without Mariamne would not be heaven at all.

He thought about the men his wife had invited into her bedchamber over the years, Yusef and the many other lovers Salome had told him about. Of course, Mariamne vehemently denied she had taken lovers, but why would he believe her words over those of his own blood? Sure, he had caught his sister in countless lies when they were children, but that was long ago. Now, he knew she desired nothing more than his survival in a sea of deceitful Maccabees.

However, he had to concede that it was possible that Salome did not know the entire story. Perhaps the beasts his sister had called Mariamne's lovers had forced themselves upon her, and his beloved bore no blame. He would find those men and slice them to shreds and then pluck out their hearts and feed them to the wolves howling in the canyon.

50

MARIAMNE, 29 BCE, JERUSALEM

*L*ila finally returned from her village, bearing a covered basket stuffed with well-worn peasant clothing. Relieved that she made it back without mishap, I embraced her. "I hope you have good news," I said.

"I do. My uncle has leased a cottage for you near the citron groves."

A swell of hope rose inside me. Perhaps I could save my family. I thanked Lila and placed another coin in the palm of her hand.

The homespun robe Lila had brought hung loosely on me, but it would suffice. There was more than enough attire for the boys, but none for the girls. Perhaps it was better this way. I could disguise my girls as boys.

Lila held out a small vessel. "Here is a sleeping potion. It's made from mandragora bark. Sprinkle two drops, and no more, in each wine goblet. They say even the biggest guard will sleep like a newborn."

"Who gave you this?" I asked. "Better that you not know," said Lila.

Tonight, we were going to leave Antonia Fortress, forever.

~

*H*ours later, a servant I had previously bribed slipped a wine vessel into my bedchamber. I poured the fragrant, crimson liquid into three goblets, and carefully added a few drops of potion to two of them. I shuddered to think of what might happen if I put in too much. After I carried them into the dining chamber, I pushed the two altered goblets across the table from my own unsullied one. I did not want to confuse them. It was time to invite in the guards.

"Phoebus, Reavus, please come join me," I said. "Join me for a goblet of wine."

The guards exchanged perplexed glances. "Thank you, your Majesty," Phoebus said, "but we can't. We're on duty tonight."

"Oh, come in. Sit down," I said. "Indulge your queen."

The guards sank into my chaises' deep cushions. I smiled and gave them full goblets of wine. I took a few sips of mine while they quaffed theirs.

The men thanked me and returned to their post. Minutes later, both lay splayed out on the hallway floor, snoring raucously.

"It's time, Mother," I whispered. "We'll bring the children here to dress them in their disguises. The night guards will look the other way as we leave from the open window. They have tied bed linens together sheets, and they will secure both ends. We will slide down. You and the boys will go down by yourselves. Lila, you carry baby Cypros. I will carry Salampsio."

~

*W*e crept down the hallway to the West wing, where my children were sleeping in their nursery. We dared not carry torches for fear of attracting attention. I knew my way well enough to navigate the dark passageways. We were nearly there when a chamber door creaked open. My neck prickled. Seconds later, I heard the door shut closed. Had we been detected?

We neared the royal apartments where Herod slept. I had a

strong urge to bolt back to the safety of the East wing. Then, I thought of my children's young, smooth faces, their innocent smiles. I had to get them away from their deranged father before he added them to his list of enemies to eliminate. Armed with a mother's courage, I carried on.

At the nursery's entrance, my heart thrashed. I opened the door with the nursery key I had hidden. Alexander stirred, and then stilled. Salampsio flipped onto her back. I could see her little belly rise and fall with each breath she took. All four of my children were sleeping, each face a mirror of peace and innocence.

A sudden chill raced down my spine. Was it right to endanger them? How could I pluck them from their warm beds and force them to take this perilous flight with me? Even if we managed to slip out of the fortress without getting caught, Herod would relentlessly pursue us. Even with disguises and assumed names, my family would never be safe from his vast network of spies and informers. Even if we managed to reach the cottage, what sort of life would my children be able to lead? How could I sentence them to a lifetime in hiding? If we left, Herod would marry again, and another woman's son would take Judea's throne. How could I deprive Alexander of his legacy as the crown prince?

"Hurry!" my mother hissed.

I shook my head and stopped walking. "No," I whispered. "I've changed my mind. We're not going."

She stared at me with astonishment. "Why?"

"I cannot subject my children to Herod's wrath. He will catch us, you know he will."

"Come now, Marianne. You don't think your husband would harm his own children?"

"Nothing would surprise me."

"All right, we will go without them," my mother snapped. "You, me, and Lila."

"No," I said, feeling defeated. "I won't leave without my children, so I won't leave at all. Come, Mother," I added, more gently, putting an arm around her. "We must return to our chambers."

"I'll go without you, then."

I took her hand. "You are no match for Herod, Mother. He has stopped you from leaving before. Remember when you tried to escape inside a coffin? He will catch you, and this time, he will kill you. Please, stay with your grandchildren and me."

My mother's crestfallen face made me feel even worse. The walk back to the East wing seemed endless. A chamber door opened, startling me.

Salome stood in the doorway holding a torch. "Mariamne? Alexandra? What are you doing in the West wing?"

I grabbed my mother's hand, and we ran.

In the hallway in front of our apartments, the guards were still unconscious. I stepped over them and headed for my bedchamber, where I peeled off my ill-fitting peasant garb and threw it, along with the other ragged disguises, into the capering flames of the hearth. I watched our freedom burn to ash.

The sudden rumble of male voices outside our apartments frightened me. I opened the door to find Phoebus sitting up against the wall with a dazed expression. "What happened?"

Reavus opened his eyes and stretched. Both men struggled to their feet.

"You were asleep for only a minute, I think," I said. "I'll never tell anyone."

Both disappointed and relieved, I climbed into bed. Dream images were beginning to drift into my mind when I heard someone throwing open my bedchamber door. I looked up to see Salome, flanked by my guards.

"We told her she couldn't enter," Phoebus said.

"What were you and your mother doing near the nursery in the middle of the night?" demanded Salome. "Herod ordered you to stay in your own wing. I'm going to tell him of your disobedience."

"How dare you come here and make accusations," I said, hoping I had sounded sufficiently outraged.

My mother stumbled into my bedchamber, yawning. "What is this noise about?"

"You must have been dreaming, Salome, if you thought you saw us near the nursery," I said, staring pointedly at my mother. "We couldn't have left this wing if we'd wanted to. You did notice the guards, did you not?"

Salome cocked her head, skeptically.

I nodded to the guards. "My guards will tell you we've been here since they went on duty early this evening."

"It's true," said Phoebus, with a sheepish shrug. "They were here."

I hoped Salome did not notice Reavus's smirk. With a frustrated cry, she stormed out.

51

HEROD, 29 BCE, JERUSALEM

erod sat in a gilded, open-air carriage rolling down the flagstone Streets of Jerusalem. People packed both sides of the road, but no one cheered him. He knew they would call out their praises if only they could see him, but they could not. He was invisible. They looked right through him. What agony!

～

*H*e woke up with a dull headache. He did not take the time to break his fast but went straight to the library to meet with his new spymaster, an oft-changed, secret appointment culled from his most elite men. He could not remember this current one's name.

"We've uncovered another plot against you," the spymaster said. He seemed nervous, bouncing a knee repeatedly. The man's eyes shifted around, never entirely focusing on him. Had he something to hide? In this treacherous world, few were worthy of a king's trust.

"Some religious aristocrats have secretly banded together to organize a coup against you."

"Another one?" Herod mumbled with a weary sigh. "Everyone has a dagger aimed at my chest. What is their complaint this time?"

"At their meeting last night, their leader ranted about the new amphitheater and hippodrome you have built. He said you had made Jerusalem too much like Rome. He also complained about the pagan temples you have built in Caesarea and Sebaste."

Herod chuckled. "They think they can plan my demise with impunity? Do go on."

"He says you are corrupting our land and leading us away from Jewish traditions."

"Those ingrates ought to thank me for the many ways I have advanced this backward country."

"These men have no use for chariot races or theater. They think contests between wild animals and gladiator matches are sinful. They want to stop you."

He would have his revenge on these small-minded men, blind to the benefits of progress. "I want this rebel and his followers condemned for treason. Kill them all."

The spymaster nodded. "I've also heard some rumblings of rebellion among some of the Pharisees."

"Again?" Herod asked. "Some of those priests are insufferable troublemakers."

He knew people thought he was overanxious about the security of his throne, yet intelligence had uncovered no less than six separate plots to assassinate him this past year. "What do the rebels want this time, besides my head?"

The spymaster shrugged his muscled shoulders. "They oppose foreign rule in Judea."

"Foreign rule?" Herod thundered. "I'm Judean born! Rome has appointed me to rule!"

"Yes, but they don't consider you ..."

Herod had heard enough. "I also want you to summon every male subject in Judea to come before me and swear an oath of loyalty. If any man refuses, execute him."

*I*t happened just inside the entrance to Antonia Fortress's west wing. Herod had just returned home, drained after a long day of meetings with his builders. He was anticipating a restful soak in the bathhouse when he heard the sound of draperies rustling. He pulled out his dagger and strode toward the noise. From behind the floor-length silk, a giant of a man leaped into his path, brandishing a dagger.

Herod swiftly blocked the stranger's thrust with his own weapon, knocking the dagger from his assailant's hand. It clattered to the floor. Both men reached to grab it, but Herod reached it first. He stabbed the stranger in his prodigious gut. The man cried out and fell to the floor with a sickening thud. Herod pulled his weapon from the gushing wound and repeatedly thrust it into the stranger's abdomen. He did not stop until the man gushing blood stared up at him with unblinking eyes.

Herod had come close to death before, but this time he had felt its fiery breath on his neck. His enemies were never going to stop coming for him. He shouted to summon his errant guards, ready to send them to their execution for failing to protect him. Where were they? Why had they failed to stop the intruder from entering the fortress? It was not until he had reached the keep that he saw the grisly sight. Four guards lay slaughtered. Their blood seeped through the wooden slats in the floor.

∾

*L*ate one winter evening, rain hammered on the fortress windows while Herod and Nicholas of Damascus swilled beer and debated some of the finer points of Greek Philosophy. Such erudite amusement usually served as a welcome refuge after long days of governing and fending off usurpers. Tonight, however, he was finding it difficult to leave his troubles behind.

"Aristotle says that the validity of any argument can be determined by its structure rather than its content," said Nicholas. "Do you agree?"

Herod jumped up and paced. "What's the matter?" asked Nicholas.

"My people want me dead."

Nicholas nodded. "It's good that you have tasters for your food and drink."

"Yes, not a sip or morsel escapes their vigilance."

"Have any yet fallen?"

Herod shook his head. "No, but I cannot let down my guard."

Nicholas cleared his throat. "You have done well in keeping your enemies at bay."

"My informants hunt down those who dare to criticize me, and I kill them. I think my own guards are conspiring to oust me."

Nicholas crossed and uncrossed his legs. "Good King, perhaps you are being …overly cautious."

Now, Herod knew. His trusted friend and court historian was just another enemy who wanted him gone. He must keep a close watch on this snake.

"Take no offense, please, King Herod," said Nicholas as he drew back. "I'm telling you the truth. Your guards are loyal to you."

"It takes only one disloyal guard to expose me to an assassin." Herod jumped up and paced. Then, the idea occurred to him. "I will execute my guards, hire new ones, and bribe them to be loyal."

"If you kill all your guards, you will be killing many innocent men. Please, King Herod, I beg you to reconsider."

"You don't know what it's like, Nicholas. You have never been at the helm of a nation. I have given my people so much, yet they despise me. The Maccabees left the treasury in shambles with their pointless dynastic wars. I have made Judea great. Our trade is strong. Those who seek work can find it. I have expanded our borders and brought Rome's law to our land. Still, they fail to recognize I am Judea's most excellent king."

"I have recorded your many accomplishments. History will judge you well."

"So, why do my people despise me? My wife blames me for her grandfather's execution. She thinks I arranged her brother's drowning—preposterous. She's furious I'd ordered Yusef to end her life if I didn't survive my journey to Rhodes."

Nicholas sat up straighter. Why did he look so astounded?

"She doesn't understand I issued those orders because of my deep and abiding love for her," he added. "How can she expect me to enter the Kingdom of Heaven without her? I want her all of the time. It tortures me."

Nicholas shifted in his chair.

"My courtiers constantly wag their tongues behind my back. They tell disgraceful lies about me. Scores of aristocrats have journeyed to Rome to see Augustus and criticize me."

"It's unfair, Herod." He sounded tired and strained.

"Ah, memories are short, Nicholas. Do you think they remember how I bought them grain with my own gold when they were near starvation during the drought? Do they appreciate how I funded the rebuilding after the great earthquake? Do they thank me for lessening their taxes? No, they do not."

Nicholas nodded.

"No matter what I do, no matter how my subjects thrive and their animals grow fat from the life of plenty I have made possible, they still want me dead. I see their jealous looks. I feel the contempt beneath the surface of their civility. They want a Maccabee on the throne. They will never consider me a part of the Maccabee family."

"They can't deny your sons' veins course with Maccabee blood," said Nicholas. "Perhaps you might consider passing the crown to Prince Alexander. You could serve as his regent until he comes of age."

Herod's eyes flashed fire. Nicholas was not his friend, just another enemy, scheming to cast him out. What a disappointment. "Leave now, Nicholas, before I kill you. If you are not on a ship out of Judea tomorrow morning, I will have you executed."

Nicholas lifted his brow in surprise. "But I have not yet completed your court history…"

Herod came towards him, brandishing his dagger. Swiftly, Nicholas left.

~

*T*he idea occurred to Herod the next morning as he drank his beer. He must personally uncover his subjects' plots to overthrow him. He could no longer rely on spies and informers to keep him safe, because they, too, wanted his head. There was no man Herod could trust to uncover the growing number of conspiracies brewing against him. He must go out into the marketplace himself, and walk among his people, and conduct his own investigation.

Herod insisted his servant dye his dark beard red with henna, and he dressed as a peasant in brown-striped homespun. The fabric felt rough against his skin. He wondered how anyone could tolerate it. He concealed most of his face with an oversize headdress and hired a farmer to take him to the market in a plain wooden cart. No one accompanied him; this was something he must do alone.

"Return for me at sunset," he called out to the driver, who nodded, whipped his mules, and rolled away.

Never before had Herod packed in with the masses in the crowded marketplace. His bare feet, smooth and soft from the nightly olive oil massages his concubines had given him, hurt with every step he took down the hot flagstones of the Cardo. The air was thick with smoke from the sacrificial offerings on the Temple Mount. He was subjected to the incessant cacophony of vendors calling out their wares.

"Fresh barbels from the Galilee!" trilled a barefoot young boy.

Herod approached the market stall heaped high with fish.

"Care to buy one, sir?"

Herod rarely saw fish before they appeared on his dinner plate. Their dead-eyed stares made his stomach churn. With a curled lip, he looked down at the young fishmonger and his vile wares. He must remember to comport himself as a simple peasant. Perhaps he ought to buy one. He reached for the silk bag that usually hung from his belt but felt only the rough homespun of his peasant tunic. His servants had neglected to send him with enough coin. He had given the few he had to the farmer who had driven him to the market. He must remember to punish his servants when he returned to Antonia Fortress.

"I have no money," Herod said with a shrug.

The boy glared at him. "Move away from here, old man. Do you think fish are free?"

"Benjamin, don't be rude," said a squat, olive-complected woman perched on a stool behind the boy. "Sir, come back just before the market closes. If we have any fish left, I will gladly give you one."

Ah, the kindness of the salt of the earth. Herod had heard of it, but he had never before experienced it. He nodded his thanks and trudged on. Further down the Cardo, a woman was ladling out aromatic lentil stew. His belly rumbled with hunger. If only he could buy a bowl.

Near the soup stall, a group of men had gathered. Herod envied their laughter and easy camaraderie. He approached them. "What do you think of our king?" asked Herod, feigning a high voice.

The youngest turned to him, shaking his head. "King Herod is—"

An old man stepped in front of the lad. "My grandson—he's too young to have opinions."

"And you, Sir, do you think King Herod is generous and fair?" he asked the older man.

"H-h-he's a fine King," the man stammered, slowly backing away.

Satisfied, Herod moved on. He tried to listen to the conversation of other gatherings he passed. Despite the din of the blacksmith's hammer and the calls of the baker selling bread, he managed to catch part of a discussion.

"Go to Hyram's Vineyard at nine tonight. We're planning...."

Herod could not decipher any other words, but he thought he heard the man saying, "King." He would attend this meeting and learn of the traitors' plans to murder him. The cart driver, who was to return for him at sunset, would have to wait. He asked for directions to Hyram's Vineyard and hobbled the long way there on bare and aching feet, yet he felt invigorated, as if he was going into battle.

He approached the gated entrance to Hyram's Vineyard, and avoided looking directly at the two men standing guard. Still, they rudely blocked his entry and turned him away. It did not matter. He had already heard enough to execute them for treason. By the pearly sheen of the full moon, Herod limped back to the market to meet the cart driver, and he returned home.

As soon as he arrived at Antonia Fortress, he sent soldiers to Hyram's Vineyard with orders to arrest every man who was attending the meeting. Hyram suffered hours of torture before he confessed the men were scheming to murder him. Herod ordered Hyram crucified. By dawn, Herod's guards, on his orders, had executed every one of the vineyard traitors.

~

On a spring night, Herod walked the battlements. The winking points of light in the sky looked close enough to count. If only Mariamne, in all of her grace and beauty, was there, beside him. Of course, she ought to be with him. She belonged to him, and she was just corridors away. He would go to her again. Perhaps, this time, she would relent, and invite him into her bed.

MARIAMNE, 29 BCE, JERSUALEM

*S*oon after I rejected Herod's advances the first time, he had left. Then it occurred to me that I should use the only power I had to attain freedom.

To my surprise, Herod did not try to visit me again the next night, or the one after that. A week after his visit, I sent him a message, inviting him to come to me again. He did. This time, I did not turn him away. I lifted my silk covers to let him into my bed. He climbed in and began to embrace me.

With eyebrows raised, I sat up straight. "Wait. We can be together as man and wife, but first, you must agree to let me see my children every day, and allow Mother and me to return to our quarters in the West wing."

"Hmmm, yes," he said, staring at my breasts.

At that point, he would promise me Rome itself if necessary to get back into my bed. "Are you listening, Herod? Do you agree?"

"Of course," he said, flushed with lust, his eyes fixed on my body.

"Good. At first light, send servants to move our possessions back to the West wing. I will spend the morning with our children. After that, I'm all yours."

HEROD, 29 BCE, JERUSALEM

*H*is first time with Mariamne, after their long separation, was as close to heaven as Herod had ever experienced. His beloved, in all her delectable flesh, was his. He took her, again and again.

However, in both boudoir and banqueting hall, his wife barely uttered a word to him. He was certain her reserve was temporary. Still, it stung. Only with their children did she smile and laugh. He would try to make her love him, to show him the same tenderness and passion he felt for her. Meanwhile, he had Mariamne back in body, if not yet in soul.

~

*T*hat summer, Herod was designing his most important building project, the expansive new Temple. It was going to replace the present one, which was too small to accommodate the burgeoning population and crumbling from hundreds of years of use. With a dome of pure gold, it was going to be the most massive and beautiful structure known to man. If Judea's treasury was insuf-

ficient to fund the building supplies and labor, Herod pledged to pay
the balance.

After an interminable day of meetings with builders, he
returned to the royal quarters. He was about to call for Mariamne
to join him on the terrace for wine when Salome rushed at him, pale
and panting. His sister's face was flushed in fury, yet she appeared
strangely exhilarated.

"Thank the Lord I found you before…Oh, Herod, I have something terrible to tell you," said Salome. "You must brace yourself."

He was in no mood for his sister's theatrics, which invariably
involved some clash with his beloved. "What is it now, Salome?"

"Summon your wife. I want her here when I tell you this."

Herod sent his guard for Mariamne. Moments later, the queen
stood before him. Her expression was as pure as it had been on their
wedding day. Her face, faintly lined now, was every bit as beautiful.

Salome pointed her finger at his wife. "Mariamne tried to
poison your wine."

Herod felt the blood drain from his face. His heart hammered.
Mariamne's cheeks reddened, yet she had a calmness about her
Herod found disturbing. "I would never do such a thing, Herod.
You can't possibly believe your sister's vicious lie."

"I'm telling the truth," said Salome. "This morning your wife
asked my handmaiden Dreya to find her wolfsbane poison. Dreya
can tell you so herself."

"I've never once spoken to your handmaiden," said Mariamne.
Though her face was a picture of serenity, Herod noticed how
quickly her chest rose and fell with each shallow breath she took.
Was she masking her guilt?

"Come, Dreya!" shouted Salome.

The girl, barely a teenager, emerged from the shadows. Sweat
beads clung to her spotty forehead.

Herod glared at the girl. "What is this accusation you have made
against my wife?"

Mariamne caught Salome's almost imperceptible nod to her
handmaiden.

"What Princess Salome says is true…" whispered Dreya.

"Tell King Herod what happened," said Salome, slowly and gently, as though speaking to a small child.

Dreya's eyes darted between Salome and Mariamne. "The queen summoned me this morning and ordered me to find her poison. I couldn't refuse her royal highness. I went to a meadow outside the city walls where my mother used to collect herbs to help sick people. I found some wolfsbane growing there. I remembered my mother saying wolfsbane is so poisonous it will kill quickly." Dreya was sobbing so hard she could barely speak. "I picked a bunch and gave her the poison. The queen gave me this to reward me." The handmaiden opened her small hand and held out a golden hare with sapphire eyes that hung from a gold chain.

Herod felt as though Mariamne had ripped his heart from his chest. He had given her the pendant only days before. He had seen it on her dressing table before leaving their apartment that morning. Mariamne was a false, deceitful woman.

"Go on, Dreya," said Salome. "The king must hear what his evil wife did to him."

Dreya fell to her knees, sobbing. "I saw Queen Mariamne put the poison in the king's wine vessel—the one on the table on the terrace."

"Salome and her servant are lying to you, Herod," said Mariamne, with eerie composure. "I've never asked Dreya or anyone else to find poison. Of course, I didn't poison your wine. Either Salome or Dreya must have stolen my necklace."

Herod snatched the necklace from Dreya and dangled it in her face. "Did you steal this?" he demanded.

"No!" the girl cried, her eyes cast downward.

Herod glowered at the trembling girl. "Did the Queen give it to you?"

Dreya sank to her knees, crying. "Answer me!" Herod bellowed.

"My servant is shy," said Salome, soothingly.

"Tell me, Sister, do you trust this Dreya?" he asked.

"She's never once lied to me. Go on, Dreya. Tell the king what Queen Mariamne said to you."

The girl shuddered. "She threatened to kill me if I refused to bring her poison."

Mariamne coolly shook her head. "That's not true."

"Where is my cupbearer?" Herod demanded.

His Galician cupbearer presented himself. This man had sipped his drinks and tasted his meals for years. No fear was evident on his pockmarked face. Herod respected him for that.

"Come with me," Herod said.

They followed him out to the terrace where he and Mariamne had taken libations together on many happier evenings. The vessel in question was on the table. Herod poured some wine into a goblet and handed it to his cupbearer. "Drink it," he said.

The cupbearer looked up to the sky, indigo in the twilight, and mumbled a prayer. He took a sip of wine. With a tortured groan, he collapsed to the floor.

"That would have been you, Herod!" screamed Salome, pointing to his lifeless body, tears spilling down her cheeks.

"Take him away," Herod said to the servants hovering in the doorway, their horror plain on their pallid faces. They dragged off the dead man.

Herod's fury burned like wildfire in his chest. His wife had tried to murder him. She would have succeeded if not for Salome's loyal intuition. An innocent woman would have been vociferously indignant and outraged when faced with such an accusation. Mariamne, however, was not. Her unnatural composure exposed her guilt. He turned to his sister. "Salome, you have always looked after me."

With a smug glance at Mariamne, Salome hooked her arm through Herod's.

Mariamne gave Salome a withering look. "You want to get rid of me. You want Herod all for yourself."

"And you—you want to murder him."

Mariamne turned to her husband. "Don't you see, Herod? Salome is behind this scheme. She has forced Dreya to find wolfsbane and poison your wine, and lie to you about who ordered her to do it. She paid Dreya for her services with the necklace stolen from me."

"Don't waste your breath denying your treason," said Salome.

"You know me, Herod. I would never attempt murder. I follow God's Commandments."

"You will pay for this," said Salome. "Herod, send the Maccabee woman to the prison tower."

He could hardly bear the thought of his most beloved treasure moldering in the tower prison. His agony was unbearable. But he was not going to let her kill him.

"Herod, did you not hear me?" Salome asked. "I told you to send your wife to the prison tower while she awaits her trial."

Mariamne, her head held high, did not utter another word. Her expression held no remorse, only Maccabee pride.

"Mariamne must die," Salome whispered in his ear. Herod nodded to his guards. They took her away.

MARIAMNE, 29 BCE, JERUSALEM

*H*erod's guards led me to a small, round cell in the prison tower. The chamber was in near darkness, though it was noon and the sun shone brightly outside these walls. There was only a wooden stool, a small table, and a straw mattress on the bare floor for my comfort. Water from recent rains trickled down the walls.

I shivered under a thin, tattered blanket. Winter was upon us, and nights were long and cold. There was no hearth or brazier to warm me. I was going to die, and my children were going to grow up without their mother if Herod deigned to let them live. I cried until no more tears would come. At dawn, an ancient guard tottered in with my breakfast, a thin gruel. He left it on the table and headed for the door.

"Wait!" I cried.

The old man turned to me with a blank expression.

"Bring my children to me, please," I said. "I must see them."

He shook his head. "No visitors."

Tears started to rise. "I heard them calling for me in the night."

The old man grinned, showing his two yellowed teeth. "I don't know what you heard, but it wasn't your children calling. The nursery is too far away from here. You must have been dreaming."

"Please, bring them here. They need me."

He did not even look at me.

"It's cruel to keep a mother from her children."

"I take my commands only from the king."

"Please, I need a brazier and another blanket, and prayer scrolls from the library."

Without so much as a glance, the old man locked the cell door and disappeared.

❧

*T*he winter deluge came. Rain pelted the tower for days. The walls grew sodden and moldy, and the musty odor made me sneeze all night. Adding to my despair, I was not permitted to sew or read; there was nothing to stop my mind from racing to the accursed night Herod sent me here. The fact that he believed his sister's malicious and ludicrous lies made it clear that the sickness of his mind had now blinded him. My life was in the hands of a madman.

❧

*W*eeks passed. I was certain Herod was going to leave me in the tower prison to grow old and die alone, with my children mere passages away. In my desolation, I struggled not to sink into insanity. I tried to recall happier times, but in my deep sadness, it was impossible.

Late one night, I heard the keys jingle. The door opened. How strange. No one had ever come after dinner. The guard handed me a scroll.

"It's from His Majesty, King Herod." My heart raced as I read.

Dearest Mariamne,
   You will soon go to trial for your treasonous act

against me. However, I will consider allowing you your
life if, at trial, you prostrate yourself before me, confess
your guilt, and beg me to let you live. It is my fervent
hope you will do this.
　　Your Herod

My stomach lurched, and I threw up in the slop bucket in the corner of my cell. What chance did I have of surviving a trial with Salome determined to see me executed? I could not lower myself to respond to this false accusation with histrionics. I was the last Maccabee Princess and the Queen, the progeny of the most high-born family in the land. Not even Herod could make me, an innocent woman, endure the humiliation of prostrating myself before him and confessing to a crime I did not commit. I would beg no one for exoneration.

～

A few days later, I woke up to a gray dawn and found breakfast waiting for me, a full bowl of plump, juicy citron sections, and steaming-fresh bread slathered with date butter and honey. Was this lavish meal an ominous sign my trial would soon begin? I lost my appetite. Pulling away from the table, I heard the clink of keys opening the door. A guard stood before me.

"Orders," he said apologetically, binding my hands with a leather cord.

"Where are you taking me?" I asked, feeling light-headed.

"To trial," he said.

The time had come. The guard followed close behind me. My legs, weak from lack of use, awkwardly navigated the stairways and long halls. In the king's the presence chamber, Herod's mother and sister, and his courtiers and kinsmen sat on benches along the walls. I saw my scowling mother in the front row, and Lila, a bright spot in the darkness, in the back corner. Across from the long row of judges was Herod's empty throne. A hush fell over the chamber as the guard led me to the podium that stood between the judges and the throne.

In my abject terror, I could barely breathe. I desperately needed fresh air. In a hoarse whisper, I asked the guard to open the shutters. He nodded, and did so, leaving me standing alone at the podium. In my nervousness, I counted the judges. There were twenty-three.

A sea of disapproving faces in the audience stared at me for what seemed like an eternity. I had never felt so exposed and the vulnerable. At last, Herod swaggered in, dressed in his gold-cloth robe lined with ermine fur. He tried to catch my eye. I refused to look at him.

The chief judge, an elderly aristocrat with a wispy beard, rose from his seat. "We're here today for the trial of Queen Mariamne for treason against King Herod." His deep voice echoed off the walls. "The Crown alleges that the accused forced a servant, by threat of execution, to find wolfsbane poison. The queen then poisoned King Herod's wine in a failed attempt at regicide. Princess Salome, Daughter of Antipater, please come forward."

Salome approached the judges' table. Her expression was smug, her posture, regal.

"Your name?" the chief judge asked. "Salome, sister of King Herod."

"Do you recognize the accused?"

"Oh yes. She's Mariamne, my brother's Maccabee wife." She pointed her forefinger at me and burst into tears. "That woman tried to kill my brother the king."

I tried to shut out the din rising in the audience. My stomach was cramping badly, but I held my spine straight and my head high.

"On what day did this attempted poisoning occur?"

"On the third day of *Tevet*, in the early evening."

"What happened?"

"My handmaiden, Dreya, came to me quite distraught. She told me that earlier in the day Queen Mariamne had ordered her to find her wolfsbane poison in the meadow beyond city walls. The queen threatened to end Dreya's life if she refused her orders, and offered to reward her with the jeweled necklace if she found the poison.

Dreya found wolfsbane, and she gave it to the queen. The queen, in turn, gave Dreya the promised necklace. Here it is."

Salome held out the necklace in front of her like a trophy. The audience gasped. "Soon after that, my handmaiden saw the queen adding the wolfsbane poison to the king's wine." Salome began to weep. "Dreya told me about it right afterward. At first opportunity, I told King Herod of the queen's treason."

"I summon the servant Dreya to give testimony," said the chief judge.

Salome paled. "It's not possible. Dreya died of fever this morning."

Again, voices rumbled from the hall's perimeter. I was certain Salome was responsible for her absence. Perhaps Dreya had refused to lie to the judges, and Salome killed her.

"There is more, Your Honor," said Salome. "Please proceed."

"The king asked his cupbearer to pour the wine from the vessel into a goblet and to drink it. The cupbearer did as ordered. He died, instantly."

The outraged in the audience called out curses to me.

"Quiet!" thundered the chief judge. He turned his terrifying countenance to me. "How do you answer this charge, Queen Mariamne?"

I felt the sudden presence of my Maccabee ancestor, Queen Alexandra Janneas, once the strong and powerful ruler of Judea, hovering over me, giving me strength. "I'm completely innocent of these charges," I said, in a strong, clear voice. "I did not ask Salome's servant, Dreya, to bring me wolfsbane or any other poison. I did not poison King Herod's wine. I would not violate a Commandment of our Lord. My necklace was missing from the table where I kept it. I never offered it to Dreya. Salome has lied to the king and to this court."

King Herod rose from his throne and looked at me, his eyes soft, and his expression hopeful. "If the accused will prostrate yourself before this court and me, and beg me for forgiveness, I will consider asking the court to spare her life."

"What says the accused?" asked the chief judge.

There was a quiet, tense moment. "I have done nothing for which I could ask forgiveness."

Herod was going to believe what he wanted to believe, and his version was the only one that counted.

"She's too proud," called an old crone in the first row. "The Maccabee Princess thinks she's too good to beg for forgiveness. Shame on her!"

A din rose. Lila came forward. She looked as though she had not slept in weeks. Dark half-moons hung under eyes. The rest of her face was ghostly pale. "May I speak to the court?" she asked.

"Who are you?" the chief judge asked.

"My name is Lila. I'm Queen Mariamne's handmaiden."

"Allow her to speak," said the king.

The chief judge nodded to Lila.

"I was with Queen Mariamne on the third day of *Tevet* from the moment she woke up until the time King Herod called her to the terrace. The queen and I had embroidered and played board games all that day. I even accompanied her to the privy. In God's truth, Queen Mariamne never spoke to Dreya or to any of Salome's servants. Nor did she ask anyone to find poison, nor did she poison the king's wine."

The chief judge turned to face his colleagues. "Judges of the High Court, have you any further questions for these witnesses or the accused?"

The judges conferred in low voices. I saw the chief judge whisper to his scribe, who wrote something down on papyrus. Ice encased my heart. I felt numb.

At last, the chief judge stood up and cleared his throat. "We have a verdict." Slowly, he unfurled the scroll. "We find the accused, Mariamne the Maccabee, Granddaughter of Hyrcanus, wife of King Herod, and Queen of Judea, guilty of treason for attempted murder of King Herod. We sentence her to death by strangulation."

I staggered backward.

"Good!" my mother cried. "Mariamne should have been a better wife to the king!"

My mother, trying to save her own skin, was pandering to

Herod. I knew that. Still, her words fell on me like knives. Her
expression of rage and loathing was the last thing I saw before I
fainted. When consciousness returned to me, I was lying on the
courtyard lawn. I did not know how I got there. Angry voices rose
from beyond the walls surrounding Antonia Fortress.

"Free Mariamne! Free Mariamne!" people chanted. "The queen
is innocent!" others shouted.

The cheers of my people melted some of the ice around my
heart, but that was not good, because the thaw ushered in sheer
terror. I was going to die and leave my children in the hands of their
brutal, deranged father.

Someone reached a hand over the wall. One of Herod's archers
struck it with an arrow. The wounded man screamed in agony.
People began to hurl stones over the fortress walls. They were
fighting for me. They loved me, those people whom I had considered to be beneath me. I was wrong. They were good people. I was
above no one, and no one was above me. We were all God's
children.

Herod's archers began shooting arrows over the wall, and the
courtyard was in chaos as more soldiers rushed in. The ensuing
bedlam diverted the guards' attention. I had an overwhelming urge
to break away from my executioners. I raced to the nearest tower
and bolted up the stairway, taking the steps two at a time. At the top,
I heard footsteps behind me. I turned to see Lila at my heels. I
climbed out on the parapets and stood on the rim.

"What are you doing?" cried Lila, panting hard.

"Go find Samuel, Lila. Be well. I love you."

Over Lila's sobs, I heard the heavy footfall of soldiers ascending
the stairs. Herod's strongmen were coming for me. I rested my eyes
on a dove soaring above the canyon. The bird was free. I wanted to
join her in the sky, so blindingly blue. Herod could take my life, but I
was the master of my own death.

I opened my arms, and I flew.

ACKNOWLEDGMENTS

I am grateful for my wonderful husband, Neil Okun, and my beloved grown children, David and Sarah, who have given me love, support, and encouragement as I planned, researched, and wrote this book. Neil's countless manuscript readings and astute editorial suggestions have been invaluable to me.

Also acknowledged are renowned Author Caroline Leavitt, who helped me with early story development, and Editor Richard Marek, who gave me vital plot advice, and Editor Diane Higgins. Others whom I thank are Author Joyce Sweeney, Jamie Morris, and the Stegner Fellows of Stanford University, for teaching me the craft of writing. My beta readers, Maxine Tabas, Milly Dawson, Gloria Newberger, Alice Friedman, Olive Pollack, and Cori Baill, made brilliant suggestions and supported me immeasurably.

Professor Jodi Magness of The Great Courses, who taught *The Holy Land Revealed*, inspired and compelled me to write about the fascinating marriage of the last Maccabee Princess and King Herod the Great.

DISCUSSION QUESTIONS

(1) Why didn't Mariamne's grandfather, Governor Hyrcanus, listen to her when she said she didn't want to marry Herod? How did the *ketubah* illustrate how women were considered property in ancient times?

(2) Princess Alexandra has been called, "The worst mother in history." Do you agree with the assessment?

(3) Education for girls was sorely lacking in the Roman Era. So why did Herod respect Mariamne's intelligence and learning?

(4) Did Mariamne ever love Herod? Were there times when her feelings came "close to love" like Herod's feelings for his ex-wife, Doress?

(5) Why did Salome dislike Mariamne? Would she have been more receptive to a bride from a different family?

(6) Why did Herod mistrust everyone except for his own family? Was it mental disease only, or was any of it grounded in reason? What in his background played into it?

(7) **SPOILER ALERT** What would have happened to Mariamne and her family had they made a successful escape? Do you think Herod would have found them? If he did find them, what do

you think he would have done? Did Mariamne make the right decision in scrapping the escape attempt?

(8) **SPOILER ALERT** Why didn't Mariamne lie and confess her guilt to Herod rather than go to her death and leave her children motherless?

(9) How did Herod juggle the demands of the Roman Empire and the needs of his subjects? Would you say he did it well?

(10) How did Mariamne change over the course of the book? How did Herod change?

AFTERWORD

To Hold the Throne is a work of historical fiction.

Aside from the well-known historical figures and events portrayed in the narrative, the characters, places, and incidents are fictitious creations of the author's imagination. Any similarity or connection to living persons is entirely coincidental.

Please note that the Maccabee Family is also known as the Hasmoneans.

Kindly click the link to my website and add your name to my mailing list so we can keep in touch:
https://joniokun.com/

It would make this author very happy if you would write Amazon and Goodreads book reviews for her.

Made in the USA
Middletown, DE
22 February 2020